THE SOLDIER'S STORY

Fiction

Truth Lies Sleeping

The Distant Laughter

Familiar Strangers

The Rewrite Man

The Endless Game

A Song at Twilight

Quicksand

The Twisted Playground

Partly Cloudy

International Velvet

The Memory of All That

Non-Fiction

Notes For a Life (*autobiography*)

A Divided Life (*autobiography*)

Ned's Girl: The Life of Edith Evans

That Despicable Race:
A History of the British Acting Tradition

Children's Fiction

The Slipper and the Rose

THE SOLDIER'S STORY

BRYAN FORBES

QUARTET

First published in 2012 by
Quartet Books Limited
A member of the Namara Group
27 Goodge Street, London W1T 2LD

A catalogue record for this book
is available from the British Library

ISBN 978 0 7043 7280 1

Typeset by Antony Gray
Printed and bound in Great Britain by
T J International Ltd, Padstow, Cornwall

Yet again for
Nanette
with half a century of love

THE SOLDIER'S STORY

ONE

It has to be one of the ironies of life that none of us are ever rich enough to buy back our pasts.

It would be so simple to pretend this is just a story of lost illusions, of wrong choices made. Human experience, I am told, is only understandable as a state of transition. Whether or not that's true, I'm not clever enough to decide. All I know is that, years ago, in a foreign country, I lived through events and a love that changed my life. How strange it is we can be so certain of all our actions except those that stem from affairs of the heart.

I was stationed in Hamburg during that merciless, killer winter of 1946, part of the Army of Occupation, living day to day in the stale aftermath of a long and cruel war. I had a room on the third floor of a bombed hotel, and during the coldest spell slept fully clothed with my Army greatcoat over me for extra warmth. Shards of glass from the bomb-blasted window still lodged in the walls as though a circus knife-thrower with a dodgy aim had previously occupied the room. Every morning I woke semi-frozen and shaved in icy water before facing the surly German waiters in the Sergeants' Mess; the only time I ever saw them smile was when they got the news that Goering had cheated the hangman at Nuremberg. Working for us, they were luckier than most of their compatriots, able to feed their families with the discarded contents of our swill bins. Although we didn't eat as well as the Yanks in their sector, we certainly enjoyed decent rations.

I'd had a lucky war compared to many, not crossing to Sword Beach as part of a Field Security section until D+5, thus missing the initial carnage. Years later, reading histories of the invasion I realised that true descriptions had been deliberately concealed from those at home. Newsreel footage of the real horrors had been edited out, for the public could not have taken pictures of men hosed down by the German MG-42 machine guns as, seasick and crapping themselves, they jumped from the landing craft and were immediately taken out, pierced through the eyes or testicles, their faces blown off, heads disintegrating into myriad red dots, the sea around them lapping into a tide of frothy blood. At the time the actuality was sanitised to preserve the fiction of brave Allied troops being cleanly and surgically killed, not atomised by accurate machine gun fire; even strong swimmers drowned in waves five feet high sucked down by the weight of the equipment they carried. I came through the subsequent advance into Benouville with nothing more serious than temporary deafness when a sapper ahead of me stepped on a Schu mine that blew his foot off, the severed extremity hitting me on the side of my head. Even so, I saw too much death; death of the enemy, death of our own troops and death of the French civilians, poor sods, who died during the bitter-sweet recovery of freedom, since I later read that during the first twenty-four hours of the invasion the same number of French civilians died as we suffered during the Blitz, mostly as a result of our bombing. So, as we painfully fought our way inland, it didn't escape us that some of the local inhabitants might have preferred the polite Krauts they had endured during four years of occupation to those who finally came to liberate them. For many we must have been just the bringers of destruction and pain.

They say that you become a man the moment you see your first corpse, but I never got used to the rotting bodies, our own and German, in the ditches and Normandy hedgerows. As I came to terms with the fact that the lives around me could be blotted out in an instant, I knew with a terrible certainty that my life had changed forever. Some nights I dreamt of my own corpse lying like the others, rotting, with maggots seeping from my open wounds. I never felt completely safe or brave. There were many who could stifle fear, but I wasn't one of them.

The other members of my section were an easygoing lot. We

survived the invasion and the subsequent advances through France and Germany more or less intact, only losing our CSM to a sniper's bullet in the battle for Abbeville, which resulted in my being promoted in the field. Our commanding officer was Lieutenant Colonel Machell, an amiable, middle-aged character, ex-Indian Army, fluent in fourteen languages. His favourite tipple was heroic slugs of neat Scotch which he termed "mahoganies", for he took his poison neat and often. Once, when pissed, he confessed that he had left behind a love child while serving pre-war in the Punjab ('The Monsoons always made me randy, dear boy'). He referred to us as his "Battersea Dogs Home" with some justification because we were certainly a mongrel bunch drawn, in the way the Intelligence Corps operated, from widely different backgrounds. No stickler for infantry-style discipline, Machell was content to leave most day-to-day operational matters to his second in command, Lieutenant Grable, a much younger man who let everybody know he had a Cambridge degree in modern history, was generally regarded as a pedant and inevitably nicknamed, "Betty". The chain of command then descended from me to Sergeant Armstrong, older than the rest of us, a regular who had survived Dunkirk, and two corporals: Groves, a ponderous character who endlessly whistled Bach, and Sasdy, a Czech who had escaped to England after Munich by swimming the Danube. Since he valued his own creature comforts, Machell always made it his business to locate and commandeer the best billets he could find as we progressed deeper into Germany. When we finally arrived in the gutted nightmare of Hamburg he somehow obtained us a base in the *Hotel zum Kronprinzen* which fronted onto the *Haupt-Bahnhof Platz*. The battered railway station had partially survived Operation Gomorrah, the great firestorm raid that blotted out the sun for four days and left thirty thousand Hamburg citizens incinerated. Those who survived still lived as troglodytes, emerging from their underground holes every day and trundling their remaining possessions through still rubbled streets to barter for bare essentials. In the uneasy peace that belonged to neither the victors nor the vanquished, many of them starved or froze to death during that first post-war winter.

Our main job was to sift through the lies of a Third Reich that hadn't lasted for a thousand years. For the most part we went our own way and made our own rules. I have to admit that most of the erstwhile enemy I interrogated sickened me for they stressed their own suffering rather than admitting any guilt for the crimes we had uncovered. The discovery and liberation of Belsen in our sector had further hardened our dealings with the locals. 'Don't let them fob you off with the usual "we had no idea" crap,' Machell instructed. 'How could they not be aware of what was happening in their midst?' We had forcibly marched the local inhabitants from Celle to the camp and made them see at first hand what had been done in their name. Even then some still refused to admit any guilt and those we made bury the decomposing dead into mass graves. I don't think any of us who witnessed those first sickening scenes ever forgot them, and for years after it only needed the smell of pork searing on a barbeque to immediately bring back a surge of memory.

Unlike the chain-smoking Eisenhower who made sure he regularly got his sexual oats throughout the entire campaign by having his mistress on the staff, prior to the British Army crossing the Rhine our celibate Monty issued one of his famous edicts, spelling out a code of behaviour we were ordered to obey once on the enemy's home territory. 'It is too soon,' he told us in his high-pitched voice, 'for you to distinguish between good and bad Germans. In streets, houses, cafes, cinemas etc, you must keep clear of them, man, woman and child. You must not walk out with them, or shake hands, or visit their homes, or make them gifts, or take gifts from them. In short, you must not fraternise with Germans.' He was too straight-laced to use the word "fuck" instead of fraternise. Eisenhower, on the other hand, sat on the fence and merely issued orders that any pictures of American troops fraternising with the German population were to be censored. The ban was more less adhered to while the fighting lasted, but within a few weeks of VE Day our vast occupying armies, for so long deprived of female company, were in no mood to continue a monastic existence. Brothels flourished but those who wanted more than transient lust had little difficulty finding and bedding compliant German girls: hate on either side was difficult to sustain when stomachs were empty and long-dormant gonads stirred again. If sex wasn't the panacea for post-victory angst, others took solace by soaking their brains in wood alcohol that sent them blind. The Yanks had their own tipple called Swipe, just as lethal, while other foolhardy souls left this life asshole drunk on buzz bomb fuel, quantities of which some-how found their way onto the black market.

For myself, I found living amongst the everyday misery of the barbequed city of Hamburg very difficult. Back home the new Labour government promised a welfare state flowing with milk, honey and free dentures to return to, but it was hard to believe in such a rosy future when reminders of recent horrors confronted you from every street corner. Likewise it was of little solace to remind yourself that the Nazis had begun it all, that way back in the Spanish civil war when I was still at school, they had perfected their dark arts on Guernica. Allied bombers had paid them back in spades, eviscerating city after city.

When hostilities ended the official exchange rate was around 13 old Reich marks to the pound, but nobody wanted that money; they wanted goods and immediately a barter system sprang up. A single cigarette commanded 20 marks, a pound of coffee beans could be exchanged for a Leica or a Rolleiflex, a bar of soap meant your laundry was done for a month, non-smokers hoarded their weekly tin of 50 free cigarettes until some had enough to acquire a Mercedes. Those of us lucky enough to gain entry to a Yank PX could buy nylon stockings which guaranteed you'd get laid. In the British sector other ranks could enjoy the humbler, basic comforts provided by the Salvation Army and Nuffield canteens; ENSA provided entertainment and most concert parties included a soubrette singing, ironically, *Lily Marlene*, that sad lament purloined from the Rommel's Africa Corps, the sentiments of which fitted all armies. When ENSA was disbanded, the Ministry of Defence replaced it with an outfit called "Combined Services Entertainment Unit" made up of officers and other ranks from all three Services who had some connection, however tenuous, with show business. Even so the class status quo was kept inviolate because officers were only allowed to produce shows and concert parties, humble squaddies and NCOs being the only ones permitted to perform.

It was at a production of that old chestnut *Charley's Aunt* given by an Army and ATS cast in the local Opera House (which had miraculously escaped total destruction), that a character called Chivers first crossed my path and was destined to become my nemesis. Seated a row in front of me with a very beddable Wren officer (the Senior Service always seemed to recruit the best lookers) and wearing the uniform of the newly established Control Commission with the equivalent rank of Major, he had his arm around the Wren, from time to time possessively stroking her neck. The play's creaky plot and stilted dialogue from a by-gone age bored rather than amused me – my humour had become more graveyard by then. Staring at the Wren's delectable neck rather than following the play, I felt an irrational resentment. Some of the Control Commission types took the superior attitude of 'Well, you brown jobs have done your stint and now you can move over and leave it to us to bring some order.' We who had come through the whole shooting match took it for granted that some of them had sat out the war in cushy civvy street jobs and, now that the danger had passed, wanted their share of the spoils, though to be fair the majority were probably motivated by a genuine desire to administer a conquered country fairly.

My first impressions of Chivers grated. His brand new uniform and insignia, his clean-shaven, almost babyish face and sleek, Brycreemed hair brought to mind a character in a pre-war American gangster film as played by George Raft. The contrast between his appearance and my statutory shorn-back-

and-sides haircut put me firmly in a lower social caste. I judged him to be in his late thirties, some ten years older than me. At the interval he got up to stretch his legs and gave me a smug look as he and the Wren edged along the row of seats. 'Enjoying it, soldier?' he said.

I heard the Wren whisper my rank to him as they left. Returning for the second act Chivers leaned back over his seat to say: 'Sorry for the gaffe in not addressing you by your correct rank, CSM. Babs here put me right. Can I make amends by offering you a snifter after the show? Come and share a dram of Johnny Walker with us back at my hotel.'

I felt an urge to reply: 'People kill for real Scotch in this town' but instead I thought, Why Not? A free drink was a free drink and there was always the remote chance Babs might be persuaded to switch partners by the end of the evening. 'Thanks,' I said, 'I'll take you up on that.'

'Splendid.' His plummy, fake upper-class accent slipped occasionally, betraying the fact it was assumed. 'Good fun, didn't you think?' he said, as we filed out at the finale. 'Very droll. I thought the chappie who played the Aunt was top hole, considering the programme says he's only a corporal in the Green Howards. Granted a bit down-market from Olivier, but we can't have everything, can we?' His dialogue was straight out of P. G. Wodehouse. 'Sorry. Haven't introduced ourselves. This is First Officer Wilson, known as Babs to a privileged few, and I'm Major Kenneth Chivers. And your name?'

'Seaton. Alex Seaton.'

'Company Sergeant Major Seaton that is. Get it right this time, Kenneth.'

'Alex will do.'

'I thought all sergeant majors were meant to look fearsome,' Babs said with a sidelong smile I felt held out promise.

'Only those in the infantry,' I said.

While we walked to his billet Chivers remarked, 'I'm told there's going to be a classical symphony concert here next week. I like a bit of Beethoven, much more my bag. He was a good German.'

'How would you know?'

'Sorry?'

'Nothing,' I said. 'Just a joke.'

He gave me an old-fashioned look but did not pursue the topic. He had been given accommodation in an officer-only hotel which had been repaired and smartened up. Unlike what I lived with, the windows of his room were intact and he even had the luxury of his own bathroom. Producing three odd glasses, he poured generous tots of Black Label. With a lack of gallantry which didn't surprise me, he took the only chair while Babs perched on the lumpy bed. Close to, she smelt delicious of French perfume doubtless gifted by another admirer – girls like her were never denied luxuries for long.

'So, here's to life to come,' Chivers toasted with a knowing grin. 'I think I'm going to enjoy living here.'

'When did you arrive?' I asked.

'Got into Flensburg a couple of weeks ago. Still finding my feet. From the first look of this place, I've got a big job to do. A big job.' He made it sound as though he alone had the responsibility for putting Germany back on its feet. 'Of course, you know who we've got to be on our guard against, don't you?'

'Tell me.'

'The Soviets.'

'You think so?'

'I know so. Don't be blinkered. Nazi Germany may be finished, but the enemy is still the Russian bear.'

'What makes you say that?'

'Because, basically, they have a more or less Oriental mentality as you may or may not know. To have America steal the march didn't go down well. Hiroshima was a big loss of face for them. Suddenly they're behind in the race for world domination. Not a good omen.' He imparted this wisdom as though he alone had the inside track. I tried to think what it was about him that had inspired such an instant dislike and decided it was his entire personality.

Now he went to the wardrobe, and produced a full tin of Passing Cloud cigarettes, authentic, superior coffin nails, and offered them around, lighting them for Babs and me with an American Zippo. 'Bit of Lend Lease in reverse,' he said. 'About time we got something back from the Yanks.' Abruptly he switched to ask: 'What's the going rate for cigarettes? They're the standard currency here, I understand.'

'A tin like that will get you a Rolleiflex,' I said. 'Or a quick trip home if you aren't careful, but I'll let you off with a caution.'

He faltered, blinked and then recovered. 'Oh, I'm careful. Caution is my middle name. I'm told that what really makes the Krauts salivate are coffee beans, so I came armed with a few pounds.'

'You'd salivate,' I said, 'if you'd been drinking roasted acorns for years.'

'I suppose so, but mind you the coffee at my favourite watering hole, the Savoy Grill, wasn't anything to write home about during the jolly old *krieg*.'

'Really? How was your jolly old *krieg*?' I asked, but any attempt at sarcasm was lost on him

'Can't complain, sport, though to my lasting regret I never saw action. Desperate to be a fighter pilot, but failed the medical. Dicky eyesight, I'm afraid. They only took those with 20-20 vision.'

Or maybe you shaved your armpits, I thought.

'So because of my background,' he continued, his free hand resting on Babs' thigh, 'they put me into Bletchley.'

'Bletchley?'

'Yes. Hush-hush outfit, still on the secret list, so I can't say much. It'll all come out one day. Until then mum's the word. Careless talk can still cost lives.'

'What was your background?'

'Academic. Senior Wrangler.'

'Really?' I had no idea what a Senior Wrangler was except that it suggested something to do with horses.

'When the shooting match over, felt I ought to do my bit over here. They were looking for chaps of my calibre. What are you going back to, by the way?'

'Going back to?'

'Yes, what career?'

'No idea. I never had the chance to start one.'

'No, I suppose not. Give you a tip. Get into property. Going to be rich pickings for anybody with their eyes open for the main chance.'

His self-satisfaction began to depress me and I regretted having accepted his hospitality, although the thin possibility of being able to shag the delectable Babs kept me there. I wished I had the nerve to make a pass at her, but I was savvy enough to know Chivers had more to offer. I turned to her. 'How long before you're demobbed, Babs?'

'Oh, I've volunteered to stay on and take a short commission. Anything rather than face going back to dreary old England. Everybody I saw on my last leave was so dowdy and depressing,' she said. 'All those pinched, grey faces and hideous fashions, plus the ghastly government. You didn't vote Labour, did you?'

'Yes, as a matter of fact.'

'Oh, are we sharing a drink with the proletariat?' Chivers said. 'We've got you to thank for them, have we? You'll live to regret it, because they'll fuck up big time. Pardon my French, Babs. That awful little creep Attlee looks like Uriah Heep in a trilby hat. And, Babs darling, I completely agree about the women. Can't wait for them to look sexy again. Present company excepted of course.'

'Watch it, Major,' Babs replied. 'You nearly blotted your copy book then.'

She gave me a knowing smile and for a brief moment I fancied my chances, but given her general air of superiority she probably didn't rate me. Chivers topped up her glass. He's welcome to her,

I thought, and then changed my mind again as she removed her uniform jacket, revealing the nipples of her prominent breasts straining against the crisp, regulation white shirt. I tried not to think about Chivers pasturing on them when I left. There are few things more depressing than being in the company of potential lovers. I downed the remainder of my whisky and stood up. 'Thanks for the drink. It's nice to see how the other half live. Excuse me if I call it day, I have to be on the road early tomorrow.'

'What does your work entail?' Chivers enquired.

'Catching the perpetrators who are still at large.'

'I hope we don't make the same mistake as last time. Be too harsh on them. They lost in a straight fight and now we must get them back on their feet.'

'You thought it was "straight", did you?'

Chivers flushed and I knew I had finally scored a point.

'I meant we traded blow for blow.'

'Did we? Maybe eventually. Most of the war we were boxing above our weight. If you'd been here you'd have known it was often touch and go.'

'Yes, well unfortunately I missed the big party doing another vital job.'

As I put my glass down I brushed against Babs. 'Always a pleasure to meet the Senior Service,' I said. 'Be careful going back to your billet, there are some ugly characters around at night, but I'm sure you can take care of yourself. Nice to have met you, Babs.'

As I left, she was kicking off her shoes and I glimpsed her perfect legs in the regulation black stockings. I walked back to my own hotel with the safety catch off on my Walther. An elderly couple pushing a wooden cart stepped off the pavement into the roadway as I approached. The man bowed, removed his hat and whispered 'guten abend', then waited, his expression fearful, expecting to be questioned. The homeless and tarts often took their chances and ignored the curfew. I waved them to continue. Outside my hotel two Military Police with stark white, fluorescent webbing belts were pushing a teenage youth against the wall.

Inside the Sergeants' Mess, a three-piece German band was attempting to play one of the current American hits to a sparse audience of drunks. I ordered a beer but after Chivers' whisky it tasted like weak piss and I left it unfinished and went upstairs to my room feeling deflated. I thought of all the things I could have said to counter his insufferable air of superiority, but most of all I thought what Babs would look like naked.

TWO

The next morning I began a journey that was to take me all the way to Graz in Austria, charged with a no-win mission. Group HQ had passed on evidence that the British brigadier commanding the Graz salient was deeply involved in an ingenious black market scam, masterminded by a similar high-ranking Yank officer in charge of the marshalling yards at Antwerp docks. The scam was simplicity itself: from every new shipment of booze, cigarettes and nylons arriving for American PX stores, one truckload would be diverted and disappear. That wasn't difficult, given the vast quantities being handled. If the loss was reported, it was put down to a highjack by one of the many marauding gangs of deserters still at large. The booty would be quickly disposed of to a chain of willing customers and vanish into the black market. The beauty of the scheme was in the final stage: all proceeds were used to buy Dutch tulip bulbs, which were then shipped to an England deprived of them for five years where they fetched a high price. To all appearances they were legitimate transactions paid for in sterling. The major players, including our brigadier who ran our end of the operation, were getting very rich. The break only came when one of the contraband trucks was involved in an autobahn pile-up and the GI driver sang to save his skin. His story was quickly traced to source.

My brief was to face down our erstwhile war hero and offer him a deal: in return for turning King's evidence and revealing names, he was to be allowed to resign with an honourable discharge and draw his pension from a grateful nation. That was the way it worked in those days and maybe still does, for all I know: it was a case of 'Don't, in the flush of victory, humiliate the good and the great for the sake of a cheap headline.' How the Yanks handled their end was not our concern.

I was savvy enough to know why I had been picked for the assignment. Sending a warrant officer from the Intelligence Corps instead of somebody of superior rank from an infantry regiment ensured the top brass could wash their hands of it if something went wrong – any snafu could be put down to me. I was expendable. Machell, knowing the score, had protested the assignment on my behalf but had been overruled.

My Jeep driver that morning was a Corporal Charlie Boag. He had been seconded to us since it was the form to use drivers from REME once hostilities ended. Charlie was a loquacious character of mongrel extraction, part Maltese, part North African on his mother's side. Squat and muscular, with a face that was seldom without a smile, I frequently chose him over others. He had volunteered to join the British Army at the outbreak of the war, fought his way through Italy and had twice been recommended for bravery. History not being his strong point, he constantly pumped me about the rise of Nazi Germany, punctuating his responses with his favourite expression of 'Mine bloody godfathers, you don't say?' Fanatically patriotic, his hero was Churchill, his one ambition to get to England and open a restaurant. I enjoyed his company. He wasn't the greatest driver, but he could fix anything mechanical and was always cheerful.

We had been on the road for about five hours and making good progress, only stopping once to refuel and eat a packed meal, when we struck a patch of bad road. During our break the weather had shut in, and now slanting sleet reduced visibility and the route became treacherous. The maps we had were unreliable and we found ourselves on a road pitted with craters that necessitated back-tracking on a complicated diversion.

Afterwards, neither of us remembered much about the skid. I vaguely recalled us turning a concealed corner and then seeing the shape of an oncoming vehicle coming at us very fast, well over on the wrong side. Charlie swung the wheel violently, but there wasn't enough room to avoid the other vehicle and we side-swiped it, ending up with our Jeep on its side in a ditch. Both of us had been smoking and my first instinctive reaction was to grope for the ignition key and kill the engine.

We disentangled ourselves, helped each other out and took stock of the damage. Charlie walked up and down cursing. He had a cut on his forehead, but refused my offer of a field dressing. I had a few minor abrasions and the odd bruise but was otherwise unscathed. 'Try and get it back on the road,' I told him, then went to see how the other vehicle had fared. It was a vintage Mercedes with chrome exterior superchargers, a model historically favoured by high-ranking Nazi officers, and had come to rest sideways across the road, with the driver's side panel crumpled and a front wheel tyre guard hanging loose. A burly, uniformed GI was standing by it inspecting the damage. He swung around and came straight for me.

'You the driver?' he said.

'No. I have a driver.'

'You don't say? Well, I'm gonna to kick him in the crotch. What outfit you both with?'

'I'm British Intelligence.'

'But not intelligent enough to drive straight.'

'Let's not get personal,' I said. 'You were coming too fast and we couldn't avoid you. It was fifty-fifty.'

'You hear that, honey? This asshole's saying it was my fault.'

'No, I'm not. I'm saying we share the blame.' I saw "honey" for the first time as she got out of the front passenger seat. She was auburn-haired, petite, wearing a WAC uniform and ignored my tentative smile. 'Is your girlfriend OK?'

'She ain't my girlfriend, asshole, she's my wife and she's pregnant, that's what,' he said. 'We were on our way to the boat and then Stateside. If she loses the baby I'm gonna start another war. Jesus fucking wept!'

'Look, we both should have been more careful. These icy roads are a death trap, so calm down and first make sure your wife's OK.'

'I'll take care of my bride, don't you worry.' He looked me up and down. 'You an officer?'

'Warrant Officer. Top Sergeant in your Army.'

'What's your name?'

'Seaton.'

'I'm Steinmetz, 12th Army Group. You ever killed anybody?'

'Killed anybody? What's that got to do with it?'

'Well, have you?'

'I wasn't infantry.'

'That figures. You don't look man enough. Well, I killed plenty, so don't get in my way because I'm going to kick your driver's brains in.'

'I don't think you're going to do that,' I replied flatly. 'If you lay a hand on him, I'll arrest you, you're in our sector and it's my call.' I rested a hand on my revolver holster and edged into the centre of the road to put myself between him and Charlie who had managed to right the Jeep and was revving the engine. 'Let's not trade threats. We're supposed to be allies, so let's act the part. We both got off lightly, considering, could have been a lot worse. Why don't we take a look at your vehicle and see if it still works? If it doesn't, I've got a field telephone and I'll send for help.'

The offer seemed to calm him momentarily. He hesitated, and then walked back to the Merc. I followed him. 'Try it,' I said.

'Don't tell me what to do.' Despite his continued show of truculence, he got in behind the wheel and tried the ignition. The engine spluttered a few times before it fired, then ticked over quietly. 'There are some things which aren't too bad about Germany,' I said. 'They make decent cars.'

'They make shit!' Steinmetz killed and then restarted the engine. Looking under the chassis, I couldn't see any sign of petrol leaking.

'So far so good,' I said.

At that moment Charlie joined us and straight away lay down on the slushy road and began straightening the crumpled mud-guard. Steinmetz was out of the Merc in a flash and kicked him in the groin before I could do anything. Charlie doubled up and lay with his head drawn in and almost touching his knees, rocking backwards and forwards with the pain of the blow. As Steinmetz moved to aim another kick, I drew my Walther out and fired a shot into the air. Steinmetz froze, squinting at me and for a second he seemed angry enough to risk anything.

'Back off,' I said and ordered Charlie to return to our Jeep. He belly-crabbed a few yards on the icy road before he recovered enough to get to his feet.

'You won't get away with this, I'll make sure of that,' Steinmetz said. 'I'll have you busted, you fucking British piece of crud.'

'What are you going to bust me for?'

'Shooting at me, that's what.'

'Well, this fucking piece of British crud didn't shoot at you. He fired a warning shot in the air to stop you kicking his driver's brains in as you threatened. That wouldn't look too good on your charge sheet. So don't push your luck any further, soldier. Let's both leave it at that and get ourselves back on the road.'

'Yeah, let's go,' his wife, said. 'Don't waste your time talking to him.'

'How are you, hon?' Steinmetz said, finally putting the question to her.

'I'm fine, just cold, let's go.'

For a second he seemed about to prolong the debate, but his wife repeated, 'Let's go! I'm frozen,' and he surrendered to her. I stood my ground until they both got back into the Merc and, after spinning the wheels, he managed to get it pointing in the right direction and drove off.

Charlie was bent over the bonnet, throwing up, when I rejoined him. 'How is it?' I asked.

'I might never have it away again,' Charlie said. He nursed his groin with both hands.

'Might keep you out of trouble for a change. Get in, I'll drive.'

Charlie protested, but without much conviction. I dropped a bar of chocolate in his lap. 'Eat that. Sugar's good for shock.'

The steering on the Jeep was a little dodgy and I tested the brakes a couple of times before setting it off, taking it slowly for the first few miles until the diversion ended and we were able to rejoin the autobahn.

For half an hour Charlie said nothing, then it all burst out of him. 'Why the fuck did he do that? Mine bloody Godfathers, we're fucking supposed to be on the same fucking side, for fuck's sake.'

'The war's over, Charlie. Things are getting back to normal.'

'I was only fucking trying to help,' Charlie said finally, baffled, as ever, by a world of inconsistencies.

THREE

Because of the accident we didn't reach Graz that night, and were forced to stop in a small village where there was a transit hostel for Allied personnel run by the Church Army. A crucifix and religious inscription over the main door denoted the building had once been a convent.

Charlie usually liked to be left to his own devices, so I gave him a pack of cigarettes, knowing he would use them to find a bed somewhere – he was never down for long. 'I might test the love muscles if I get lucky,' he said.

'Just be careful. You've had all your luck for one day. And be ready to move off at seven tomorrow after you've checked the Jeep.'

Everything in the hostel was utilitarian, but it was warm and the comfort food they provided reminded me of my mother's cooking. That night I slept without my greatcoat over me for once, and slipped into one of those recurring, confused dreams from which there is no escape. When I finally managed to drag myself awake it was still dark, but I found a bathroom and showered in hot water, a real luxury. Going downstairs I found a middle-aged woman already at work in the kitchen. She was one of those easily recognisable, typical English characters from the Women's Institute, the kind who sold home-made jam and tea cosies at village fetes – often derided, but who could always be relied upon to come up trumps in an emergency. She told me to call her Audrey, and confided that she was having the time of her life. 'It took a war to get me out of Cheltenham, don't know how I'll settle down again when eventually I return home. Do you know Cheltenham?'

'No, 'fraid not.'

'Nice, but stuffy. Some people call it God's waiting room.

Haven't got a husband and the children fled the nest as soon as they could. Couldn't blame them. You married?'

'No.'

'I had a good marriage, but he was killed early on. One of those who didn't benefit from the miracle of Dunkirk. Nice man, smoked a pipe and collected stamps. Such a boring hobby, I always thought, but, bless him, he was passionate about his stamps. Sticking them in, then taking them out again with his tweezers. Could have been worse, I suppose. He could have taken up growing dahlias. Vulgar flowers, to my mind. Too many garish colours and no scent. One of these days I must try and find his grave. That is if he has one. Now, stop it, Audrey, don't get maudlin in your old age. How d'you like your eggs?'

'Eggs, plural?'

'Yes.'

'Fried, please.'

'Sunny side up or easy over?'

'What's that mean?'

'Expression the doughboys taught me. Such a quaint way of saying things, the Americans. But I like Americans, don't you?'

'Yes,' I replied without too much conviction, the memory of our encounter with Steinmetz still raw. 'You decide on the eggs.'

I ate the best breakfast I had had in months. When I said goodbye she produced a bottle of brandy. 'Here. I was given this but don't touch it myself, gin's my ruin, but I'm told it warms your toes in this weather.'

'You're spoiling me, Audrey.'

'Got to spoil somebody,' she said and kissed me. She smelt of lavender like my mother.

Outside, Charlie had the Jeep's engine running. 'Doesn't seem to have done any damage, boss,' he said.

'Good. How was your night?'

'No problem, boss, everything still in working order, and it only cost me ten fags.'

'How d'you manage to score every time, Charlie? Let me in on your secret.'

'I laugh them into bed, boss. I reckon they haven't had too many laughs around here recently.'

Austria, in contrast to Germany, was remarkably unscathed; the farms we passed in a near-deserted, pristine landscape were laid out like displays in a toy shop – geometrically neat, smoke rising straight from chimneys, wood stacked with military precision, pale beige cows looking as though they had been freshly polished. 'Mine bloody Godfathers,' Charlie observed. 'Like they never had a war.'

We made the outskirts of Graz before nightfall, and located the local Field Security unit housed in a commandeered farm-house. A portly sergeant named Hargreaves with a pronounced North Country accent greeted me. 'We were expecting you yesterday, Warrant.'

'Yes, unfortunately we ran into a bit of bother with one of our American friends. Quite ugly while it lasted.'

'Funny lot, the Yanks. Nice as pie until they suddenly turn. Think they eat too much red meat. Talking of which, I'm sure you're famished. How would a steak sit with you?'

'You kidding?'

'Oh, no. We don't do things by halves here. What's the point of winning a war if you can't live well? Come over to the Mess. Not much but we're proud of it.'

'This place reminds me of home. Same atmosphere,' I said.

'Where's home?'

'Lincolnshire.'

'Don't know it myself. Never strayed far from Sussex until I was called up.' He led me to an adjacent stable block that had been roughly converted and made habitable with odds and ends of rustic furniture. There was a framed picture of our King and Queen on one of the walls, hung alongside a Nazi flag with bullet holes in it. Hargreaves introduced me to two other sergeants, Mathews and Lewis, who were helping themselves to a beer from a keg on top of a makeshift bar, behind which was a selection of different wines. Seeing my eye go to them, Hargreaves explained: 'The local Gestapo had accumulated quite a cellar, which we appropriated. Some nice French reds, which go down a treat with a steak.'

He selected a bottle and showed me the label. 'Nineteen forty. A good year for Margaux, if not for the French Army.'

A stranger to such vintage wines, I thought it was like velvet and we killed a second bottle over a relaxed meal. I remained deliberately vague about the real purpose of my visit, but pumped the other three for local information. 'What's the local Brigadier like?'

'Hirst? What would you say, Bert?' Hargreaves asked, turning to Mathews.

'Bit of a martinet. Well, definitely a martinet.'

'Yes, definitely,' Lewis chipped in. 'Pre-war professional soldier, took the honour sword at Sandhurst in his year, collected an MC at Anzio, well connected, friends in high places, played polo with the Prince of Wales, so I'm told.'

'D'you have much to do with him?'

'No more than we have to. He's not our number one fan. We usually deal with Wadham, his Adjutant.'

'A real pompous prick, that one,' Mathews said. 'Together they run this area like a personal fiefdom.'

That night I slept soundly in a loft above the stables which smelt of musty hay. After a substantial breakfast I found Charlie hosing the dust off the Jeep. 'How was your night?' I asked.'

'Got my oats again, boss. No problem.'

'What about your wife back In Malta? Don't you ever have a conscience?'

'I ain't seen the missus in four years, haven't had a letter from her in two, maybe she's gone walkabout. In any case I'm not going back to Malta. No future there. England, that's where I'm heading after this.'

Arriving at the camp our identity passes were closely scrutinised before we were allowed to proceed. Hargreaves was right about Hirst being a bullshit artist – the camp looked as though it had been prepared for a visit from royalty. I was directed to Wadham's office where, again, a sentry stood guard and I was required to produce my pass once more. Major Wadham turned out to be a dapper little individual with a trimmed toothbrush moustache and a clipped accent. He immediately made me aware that my presence wasn't welcome.

'I fail to understand why Hamburg didn't inform us you were coming, Sergeant Major,' he said after I'd thrown him a crisp salute. 'What is the purpose of this visit?'

'We've had reports of Martin Bormann being sighted in this area,' I lied, having decided this was a good opening ploy.

'So?'

'I was sent to check them out, sir. Amongst other things.'

'You don't think we're capable of doing that ourselves?'

'Mine not to question orders, sir.'

'You said "other things". What other things?' he snapped.

An orderly interrupted, bringing a cup of tea for Wadham who pointedly didn't offer me one. 'What other things?' he repeated, stirring his cup and dumping in enough sugar to bring on instant diabetes.

'General security matters, sir. Making sure everybody's on their toes.'

'That's a bloody impertinence. You can go back and inform Group that had Bormann been seen in this sector I would have known and dealt with it. Everything comes through my office, I make certain of that. You've had a wasted trip.'

'You could be right, sir.'

'I shall certainly take this up with Group and make my views known.'

I began to get the distinct impression there was unease behind his bluster and suspected that somehow he had got wind of the true purpose for my visit.

'I was told to request a meeting with the Brigadier, sir.'

'That won't be necessary. You can get all you need from me.'

'My orders were specific, sir, and were signed by the General commanding 30 Corps. Perhaps you'd like to see a copy?'

'I certainly would,' Wadham said, his expression betraying the fact that this was something he had not allowed for. He studied the document and handed it back to me. 'Well, Brigadier Hirst is not available today. He's in Vienna attending a tri-party conference on the refugee situation.'

'My orders are to stay in the area until I have a personal meeting, sir, so will you be good enough to let me know when he returns? I'm contactable at local Field Security.'

'I'll do that,' Wadham said tersely and brought the meeting to an end. I saluted and withdrew.

'How did you make out?' Hargreaves asked.

'I didn't get very far because Hirst is away in Vienna, so you're going to have to put up with me for a while longer. I agree with you about Wadham. Puffed up little sod.'

'I don't want to push you, but would I be right in guessing that this isn't a casual, routine visit?'

'No, it isn't. I'll explain when I've seen Hirst. In the meantime what d'you lot do for relaxation around here?'

'Usually we take a ride into Krumpendorf, where Bert here discovered a super little *Gasthof*. Pretty setting, overlooking a lake.

Good grub, lethal brew of home-made cider and usually a clutch of local talent to suit most tastes – war widows looking for company and a free meal.'

'Lead me to it,' I said.

FOUR

I reported the lack of progress to Group and was told that on no account was I to return until Hirst had been confronted with the charges. Suddenly handed a few days unexpected French leave and having been introduced to the *Gasthof* at Krumpendorf I decided to move in and enjoy a complete change of scenery. After the dirt and squalor of Hamburg, to be able to recapture an almost forgotten freedom brought back the feeling of the first day after school broke up for the holidays.

The *Gasthof* nestled in a thickly wooded area of pine and had a quality about it, which reminded me of an illustration from a childhood fairytale book. The proprietor, Herr Wohlbrueck and his wife allocated me the best room, while Charlie was given one in the eaves. The Wohlbruecks were hospitable without being servile, though I couldn't make up my mind whether their attitude was genuine or calculated. There was a photograph of a young soldier in Wehrmacht uniform on a table in the entrance hallway that I took to be a portrait of their dead son because a candle was always burning in front of it along with a vase of fresh flowers. The food they served was simple but good. I gave Frau Wohlbrueck a bar of soap with which to do my laundry and a tin of pipe tobacco to her husband, having been nauseated by the odour of the herbal mixture he smoked.

In the evenings half a dozen women of varying ages frequented the small bar. Hargreaves had described them accurately: they were widows, lonely and looking for companionship. Some of them came in traditional Austrian costumes, their scrubbed, peasant faces devoid of make-up reminding me of Lincolnshire girls at a village hop. I chatted in German with them and bought them drinks, enjoying feminine company after such a long absence, but, unlike Mathews and Lewis, I shied away from any more

33

intimate involvement. The idea of sleeping with the enemy was still alien to me.

During the three days I spent there I had the luxury of a fire in my bedroom. Pleasantly drunk every night but becalmed under the feather duvet, I retraced my life to date, pondering what a long journey it had been from the Normandy beaches to this moment. A line had been drawn between my childhood and forced maturity; everything in between was a void. I was a stranger to myself, unsure what was normal any more. I tried to imagine how others – Charlie, Hargreaves, Wadham – made sense of the lives they had been compelled to live and what plans they had for the life beyond the Army. I couldn't imagine what the rest of my life would be, how I would fill my civilian days. The scent of pine from the hissing logs in the tiled stove eventually lulled me to sleep and I awoke to the sound of distant cowbells.

After breakfast and having checked that there was no word of Hirst's return, I would go for long walks, taking the icy path that skirted the dark waters of the nearby lake – a black wound in a landscape blanketed by dazzling snow. Apart from the sound of my boots crunching the packed snow, I was alone in a country of stillness.

Finally I was informed that Hirst was back and prepared to grant me an interview. In preparation for the meeting I had folded my uniform every night and slept with it under the mattress to ensure that the trouser creases were straight. I spit-polished my boots, blancoed my webbing and when satisfied that Charlie's appearance was likewise parade-ground perfect, drove back to Brigade HQ, arriving ahead of the prescribed time.

Wadham greeted me with a curt, 'The Brigadier will see you when he's finished with daily orders,' and I was left to cool my heels for the best part of an hour before the phone on his desk rang and I was marched into the presence. Hirst's room was dominated by a looted partner's desk and other antique pieces, giving it the look of a successful lawyer's chambers rather than an Army office. My eye went to several silver photo frames displayed on the desk, one showing Hirst in polo gear receiving a cup from Edward VIII, another a family portrait of his wife and two young sons.

Hirst was a tall man, handsome in a period way, the sort of Anthony Eden good looks that found favour with pre-war debutantes. He wore a well-tailored uniform with the MC ribbon on his chest. In contrast to Wadham he received me with a smile and from the start he conducted the meeting with studied politeness.

'At ease, Sergeant Major. Apologies for keeping you hanging about, rather heavy schedule this morning. However, I did find time to make enquiries about you. You have an exemplary record so far.' He gave a slight emphasis to "so far". 'Always a good thing, don't you agree, to know who one's dealing with?'

'Yes, sir.'

'The fact that you were promoted in the field speaks volumes. Where did that happen?'

'Outside Abbeville, sir,' I replied, 'When our previous CSM bought it.'

'I wasn't at the Normandy party. From all reports a good show.' Many of the top brass aped Montgomery's cricket-commentary-style of speech when talking about battles – 'We're going to knock them for six,' and so forth. 'Not that Italy was a cakewalk,' he added.

'No, I'm sure not, sir.'

'I understand you were educated at a grammar school and came away fluent in two languages.'

'Wouldn't say fluent, sir. I get by.'

There was something too studied about this opening exchange, as though from the outset he wanted to establish the social difference between us.

'Do stand at ease. Why weren't you ever considered for a commission?'

'No idea, sir.'

'Obviously an oversight. I would have thought you're obvious officer material. Has anybody offered you any refreshment, by the way?'

'No, but I'm fine, sir.'

'How old are you?'

'Twenty-four, sir.'

'Ever thought of staying on in the Army?'

'No, I haven't, sir.'

'What are you going back to when you get demobbed? Got a job waiting?'

'In a way, sir. My people are farmers.'

'Is that what you want to do?'

'It's sort of taken for granted, sir.'

'Never take anything for granted. The Army can use intelligent officers of your calibre. If you're keen, I'd be happy to put forward a recommendation for a peacetime commission.'

'That's kind of you, sir, but I'm looking forward to getting demobbed.'

'Well, bear it in mind. The offer's there if you want it. And coming from me, it would carry weight . . . Now, I understand from my Adjutant you're here to see if we're up to scratch on security matters.'

'It's part of my brief, yes, sir.'

'Any particular area you're concerned about?'

He was going out of his way to be pleasant to me, as though he had determined charm was his best defence, but as we edged closer to the crux of the matter, I was aware of tightness in his voice.

'One of the leads I was asked to follow up concerns a reported sighting of Martin Bormann in your sector, sir,' I answered.

'I thought he was presumed dead?'

'He can't be accounted dead, sir, until we've captured him or found his corpse. There are conflicting stories about his last days in Berlin and the Russians are not sharing any information they have.'

'And you say he's been sighted around here? '

'Allegedly once in Villach, sir, and once in Werfen.'

'Were we circulated?'

'I believe so, sir.'

'Not to my knowledge.' He frowned and scribbled something on a notepad. 'I'll look into it straight away. Is that all?'

I took a deep breath and plunged. 'There is another matter, sir, of a more personal nature.'

'Personal?'

'Yes, sir.'

'And what would that be?' His voice remained flat.

'Your name has cropped up in connection with an ongoing investigation, sir.'

There was the slightest of pauses. 'What does that mean, Sergeant Major?' The sudden reversion to my rank was indicative of his unease.

'Well, sir, for some months now we've been involved in a combined operation between ourselves and the American special branch to crack a major scam.'

'Scam'? What does that mean?'

'An American expression, sir, for an illegal scheme. In this case it carries criminal charges,' I added for emphasis.

'What have the Yanks got to do with it?'

'Their prime suspect was in charge of the marshalling yards at Antwerp where the chain originated.'

'You said "was" in charge.'

'He's currently under arrest, sir, awaiting trial.'

'I still don't understand what this has to do with me or my command.'

'We have been given to believe, sir, that you form part of that chain.'

Hirst did not flinch, or lose his thin smile. 'That's a very serious allegation, Sergeant Major. In the circumstances, you'd better repeat it in front of Major Wadham.'

'Of course, sir.'

He pressed a button on his internal phone. 'Come in, Wadham.'

Wadham entered immediately as though he had been listening for the summons on the other side of the door. 'Brigadier?'

'The Sergeant Major here has just made an extraordinary allegation which I would like repeated in the presence of a witness. Continue, Sergeant Major.'

'I am under orders to inform Brigadier Hirst, that he is implicated in a serious breach of King's Regulations which, if substantiated, would lead to a court martial.'

Wadham's response had menace in it. 'I hope you are aware of the gravity of that statement, Sergeant Major.'

'I am, sir.' The whole atmosphere in the room had undergone a change.

'Should you repeat it outside this room, you'll find yourself under arrest,' Wadham said.

'Well, let's not be too hasty,' Hirst said, jumping in. 'First of all I need to know how I am supposedly implicated.' He still maintained a calm façade, though by now I was convinced that he and Wadham were in cahoots.

I began a carefully prepared speech, memorised from the full briefing I had been given in Hamburg. 'Sir, a GI truck driver was recently detained outside Vienna. Under interrogation he gave names and full details of a widespread scheme involving participants in both the American and British sectors. The consignment of cigarettes, liquor and other goods he was transporting were intended as stock for American PX stores, but would never find their way there. Instead, the goods would be diverted and disappear into the black market and quickly disposed of. A bogus trading company had been set up in Holland to handle the proceeds; the money fed to this company was then used to purchase and ship to England large quantities of tulip bulbs. The scheme was operated on a regular basis and until recently the considerable profits generated could not be traced back to their source.'

Hirst heard me out. 'Yes,' he said, 'very ingenious, but I fail to see what it has to do with me.' He took a cigarette from the silver box on his desk and lit it.

'The driver gave a number of names, sir. One of the names was yours.'

I caught a quick glance between them. Wadham immediately responded with, 'Are you telling us that this GI's word is the sole basis for a monstrous accusation against a senior British officer?'

'No, sir. It isn't just this man's word. At least a dozen others involved have already been rounded up, including an American Colonel. He also implicated Brigadier Hirst.'

Hirst took his time before speaking again. 'I take it you came with written authority to put these allegations before me?'

'Yes, sir. My authority was signed by the GOC 30 Corps. I have already shown it to Major Wadham.'

'Let me see it.'

I produced the document and he studied it, then got up from his desk and went to the window. There was an appreciable silence before he said: 'Wadham, leave this with me, will you?' Wadham hesitated, seemingly about to say something else before withdrawing as ordered. When we were alone once again, Hirst returned to his desk and slumped into his swivel chair, staring past me for a few moments before looking me in the face. 'You appreciate, Sergeant Major Seaton, that I have no intention of responding to the charge you have laid against me. That will have to wait until I am dignified by a higher authority than you. But I would value talking to you off the record, as soldier to soldier.'

'By all means, sir.'

'Without prejudice.'

'As you wish, sir.'

Hirst began slowly, picking his words carefully. 'We're living in turbulent times, Seaton, the best of times and the worst of times, in many ways times none of us could have envisaged a few years back. We're all at the end of a long war, fought against a terrible enemy. A terrible enemy,' he repeated, 'and many, too many, good men paid the ultimate price to put us where we are. But those of us lucky enough to come through it didn't escape unscarred. I know I didn't, and I suspect you didn't either. Or perhaps you did? Only you can decide that. There were many moments, especially when things were not going our way, when I tried to imagine how I would react to defeat. I never came up with an answer. All I did know was that if I came out unscathed I had no intention of letting myself be sold down the river like my father. The signs are already there. It's highly unlikely this new Labour government will retain a large standing army unless they've changed their spots. Chaps like me will soon be forgotten, despite this.' He tapped the Military Cross ribbon on his chest. 'My father won a DSO and bar at Ypres and a damn lot of good it did him. He wore a tin mask to hide his shattered face before he died of his wounds and my mother had to sell his medals to put me through college. I long ago determined I would not condemn my own children to live on charity.' He stopped and seemed at a loss to know how to conclude. 'What I'm trying to say is, we've all had to reconcile ourselves to the fact that nothing is ever black and white. Wouldn't you agree?'

'I'm not sure that I follow you, sir,' I said.

'Those who didn't go through what you and I went through, find it easy to make moral judgements about our behaviour. But they weren't there; they didn't see men die as we did. They think the annual laying of wreaths at the Cenotaph is repayment enough. Well, I beg to differ. They owe us, and if we believe, as I believe, they will choose to ignore us, as in the past, then we have the right to take matters into our own hands.'

'Sir, with respect, although I appreciate your views, I did not lay the charges against you, I'm only the messenger.'

His mood changed abruptly. 'Don't patronise me,' he barked. 'I know you're the bloody messenger and I've eaten types like you for breakfast. They sent small fry like you because those bloody desk wallers don't have the balls to face me themselves. What else were you instructed to say? I'm sure they didn't let you come empty-handed.'

'I wasn't told the nuts and bolts, sir, but I was given to understand that, if you co-operated, a compromise could be reached.'

'Compromise? What does that imply?'

'That the matter could be settled without dragging anybody down.'

'Come on, man, be more explicit, spell it out.'

'You'd be offered early retirement, with all charges dropped.'

Much to my surprise, Hirst snorted with laughter. 'Oh, that's rich. One of their typical stitch-ups. Push everything under the carpet. So, if I co-operate, as they put it, admit guilt, I can be shunted off into oblivion. And what if I don't accept their bloody compromise?'

'I can't answer that, sir.'

He got up and walked around the room. 'Well, so be it. You've carried out your brief and can report back that I admitted nothing, nor agreed to anything, and that I will give my response when formal charges are lodged. Is that understood?'

'Understood, sir.'

'Do you? Do you? I doubt it. I doubt if you're capable of understanding my situation, given your background.' He stared hard at me for a few seconds. 'You've carried out your orders, now leave me with it.'

I saluted and left the room. Wadham eyed me as I went through, but said nothing.

FIVE

My run-in with Hirst left me angry. I suppose it was his parting shot about my background that really rankled. He was right, of course; I was unable fully to understand his world. It was difficult for a Lincolnshire grammar-school boy to comprehend the life of a red-tab officer schooled at Sandhurst who played polo with royalty. Doubtless certain codes of conduct had been instilled in him from birth as surely as coal dust is engrained in a miner's face, and he lived by them come what may. I felt no personal animosity towards him; if anything my bile was reserved for Wadham and his kind, the arse-licking time servers.

That night, hunched beside the warmth of the tiled stove, I made an effort to remember everything that he and Wadham had said to me as I wrote my report. I put in I suspected Hirst had known the real purpose of my visit from the start, and had prepared his careful responses. I also included that I viewed his offer to obtain a commission for me as a not too subtle ploy to win me over to his side and I summed up by saying that I had come away convinced that both he and Wadham were involved.

The following morning after organising for the report to be couriered back to Group, I stopped Charlie preparing for our departure.

'We're not moving out just yet, Charlie. I have to wait here until I get further orders.'

'Suits me, boss. Can I ask you something? Are you believing in love at first sight?'

'I suppose so, a lot of people claim it does happen. Why?'

'I've got it bad,' Charlie said. 'Mine bloody Godfathers, have I got it bad. She's the real thing for me.'

'What're you talking about?'

'Anna. I see her and suddenly I can't breathe.'

'Charlie, wait a minute, you're going too fast for me. Who's Anna?' I was alarmed. I had never seen him so animated.

'My bride to be. This time it's the full works.'

'How d'you mean, "your bride to be"? Slow down. You're already married. You've got a wife back in Malta'

'Maybe. Maybe not, boss. '

'No, not "maybe". You're married, you silly sod.'

'OK, you're right, boss. But now I am not going back there. Next stop England, with Anna.'

'Charlie, listen. Calm down and listen to me. Marriage, England, what the fuck are you talking about? You'd never met this Anna before we got here, for Christ's sake.'

'A few days are plenty for the real thing.'

'Who is this Anna?'

'Tonight, I show you her, then you understand.'

'Is she Austrian?'

'No, she ain't anything right now, but after we marry she gets British papers like me.'

'What d'you mean "like you"? You don't have British papers. You're Maltese.'

He grinned, shook his head and produced a British passport from his battledress pocket. 'I buy this in Hamburg for just such an occasion.'

'What about your Army documents? They show you as Maltese.'

'You want to bet, boss?'

'I shouldn't be listening to this,' I said. 'You're going to end up in the slammer.'

'I tell you, boss, my life up to now has been a bloody bummer, I need to change it before it's too late.'

'A prison cell, that's what you'll change it for.'

'I'll take my chances, boss,' he said, but for the first time his voice betrayed the fact that his convictions had been dented.

'Well, I never heard this conversation. You're crazy.'

'Ain't you ever been crazy, boss?'

'Not that crazy. Just think it through is my advice.'

That evening he brought his prospective bride into the small dining room and introduced her. I've never been able to fathom what determines selection in the human mating game. By any criteria Charlie and the stateless girl he called Anna were worlds apart. Anna was in her twenties, Charlie approaching forty. She wasn't sexy, just pleasantly attractive with deep-set, dark eyes under auburn hair, a small Cupid's bow mouth. I saw history and tragedy in her wan face, the legacy that the war had etched into it. I did my best to put her at ease but she carried the wariness of the dispossessed like a birthmark to anybody who showed kindness; kindness, she had learned, always had a price. I made some innocuous remarks to Charlie, complimenting him on his choice, which he accepted with eagerness. Anna made little or no conversation during the meal and it did not escape me that Wohlbrueck served her with smaller portions than Charlie or me, offended I suppose that he had been forced to be polite to an inferior displaced person.

There was no way of telling whether Anna's feelings matched Charlie's; perhaps, like so many women in her situation, she saw him as a lifebelt miraculously thrown her way. Aware that Charlie was desperate for me to be impressed, I went along with the charade as he frequently raised Anna's hand to his lips and kissed it.

'All night I don't sleep, boss,' he said. 'But love is a debt you got to pay, right? So I fix everything.' He drained his wine glass. 'Am I getting processed, boss?'

'I think so, just a bit. What're you talking about now? What have you fixed?'

'You can't have no idea what's going through my head. I have a big favour to ask, boss.' He stood up. 'I hope I put it to you right, because I got to do this. Although I've fixed it, I need two.'

'Two what?'

'Witnesses, boss. Right now I only got one, a friend of Anna's.' From habit, he drew himself up to attention. 'The favour is, boss, I need you to make it legit.'

'Sit down, Charlie. Sit down and let's talk this through.' I felt uneasy discussing the situation in front of Anna, whether she understood or not. 'We've already been over the pros and cons and I've told you what I think. I accept you feel this way about Anna, and having met her, I agree she's a very nice girl. But taking it further until you're free isn't a good idea. It'll lead to nothing but trouble for you both.' I shot a look at Anna and smiled at her.

'Boss, sir, with respect always, it's a matter of honour. I've given my word.' He reached for Anna's hand again. 'I have made the marriage proposal.'

'I appreciate that, I appreciate you're acting with the best intentions, but sometimes best intentions aren't enough, even in matters of the heart . . . especially in matters of the heart. Because sometimes we let our hearts rule our heads and we need to stop and think very carefully.' I realised I had begun to sound like a bank manager discussing a dubious request for an overdraft. 'You know it would be wrong of me to pretend I think this is a good idea.' Seeing the look of hopelessness in both their faces, I faltered. 'You say you've "fixed everything", what exactly does that mean?'

'The time, the place, boss, for tomorrow.'

'Tomorrow?'

'Yes, boss.' His eyes pleaded. 'Tomorrow we get hitched, legitimate, at the town hall. I paid good money in advance.'

Anna had the expression of somebody who had just been told of a death in the family and I could imagine what her future would be if Charlie's scheme fell apart. Life for the stateless was a living nightmare: without papers they didn't exist. They both stared at me with the hurt eyes of dogs waiting to see if they would be put down, and I didn't have the heart to fight any longer.

'OK,' I said, 'let's have another drink, you crazy sod. I don't know why I'm saying this, but I'll go along, I'll do it.'

For a moment I thought Charlie might throw his arms around

me, but discipline kicked in and he hugged Anna instead. For the rest of the evening I tried to enter into the spirit of the thing and share their happiness, but it required an effort. I could see nothing but disaster ahead. The only way I reconciled myself to their madness was that, as far as I knew, nothing in King's Regulations forbade me merely witnessing a marriage, albeit a bigamous one.

SIX

Hargreaves rang while I was having breakfast the next morning and said: 'Has the news reached you yet?'

'What news?'

'About Hirst?'

'No.'

'He's out of the reckoning.'

'In what way?'

'Dead.'

'Dead?'

'Found in his staff car with his brains splattered all over the windscreen.'

'Jesus!' I exclaimed. 'Where?'

'Not far from you, on the road to Klagenfurt.'

'Jesus!' I repeated.

'My bet is he pulled the trigger himself, but they're already covering their tracks. The story we have to stick to is that he was ambushed and killed by a band of last-ditch SS.'

'He was in deep shit, you know.'

'I didn't, but I guessed as much. We figured your trip here wasn't a courtesy call. You didn't let on, but what was he facing, a wrist-slap or the chop?'

'The chop. But I thought he'd find a way of beating the rap.'

'Well, I guess you could say he did in a way. But, watch this space. You wait; they'll bury him with full military honours. Tragic murder of decorated hero.'

'You think?'

'I bloody know. Look, before you disappear let's all have a farewell dinner and you can tell us the full story.'

My appetite gone, I pushed the rest of my breakfast to one side. Irrationally, I felt I was responsible for Hirst's end. 'We have to take matters into our own hands,' he had said. At that moment, had he already decided what to do?

I telephoned Wadham. 'CSM Seaton, sir. I've just learned the tragic news about Brigadier Hirst and wanted to offer my sympathy and give any help I can.'

'I think we can get along without your help, Sergeant Major,' he said tersely.

'Have you established what happened, sir?'

He hesitated before answering. 'From what we've been able to piece together it would appear that he was struck down by enemy elements still at large. I have already mounted a full-scale search and destroy operation.'

'I hope you succeed, sir.'

'I have no doubt we will.'

'A great loss, sir.'

'Yes. Do you have anything else you wish to discuss with me? I'm a busy man.'

'No, sir.'

'Good.' The line went dead.

Hargreaves was right. The Establishment moved quickly to protect their own. Doubtless Wadham would stage manage the rest of the charade, arrange for the corpse to be flown home, a flag draped on the coffin for the full ceremonial funeral, ensure that any remaining evidence was destroyed, and eventually be rewarded with his own red tabs in return for keeping his mouth shut. Death was preferable to disgrace in the book they all read from.

It was only then that I remembered what I had to do that morning. I found the nervous bridegroom, and told him the news without elaboration, sticking to the official line. Charlie took it philosophically, his mind on more pressing matters. 'Poor fucker, boss,' he said. 'That's a bad omen on my wedding day.'

'And you're still going through with it? No second thoughts?'

'No, boss. Like I said, love is a debt you've got to honour.' I wasn't sure what debt Charlie had to repay. He was prepared to

48

risk his and Anna's future for a love that hadn't existed a week ago.

'How do I look, boss?' he asked me.

He was wearing his best battledress, his hair was slicked down and he had half a dozen shaving cuts dotted around his chin, each one with a piece of toilet paper stuck on them.

'Apart from the sabre wounds, not too bad.'

'I want to be smooth for my wedding night.'

'You're smooth all right, Charlie.' I said. 'Too smooth for your own good.'

'Hey, boss, you think we could have a drink before we set off?'

'Meaning you want one? OK, but just a small one.'

'And, boss, one last favour. Tell me the German words I got to say. Anna went through them last night, but I forgot already.'

Over the drink, I told him, 'You know what you're going to be after this, don't you? By the end of today you're going to be a Maltese citizen holding a fake British passport bigamously married under Austrian law to a stateless girl. That's some big shit list.'

'Boss, how I look at it, if you're going to take a risk, take a big one.' He produced a crumpled piece of paper from his breast pocket. 'This is the stuff I have to say.'

I did my best to take him through his responses which he repeated after me in halting German. There was no point any longer in persuading him against it; like Hirst he was determined to put a gun to his head and pull the trigger. He had an *amour fou*, as the French put it.

There were only four people at the ceremony: the bride and groom, me and the second witness – a drab, starved little woman, recruited by Anna, who disappeared the moment the proceedings were concluded. The knot was tied in a bare, first-floor room in the Town Hall, conducted by the Burgermeister, Herr Kruger, who scowled at Charlie throughout. It was hardly a joyous occasion, more like applying for a driving licence. A section of ceiling plaster fell down just as Charlie and Anna were pronounced man and wife, which was as close as it got to being a white wedding. We two witnesses signed the certificates and Register, then Kruger rubber-stamped everything, the only part of the proceedings he appeared to enjoy. Charlie slipped my fellow witness some money and she disappeared.

Back at the Gasthof, I shared what passed for a wedding breakfast with the happy couple. Throughout the meal Charlie repeatedly kissed his bride, leaving specks of blood on her face from his shaving cuts. 'How could I be this lucky?' he said. 'What did I do to deserve this angel?' He kept the marriage certificate beside his plate and from time to time studied it as though he couldn't quite believe it existed. As they nuzzled each, I began to feel like an intruder and excused myself. 'May you both be very happy,' I said.

'Boss,' Charlie said, 'I never forget what you do for me.' I saw that he had tears in his eyes. 'You always have a best friend in me and when I have my restaurant in London, every day you eat for free.'

'You'd soon go broke. Have a great day, but don't forget we have to leave first thing in the morning.'

It was only when I had left them that I realised he had never mentioned how Anna was going to live with him in Hamburg, or indeed how she was going to get to Hamburg. She couldn't travel back with us in an Army Jeep.

Next morning a tearful Anna saw us off and it wasn't until we had been on the road half an hour that I broached the question.

'I left money for her keep and the train ticket,' Charlie said. 'When I've found a place for her she'll join me. I've got contacts.'

'Then what? What's the long-term plan?'

He stared ahead, gripping the driving wheel. 'That's going to take a bit of working out, boss. But I got it going round in my head. I ain't worried long term. Where there's a will there's a way, ain't that the British saying?'

But some of the old ebullience had gone out of his voice.

SEVEN

It was grim to be back in my cheerless Hamburg bedroom after the comforts of the Gasthof and having to resume the daily round of interrogations. The onus of having to make spot decisions about the probability of innocence, the possibility of guilt, was never easy. If they were to be believed, few of those who came before me ever admitted to having supported Hitler: as they told it, the dead Fuehrer was a regretted genetic aberration thrown up by mistake. As the first chill winds of the Cold War started to blow across the political landscape, many now denied they had ever wished to fight the British. Historically, they insisted, we are blood brothers who have always been allies. ('We were at your side at Waterloo, don't forget.' 'Your Royal family is German.' 'The real enemy is Bolshevism.')

Listening to the same pleadings day after day wore me down and what truly pissed me off was that we were under unwritten orders to operate double standards. On the one hand we were supposed to be ruthless in rooting out Nazis guilty of crimes against humanity, yet allowed to turn a blind eye if we thought any of them had the necessary qualifications to help get Germany back on its feet. It was an open secret that the Yanks were granting amnesty and shipping the rocket scientists home. Whereas I had power over the lives of others, my own life was in what the airlines call a holding pattern. Many of us had been promised we would soon be demobbed, but somewhere, someone decided our services were too valuable to lose. Before the election we had been told 'Vote Labour and you'll go to the head of the queue' – a con which drove Grable into paroxysms, but which Machell accepted with his usual equanimity. 'Rule one,' he said. 'Never believe anything that isn't written down in triplicate and signed by your mother. Have it framed and nail it above your bed.' Unlike the rest of us he was quite content to be left in harness. 'You lot may be anxious to see the back of me, but personally I'm quite happy to keep my head below the parapet until somebody wakes up to the fact that I am long overdue for putting out to pasture. What have I got to go back to? Just the prospect of joining a tribe of fellow geriatrics in some seaside guest house and boring them rigid with reminiscences of the glory days of the Raj.'

Allied to his cheerful cynicism, I envied him having a past. My own, as the only son of aged parents reared on a small Lincolnshire farm, was hardly the stuff of legend. Schooling had ended for me at age sixteen, for then the war seemed destined to last forever and I counted on being called up in a year's time. Denied the chance to go to university, I was lucky in that Mr Bennet, the headmaster, was passionate about literature and the English language. An odd character, crippled from a First World War wound so that he walked with a lopsided gait, unmarried, certainly not everybody's cup of tea, his temper was always on a short fuse. To most of my classmates he was an ogre, but curiously he was always prepared to take pains over me. I don't think I was particularly bright, maybe a little brighter than the rest, but, presumably, Bennet must have detected some potential because he gave me special tuition in French and German, a grounding later honed by Machell. He also allowed me the run of his eclectic library, which was manna in my eyes, my home being devoid of books. He lifted me out of the set school curriculum, and guided me towards authors such as Aldous Huxley, Aldington and D. H. Lawrence, instilling in me a reverence for the written word. I went to war with his well-thumbed copy of *Death of a Hero* in my knapsack. 'Don't ever be fooled by what authority wants you to believe in,' he told me, curiously anticipating Machell's advice. 'Put not your faith in politicians or archbishops, question everything, never become the passive cannon fodder they want you to be.'

On the long haul from the Normandy beaches I could endure most privations providing I had a book to read; occasionally I was lucky enough to come across an odd volume in the debris of a bombed-out house, but it wasn't until the unit had a base in Hamburg that I had the opportunity to seek out the few book-shops that remained in business.

Chance so often changes the compass bearings of our lives, pointing us in directions we would otherwise never have taken. Who knows what led me one afternoon to the shabby exterior of a small backstreet shop where I spied an English copy of *The Scarlet Letter* that had somehow escaped the Nazi book burnings. There was another customer in the dim interior when I went in to enquire the price and was quoted the equivalent of three pounds sterling. 'I'll take it,' I said. While my purchase was being retrieved from the window, the other customer, a middle-aged man of unprepossessing appearance, addressed me deferentially in English: 'You have made a good choice, sir. I myself was tempted, but alas the price was beyond my means.'

My trained, suspicious mind noted his ingratiating smile and command of English, and I took him to be another black market operator, albeit more cultivated than average, since most did not frequent antiquarian bookshops. I waited for the inevitable – "Do you by any chance have cigarettes for sale?" – but he surprised me by saying: 'Allow me to introduce myself. Professor Grundwall.'

I shook his proffered hand and asked: 'A professor of literature?'

'A lover of literature, a professor of philosophy,' he answered.

'Here in Hamburg?'

'Yes, at the university. The faculty is gradually getting back to normal. Well, as normal as can be expected in the circumstances.'

After I had paid for my purchase, he left the shop with me. 'It's not usual to find British soldiers in a bookshop,' he said.

'Really? We're not all philistines.'

'Of course, forgive me, I had not intended to be rude. Just an observation.' Now that we were outside in the daylight I saw that his shabby suit seemed a size too large for his frame and his shirt collar was frayed. He seemed anxious to keep me in conversation.

'The novel you have just purchased created a stir, I believe, when it was first published.'

'Yes,' I said, 'I believe it did. The branding of sinners was a shameful stigma.' I decided to test him closer to home. 'In the same way as forcing Jews to wear the Yellow star.'

He took this. 'Indeed. A shameful act which can never be written out of our history.'

I wanted to get behind his mask, if mask it was. I had become programmed to suspect everybody as a matter of course, but his answer, although predictable, seemed genuine. Then he asked: 'Do you write, by any chance?'

'No. I don't have any talent in that direction. But I love books.'

'Well, to make amends for my rudeness just now, perhaps you will allow me to lend you a volume or two from my own, modest library? I know what it is to be deprived of reading matter, even though I was fortunate and came through the war with most of my collection more or less intact. The destruction of books is another blot we would like to expunge.'

'Were you still teaching at the university throughout the war?'

'No. I had to serve in the forces like everybody else. Not as a fighting soldier I'm happy to say. I was in communications, monitoring foreign broadcasts like your BBC.'

'That must have given you a different slant on the news compared to that put out by Goebbels.'

'Yes, but too dangerous to share. Should you ever wish to look at my library, allow me to give you my address.' He wrote it down on a scrap of paper and handed it to me before we parted company.

The address lay forgotten in my pocket for a couple of weeks, then, when pressure of work eased for a day, I remembered the invitation and, being at a loose end, had Charlie find the location on the map and drive me there. He took me to an area that I suppose must have been considered middle class before the war with solid, dull architecture. Now there were gaps and the exterior of the house where Grundwall lived was smoke blackened still and stood isolated, with gutted shells on either side. The main door swung open on damaged hinges and the first thing that struck me as I stepped over the threshold was the scent of charred wood as though the very walls had been impregnated. There was also the repellent smell of boiled cabbage, taking me back to childhood visits to an elderly aunt. From the name plate there appeared to be half a dozen families sharing the house. The Grundwalls were on the first floor. There was no name on their door, but I knocked twice and it was eventually opened by a small, bird-like woman, dressed in old clothes that, like her husband's, hung loose on her sparse frame.

'Frau Grundwall?'

Confronted by a stranger in uniform, her expression was immediately fearful.

'*Ja, mein Herr.*'

'Is Professor Grundwall at home?'

'*Ja, mein Herr.*'

Behind her Grundwall came into view and peered at me, his expression likewise wary until he recognised me. 'It's all right, Gerta,' he said in German, 'the officer is somebody I met in a bookshop. Please, sir, do come in. I'm sorry, but I don't know your name or rank.'

'My rank doesn't matter. My name's Alex.'

I stepped straight into the dimly lit main room, which was crammed with ill-assorted furniture as though, in their reduced circumstances, they had retained the sentimental rather than the functional. Three odd chairs were grouped around a central table covered with a moquette cloth and strewn with papers.

As I was ushered inside he volunteered the information that this was the day in the week when he stayed at home to mark his pupils' test papers. I sat at the table and he produced an opened bottle of hock and his wife brought a plate of pieces of dry, plain cake. She poured the wine in two odd glasses and then sat quietly in a corner of the room. The wine had little taste.

'There is my library, such as it is,' Grundwall said, indicating a small, glass-fronted bookcase which also housed a few china ornaments. It could scarcely be termed a library, since there were fewer than fifty volumes in shabby bindings, of which only a score were in English. Grundwall took out a selection of these and laid them on the table for my inspection.

'As a teacher I was permitted to retain those not deemed subversive. At one time I had the complete works of Shakespeare, but was forced to sell most of them.'

Before starting to examine the books I took out a packet of cigarettes and offered one to him. He extracted it with care, and then turned it over and over between his fingers, studying it as he would some rare clinical specimen.

'Please do not be offended if I don't smoke it now, but save it for later.'

'Don't save it. You're welcome to the whole packet.'

He acquiesced and let me light it for him, inhaling deeply with an expression of bliss. We sat and talked about authors we both admired, though some names he mentioned were unknown to me.

'There are likewise many blanks in my own knowledge,' he confessed. 'We lived in a vacuum for a decade. You have no idea what it was like to be cut off from the world of culture. We had our own culture, of course, the one designed by Speer. A Utopia built on sand.'

I discovered that poets were his great love, especially Rilke and Heine, and he waxed lyrical about 'your all-but-forgotten Edward Young whom Johnson described as a genius. Does anybody read him now?'

'I can't say. Certainly I haven't.'

'Then, *bitte*, borrow my copy because he won't disappoint you. And if I may presume further, please have this too.' He handed me a slim volume. The title on the spine was *Wanderschaft* but gave no clue as to the author. It wasn't until I opened it and turned to the title page that I saw it bore his name.

'Privately printed for friends,' he said. 'You will find it is the ramblings of a once romantic young man. My only opus. Wasn't it your great novelist, Forster, who said, "Write one book and rest on your oars forever?" I took his advice.'

'Are you sure you can spare this?'

'Oh, yes. I still have a few more copies.'

Not since the days when old Bennet had taken me under his wing, had I spent an afternoon talking of literature and for the first time in ages I relaxed, taking Grundwall's answers at face value, not looking for hidden meanings as perforce I had to during the course of my everyday duties. Conscious that Charlie was waiting for me outside, I did not prolong the visit any further, thanked them both for their hospitality and left.

I thought about the interlude a lot and decided to pay a second visit a week or so later. This time I went armed with a small collection of luxuries – a tin of corned beef, a bag of coffee beans, a tablet of Sunlight soap, a bar of chocolate, a razor blade, and two ragged Penguin paperbacks I was finished with. Grundwall and his wife spread the gifts out on the table and regarded them with reverence.

'The razor blade is especially welcome,' Grundwall said. 'The one I have is six months old, carefully sharpened every day on a piece of leather.'

Frau Grundwall immediately wanted to brew the coffee. 'Please,' I said, 'save it for yourselves,' but she insisted. While she busied herself I complimented her husband on his poems. 'I've read them twice, they're so fresh and lyrical.'

'Perhaps that's because at the time I wrote them, I was fresh and lyrical,' he said with a smile. 'Alas, no longer.'

'Nonsense, you still are, Karl,' his wife said in German, calling from the small kitchen.

'Perhaps to my dear wife,' he said to me with a smile.

It was at this moment a young girl let herself into the apartment. Grundwall introduced her. 'This is our only daughter, Lisa. Lisa, please meet our new British friend, Alex.'

Like her mother Lisa wore nondescript clothes that made her look older than her years. I guessed she was on the brink of womanhood. She was obviously disconcerted to be confronted by a strange British soldier in her home. I had to make a conscious effort not to gape, for her delicate beauty took me unawares. There was a pallor to her cheeks, denoting under-nourishment; only her full mouth, although devoid of lipstick, had colour. When we had exchanged greetings, her eyes flicked past me to the gifts on the table.

'Chocolate,' she said. 'Is it real, Mutti?'

Her mother nodded.

'Have some,' I said. 'It's there to be eaten.' I spoke to her in German, but her father interjected. 'I am proud to say that she had a good education and speaks, I think, very good English.'

Lisa handled the bar of chocolate as though it might suddenly slip through her fingers and disappear. Carefully removing the end of the wrapper, she broke off a single portion, looking at it closely before putting it in her mouth and savouring the moment. 'Oh, it's just wonderful.'

'Eat it all,' I said, now offering her a cigarette. 'I can always bring you some more.'

'Thank you, but I don't smoke,' she said.

'As your father says, you speak good English. Are you a student at his university?'

'She is an actress,' Grundwall answered.

'Really? Are you acting anywhere at the moment?'

'Now we are still rehearsing.'

'What play is it?'

'Not a play, an operetta. *The White Horse Inn.*'

'I don't know it,' I said. 'Should I? Is it very famous?'

'I'm not sure. I think it was very popular before the war.'

The exchange petered out and while I searched for something else to say, her father informed me that the production would have its first night at the Stadt Opera House in ten days time.

'I must come and see you,' I said to her, perhaps a shade too quickly for I caught the look that passed between her parents. Did they think I was just another soldier on the make for their daughter? My gifts suddenly took on the appearance of bribes.

Grundwall said: '*The White Horse Inn* was always a favourite of mine. You remember, Gerta, we saw it together before we were married?' He hummed a few bars of one of the numbers. 'That song in particular has special memories for us, doesn't it, dear?'

His wife smiled and shook her head as if to say, 'Yes, but don't try and sing it now.'

Grundwall shrugged. 'Lisa, you sing it.'

'No, please, Vater, don't embarrass me.'

'Then, despite advance criticism, I shall.' He sang one stanza in a croaky voice before admitting defeat. 'Well, something like that.' The stanza he had sung translated as: 'It would be wonderful indeed if you loved me as I love you.'

'Is that one of the numbers you sing that in the show?' I asked Lisa.

'Oh, no, I am not one of the principals. I just have a small role.'

The pungent smell of coffee filled the room and sent them all into a sort of trance. 'What a day this is,' Grundwall said. 'A cigarette, coffee, and of course the books you brought. I have to pinch myself to believe I'm not dreaming.' He cradled his cup in both hands and bent his head down, inhaling the aroma.

'Aren't we lucky,' Lisa said.

'We are, we are. Such kindness.'

Given the paucity of my gifts their pleasure and gratitude seemed out of all proportion. It suddenly struck me that, for the first time since I had entered Germany, I was enjoying an ordinary conversation with an erstwhile enemy family. But, more importantly I could not see anybody but Lisa in the room.

'What date does the play open?' I asked.

'The fourteenth.'

'The fourteenth? I must make sure I'm not on duty that night. Perhaps, I could take you for a meal after the show? If your mother and father don't object.'

Lisa immediately looked to her parents. 'I don't see why not, do you, Gerta?' her father said.

Frau Grundwall expressed agreement, but there was a note of doubt in her voice.

'Although an actress, our daughter is not all that worldly,' Grundwall added ambiguously.

Their replies betrayed the fact that they had fears. Understandably. Soldiers were usually only out for one thing and my eagerness was too blatant. 'Of course, only if Lisa wants to,' I said. I smiled at her across the table.

Her response hung in the air for a few moments and again she looked to her parents. 'Yes,' she said. 'Yes, that would be nice.'

I made my excuses shortly afterwards and left, hoping none of them would have a change of heart.

EIGHT

The following day I was detailed to escort a high-ranking SS prisoner to the dustbin in Celle. I requested Charlie as my driver as usual, but when I went to the garage I found he hadn't reported in for duty.

'Haven't seen him, CSM,' the duty corporal told me.

'See if he's still in the sack and, if he is, give him a bollocking and get him here double quick.'

'No sign, sir,' the Corporal said when he returned. 'His bed hasn't been slept in. Think he's gone AWOL, sir?'

'If he has, the stupid sod's going to be on a fizzer.' I took another driver in his place, but later in the day, Charlie was still missing and there was a message for me to contact the Military Police. I discovered that he had been picked up the night before in the off-limits, red-light district and held on several charges, the most serious being in possession of forged papers. I obtained permission to visit him in the cells.

Crestfallen, he greeted me with, 'Boss, I let you down big time.'

'Never mind that, why on ever did you take such a chance?'

'No choice, boss.'

'What d'you mean, no choice? You didn't need to go whoring.'

'No whoring, boss. I had to see Anna.'

'Anna? What's she got to do with it?'

'It's where she is, boss.'

'In the red light district?'

'Yes, boss.'

'You mean in a brothel?'

'Yes, boss, but she's not on the game, don't think that. Not my Anna. I thought it was the safest place, until I make other arrangements. I've visited her there before, just got unlucky this time. When she made her way to Hamburg I bribed one of the pimps

61

to find her a safe room. What will happen to me, boss?' The words tumbled out, all his old assurance gone.

'You're in a fucking mess, Charlie, and I wouldn't like to predict the outcome. If it had just been a brothel visit and left up to Colonel Machell to deal with, you'd have got off with a few days jankers and loss of pay, but this is dead serious, it's now in the Provost Marshal's hands. Why on earth did you have those fake papers on you?'

'Nowhere else safe to hide them,' he said lamely.

'Do they know about Anna?'

'No way am I telling them about her. No way.'

'You never listened to me, did you, Charlie? I warned you way back in Austria.'

'I love her,' he said simply. 'She's my wife.'

'Well, let's not open that can of peas. I'll do my best to help, but don't expect any miracles.'

When his case came up I attended the hearing as a character witness and pleaded for his previous good record to be taken into account, citing his bravery during the Italian campaign, but the court was not persuaded to leniency. Possession of forged papers could not be ignored, especially when the accused was serving with an Intelligence unit and therefore could come in contact with undesirables anxious to acquire counterfeit identities. Even though the marriage certificate had been found amongst his forged papers Charlie refused to betray Anna's whereabouts. He was sentenced to eighteen months in the glasshouse to be served in England, at the end of which he would be given a dishonourable discharge and deported back to Malta.

I managed to see him one last time before he was shipped across the Channel and he gave me the address where Anna was being hidden, together with a letter for her. The only way in which I could get this to her was by bribing one of our waiters to deliver it. I included some money with a note of my own breaking the news of Charlie's fate. They had become just two more pieces of human flotsam and the irony was that Charlie's cherished dream of getting to England had finally been realised.

On my next free day I paid another visit to Lisa's home, taking another bar of chocolate, hoping that she would be there, but she was rehearsing and I found her father alone, his wife having gone out to queue for bread. 'I'm sorry to disturb you,' I said.

'No, please, I welcome the chance to stop work.'

I offered him a cigarette and studied his narrow, bespectacled face as he allowed me to light it for him. One broken arm of his spectacles was held in place with an elastic band and there were flakes of dandruff on the shoulders of his shabby jacket. It was difficult for me to comprehend what life must have been like during the Nazi years for a man of his intellect. The months I had spent interrogating had gone a long way to convince me that there was little honesty in post-war Germany. The majority of Germans were in denial. Yet here I was sitting down in the company of a man who, from my admittedly brief acquaintance, had shown none of the characteristics I had grown to auto-matically suspect during interrogation.

'How are Lisa's rehearsals going?' I asked.

'Well, I believe. Not that I understand much of what she tells me. The world of the theatre is a foreign country to me and Gerta. I had always thought Lisa might have followed me into an academic career, but today young people have to go wherever the work is. But then again I find a much that is foreign these days. It must be odd for you too, a long way from home, thrown into this chaos, compelled to live amongst people you previously sought to kill.'

'I didn't do any killing,' I said. 'I was lucky, I wasn't in the infantry. You neither, right?' From long habit I could not help myself double-checking on people's stories.

'Yes,' he said carefully. 'We were both lucky.'

'I have to say, you and your family are the only Germans I've met socially. My work normally doesn't bring me into contact with somebody like yourself.'

'And what is your work, if I may ask?'

'I'm in administration,' I said, deliberately evading a true answer since it was never a good idea to reveal one's real function.

'Gerta and I are glad we are in the British zone. We expected draconian retribution, but you treat us fairly. There are hardships, shortages of food, of course, but we are used to that. At least we did not exchange one police state for another. And on your side, are we what you expected? You must have had preconceived ideas of our society before being forced into contact with our worst elements.'

'Yes,' I said, not wishing to be drawn. 'But it's not all bad. By sheer luck I've met you and your family.'

'Thank you.' He appeared disconcerted by the compliment. 'Shall we have a cup of coffee? We have been rationing it, but there is still enough of your kind gift left.'

'I'll bring you some more.'

'No, no, please, I mustn't abuse our new friendship.'

For the first time I glimpsed another side to him, an obsequiousness that seemed assumed for the occasion. While he busied himself boiling the water and preparing two small cups he again spoke of his hatred and fear many Germans had felt for the SS and Gestapo. 'How far into the abyss of tyranny we descended. They turned us into a nation of informers. Neighbour against neighbour. Nobody was safe. It was hateful.' He spoke in a low voice like somebody long schooled to be cautious in case overheard.

We both savoured the coffee, then he said: 'Can I ask you something, something that is seldom out of my thoughts? I have to know the true facts about Belsen and such places. Please say if you do not wish to talk about such matters, but I have a great need to hear the truth from somebody like yourself.'

'What exactly do you want to know?'

'The photographs we were shown, were they authentic? Some still choose to believe they were fakes, products of Anglo-Jewish propaganda.'

'They are wrong,' I said. 'You couldn't fake horror like that. It so happens I was part of the British contingent that liberated Belsen.'

Grundwall stared at me across the table. 'You? *Grus Gott!*'

'I can assure you the photos did not lie. If anything they only showed the tip of the horror. We found thousands of unburied dead, hundreds of others dying of typhus, cholera and dysentery. And the deaths continued after liberation, five hundred a day for weeks. Sadly, we contributed to the death toll.'

'How so?'

'Being misguided Good Samaritans, giving them some of our own rations, but they couldn't handle proper food. The medical teams arrived and stopped us, but by then it were too late, our good intentions had done the damage.'

As I described the remembered scene to him, one skeletal face out of so many hung before me, like Banquo's ghost.

Grundwall was silent for a while, then asked: 'How could it be that we allowed such bestial places to come into being?'

'You tell me. Didn't you ever suspect they existed?'

'I would be a liar if I denied knowing nothing of the policies being pursued. How could we not know? From the moment the Nazis took power, the dream of Aryan purity became central to their ideal of a master race, all set down in Hitler's wretched, ill-written book we were required to read. His bible of hatred was mostly directed against those he held responsible for our defeat in the First World War, the Jews and Bolsheviks. Later, the net was extended to include the mentally ill, the sub-normal, homo-sexuals, gypsies, anybody in fact the authorities deemed imperfect. By then nobody except the totally blind could have been unaware. It was happening all around us: Jewish shops smashed, Jewish books burned, synagogues destroyed, individual Jews humiliated, made to perform the most degrading tasks in public.'

'You must have had some Jewish colleagues in the university faculty.'

'Yes, several. One by one they disappeared. The story we were given, the story I and others allowed ourselves to believe, was they were leaving the homeland voluntarily to seek a new life abroad. I am ashamed now, ashamed of my passive acceptance, of permitting myself to swallow the official lies. I could not allow myself to accept that our government was deliberately carrying out a policy of sustained mass murder, that my country, the country that gave the world Goethe, Beethoven, Thomas Mann, could be capable of exterminating a whole race. It was . . . It is, beyond comprehension . . . And yet . . . and yet . . . ' he trailed off.

'And now? Can you accept the world's verdict?'

'I must, and I will never forgive myself for my silence, my cowardice.' He struck his head with a bony, white hand. 'I should not say this of the land of my fathers, but it will take a hundred years to atone, and even then we should not be forgiven.' He removed his ancient, spectacles and wiped his eyes.

His remorse seemed genuine and I wanted to believe him – the admission of a man of conscience finally prepared to accept the unacceptable.

'Did you ever discuss these things with your wife and Lisa?'

'Gerta, yes, but not Lisa. I protected her, and in any case she was not living with us for most of the war. We sent her away to be safe from your bombing.'

'But, presumably, she had to join the *Bund Deutcher Madel*?' I probed. 'I understand girls as young as ten were compelled to belong.'

He thumped the table with his fist. 'Ah! The Hitler Youth movement, another madness. Mere boys made to take up arms and sent to die in the streets when the war was already lost.'

From long habit I slipped into interrogation mode. 'And young girls like Lisa were required to read *Der Sturmer*, weren't they?'

'It was compulsory reading. Can you imagine the mentality of those responsible for poisoning the minds of children with such filth?' he said vehemently. 'You can't. I have spent most of life trying to teach young people the truth, but those were the lost years when we were pushed back into the dark ages.'

The conversation we had that afternoon was still with me when

I took myself to a performance of *The White Horse Inn*. Apart from one occasion when I had been taken to an amateur production of *The Pirates of Penzance* performed in a village hall, I had never before seen a full-blown stage musical. Taking my seat, a front row stall reserved for Allied personnel, I felt how racy it was to actually know one of the actresses in the cast. As she had told me, Lisa only had a minor role and it took me a while to pick her out in the ensemble. Her heavy theatrical make-up masked her usual pallor, but she moved and danced with grace and I never took my eyes off her whenever she was on stage. The spectacle of a lyrical, peasant community singing the romantic tunes utterly seduced me; by the final curtain I was in love not only with Lisa but with the whole cast and joined in the standing ovation.

I waited outside the stage door for her. It was some twenty minutes before she came out, denuded now of greasepaint, the stage illusion gone, transformed back into an absurdly young girl.

'You were so good,' I said, 'and you looked so pretty.'

She coloured at the compliment. 'A lot of things went wrong tonight.'

'Really? Well, I didn't notice, because I only had eyes for you. I shall come to see it again.' I took her arm: so thin, so weightless. 'Let's go and have that meal I promised.'

I took her to the Nuffield Club which was crowded as usual, the dance floor packed with Service personnel; confronted by the noisy throng of bodies Lisa drew back on the threshold.

'I am allowed?' she asked.

'Of course. You're with me.'

I threaded our way through the crush and secured an empty table. 'Now, what would you like to eat?'

'There is a choice?'

'Oh, sure.'

'You choose for me,' she said.

'Would you like wine or beer with your food?'

'I don't drink,' she said.

'How about a Coca Cola then?'

'I've never tried it, but I've heard that it is very nice.'

I went to the service counter, light-headed and happier than I had been for months and ordered two mixed grills, not exactly gourmet fare for a first date, but I hoped that eggs, sausage, chips and a rasher of bacon would prove a feast in her eyes. Taking the plates back to our table I found her being chatted up by a suave RAF type.

'This lady's with me,' I said.

'Just testing, Sergeant Major.' He gave a conspiratorial leer. 'Get in, it's your birthday.'

'Why did he say that?' Lisa queried. 'Is it your birthday?'

'No, just a silly expression.' I put her plate down in front of her. 'I hope I've chosen something you'll like. Tell me if you don't and I'll change it.'

'It looks wonderful.'

'Well, here's to your performance.' I clinked my beer glass against her Cola. She took a tentative sip. 'OK?'

'Yes, thank you. I love sweet things, like the chocolate you brought that day. You're spoiling me.'

'That's the idea.'

It was touching to watch her savouring each mouthful of our taken-for-granted canteen food as though it was something extra special which would never again be put in front of her. I suppose it was special to her, just as being with her was special to me. Everything about her was delicate and vulnerable and I was filled with a desire to protect her. My emotions and anxiousness made me tongue-tied; I couldn't find the right words to express what I wanted to say. I didn't want to scare her by revealing too much, too soon, for on that first occasion I had no idea what she felt about me; perhaps she had only accepted my invitation out of deference to her parents' wishes. I had little or no experience of falling in love other than the fumbled encounters of my pre-Army adolescence. What I felt now was different, life enhancing. Every instinct willed me to reveal myself, but I held back, frightened of making the wrong move and ruining the moment. Instead I made small talk. 'Did you always want to be an actress? You seem so at home on the stage, as though born to it. I'm sure they'll give you a bigger role soon. Are you in the next play?' I gabbled on.

'It hasn't been decided yet. I don't mind if they don't choose me. I think I'm just lucky to be in work.'

'Do they pay well?'

'Nobody pays well any more, but we get some luxuries.'

'Such as?'

'A bar of soap every month,' she said as though describing a gift of caviar. 'And the dressing rooms are heated.'

'I'm sure that's welcome.'

'Oh, yes. At home we go to bed with our clothes on.'

'I did too when I first came to Hamburg. Do you think it's funny, sitting here with me?'

'Funny?'

'Well, strange then? Did you ever think you'd have a date with a British soldier?'

'No.'

'What about the other girls in the cast, do they get taken out?'

'Some of them,' she said.

'And what do they think?'

'I don't know. Most of them are older than me and some of them lost their husbands in the fighting.'

'I expect they resent us. It can't be easy to have your country occupied. Are we different from what you expected?' My probing seemed to embarrass her.

'I don't know what I expected,' she said dodging the question directly. 'My parents think you are very kind. My father always says he was so fortunate to meet you the way he did. He respects you.'

'But what do you think?'

'I too think you're very kind.'

'And do you like me?'

She looked down at her empty plate and put her knife and fork neatly together. I waited 'Yes,' she said finally, scarcely audible and without looking at me. I reached across the table and took her hand. 'Would you like to dance? I'm a long way from Fred Astaire.' She looked blank. 'Fred Astaire,' I repeated. 'American film star.'

'We were only allowed to watch German films.'

'Well, next time one of his films comes to our Army cinema, I'll take you.' I led her onto the crowded dance floor as the band struck up Glenn Miller's iconic *Moonlight Serenade*, a composition that evoked romanticism for my generation. Holding Lisa in my arms for the first time was like dancing with somebody weightless. The same RAF bod who earlier had tried to chat her up now had a pert little blond clinging to him; he gave me a leery, con-spiratorial look as we edged past each other. After two more dances I felt it would earn me brownie points if I did not keep her out too late. I had arranged for one of our drivers to have a Jeep waiting outside so that I could deliver her home.

When we parted at the darkened entrance to her block of flats, I said: 'I could see you again on Sunday if you're not rehearsing.'

'No.'

' "No, I can't see you again" or "no, I'm not rehearsing"?'

'We don't rehearse on Sunday,' she said.

'So, shall I call for you?'

'If you want to.'

'I want to.'

'You have given me such a best time tonight. I feel alive again,' she said.

I kissed her lightly on the cheek. 'I'm glad,' I said.

And so it was that we began.

NINE

My blossoming feelings for Lisa changed everything. Now I no longer fretted about when my demob number would come out of the hat; on the contrary I was happy to stay on in Germany for as long as the Army decreed. I saw Lisa whenever our various commitments allowed and shamefully ingratiated myself with her parents, taking them regular gifts of food and cigarettes. With winter finally retreating and bringing longer hours of daylight there was a more hopeful atmosphere in the city; the number of night murders went down for the first time since we took up occupation. The *trummefrau*, or "rubble women", worked to clear the streets and bombsites, spurred on by an imaginative scheme devised by the British Town Major: every half a dozen clean bricks brought in to the collection points entitled the workers to a bowl of soup; they and their families could return with more bricks as many times as they liked. By this method many of the worst streets became passable again and the number of violent crimes went down.

Sometimes on warm spring days Lisa and I picnicked by the Alster. Through the generosity of a Yank colleague I wangled a visit to a PX stores in their zone and bought Lisa her first bottle of French perfume and two pairs of nylon stockings – at that time the equivalent of gold dust. Because I saw to it that she ate regularly she gradually put on weight, colour returned to her cheeks and her small breasts began to fill out. My leave was coming up but instead of going home to see my aged parents, I decided I would try and spend it with her – love makes you conniving and selfish. For my plan to succeed, my leave had to coincide with a period when she was not appearing in or rehearsing for a new play. I waited until her current play finished its run before I casually mentioned that I could take some of the leave due to me.

Her face fell. 'I expect you'll be going back to England?'

'I don't have to, nor do I want to. I had a better idea, I thought maybe we could both have a holiday together in Austria.'

'Austria?'

'Yes.'

'Where in Austria?'

'A place I know.'

'With me? D'you mean it?

'Of course I mean it. Providing your parents allow it. D'you think they will?'

'I don't know. They can be very old fashioned about certain things. Especially my father.'

'D'you want me to ask their permission?'

She thought for a long time before saying, 'No, it's better that I do. I know how to put it.'

I never discovered how she squared it with them, if indeed she ever told them the truth – lies come easily for lovers.

I drove us in a borrowed unit Jeep back to Herr Wohlbrueck's *Gasthof* at Krumpendorf, back to the same dining room where Charlie had introduced me to his doomed Anna and where, in the hallway, a candle still burned in front of the portrait of the Wohlbrueck's dead soldier son. It was there, in that same bedroom I had previously occupied alone, and where the tiled stove still burned at night, that we slept together for the first time. I've known men who boasted that taking a girl's virginity was their supreme achievement, the crowning macho moment, but now, after so many years when I relive that defining moment as, sleepless, I often do, it isn't a sordid triumph I remember, but a sort of wonder achieved with tenderness and never repeated. Even now I can't ever catch the scent of pine without being transported back to that room and that moment.

That first night she asked me: 'Will people know I'm different now? Will it show on my face?'

'What're you talking about?'

'I was told people always know when you've stopped being a virgin.'

I pretended to study her closely. 'Yes, there's definitely a change which everybody will see.'

'You mean it?'

'It's frightening,' I teased. 'A transformation.'

'Don't tease me, please. Tell me the truth.'

'OK, the only change I can see is that you've become even more beautiful.'

The weather stayed fine the entire time we were there and often we ate outside on a small terrace and three ponies would wander up through the orchard and stand quietly until we fed them with fallen apples. There was an old dog, blind and mangy, who lay on the stone steps of the terrace and remembered his croaky bark whenever the ponies came near. Some mornings, after making love, we took the path up into the hills, past the roofless church, the garish shrines, and the cider factory stinking of putrid apples. From the summit we could look down on Krumpendorf and try to pick out our room in the *Gasthof*, but the reflected glare from the lake was too strong, blurring our vision. Descending, we skirted around the ruins of a castle that reminded me of Gibbs toothpaste advertisements, and stumbled across rutted fields, the ground soggy with decaying pine needles. On our third evening there I persuaded Lisa to take a first taste of the local wine. She sipped it delicately, like a bird at a pool, but wouldn't try a cigarette although she didn't mind me smoking and said the smell reminded her of her father. There were no health warnings on the packets in those days: the only warning I heeded came from my heart, I was so anxious that nothing should ever harm what I felt for her.

On our last night there we made love by moonlight, the shutters flung open, the air chill on our hot bodies. With my face close to hers I asked: 'Did you ever think you'd fall in love with one of the dreaded ravagers of your country?'

'How about you? Did you ever think you'd fall in love with a Nazi *machen*, the terrible enemy?

'Maybe.'

'Oh, I don't like "maybe",' she pouted. 'It means you must have been looking for somebody else.'

'Well, if I was, I never found her.'

'But you tried?'

'I admit nothing,' I said. 'And in any case the past is unimportant now, nothing is going to come between us ever again. I want to marry you, if you'll have me.'

She lifted her head from the pillow and stared at me. 'Do you really mean that? Is it allowed by your Army?'

'It's allowed. What will your parents say when I ask them?'

'They'll be happy.'

'You're sure?'

'Oh, yes. Otherwise I wouldn't be here, would I?' she said.

Awake when she slept, her nakedness touching my own, I thought, a new journey without maps begins. Some people had God to accompany them, guide them. I didn't. I was on my own in love and in a foreign country.

TEN

The moment we returned from Krumpendorf, I was directed to take part in one of our periodic hunts for deserters and other undesirables. The target area this time was the Hamburg dock area, a rabbit warren of bombed and derelict warehouses where many of those intent on trying to escape out of the country holed up. The task force consisted of a platoon of infantry supplemented by Military Police, with our Field Security unit as back-up should they ferret out any ex-SS or Gestapo still on the run.

The entire area was sealed off just before dawn to achieve maximum surprise and the raid proved a limited success, ending with some fifteen Allied deserters in the bag. We flushed out a solitary Waffen SS veteran who invited his own death by wounding a Military Policeman before being shot dead. We had come to recognise that the love of death was an integral part of the under-pattern of the Nazi character. Apart from this man there was nothing for us to deal with but, as we were leaving, the Provost Marshal handed me a battered leather pouch.

'This could be of interest to your lot,' he said. The pouch looked as though an attempt had been made to burn it, but a faded SS insignia was still discernible on the cover. I took it back to the office for closer examination. Inside were some scorched documents, typed on official SS headed notepaper. Grable made out the name Auschwitz-Birkenau on several of them and by piecing together the fragments we reconstructed two or three complete documents. They were dated early 1945, one signed by Himmler to the Commandant of the camp ordering him to eliminate as many of the remaining inmates as he could before the Allies arrived. Machell had everything photographed and the originals sent to Group Intelligence to be crosschecked against the master files.

'I've always thought it extraordinary,' he remarked, 'this compulsion the Nazis felt to document their crimes. I mean, why write an incriminating order like that? Would you? If you look at the date, it was obvious the war was lost by then, so why not pass the order by phone instead of in writing? No, even at the eleventh hour in the final panic they continued to rubber stamp everything. What a mentality.'

'They believed they had a God-given right to eliminate the Jews,' Grable said.

'Except they didn't believe in God.'

'Hitler was the Christ who had led them out of the wilderness. Accept that and everything else falls into place,' Grable replied. 'Who else could have persuaded pathetic children to fight Russian tanks with rifles in Berlin?'

Grable was often given to joshing me about what in his upper-class way he referred to as my piece of German totty. 'How's the frat going?' Although I am sure that Machell and the others were aware that I had a girl friend, I was at some pains to ignore Grable's predictable sexual banter. Lisa was not for sharing. I made sure we spent every snatched hour together and, having drawn out some back pay, I rented a room in a renovated apartment building. Whenever I was off-duty and Lisa was not rehearsing, we went there and made love, the element of furtiveness giving a fillip to the liaisons. Lisa never wanted to leave; I would have to plead, and threaten her. 'Darling, we have to go, I'm on duty in an hour's time.'

'Tell them you were taken sick.'

'You're shameless.'

'Yes.'

'I'd much rather stay here, too, but I can't. Aren't your parents suspicious when you don't go home in the afternoons?'

'I pretend we have extra rehearsals,' she said, trying to draw me back down on the bed.

'Now, behave. You must get up, please. Lisa, please, be good for once.'

'I will get up, but only if you make love to me again.'

'I'd like to but it would land me in trouble.'

It was after one such episode that I returned to the office and found the others studying a new set of photographs passed to us by our American counterparts for checking against our own records. Although we were long since inured to the horrors of such material, this latest batch was especially nauseating. They all related to the hideous experiments carried out on children by Dr Mengele and his team. Included in this batch were photographs of infant victims strapped down on the operating table while operations were performed without anaesthetics. There were also shots of body parts preserved in formaldehyde – human brains and hearts, even the severed head of a Mongoloid girl, the sort of material that normally would only be kept in a black museum.

It was unlike Machell to show any emotion, but that day he could not conceal his anger. 'What sort of man can bring himself to torture children? How do go about your daily routine and function normally after that? Tell me, somebody. Did he get up every morning, wash, shave, take a crap, and then think nothing of going to work and defiling these tiny defenceless bodies in his smart uniform and highly polished boots? Just another ordinary working day. It defies belief,' he said in a choked voice. 'I thought I knew everything about evil but these acts are beyond my imagination.'

The print that provoked this outburst showed four men standing around on an operating table on which what looked like a dead child.

Grable asked: 'Where was this taken?'

Machell turned it over and read out what was written on the reverse: 'Mengele and three members of his special SS unit known to have carried out experiments on children at Auschwitz-Birkenau under Mengele's supervision. Date of photograph unknown. Figure far left identified as Karl Off, committed suicide April 1945, Lunenburg Ref 2786-SS7A. The other two suspects currently unidentified. Further information urgently needed. Ongoing.'

The photograph was handed to me. It was the first time I had seen a photograph of Mengele and I found myself surprised by how young he looked – relaxed, smiling, at ease, so confident and well groomed in his smart uniform. Two of the four men were smoking, for all the world like a group of friends taking a relaxing break from the chores of the day.

'If those other two are ever found I want to be there when they take the hangman's drop,' Machell said.

I stared at the print for a long time with a growing sense of foreboding before giving it back. I said nothing to the others but later that night I returned to the office, found the same incriminating print and took it to my room. I locked the door, poured myself a stiff whisky and scrutinised the print again, this time using a magnifying glass. Although it was creased, the three faces were in the clear. From the moment I had first seen it I had prayed that my suspicion would be proved wrong, but it was not to be. I sat staring at it, refilling my whisky glass more than once, but the alcohol did nothing. I sat there, coldly sober, no longer in any doubt: the man in the centre of the group was Lisa's father.

ELEVEN

That night I drank myself to sleep and closed my eyes to a recurring nightmare.

My world, which a few hours before in our rented love nest had seemed so perfect, had been snatched from me. I cursed myself for my stupidity, the blind, careless naïvety that had allowed me to ignore rule one drummed into us from the moment we crossed the Rhine: this was a ruthless enemy, never accept anything or anybody at face value, question everything.

The long months I had spent listening to lies and evasions had taught me that the death camps had been staffed by second-string SS, recruited from every section of German society – bank clerks, lawyers, waiters, nurses, bookkeepers, carpenters, locksmiths, petty customs officials, even restaurant owners – so indoctrinated, so warped by the ex-chicken farmer, Himmler, they had persuaded themselves they were carrying out a divine mission to cleanse the fatherland. To that corrupted band could now be added a university professor, the plausible family man and one-time poet, the father of the girl I loved.

The shock of events spared me a hangover next morning. I replaced the photograph in our files before going to the Mess for breakfast, but I was still trying to decide how could deal with the revelation.

Grable joined me with the greeting: 'You look rough, Alex.'

'Do I? Slept badly.'

'Never have that problem myself. Sleep like a baby the moment my head hits the pillow. You must have a guilty conscience about something.'

He babbled on with his usual small talk until I could have hit him. All my thoughts were centred on what I should do next. A line had been drawn in the sand between my love for Lisa and my

79

duty. I wanted to believe that I had not been taken in by her in the same way that her father had deceived me. Or did she wear a mask like him? The sense of horror that now consumed me did not remove the necessity that, whatever the personal consequences, sooner or later I had to share my conviction with Machell. I still hesitated, wanting to delay the inevitable as long as possible and drove to the university campus, determined to verify one aspect of her father's story. I was shown into the presence of the Registrar, a woman of indeterminate age with a well-oiled servile manner. She confirmed that Professor Grundwall was an active member of the faculty. Consulting her wall chart she said: 'He is taking a class at the moment, but of course Herr Captain, I can interrupt him if it's urgent.'

'I'm not a Captain and that isn't necessary. Can you tell me how long has he been a member of the staff?'

'Let me consult his file to make sure, sir. I wish always to be accurate.' She went to a steel cabinet and took out a folder. 'Ah, yes, it says Herr Professor Grundwall taught here from 1934 until 1939.'

'And does it give details of his war service?'

'Yes, sir. He served in the Wehrmacht with the rank of Haupsturmfuhrer.'

'And where did he serve?'

'It says he was on attachment to the Ministry of Communications. As a translator, because of his academic and linguistic abilities,' she added, then seemed suddenly nervous and flustered. She dropped the file and, in bending to retrieve it, dislodged her rimless spectacles. 'There's nothing wrong, is there, sir? Professor Grundwall was given clearance by your people before he was allowed to resume his position here.'

'We have to carry out these periodic enquiries to ensure that the details we have been given are correct. Can I see the file, please?'

She handed it to me. It gave his age, marital status the names of his wife and daughter and inserted into the body of the file were the official notifications that, following the cessation of hostilities, he had twice appeared before de-Nazification Tribunals and had been cleared to return to his peacetime occupation. Details of his war service were as she had said, but what jolted me was a footnote stating that before taking up an academic career he had been a medical student, had qualified and indeed obtained a position as a general practitioner for a short period.

The Registrar watched me anxiously. '*Alles in ordnung?*' she asked, reverting to German.

'Yes, it all seems in order. I note that, in addition to his academic honours, he is also a doctor of medicine who once practised.'

'I believe that is so, sir.'

'But he doesn't teach medicine here, does he?'

'No, sir.'

'What does he teach?'

'Philosophy, sir,'

'Is that a popular subject?'

'Oh, yes, sir. His lectures are always well attended.'

I said, 'I will have to take the file away and check the details against our records, but there is no need to inform Professor Grundwall. It's just a periodic routine check. This file will be returned in due course.

'I understand, sir.'

I wondered if she could be trusted not to discuss our meeting with Grundwall; the need to inform on others had been so ingrained into the German character over a decade or more that one could never be sure.

I drove away from the campus knowing that I could no longer delay revealing my conviction that Lisa's father and the man in the photograph were one and the same. The fact that he had twice been cleared was no guarantee of innocence. From the many interrogations I had carried out I knew that lying was the norm, that in the chaos that followed the end of hostilities many records had been lost or deliberately destroyed and that many a suspect escaped because discrepancies in their accounts would never come to light. Sometimes we got lucky and scattered pieces of the jigsaw we were trying to fit together suddenly slotted into place, but most of the time we had to rely on a gut instinct to decide between lies and truth. In the immediate aftermath the whole of Germany had been thrown into the melting pot with four million people on the move. None of the victorious four powers had worked by the book because there was no book, all four wrote the scenario as they went along and hoped for the best. Until some semblance of law and order was patchily established, it was inevitable that many of those we needed to apprehend slipped through the net. Had I not visited that bookshop the photograph that came to us by chance would have had no significance for me. Grundwall would have continued to believe his past was secure, that he had made the transition back into the world of academia, not an obvious location for war criminals.

I had arranged to meet Lisa later that afternoon after she finished rehearsals and although I knew what course I now had to take, I still stayed my hand and collected her at the stage door, determined to quell one last doubt. I loved her and I owed her that.

We walked the short distance to the Salvation Army canteen and I made an effort to act normally. Lisa immediately spotted something different about me and reached for my hand across the table.

'You look so worried,' she said. 'Has anything happened?'

'It's been a pig of a day. How's yours been?'

'Oh, so so. I couldn't remember my lines.'

'Have you got a lot to learn in this one?'

'Enough. I knew them perfectly last night, but when I got on stage I had a complete blank.'

Looking at her sweet, trusting face I willed myself to believe that she knew nothing of her father's past.

Oblivious of my thoughts, she said: 'I've got Friday afternoon off while the new set is put up, so we could go to our room and make love.'

'Friday? Let me think. I'll have to check. This is a heavy week for me, we've got to prepare for an inspection.'

'Try,' she said.

'Of course, darling, of course I'll try and make it. If Friday's not possible, then sometime soon.'

'Very soon,' she said. 'Please.'

'How are things at home?'

'Good. My mother has put on weight. The only thing she says is that because you supply my father with cigarettes, he smokes too much.'

'There are worse things,' I said. 'I smoke too much.' I tried a tentative ploy; 'Tell me, because I'm interested, does he ever talk about the war, what he did in the war?'

She shook her head. 'No, he wants to forget all about it. I'm so happy he didn't have to fight.'

'That's right. He had a desk job, didn't he? Listening to and translating our forbidden broadcasts. I don't suppose you saw much of him after you were evacuated.'

'No, mother visited me when she could, but you had to get special permission to travel.'

'So I imagine he was a sort of stranger to you when eventually you returned home?'

She nodded. 'Yes, he seemed so different. Well, he was different. Everybody was different. All my father ever said was that he was glad it was over and all three of us had survived.'

After that meeting I agonised for a second night, but I woke the next morning knowing I could delay no longer. I went straight to Machell and before I could put my suspicions to him, he pre-empted me.

'D'you want the good news first, or the bad?' he said cheerfully.

Taken off guard, I said, 'Give me the bad.'

'Your demob has been delayed again. Don't ask me why, but somebody must think your services are too valuable to lose. The good news, but sad for me, is you're being transferred to MI6.'

'What does that mean?'

'It means you're being transferred.'

'But beyond that?'

'God knows, dear boy. We are but pawns, to be dismissed or advanced at a whim. However, and I've saved this until last, there's a sweetener – an extra three weeks home leave, a posting to Berlin and an immediate commission. You can put up three pips. Official confirmation will follow you home. Congratulations, Captain Seaton.'

'Did you fix that? '

'Good God, no. Beyond my limited influence.' He waved my furlough documents. 'I checked for you. There's a Blighty boat sailing in four hours, so get your skates on.'

'Sir, that's amazing news. Amazing. Haven't taken it all in yet because before you sprang it on me, I came to discuss something vitally important.' I put Grundwall's file on his desk. 'That print of Mengele's team at Auschwitz the Yanks sent us and we all examined.'

'What about it?'

'I believe I've identified one of them. Is it still with you?'

'Yes,' he said. He extracted it from the pile on his desk. I pointed to Grundwall. 'I'm pretty sure I interrogated that man when we first set up shop here,' I lied. 'Once he'd been cleared by our people he was allowed to resume his pre-war post as a member of the university faculty. But I don't want to jump the gun, so before putting my suspicions to you I double checked, and yesterday I went to the campus to make sure he was still on the staff there and questioned the Registrar, giving her the excuse we were following through a periodic routine enquiry.'

'And? Did you see the man himself?'

'No, didn't want to risk alerting him. I established he is on the faculty as a Professor of Philosophy, but as you'll note from his CV he once trained as a doctor, which is material in view of the photograph. If I'm right, he's the one standing next to Mengele. They're all doctors together.'

'How sure are you ?'

'Ninety per cent. I'd take the investigation further myself, but if I'm not to miss the boat, I'll have to dump it on you, sir.'

Machell studied the photograph anew. 'Right, will do. I'll have him brought in, confront him with this and have Grable give him another going over. If Grable believes there's a case to answer, our findings will be passed to the Jewish War Crimes Commission. They have survivors they can tap for positive identification, make it watertight. It was smart of you to spot him. Good man.'

I didn't feel like a good man; because of Lisa I felt like Judas. I prayed that in time I would be proved wrong and that nothing would destroy the love we had for each other. Going to my room, I packed and hastily penned a note to her telling her why I wouldn't be around for a bit but would write again as soon as I got home. After handing in the letter at the post room, I caught the train to the port.

A couple of hours later I was standing on the dock waiting to embark when somebody called my name. I swung around to find Chivers behind me. He now sported a moustache and a swagger stick.

'CSM Seaton,' he repeated. 'How about that? I never forget a face or a name. You off home for good?'

'No, just a spot of leave. Are you catching this boat too?'

'Lord, no. Too much to do over here. Enormous job, you know, but I'm getting on top of it.'

His attitude was as insufferable as ever, behaving as though he was single-handedly responsible for the whole burden of putting Germany back on its feet.

'A bit of luck bumping into you like this, because I was hoping to find someone to run an errand for me and you'll do nicely. I've got a letter that urgently needs to get to my London bank and the Army mail is so bloody unreliable.' He opened his briefcase and took out an envelope. 'This is hot stuff. Between you, me and the gatepost, I was given a nod and a wink the other night dining with some City heavy hitters who were over here sussing out business opportunities. I did them a few favours and, quid pro

quo, they told me about a killing waiting to be made back home.'
He looked over his shoulder and tapped the side of his nose.
'Property.'

'Property?'

'Yes. All those empty bombsites sitting there.'

Seeing my blank expression, he elaborated. 'I'm reliably told
they can be had dirt cheap. Vacant land is prime building material,
sport. Attlee's proletariat are going to need houses, lots of real
flats and houses, not those bloody pre-fabs. These characters I
met said they're picking up freeholds all over London for a few
thou a go. Copper-bottomed investments. There's nothing like
getting in on the ground floor. He who hesitates etcetera.' He
pushed the envelope at me. 'I want to get my money down double
quick, so, if you could post this the moment you land, you'll
forever be on my Christmas card list.'

I accepted the letter with nil enthusiasm.

'My address is on the back of the envelope. Make a note of it
because we must keep in touch. Never know, I might be able to
row you in one day. I'd row you in on this, but I was sworn to
secrecy. They don't want too many punters getting their noses in
the trough. Really good to see you again, sport. Have a good
leave.'

He turned and walked away, as though, having dealt with the
messenger boy, no further dialogue was necessary. I wanted to
shout after him, 'Say, thank you,' but he was already lost in the
crowd.

On the sea voyage thoughts of the unfinished business I was
leaving behind never left me. I wanted to believe that, on my
return, nothing would have changed, my naming of Grundwall
would have proved to be wrong and Lisa and I would be as before,
but doubts blurred my vision as I stared towards the approaching
English coast. What lay ahead was as impenetrable as a dark
forest.

TWELVE

The moment the boat docked and before catching a slow train, I telephoned home to warn my mother that I was about to appear on the doorstep; she had always been panicked by the unexpected.

My father farmed fifty leased acres of rich fenland near Tattershall with most of the acreage given over to potatoes and sugar beet, but he kept two fields for grazing a few cows to provide milk and butter for the house. During the war the area around had sprouted a number of operational airfields and on my last leave prior to D Day I watched the swarms of Lancasters, Wellingtons and Halifaxes darkening the evening skies like slow-flying geese as they lumbered off to bomb Germany. Although during the Blitz the Luftwaffe flew in the opposite direction over the Fens on their way to flatten our Midland cities, apart from the occasional Dornier jettisoning its bomb load to escape being shot down, most of Lincolnshire had been relatively unscathed. The Fens have a stark, unique quality that some find dull but, as a child knowing nothing different, I had always seen them as mysterious and enchanted. Some winters the flat landscape froze and we children could safely skate for miles across flooded fields, the grass stems protruding through the ice like petrified insects in ambergris.

As the train got closer to home I began to pick out familiar landmarks; the contrast between the devastation I had left behind and the calm of the English countryside made my heart quicken. Journey's end was Woodall Spa, a small halt rather than a full-blown station but in pre-war days it had still won prizes for its flowerbeds; the Stationmaster, always dressed in a frock coat and peaked cap, would hold the train if he saw a pony and trap approaching along the road from nearby Walcott Dales – travel was more civilised in those days. There would be a coal fire burning in the waiting room during cold spells and a porter willing to help with luggage.

After being hugged and greeted by my father, he drove me home in his battered Wolseley that stank of cattle feed. It wasn't until our farm came into view around the last bend of the single track that ran along the bank of the sluggish River Witham, that the realisation finally struck me that, unlike so many others, I had come through the war alive.

As the Wolseley bumped its way down a rutted path to the house we passed two men heaping straw onto a new potato grave.

'My German PoWs,' my father said. 'I had three at one time.'

'How d'you get on with them?'

'Oh, so, so, with a bit of give and take. Can't complain, grateful for their help. They put in a fair day's work. We fixed up one of the outhouses for them to sleep in. Nothing much, but I guess it's better than being behind barbed wire.'

When I got out of the car and looked back at them they had stopped working and were staring in our direction, concerned perhaps at the arrival of somebody in uniform.

Despite the fact that rationing was still in force my mother had assembled a feast for my homecoming: a whole ham, cold chicken, home-made bread, salad, a brick of butter, baked apples stuffed with raisins and a bowl of custard.

'They say rationing will be with us for years, would you believe?' my mother said. 'Of course we're luckier than people in towns, because we kill our own.'

'Is that allowed?'

'No, but everybody does it around here.'

'I blame the austerity on old Sir Stifford Crapps,' my father chimed in, deliberately using the rude name people used for Sir Stafford Cripps, the vegetarian, manically austere Labour Chancellor. 'They say he lives off watercress grown on blotting paper.'

As I studied them both I saw how much my father had aged, how stooped he had become. He had worked hard all his life and farming was far removed from the popular conception of a healthy open-air idyll – all the women rosy-cheeked and the men ruddy and strong. Although he owned a Fordson tractor, much of the day-to-day grind was still done with the help of two massive Shire horses. Always up before dawn, mucking out, feeding and watering the livestock, humping bales of fodder in winter, a Woodbine too often burning down to the last half inch and browning his upper lip, his life was an endless round. As he cut thick slices of ham, I noticed his hands were calloused and ingrained with soil. Although he had put on his best suit for my homecoming, it seemed alien to him – he was still unmistakably a red-necked labourer. I was well aware that for most of the war, he had needed the help a son would have given, but had somehow managed to keep everything together. My mother's role had always been to look after the score of Rhode Island hens that scratched around the house, milk the cows, churn the butter, skin the shot rabbits, boil the washing in soft rainwater from the butts and put it through a wooden mangle. It was a list of chores that would have defeated most, but I had never heard her complain. She, too, looked worn, though to greet me she had powdered her cheeks and put a smudge of lipstick on her mouth.

'How d'you get on with your Germans, Mum?'

'Don't have over much to do with them. Don't want to. In any case, we're told not to fraternalise.'

''Fraternise', mother,' my father corrected gently.

'Well, whatever they call it. I've heard some local girls walk out with them.' She lowered her voice. 'A girl over at Coningsby had a child by one of them, so they say.'

'They're allowed out then?'

'Within limits.'

'I imagined they'd have been returned home by now,'

'Old Atlee decided they must stay and help repair the damage they caused. Quite right, too. Make the buggers pay something back.'

'Now, don't use that language,' my mother said. 'I've told you before.'

'Do they resent having to work for you?'

'The first couple they sent me were hard cases, very stroppy, so I got shut of them. The two we've got now are as good as you can expect.'

After the meal I wandered around, re-familiarising myself with the rest of the house. Nothing had changed; it was just that all the furnishings now struck me as fusty and belonging to a lost age. The downstairs rooms were still lit with oil lamps, the bedrooms with candles and although there was a basic bathroom, everybody had to use the outside privy, where cut squares of newspaper, home-made toilet tissue, hung on a nail. I went upstairs to my old bedroom. The last time I had looked at myself in the mirror over the chest of drawers, I had been four years younger. The mirror had patches of brown on it where the silver backing had peeled away, aping the age spots on the back of my mother's hands. The face that now stared back at me was thinner and gaunter than the youth who had last slept in the room. I lifted the mirror from its hook and turned it over. Pasted on the reverse was a faded photograph of a nude girl cut from a magazine which I had once used as a spur to masturbation. There was a row of Penguin paperbacks stacked on the windowsill, most of them foxed; the jacket of *A Farewell to Arms* came apart as I picked it up. From the window I could see the perfect Norman keep of nearby Tattershall Castle which had mercifully escaped the attention of German bombers. Testing the springs on my old bed, I thought of nights I had lain there listening to small animals scurrying above me in the eaves. I caught the familiar smell of the lavender polish my mother always used. It was all the same, yet strangely alien, as though I had never before been there.

Downstairs, the window in the "best room", as my mother called it, remained sealed from the outside world. Pre-war it had only been used for special occasions such as christenings and funerals, for the patterned lino on the floor, considered an expensive luxury when first laid, had to be kept pristine. The single sash window still had a blanket nailed to the wooden shutter and outside it was blocked up with rotting sandbags, my father having followed government guidelines at the time of Munich urging everybody to make one room safe against gas attacks. Standing there, I thought how tragically ineffective such puny measures would have proved in the event. Now the room reeked of damp, preserved like a museum exhibit.

With the light fading I went outside and walked along the riverbank. As a child I had often earned six pence pocket money making cans of tea for the weekend fishermen who came to spin for pike. One Christmas the river had frozen over, the ice thick enough for skating, but I had been too scared to test it, just as I had been frightened to go near the Shire horses. But now when I went to their stable the current pair stopped chomping sweet hay and turned to regard me. They still looked enormous, but their noses were velvet soft when I stroked them and I no longer felt menaced. The stable had a stove for heating their bran mash, the red-hot lid of which being perfect for roasting chestnuts.

I left there and looked into the adjacent chaff house, where huge Bramley apples were buried in the chaff like hidden prizes in a circus lucky dip. Rats jumped and scurried away as I opened the door.

As I retraced my steps to the house, I came face to face with the two Germans washing themselves under a pump. They instinctively stiffened.

'Relax,' I said in German, 'The war's over for all of us. Are you happy working for my father?'

The younger-looking of the two answered: 'Is OK.'

'Does he treat you well?'

'*Ja.*'

'Where were you taken prisoner?'

This time the other man answered me in English. 'At Falaise.'

'And have you been in England ever since?'

'No. Before, we are sent to America.'

'You speak good English.'

'You speak good German,' he replied with a certain arrogance.

'What were you in?'

'12 SS Panzer. And you?'

'Intelligence.'

He shrugged, implying I was not an equal combatant. 'Why are we not treated as prisoners of war?'

'Aren't you?'

'No. We are forced labourers, this is contrary to the Geneva Convention.'

Sod you, I thought and reverted to German again. 'I thought your lot invented forced labour, or am I wrong?' I said. 'Wasn't the great Atlantic Wall built with it? You also gave the world Dachau. I'm sorry you're here and not in your own homes, but I'm sure my father treats you decently. Don't blame it on us, blame that asshole with the stupid moustache who you allowed to lord it over you.' I walked away, angry with myself for losing my temper.

That evening after my mother had gone to bed, my father produced a full bottle of whisky and a box of cigars. 'I saved these,' he said. 'Kept them moist with lettuce leaves, so I hope they're alright.'

'They're fine.' He lit two from the same match.

'Your letters didn't tell us overmuch. What's it really like over there?'

He had never travelled out of England, his most ambitious trips being visits to the seaside at Skegness and once to London for the Smithfield Cattle Show, so my descriptions of Germany and Austria amazed him. 'How about the women?' he said giving me a sly look. 'Anything you want to tell me now we're on our own? They're all blondes, aren't they?'

'Not all. Some.'

'And?' He gave me the wink. 'Have a good time, did you?'

'When we first got there we were forbidden to fraternise, but nobody took much notice and eventually the rules were relaxed. Yes, I did have a friendship with a German girl, the daughter of a professor.'

'A professor, eh? Educated girl, I take it?' he said, as though anxious to assure himself that this somehow mitigated against her nationality.

'Actually, she's an actress.'

'An actress?' His voice took on a new note of concern.

'I got to know her after seeing her in a musical play,' I said.

'Sow your oats while you can. Long as you don't marry her. Now what? You'll be home for good soon.'

'Not as soon as I'd hoped.'

'No? Why's that then?'

'They need key people like me to stay on. I should have told you before. I've been promoted again and have to take up a new job in Berlin when I get back.'

'Promoted?'

'Yes, you've got an officer in the family.'

'Well, well, that calls for another drink.' He refilled our glasses. 'What rank are you now then?'

'Captain.'

'Isn't that something? Wait 'til I tell your mother. And Berlin, eh? You're looking forward to that, I expect.'

'I imagine it's not very different from Hamburg. Most of their big cities were flattened.'

'Be funny to think of you there. Only a name to me. Well, looks as though what I've been planning will have to wait a while, but I'll show you anyway.' He got up and went to the dresser and took some papers out of a drawer. 'Take a look at these.' I saw they were bank statements. 'I've managed to salt away a few thousand.'

'Wonderful, Dad.'

'It's all yours when you finally hang up your uniform.'

'Mine?'

He grinned. 'Yes. My gift to you.'

'I couldn't take it.'

'Course you could. I've been putting it aside for you from the moment you left. What's more, there's a farm going nearby. You remember old Leggatt, don't you? Well, he died a few months back and his widow can't afford to keep it going. Not as big as this, only thirty acres, but decent soil. The house isn't up to much, but you can live here until you get it fixed.'

His face as he outlined his plan was bright with expectation. 'Sounds a very good buy,' I said.

'I thought you'd go for it.' He stubbed out his ragged cigar and downed the last of his whisky. 'That's settled then.'

That night, lying awake in the bed that should have been familiar but wasn't, I tried to think of ways to refuse his offer without hurting his feelings. The prospect of coming back to wrest a living from the earth for the rest of my days as he had done chilled me, but during the following week I went through the motions, giving the impression of being keen, and spent a morning going over the Leggatt property. It was a depressing holding, the farmhouse in urgent need of renovation like the accompanying cluster of outbuildings. I kept up the pretence of being interested by seeing the local solicitor handling the sale and was relieved to find there was another prospective purchaser prepared to pay over the asking price. I relayed this to my father.

'Well, we'll match him, top him if necessary. The bank manager owes me. I kept him in chickens and eggs during the war.'

'No, I couldn't let you do that, you're being generous enough as it is. The truth is, Dad,' I began tentatively, 'when I do get back, I want to think carefully before making up my mind. I might try my hand at something other than farming.'

He stopped what he was doing and straightened up. 'Are you saying you don't want the Leggatt farm?'

'It's just that everything's happening too quickly for me.'

'You have to act quickly sometimes, otherwise you lose the chance.'

'I'm sure you're right, but I need to think about it more if you'll let me. I'm sorry, especially because you've been so generous.'

'I'm sorry, too. It's an opportunity that won't come again in a hurry.'

He walked away from me, reached for a Woodbine and stood

staring across the fields. 'There it is then,' he said. 'I thought you'd want to get back to normal.'

'Dad, I don't know what's normal any more. I don't want to sound ungrateful.'

'No, better you should say what's on your mind. Have you mentioned anything to your mother?'

'Not yet.'

'Let me tell her. She was living for the day when you'd be back for good.'

During the remainder of my leave I spent time tidying up the "best room", removing the decayed sandbags outside and giving all the woodwork a coat of paint. I also made the social rounds, catching up with relatives and friends, and was saddened to learn Bennet, my old headmaster, to whom I owed so much, had been killed in a road accident during the blackout. My mother proudly sewed three pips on my uniform and out of curiosity more than anticipated pleasure I went to the village hop one evening and was greeted as a war hero. Dancing to music by an amateur four-piece band, I felt ever more alienated, remembering the first time I had danced with Lisa. I partnered a girl I had once been sweet on, but her early lushness had faded and I had to carefully resist her efforts to rekindle the flame. All too clearly I saw the constricting same-ness of village life, the cycle of birth, marriage and death taking place within narrow boundaries. The encounter intensified my longing to see Lisa again. I had written to her regularly since arriving home, but had received no word back. Suddenly seized by the need to hear her voice, I took my father's car and drove to Woodhall Spa. There I spent a fruitless hour using the one public call box trying to get through to the theatre stage door, but making a connection to Hamburg proved impossible.

My leave finally over, it wasn't until I was packing that I came across the envelope Chivers had entrusted me with and which I had completely forgotten. My first thought was to destroy it but in the end, I bowed to conscience and wrote him a mea culpa letter full of remorse.

THIRTEEN

The moment I arrived back in Hamburg I went straight to the theatre. Posters for the next production were displayed outside, featuring Lisa's name for the first time. The foyer doors were open and I went through into the darkened auditorium to find a rehearsal in progress on stage. After my eyes had adjusted to the gloom, I spotted Lisa sitting in the front row stalls. I took a seat in the row behind her and kissed the nape of her neck. She wheeled around, startled, and clapped a hand to her mouth when she saw it was me.

'When do you break?' I whispered.

'Soon,' she whispered back. 'But we only get half an hour for lunch.'

The director, an obvious queen, flapped a limp wrist at Lisa and shouted, 'Would it be too much to ask if we all concentrate? Lisa, you missed your cue!'

She got up quickly and mounted the steps to the stage. The queen glared at me. 'We don't allow strangers at rehearsals, so if you wouldn't mind, officer. Thank you.'

I retreated and waited for her at the stage door. When Lisa appeared, she immediately burst into tears.

'Darling,' I said, 'That was my fault, I shouldn't have barged in like that, I'm so sorry. Did he take it out on you?'

'Not him,' she said. 'I'm not upset about him.'

'What then? Tell me.'

'Don't you know?'

'Know what, darling?'

She looked over her shoulder before answering in German, something she seldom did now. 'My father was arrested. Your people came for him.'

I took her arm and hurried her into the Salvation Army canteen.

Once I had ordered sandwiches and coffees, I kept up the pretence of total ignorance. 'Don't cry any more, sweetheart. Tell me exactly what happened. Why would they arrest him?'

'I don't know. A week ago when I got home after rehearsal there were soldiers outside the door. Papa had already been taken away and they were searching the apartment.'

'Searching it for what?'

'I don't know,' she said again. 'They wouldn't tell us.'

'What about your mother? Did they arrest her as well?'

'No. She went to stay with relatives and I had to find somewhere else to live. A friend let me share with her.'

'They must have told you or your mother something, given some reason.'

'No.'

'What about the university, does anybody there know why?'

She shook her head. 'I went there, but they couldn't tell me anything.'

'It must be a mistake,' I said, 'We make mistakes like everyone else.' I felt a total shit lying as I did.

'Do you? Tell me you do,' she said clutching at straws.

'They've probably mixed up his file with somebody else's. It happens,' I told her, ashamed by my glibness. She looked so pitiful, but since I had no idea of the outcome of Grable's grilling, I had no alternative.

She withdrew her hand from my grip and wiped her wet cheeks. 'Will you find out?'

'Yes, darling, of course.'

'When? When will you do it?'

'As soon as I can,' I said. 'Try not to distress yourself any more. Drink your coffee and eat something, please.'

'It could be a mistake, couldn't it, like you said?'

'Yes.' Her trust in me to solve everything made me further ashamed. 'I'll find out whatever I can before I leave for Berlin.'

'You're going to Berlin?'

'Yes, I've been given a new posting.'

'When did that happen?'

'While I was at home,' I lied. It seemed I was lying about everything.

'Do you have to go soon?'

'Tonight, darling.' I pushed a notepad and pencil to her. 'Write down your new address. Have you got money?'

'Yes,' she said, but I persuaded her to accept some more. On the way back to the theatre she kept saying, 'Promise you'll do something, make them see it's all a mistake.'

'I love you,' I said, as though love alone could end her nightmare.

After leaving her I straightaway went to find Machell. He greeted me with, 'Alex, dear boy, you're meant to be in Berlin saving democracy from the KGB. Can I offer you a mahogany to speed you on your journey?'

'No thanks, sir, thanks all the same. I have to find out what happened to that man I picked out from the photograph. You said you'd deal with him.'

'Well, we did. Grundwall, isn't that his name? Very plausible on the surface, but Grable broke him down over three sessions. Your hunch was right, he was one of the men in the photograph, plus, although he had tried to erase his SS tattoo under his armpit, he hadn't been able to completely eradicate it. Subsequently your hunch was confirmed by two survivors of the camp who picked him out on an identity parade without hesitation.'

'They did? Oh, God,' I blurted, unable to help myself.

'Why, oh, God? I thought you'd be chuffed.'

'I am, I am. So where is he now?'

'Banged up in Nuremburg awaiting trial.'

I hesitated. 'Look, there is something more I should have told you before, but I held back hoping my hunch would be proved wrong . . . Something that complicates matters . . . I hadn't previously interrogated him, that was a lie. I recognised him because I know him.'

'You know him? How?'

'I'm having an affair with his daughter.'

'Ah,' Machell said after a long pause. 'That is definitely a complication. How much does she know about her father's past?'

'Nothing,' I said a shade too quickly.

'You're sure of that? What if she took you in? Maybe she knew and protected him?'

'I'd stake my life that she knew nothing. The question now is should I reveal my relationship with her?'

'Well, having been the instigator, you'll almost certainly be called as a witness at his trial, so my advice would be confess it now, rather than have somebody pull it out of you. Then walk away, end it. Don't see her again.'

'I can't do that,' I said slowly. 'You see, I love her.'

'Don't give yourself grief because you allowed yourself to be seduced by a piece of German skirt. You can't change anything now, the due processes have taken over and if he's proved guilty, then fuck him, he deserves whatever's coming.'

'But I started it.'

'No, you didn't. It started before you ever wore that uniform. You were just doing your job.'

'It's her father, for Christ's sake. That's the difference.'

'It's always somebody's father. Even Himmler had one,' Machell said smoothly.

I knew he was right but I still ignored his good advice and in the hours remaining before my plane took off, I commandeered a Jeep from Transport pool to set out for the address Lisa had given me, armed with a bottle of wine. I knew now that there was no turning back and that the love I had for her was greater now than ever.

The journey took me to a large tenement building in a working-class suburb, bomb-scarred like most. Climbing concrete stairs to the third floor I located the number of her apartment. Another young girl opened the door. Fear jumped into her face immediately she saw my uniform.

'I've come to see Lisa,' I said in German.

The girl did not answer and we stood facing each other until Lisa appeared behind her.

'It's alright, Greta,' she said in a flat voice. It was obvious she had been crying again.

Greta pushed past me and disappeared as I went inside. The room I found myself in was clean but sparsely furnished with odd, ill-matched pieces. There was a sepia photograph of Lisa's parents on the mantelpiece and some clothes hanging on a rope in one corner. It was a room made for bad news.

'I didn't expect to see you again so soon,' she said.

'Well, I couldn't go and leave you in that state. Have you got a corkscrew?'

She found a corkscrew and I opened the wine and filled two tumblers, all the time trying to think of the right words with which to pacify her. Yet I knew that I had to tell her. 'As promised, I found out where they've sent your father. Here, it'll do you good.' I handed her a tumbler. 'He's in a holding prison.'

'Where?'

'Nuremburg,' I said as casually as I could.

She was about to drink but stopped. 'Nuremburg?'

'Yes.'

'That's the place where they held the other trials. Why would they send him there? What for?'

'Darling, they're contending that he didn't work as a translator, but served in one of the death camps.'

Her face was becoming blotchy again and she shook her head from side to side in disbelief. 'That's not possible.'

'It's what they're saying now, but of course it has yet to be proved.'

'How can they say that?'

'Because, I gather witnesses, survivors from the camp, have identified him as being one of the SS staff.'

'But he wasn't.'

'Darling, photographs exist.'

'Then they're fakes,' she said.

'No, I've seen one of them. Taken at Auschwitz.' I finally named the camp.

Her body started to shake violently and she gave a cry like some trapped animal. 'No, no, no, don't say that, it's not true, not Vater, not him.' She fell to the floor, knocking over her wine over as she collapsed. I cradled her, attempting to stop the tremors wracking her body, but she pushed me away. 'Not Vater,' she kept repeating, 'not Vater, please no. You know what a wonderful man he is.'

'I never wanted to be the one tell you all this,' I said, but she was beyond comfort, her misery was absolute. When I finally managed to quieten her, I carried her into the tiny bedroom she shared with Greta and laid her on the double bed. She still continued to whimper the same mantra again and again.

'Don't,' I said. 'Please don't, darling.' I lay down beside her, my face close to hers until, finally exhausted, she fell silent and seemed to sleep. With my arm cramping beneath her, I lay without moving for a long time as the room gradually darkened. Then she turned into me, pressing her body against mine, seeking my mouth, kissing me with hungry desperation as if we were about to part forever. I allowed the kiss to obliterate all reason, all common sense, my sexual hunger matching hers. We tore each other's clothes off, she crying for me to take her quickly, willing me to act out a sort of rape as though only such a violation could obliterate her misery. She became in those moments somebody I did not recognise, somebody possessed. Spent, I lay with my head nestled into her damp neck as our bodies slowly relinquished each other and our hearts gradually slowed to normal.

Afterwards Lisa said: 'Will I ever see you again now?'

'Of course you will,' I said. 'I love you, nothing will change that. Being in Berlin, I won't be able to see you as easily or as often as before, but I'll come back here whenever I can and I'll write every day.' At that moment I believed I could honour such promises.

'He must have been forced to it,' she said suddenly. 'That's what must have happened.'

'Yes, I'm sure you're right. Listen, darling, I must go now. I've just about got time to catch my plane. Have you got enough money?'

'I can't take any more money from you.'

I got out of the bed and started to dress, then took my wallet from my uniform jacket. She had not noticed I was now an officer, nor had I mentioned it. 'Here, treat yourself and Greta to a meal. I want you to promise you'll eat properly and take care of yourself.'

'Come back soon,' she said.

'I promise.' I kissed her twice and then left quickly before she cried again, carrying with me the sickening realisation that, forced to make the hideous choice between love and duty when I first saw the incriminating photograph, I had ruined the life of the first person I had ever truly loved.

FOURTEEN

At that time the British zone in Berlin was a curious outpost. The division of spoils had resulted in the city being isolated within Soviet East Germany, chopped like a cake into four uneven sectors. The Russians immediately closed off their sector from the other three, renamed the streets and set about imposing communist rule in place of Hitler's failed brand of National Socialism. At night, as well as the concrete barriers, a frontier of darkness separated the Soviet zone from the deliberately highly illuminated Western sectors. Officially, we were all still buddies, but that wasn't the reality: the reality was suspicion, tension and endless bureaucratic obstruction.

My scant knowledge of pre-war Berlin had mostly been gleaned from Isherwood's novels, but Sally Bowles's world was a far cry from the city in which I now found myself. On arrival, I was billeted in a tumbledown hotel reputed to have been a luxury brothel catering for every taste. My room was lined with shabby red plush wallpaper; a broken chandelier hung from the bullet-pitted ceiling. If anything in many areas the destruction was worse than Hamburg. The bitter house-to-house fighting when the Nazis had made a final despairing effort by throwing young boys into the battle had ensured that few buildings left standing were without scars.

After stowing my gear I reported to the SIS station housed close to the old Olympic Stadium which, by some quirk of fortune, was one of the few that had escaped major damage. The SIS operated undercover as part of the Control Commission's Political Division. My Head of Station was a career diplomat called Graham Green. Middle aged, grey faced, heavy pouches under spaniel eyes, wearing a well-cut pinstripe suit, blue shirt and faded Garrick tie, he unnervingly, barked staccato non-sequiturs at me the moment we met.

'No connection, by the way. Different spelling.'

'Sir?'

'With that Catholic writer chap of the same name. Most people ask. Wrote that book about the Brighton race gangs. One of us during the war, somewhere in Africa. Freetown. That's a misnomer. Bloody awful place Africa. Spent a tour there myself. Flies, dysentery and the clap.' He looked me up and down as though I might possibly be a carrier. 'Lethal combination. So have you?'

'Sir?'

'Ever read him, my namesake?'

'I read his thriller about the Orient Express.'

'Prefer Wodehouse myself. More cheerful. But he's persona non grata now, blotted his copybook broadcasting for the Boche, stupid sod.' His dialogue hopped from subject to subject at bewildering speed. 'Took that train once pre-war. With the wife. First wife that is. She hated it. Last holiday we had together. She fell off the perch a few months later. Cancer. You religious?'

'No, sir.'

'Glad to hear it. Steer clear of the Bible punchers, especially the holy Romans. He was a convert, you know.'

'Who, sir?'

'The writer chap. Funny, the more intelligent they are, the more they buy into all that mumbo jumbo. I was cured early on, in prep school. Chaplain made a pass at me. How about clubs?'

'Clubs, sir?'

'Yes. Belong to any?'

'No, I don't.'

'White's and the Garrick, myself. By the way, do feel free to wear a suit and tie. Less conspicuous.'

'I don't possess a suit, sir.'

'Don't keep calling me "sir". First names here. What else have you read? Lawrence, the one who dressed as an Arab?'

'No, I haven't.' I was completely lost now.

'Arabia. That's another place to avoid. First posting I had. Sand and another ghastly religion. What's your first name?

'Alex.'

'You a Cambridge man, Alex?'

'No, Horncastle Grammar.'

'Really? Horncastle, eh?' For the first time he seemed stymied. 'Better advance you some pay, then point you in the right direction to get a suit made. Very reasonable here, because they're desperate for work. At one time we were paid in sovereigns, did you know that?'

'Who was paid in sovereigns, sir?'

'MI6.'

'I didn't know that.'

'Oh, yes. Gold bullion and never any questions asked in the House. Well, good to have you on board, Alex. When you've settled in, you'd better take a course in codes and ciphers with our man in Vienna. Been there, have you?'

'No, I never got further than Graz.'

'Old Hugh will show you around. Hugh Dempster-Miller. Bit of a mouthful, but you'll like him, he makes a mean bowl of flaker.' When I looked blank, he continued: 'Black coffee with a tot of rum in it. In Hugh's case two tots. By the way, never ask for *eine Tasse Kaffee* in Vienna, shows you're a stranger. It's a "bowl" of coffee always – *eine Schale*. Old hand, Hugh. Seen it all.' He broke off and stared at me as though weighing me up for a difficult decision. 'What're you doing for tiffin tonight?'

'Nothing, I haven't made any plans.'

'Right, well, to welcome you to the team, I'll take you to my favourite watering hole in the French zone. Don't get many things right, the French, but at least they know what to put on your plate. Strange bird, de Gaulle. Met him once. Thinks he can walk on water. Probably can, wouldn't put it past him.' He moved away from his desk and stared out of the window. I waited, uncertain as to whether the interview was over. 'We've got to watch our backs, Alex,' he said finally. 'This bloody place is the Last Chance saloon. We bitch this one and it's curtains. I'll fill you in over dinner. Seven o'clock. Collect you at your hotel.'

I took this as a dismissal but, as I moved to the door, Green fired a parting shot.

'I don't know what you were told about me in advance, Alex. But whatever it was, ignore it. I have one thing in my favour, I look after my own.'

I was waiting outside the hotel well before seven, still wondering what was in store for me from this odd character who was now my boss, when a car drew up and Green, leaned across and opened the passenger door for me. 'Have you got your pea-shooter?' he asked tersely.

'Yes.' I patted my Walther.

'Good. Let's go,' he said. The moment I was inside he gunned the engine and drove off at speed, gripping the steering wheel in the orthodox ten to two position and changing gear frequently with professional skill.

'I spoke too soon,' he said after when we had gone a mile or so. 'Tempted fate. Should have known better. Never take anything for granted in this town, Alex. Arrivals and departures. You arrive and another departs,' he added cryptically. After that he was silent and we drove for half an hour before he pulled up. I had expected a restaurant as he had promised, but we were outside a large nondescript apartment block where a few lights were burning in the windows. Killing the engine, he reached inside the glove compartment and took out a Mauser and clicked a full magazine into place.

'Have yours handy too. Rawnsley said it was all clear, but one never knows.'

'Rawnsley?'

'One of my team.'

'What are we doing here, sir?'

'You'll find out.'

We went into the building and climbed a dirty stairway all the way to the top floor. Bare bulbs burned on each landing. A smell of damp and rancid cooking oil filled the stairwell. I followed him with my Walther cocked. When we reached the final landing we were faced with a long corridor with identical doors at intervals on either side, all painted a drab battleship grey. Cold air blew in from a broken window at the far end as Green led the way to a door at the far end which was ajar. He gestured caution before pushing it wide open with his foot. We edged into a room which reeked of stale cigarette smoke.

Green called: 'David?' and immediately a young man appeared with a Smith and Wesson in his hand. He stared at me.

'This is Alex, our new boy,' Green said. 'Where is she?'

'Through here.' Rawnsley led the way into a bedroom. At first glance nothing seemed untoward. The only illumination was provided by a lamp on the bedside table. There was a large pink Teddy bear propped against the pillows on the neatly made bed and it wasn't until Rawnsley tilted the lamp to shine on the space between the bed and the wall that I saw the girl. She was fully clothed and very dead. Green knelt down beside her and went through the motion of feeling the side of her neck. She was pretty, her Slavic features relaxed in death, the eyes open. Green knelt beside her and passed a hand over her face to close the lids.

'She was still warm when I got here,' Rawnsley said.

'How long ago?'

'Half an hour. I'd arranged to collect her at six. I was on time,' he added.

I said, 'Can I ask who she was?'

'Somebody who ran errands for us,' Green replied. He got to his feet. 'Have the garbage collectors been alerted?'

'On their way,' Rawnsley said.

'I want a post mortem before disposal.' Green looked around the room. 'Did you find anything?'

'These.' Rawnsley produced a gold-tipped cigarette butt and a spent hypodermic syringe.

'Not like them to be that careless,' Green said.

'Must have been in a hurry.'

'When you said you'd collect her, did you telephone ahead?'

'Yes.'

'That, too, was careless. Who else knew?'

'Nobody.'

When he turned away from the scene, Green's face had sagged. 'Lock the door when everybody's finished, David, then throw away the key. We won't be using this again.' To me he said brusquely: 'Right. We're out of here.'

Once we were at ground level again, I asked: 'D'you still want to have dinner?'

'Yes,' he said flatly.

He drove in silence to a small restaurant in the French sector where the clientele was exclusively French officers and their girl friends. A group of them nearest the door looked vaguely disgruntled at our arrival. We were shown to the only vacant table and Green ordered a carafe of the house red as soon as we sat down. There was a marked change in him from earlier in the day, the pouches under his eyes had become darker, the voice was softer and he no longer used the machine-gun delivery that had so thrown me at our first meeting. 'Best kept secret in Berlin, this place, and long may it remain so. I don't go a bundle on German cuisine. Too much bloody pork.'

A waitress in a tight sweater arrived with the carafe and poured some wine for Green to taste. He sampled it and pronounced it acceptable in impeccable French. When she had filled both our glasses and withdrawn he drank a full glass and then gave himself a refill. 'I'm sorry our first meal had to start on such a down note.' He stared into his glass. 'Not what I intended.'

He picked up his menu and studied it. I did the same, but the dead girl's face swam before me, obscuring the menu text.

'I can recommend the veal,' Graham said. 'If you like veal, that is. Some people don't. My first wife didn't, had a thing about eating young animals. Or try the *coq au vin*, usually excellent.'

'Fine. Sounds good.'

He beckoned for a waiter and ordered for both of us plus another carafe of wine.

'You said the murdered girl used to run errands for you. What did that mean exactly?'

'Dead letter drops and pick-ups.'

'You'll have to forgive me, I'm not familiar with the jargon.'

'You'll learn soon enough. She was permitted to visit her mother in the Soviet sector once a month. The old woman elected to stay there when they closed it off, and the girl acted as our postman, a job she volunteered for.' He fiddled with his knife and fork, straightening them by the side of his plate.

'Do you use many like her?'

'We use who we can, Alex, those we can trust, which is a very inaccurate science.' He poured the remains of the first carafe into our glasses. 'A dangerous game for all concerned, but one, unfortunately, we have had to resume from necessity. From the moment the war ended our relationship with the Russians went off the boil.'

'So soon?'

'That surprises you?'

'Yes,' I said.

'Get used to surprises, Alex, they come thick and fast here. Just when we thought we could sit back and enjoy the fruits of victory, the rules changed again.' He stopped arranging the cutlery and looked up at me. 'This is where it might all go pear-shaped one day.'

While I tucked into my meal I noticed he only played with his food while drinking steadily and it was some time before he spoke again. 'At least they killed her by injection, which is a sort of comfort.'

'How long had she been working for you?'

'Too long it now appears. I blame myself.' Then he surprised me. 'Before somebody gets to you with the wrong version, I should tell you she was my mistress.'

'I see,' I said lamely, at a loss to find the appropriate response.

He was silent again and pushed his plate to one side. The head waiter came up to enquire whether anything was wrong.

'No,' Graham replied in French. 'It's excellent as ever. Just that I've lost my appetite.'

'You wish me to get you something else, monsieur?'

'Thank you, no. You can remove my plate.'

When we were alone again, he said, 'Funny thing, falling in love at my age. Once past the big five O one should have more sense.' Flushed of face, his features crumpled. 'I should never have used her in the way I did.' He filled his glass, and then remembered me. 'Sorry. Have some. I apologise for being such lousy company.'

'You're not. I understand completely.'

'I doubt that. The hardest thing, you see, is the thought of somebody you've made love to being cut open.'

'Who d'you suspect killed her?' I said, anxious to show sympathy.

'Oh, it was a KGB job. Bears all the hallmarks. When the shooting match stopped, Moscow Central went straight back to business as usual. They never thought of us as an ally, those wartime get-togethers of the big three were charades. Roosevelt trusted Uncle Joe Stalin. Big mistake. Churchill was pragmatic because the Russians bought us time before D Day and, let's face it, they had the worst war, even though they brought it on themselves. We tipped them off you know, told them the exact day, the exact place and hour that Germany would invade. Stalin ignored our warning, he was too busy killing most of his best generals.'

'How did we know the date?'

'The Bletchley boffins had broken the German Enigma code.'

I put my glass down. 'Bletchley,' I repeated. 'I met somebody in Hamburg who said he'd worked there, but I didn't know the significance.'

'Who told you he worked there?' There was an edge to Green's voice.'

'A Control Commission Major called Chivers. Dodgy sort of character, I thought.'

Green frowned. 'Very dodgy if he volunteered that information. Bletchley's still top secret, nobody's allowed to mention it.'

Over coffee and Armagnac he returned to the subject of his dead mistress. 'The last thing that ever entered my mind was that I'd fall for a German girl.'

'Same here,' I said, 'my problem too.' If I thought this would show solidarity, I was wrong.

'Is it?' He betrayed no interest. 'I wasn't a good adulterer. Some characters can carry it off. Not me. I could rationalise it to myself – away from home, the end of a long war, every man needs to get his oats, middle-age crisis, etcetera, but guilt was always there. Are you married?'

'No.'

'Ah! There's the rub. My wife, my second wife that is, is a good woman, deserves more. Not that she knew. And it's ended now, over, finished.'

I had the sense he might weep, but then a safety switch was pulled, and he downed his Armagnac, pushed his chair back and signalled for the bill. 'Let's go.'

He drove erratically on the way back, twice narrowly missing pedestrians. His good-night was perfunctory, more a dismissal than a social convention, as though, even full of alcohol, he was aware he had revealed too much: confidences shared stored up future problems.

FIFTEEN

That night, my brain racing from too much Armagnac, I began several letters to Lisa, but binned all of them, unable to find the right words of comfort, unwilling to lie to her.

Green made no further mention of his murdered mistress when next we met, but honoured his promise to advance me some pay together with the details of a local tailor. 'Sweeten him with a packet of cigarettes and he'll kit you out in a week. I've got a bit of a chore for you before your trip to Vienna, which is going to be delayed anyway. The Yanks have asked whether we have anybody who could escort one of their star war correspondents around our sector. Bit of a strange request to dump on us, but one likes to oblige if one can. Might also help you to get acclimatised.'

'What's his name?'

'Her.' He searched amongst the papers on his desk. 'A Beth Eriksson. Ever heard of her?'

'No. You say Vienna's delayed.'

'Yes. Old Hugh has gone on leave for a couple of weeks. Never know, you might enjoy taking this Yank floozy around.'

The Yank "floozy" turned out to be an attractive woman in her early thirties with close-cropped blond hair framing a tanned face devoid of make-up. She greeted me wearing faded US battledress, the trousers tucked into paratrooper boots. 'Hi, I'm Beth. This is so nice of you, Captain. Hope it isn't a bore.'

'Not at all. And please call me Alex. I won't be the greatest guide, because I'd better confess I'm a recent arrival myself.'

'No sweat, we'll explore together. I thought I should at least set foot in the Tiergarten before heading home.'

I had never met anybody else like her before. She was good company, her conversation a cocktail of gossip, expletives and raunchy American colloquialisms that had to be explained to me.

None of the women of my acquaintance had ever used the f-word so openly, but it was curiously inoffensive coming from her. During our tour she occasionally used her battered Leica to take a shot of a particular ruin, handling it casually, no fiddling with focus or stops but with the expertise of a professional. At one point she said: 'We sure fucked up here, didn't we?'

'You think so?'

'Yeah. In spades. Either Bradley or Montgomery could have got to Berlin first if Ike hadn't succumbed to political pressure. Would have saved us the crazy half-assed solution we're living with. Ike never rated Montgomery, they were too far apart in personality. Ike is basically a fucking lucky West Point desk job, Cary Grant with four stars who knows how to pass the cocktails around. A cold martinet like Monty, with no apparent vices, would have fazed him. For one thing Monty doesn't smoke and Ike smokes like a chimney. Plus he was humping his Wac driver throughout the war. Adultery wouldn't have sat well with Monty.' Seeing my blank look, she said: 'Didn't you know that?'

'No.'

'The Press corps were onto it, but kept it under wraps. They even put it around that Monty liked to be surrounded with good-looking fags at his command post.'

'You are an extraordinary character,' I said. 'How d'you know so much?'

'Didn't you ever learn that the first casualty of war is truth? Like, FDR was crippled by polio, wore steel braces on his legs and had to be supported in public, but that was kept under wraps. We couldn't have a great war leader who couldn't walk. I guess we'll have to wait for the memoirs to be published before the whole story comes out. Bet your bottom dollar they'll all claim the credit and none of the blame.'

She told me she had been attached to Patton's Army for most of her war. 'My personal contribution to morale was to distribute my favours, such as they were, free of charge, like extra K rations. Nothing emotional, you understand, it was strictly philanthropic.

The only one who got under my skin was this kid,' producing a photo of a young pilot: it was the face of a boy who didn't look old enough to drive a car let alone take to the skies in a Mustang. 'He was shot down over Holland. The last time we slept together I knew his luck had run out. I could always tell, it was there in their faces. It sometimes seemed I only fucked young men destined to die. Still, I guess they figured it was better to burn out like a rocket, than to fade slowly.'

I found myself becoming captivated by her; she was so alive, so emancipated. I also discovered that her gung-ho attitude was only surface deep; despite her surface toughness she had been scarred by the horrors she had photographed. She showed me some of the prints she kept in her camera bag. 'Taken at Dachau,' she said. It was a shot I had seen reproduced in a newspaper – a naked, emaciated little boy with the face of an old man sitting in the dirt beside corpses piled like some monstrous avant garde sculpture.

'How do you bring yourself take shots like that?' I asked.

'You don't think about it, if you did you'd never press the button. All war photographers will tell you the same. Just aim and hope you've got the exposure and stop right. Mind you, at Dachau I threw up every day.'

She showed me other examples of her work taken there: a garrotted concentration camp guard, his face knocked out of shape, the eyes open but frozen in a last expression of terror as he met the fate he had meted out to so many others. 'God left early in Dachau, if He was ever there,' Beth said.

'Why did you stay on this long? Surely you could have gone home the moment it all ended?'

'Yeah, I could have, but I didn't. I'd never set foot outside the States before and over here I was treated like an equal. In any case, I don't have anything to go back to. War correspondents need a war.'

'No family?'

'Put it this way, nobody's missing me.'

We had dinner together in her hotel in the American zone and she was amused when I remarked on the size of my steak. 'Everything we Yanks do is larger than life, honey. The reason the rest of the world loves us right now but will eventually hate us, is we're so fucking full of ourselves. We have too much of everything. That's the way America works. Don't fuck with the dollar, baby.'

When I pressed her to tell me more she painted an intriguing picture of life in small-town America where she had grown up, describing a closed community where everybody knew everybody and nothing ever changed.

'I'd love to get to America one day,' I said. 'All I know about it is from films.'

'Well, if you ever make it across the water, look me up.'

She chain-smoked throughout the meal and downed several neat shots of Jack Daniel's. Although I couldn't match her, I also drank too much.

'So, how can I thank you,' she said. 'Want to fuck?'

Not knowing how to reply, I tried to make a joke of it. 'Am I young enough for you?'

'I can make an exception.'

'Are you serious?' I said.

'I wouldn't have asked if I wasn't.'

'Well, I'm flattered, but I've got a girl friend.'

'I'm not looking for marriage, honey, just a bit of social lend lease. Think of it like we're just two ships that shortly will pass in the night.'

I still couldn't make up my mind whether she was serious or it was just the Jack Daniel's talking.

'Look, if the idea doesn't grab you, I won't take it personally, I'll just put it down to your famed British reserve.'

The friendly jibe struck home. Although for the last month or so my every thought had been centred around Lisa, the recollection of our last meeting together had gradually become blurred, as though acted out between, two strangers like a scene from a half-remembered movie. My life had been pirated by outside events and the shock of being witness to the murder of Green's mistress had brought a new awareness of how all our lives hung by a thread. I had to admit that I had been attracted to Beth from the moment we had met, but the idea of taking it further and being unfaithful to Lisa had not occurred. Now I felt myself being pulled towards that deciding point when lust extinguishes conscience. An inner voice said, 'Why are you hesitating, Lisa won't know?', giving myself that age-old justification for betrayal. In any case, I half believed that Lisa was probably already lost to me. I loved her but once she became aware, as undoubtedly she would, that I was the one who had triggered her father's exposure, would love be enough? In my heart I doubted it.

'Yes,' I said to Beth, before my silence became rudeness. 'Let's go up to your room.'

It proved to be the room of somebody of no fixed abode as the saying goes, the temporary occupant always in transit. Beth slung clothes, camera bags and newspapers off the unmade bed. 'The powder room's through that door,' she said and there I found the same state of disarray – wet towels littering the floor, a full ashtray on the edge of the bath, underwear strung on a string, an empty bottle of Jack Daniel's by the toilet. I undressed and took a condom from my wallet before going back to the bedroom. Her shapeless battledress had concealed her true shape and I stood transfixed by her nakedness.

'What are you staring at?' she said.

'You. Your body.'

'Haven't you seen one before?'

'Not one like yours. How lovely you are.'

'Well, it ain't going to last, honey, it's just on loan, so enjoy it while you have the chance.' After we had kissed she saw the condom in my hand. 'What's that for?'

'Shouldn't I wear one?'

'Hell no.'

'What about the risk?'

'Risk of what? You aren't about to give me a dose, are you?'

'No, of course not. I meant risk of a baby.'

'If I have a baby, honey, it'll be a medical first. I had a hysterectomy when I was twenty and never wanted children anyway. Who would want to bring them into this world?' She pulled me down on top of her and with a practised hand guided my penis inside her. 'This is the only thing God got right, don't you agree?' she said. Her love-making had an uninhibited urgency, difficult to describe without resorting to the clichés of shop-girl fiction. Her speech became louder and more incoherent as we thrashed about and I was scared that somebody would bang on the door and tell us to be quiet. Several times she cried out the name 'Steve', perhaps the name of the doomed pilot she had once loved. There was nothing fake about her orgasm when she came and my own was more intense than I had ever experienced before. Afterwards, I wish I could admit to having had remorse about Lisa but, with my racing heart slowing to normal, there was only a sensation of feeling wasted, as though I had run a long race.

When Beth also rejoined the land of the living, she padded into the bathroom, returning with two tumblers and a full bottle of Jack Daniel's. 'Pour some, honey, and let's have a Philip Morris post-coitus moment.'

She lit two cigarettes and put one in my mouth. 'You needed a fuck as much as me, didn't you?'

'Yes. Yes, I did.' I ran my hand through her thick, cropped hair, then traced with a finger traced circles around her nipples. 'Just like Miss Blandish,' I said.

'Who's Blandish, your girlfriend?'

'No, a character in a book we weren't supposed to read as kids. The author described her as having tits with nipples like Bing cherries. I thought that was the most erotic thing ever. Never knew what it meant until now.'

'Well, I'm glad I solved that for you before I leave tomorrow.'

'Why tomorrow? Why can't you stay a bit longer.'

'If I stay I might get serious about you and that wouldn't be good for either of us. There's no future in somebody like me, take my word. We had a good time in the sack, don't spoil it.'

I went to Templehof next morning and watched her Douglas DC3 lift off and climb into the sullen sky, staying there until it vanished into the clouds. Some weeks later I got a letter from her enclosing a print of her saltbox house in Maine with 'Will provide rocking chair and a crate of Jack Daniels if you ever make the trip,' written on the back. I replied, but that was the last I ever heard. Years later I picked up a copy of *Time* in a dentist's waiting room which featured an obituary saying that, after a distinguished career as a war correspondent, she had died of an embolism aged thirty-eight. A collection of her photographs was published post-humously with the shot of the child at Dachau on the cover. It received considerable critical acclaim.

SIXTEEN

Acting on Machell's advice, I volunteered a statement to the war crimes investigation team. From them I learned that several Auschwitz survivors had given evidence identifying Grundwall as a member of the SS staff, and that a damning case against him was being put together.

When next I wrote to Lisa I chose my words with extra care so as not to raise her hopes, but when I read the words back before posting the letter appeared trite and insincere; I thought of Charlie Boag who, despite his fractured, inarticulate English, had still managed to convey genuine love, whereas my own efforts had a falseness about them, as well they might.

I carried my guilt about her when I took a train to Vienna in order to be tutored by Hugh Dempster-Miller. On arrival, he treated me to a meal then gave me a potted tour of the city. 'It's important to get the feel of this place, entirely different from Germany,' he said, 'and don't be fooled by the surface atmosphere. Those with short memories still believe they can detect distant strains of Strauss and Ravel, poor souls. They can't see behind the façade. This place may once have danced to the music of history, but to me it's a sinister enclave. The Austrians have always played a double game, bending like reeds to whichever wind blows their way. Still do. Nice to your face but, believe me, not to be trusted.'

Miller was in his late fifties, a short, hyperactive man with a round, Pickwickian face; small, deep-set, but bright eyes, an engaging smile which, when he used it, concertinaed down to his double chin. There were flakes of dandruff on his shoulders, frayed cuffs to his double-breasted suit, a general crumpled look, as though he slept in his clothes. Like Beth, he chain-smoked, letting the ash fall where it may, and was never without a tin of

Wills' Capstans bulging a side pocket of his jacket. Although many of his opinions mirrored Green's, he had a more pragmatic approach to the problems now facing us, unlike the disillusionment that Green exuded like stale body odour. As a teacher he was thorough, taking me through the intricacies of the cipher code books with infinite patience. 'An old-fashioned trade ours, Alex,' he said. 'Despicable probably . . . no, correction, definitely despicable . . . but deemed necessary. We've always been amateurs at it. It's the British character to despise professionals. We prefer the Gentlemen versus the Players approach, as in cricket. Let the enemy bat first, then try and bowl them out with spin on a crumbling wicket. My station here is understaffed and underfunded, consequently we're always at a disadvantage, but try getting London to do something about it.' He gave a sudden chuckle and lit another cigarette from the one still smouldering. 'Not that I'm bothered any longer; if they don't want to listen, that's their problem and I won't be here to worry about it.'

'You're near the end of your tour, are you?'

'What a nice way of putting it. I'm living on borrowed time, Alex. Piss all night. Prostate. Could do something about it, I suppose, but I'm not keen to go under the knife, prefer to bite on this handy little comforter when it becomes too much to handle.' He fished in a coin purse and produced a small capsule. 'Cyanide. Took it off an SS prisoner.'

'I'm sure it won't come to that,' I said, at a loss to know exactly how to react to such intimate details of a stranger's life so early in the relationship. I was swiftly coming to the realisation that I had joined a band of eccentrics – first Green and now Miller. Neither had waited long before confiding their Achilles heels to me. It was if, being wedded to a secret trade, they had a burning need to confess their hidden lives.

'What exactly is our job now? Be helpful if you could tell me.'

He looked nonplussed. 'It's flattering of you to think I know.

There's a manual for codes, but no Boy Scout instruction book for the rest of our job. We've always had to work things out for ourselves as we go along. Trial and error, mostly error. Take me, for instance. Guess where my career as a Mata Hari began.'

'Foreign Office?'

'Good God, no. In prison. Wormwood Scrubs. I was recruited by one of my old tutors at Charterhouse. Immediately drafted into an outfit called Radio Security Service, a real Heath Robinson affair, one of the department's curiosities that sprang into existence at the beginning of the war. Nobody knew what we were supposed to do but, after commandeering the Scrubs, we kicked out all the inmates and used their vacated cells as offices. I don't think anybody knew we existed. Our CO was a dotty old cove, ex-actor, who had once played the Red Shadow in *The Desert Song*, hardly the best foundation for a career in espionage, would you say? But on the other hand we're all shadows in a way. When the phoney war ended they scattered us into more worthwhile causes. I wangled my way into MI6, at that time pretty much a shambles, because the moment France collapsed our European network went up the spout. After Churchill took over we slowly got our act together, but there was always too much rivalry between us and MI5. Still is. So what did you ask me, Alex? Oh, yes, I remember. What's our job now? Same as ever. To watch our backs and to shift the night soil of others. It often seems to me that the enemy within is always the one we should fear.' A glob of ash fell onto his crotch but was ignored.

'That's a fairly gloomy prognosis,' I said.

'I'm a fairly gloomy character, sport, always had a sick sense of humour. Probably because I've spent too long practising the black arts,' he said, breaking into a chin-wobbling smile. Dousing a cigarette in his coffee cup saucer he immediately lit another. 'Still, better this than a life in Barclays Bank, which might have been my lot. My father spent his entire life telling people how to use their money, but never spent any himself. "Save the pennies, Hugh," he preached to me, "and the pounds will multiply." He was a terrible bore. I'm sure I can be a bore at times, but he was a bore in spades.'

I enjoyed my stay with him, for he was a gregarious and amusing companion. Although he liked to give the impression that he had perfected the casual approach to any problem, there was a steely purpose to him which he urged me to emulate. Like Green, he was convinced that the Soviets had never had any good intentions towards us and that, even though he wouldn't live to see it, he argued the world would be lucky to escape another major conflagration in the next two decades. He appeared to be asexual, never talked about women past or present and struck me as a solitary remnant of a dying breed, the type England had always thrown up when building the Empire. Yet during the time I spent in Vienna while he taught me the ropes of my new posting, there wasn't a single night when confused dreams that mingled images of Lisa and Beth didn't trouble my rest.

Through Hugh's office I kept in touch with the Nuremburg legal team, but no date had been yet been set for Grundwall's trial. Lisa lacked a phone in the flat she shared with Greta, and although I rang the stage door number several times I failed to get her. Because of the uncertainty about the eventual fate of her father, my life had an emptiness; I had no real idea how to deal with the situation. Nobody had trained me how to heal another's unhappiness, only to cause it.

SEVENTEEN

On my return to Berlin I could not rid myself of the feeling that
the Army had manoeuvred me into a cul de sac. I missed the
comradeship of my old Field Security unit, for we had come such
a long way together, and I even mourned the bleakness of my
Hamburg bedroom in the *Hotel zum Kronprinzen*: the red wallpaper of my new billet constantly reminding me that buying that
copy of *The Scarlet Letter* had changed the direction of my entire
life. Sometimes I awoke expecting to find Lisa's face on the pillow
beside me, and sometimes, alone, I spoke my thoughts and fears
to her.

The first day back Rawnsley buttonholed me on my way to
report to Graham. 'In case you were thinking of raising the
subject, don't,' he said.

'What subject?'

'His girl,' he said with a trace of irritation as though I should
have automatically tuned in to his wavelength. 'The autopsy
confirmed they murdered her with a nerve gas, a strain developed
for the SS, which no doubt the KGB purloined and now
use. Attacks the respiratory system, causes death in a matter of
minutes.'

'I suppose there's some small comfort in that. How did Graham
receive that news?'

'He doesn't discuss it, nor should we wish to enquire.'

His note of disapproval warned me that if he ever learned of
my involvement with the Grundwall family, he would bracket me
with Graham as another who only had himself to blame for
sleeping with the enemy.

'Has anything been heard from the girl's contact since?'

'No, nothing.'

'Who is he?'

'More likely who was he? A Pole. Hugh Miller put him in place originally and passed him over for us to run. He was supposed to come in from the cold if the girl failed to make two consecutive drops.'

'Miller believes our operation over here has been infiltrated.'

'Yes, well, he's of the school that believes there's a red-under-every-bed, convinced that London has more moles than the average lawn. And he could be right. I'm never certain who we're fucking or whether we're being fucked.'

This dialogue continued later that same day when we were both parked in a nondescript Volkswagen two hundred yards from Checkpoint Charlie, keeping observation on the East German border guards as they stopped and searched the human traffic entering and exiting our zone.

'One thing I've been wanting to ask you,' I said. 'How did Graham's girl bring out the information?'

'Micro film concealed in her sanitary towel.'

'Original.'

'You could say that, but personally I prefer not to go there.' He dropped his field glasses into his lap and fished for a cigarette but didn't offer me one. 'Tell me, what did you make of old Hugh?'

'Cheerful old sod, I thought, despite the fact he believes his days are numbered.'

'Really? Why is that?'

'He told me his prostate is dodgy. Never been quite sure what the prostate is or what it does.'

'One of the Almighty's nastier tricks on us men,' Rawnsley replied. 'Only the size of a walnut apparently, but can be a killer. Poor old Hugh. Always thought him a thundering bore myself, remnant of our lost glory, but I wouldn't wish his possible end on anybody.'

As we watched, the *Vopos* dragged a young man out of a battered truck and spread-eagled him across the bonnet. An officer appeared from the blockhouse as a third *Vopo* trundled a wheeled mirror under the vehicle. Adjusting focus on my binoculars, I got a closer look at the man before he was frog-marched away.

'Why are they so bloody determined to stop their people getting to the West?' I said.

'I imagine they know that if they once allowed free passage, there'd be a mass exodus.' Rawnsley scanned the scene through his own glasses. 'I'll tell you what's wrong with the Russians. They don't play cricket. There's something fundamentally missing in a race that doesn't play cricket.'

'What a sage you are, Rawnsley,' I said, for once daring to mock him.

'I just echo our fearless leader.'

'How d'you read Graham?'

'He fancies himself as Polonius.'

'Did you ever meet his girl?'

'Once. Briefly. I bumped into them both at the cinema. Can't say I thought she was worth risking a career for, but then it takes all sorts.'

I plunged at that point, the need to confide in somebody, even Rawnsley, overcoming discretion. 'I left a girl friend in Hamburg. An actress.'

If I thought this would provoke one of his sardonic comments, I was mistaken. He surprised me by merely commenting: 'Is that so? My wife was an actress. She was in a play called *Quiet Weekend* when I met her. Ever see it?'

'No. There wasn't much theatre where I was brought up. I was taken to a pantomime once.'

Rawnsley groaned. 'Ghastly English convention, pantomimes. Likewise Peter Pan. I always prayed for Tinker Bell to die. Didn't you?'

'No.'

'You're not serious? Didn't your Nanny read the bloody book to you?'

'I didn't have a nanny.'

My answer threw him. 'Good God. Really? How extraordinary.'

He was silent for a few moments, hesitating, I imagined, between feeling sorry for me and being genuinely at a loss to understand how I had got this far without a normal upbringing.

'Is your wife in a play now?'

'Oh, no. I made her give it up when we got married and concentrate on being a proper mother.'

'Did she mind that?'

'Well, if she did, she had to lump it. You can't mix these things,' he said obliquely.

'D'you have children?'

'Yes.'

'How many?'

'Three. Needed three attempts before I produced the son and heir. Put him down for Eton the moment he was born. That's why I've got my sights fixed on the Washington desk.'

'That's a good posting, is it?'

'*La crème*. You're not Oxbridge, are you?'

'No,' I said.

'Oh, that's right, I read your file. Strange the way we recruit these days. This used to be an occupation for gentlemen, like publishing.' He seemed unaware of the offensiveness of the remark. 'So, this bit of Hamburg totty, she's German I take it?'

'Yes.'

'I've never fancied them,' he said, as though bracketing German girls with sauerkraut.

We resumed our watch. Two cyclists, a young boy and a girl, came into view and were flagged down by the *Vopos*. Instead of stopping they made an erratic dash for the frontier, peddling furiously. Shots were fired and the boy careened around in erratic circles before crashing into one of the barriers and toppling to the ground. A moment later the girl was also brought down. Through our glasses we could see no signs of life from either of them. Their bodies were quickly removed. The whole incident had been like something in a silent film. Neither of us said much after that. There wasn't much to say.

EIGHTEEN

It was a time of waiting, a feeling of not knowing which way the pendulum would swing.

In the seven weeks since we had parted in Hamburg, Lisa had only written once, a sad little letter, such as a schoolgirl might pen to a first crush: '*The rehearsals are going well but Herr Director is still picking on me and we have had foul weather the past few days which means I get drenched walking to the theatre. Greta and I have eaten out twice on the money you gave me, really good food for a change and I think some of the other members of the cast are envious that I have you. I still feel badly about taking your money but perhaps one day I will earn enough myself to treat you. Your love is everything to me and I miss you very much, especially now, so don't forget me and write very often and give me any news about Vater. I think of little else with every day that passes. I will always love you.*'

I attempted to write back something that would keep her hopes alive, though in my heart I knew that the eventual trial would almost certainly bring grief. I felt unable to confide in either Graham or Rawnsley as I once had with Machell.

Trying to push the situation to the back of my mind for a few hours, I put on my new suit and went to sample one of the night-clubs that had been permitted to open. Graham had told me that they were making an effort to recapture some of the gaiety and decadence that had characterised pre-Nazi Berlin, but there was something ersatz about the Blue Cockatoo, my random choice. It welcomed customers in the refurbished basement of a bombed building and had made an attempt to rekindle the setting of Brecht's *The Beggar's Opera*: dim lighting throwing shadows on walls decorated with crude suggestive murals, red plush banquettes circling a small dance floor which could be curtained off for clients wanting something more than the over-priced drinks.

A few couples were dancing to canned music in a desultory fashion as I was conducted to one of the banquettes past half a dozen flashily dressed girls waiting expectantly at the bar. The moment I sat down a hand came around the curtains from the adjoining banquette to tug at my sleeve and a voice said: 'Small world, eh, sport?'

I turned and found myself confronted by the unwelcome, grinning face of Chivers. He was with a girl young enough to be his daughter with a thin, lamb-to-the-slaughter expression.

'Why d'you think it is our paths cross so often?' he said.

'Sheer bad luck, I suppose.'

'Oh, full marks, I like that. You always did have a droll sense of humour. Don't sit on your own, come and join us. This is Inga. Move over, darling girl, and make room for my friend.'

Accepting the invitation with reluctance, I eased myself in beside Inga. I caught a whiff of Chivers' overpowering after-shave.

'Let me buy you a drink. I see you're back in civvy street.'

'No, just happen to be out of uniform tonight. Like you,' I said pointedly.

'Still a sergeant major?'

'No, I was promoted.

'What are you now?'

'Captain.'

'Well, congrats, sport. I should be in line for a leg up shortly. So, what's your fancy, Captain?' he asked as a waiter hovered. 'We're on champagne.'

'I'll have a Scotch.'

'Bring a Scotch and another bottle of champers,' Chivers said. He had his arm around Inga's neck and was fingering the lobe of her ear.

'Do you ever see First Officer Babs these days?' I asked.

'Who?'

'The Wren you were with the first time we met.'

'Oh, her. No. Yesterday's news, gone the way of all flesh, sport.

I've transferred my unlimited charm to the natives, like little Inga here.'

'What brings you to Berlin? Apart from the nookie that is.'

'Nookie. What a lovely word. Haven't heard that in ages. Just flew in to check out a new business proposition. And by the way, I owe you a big thank you.'

'You do? How's that?'

'Remember that letter I asked you to post way back?'

I arranged my face to express uncertainty. 'Remind me.'

'We bumped into each other at the docks and I entrusted you with an urgent letter.'

'And I stupidly forgot to post it immediately.'

'Happily, that did me a favour. Had it not been for your fortuitous loss of memory, it would have been delivered and landed me in Queer Street. The scheme I was about to join turned out to be a con, but because of you I missed the deadline and my money never went in. If it had, I'd have lost the lot.'

The drinks arrived at that moment and we clinked glasses. 'Well, thank God I had a memory lapse. And now you're onto to something new, are you?'

Chivers looked around before answering, but nobody was paying us any attention. A few couples still drifted aimlessly on the dance floor. 'Strictly entre nous,' he said confidentially, 'cameras.'

'Cameras?'

'Yes. Leitz, who made Leicas, ended up in the Soviet zone but the patents are no longer valid, so there's nothing to stop them being copied. A Yank I met here says he can cut me in and has a way to produce identical copies in Canada. People haven't been able to buy a decent camera for seven years and as you know, Leicas are the crème de la crème for the shutterbugs, sport, so one could clean up.'

Like the previous get-rich-quick scheme I had saved him from, this sounded equally dubious. I was conscious that Inga was being totally ignored. 'Are you a Berliner?' I asked her in German.

'Yes,' she answered.

'How are you finding things now?'

She shrugged. 'We have good days and bad.'

'What sort of day is this?'

With a knowing smile she said: 'It's too early to say.'

'You're not muscling in on my date, are you, sport?' Chivers said.

'Wouldn't dream of it. How's life in Hamburg these days?'

'I'm getting it sorted. And you, are you enjoying the change of scenery? This must be a strange place. I want to take a look at the Russian zone before I head back.'

I finished my whisky and stood up. 'Well, thanks for the drink.'

'Not going to make a night of it, sport? We could make it a foursome and have a good time.'

'Not tonight.' The idea of sharing his idea of a good time repelled me. 'Good luck.' My farewell was for Inga rather than Chivers.

As I climbed the stairs to the street a sudden gust of wind twisted dust and litter into a spiral that danced along the pavement ahead of me. The lights of the Western sectors bounced back off low clouds emphasising the blackness beyond. I felt my life was like that, sliced in two, darkness and light, like everybody else I knew. We were all scarred by a secret history: Machell and his lost love child, Graham mourning his murdered mistress, Beth finding a sort of fulfilment in casual sex, the smooth passage of my own life suddenly corrupted by my own actions.

Lost in such thoughts I suddenly felt something sharp being jabbed into my back. I wheeled around to find myself confronted by a ragged man of my own age.

'Give me your money,' he said in German. 'Quick!' He again prodded me with the knife. 'Give it to me or I'll kill you.'

Keeping my movements deliberate and slow, I put a hand inside my jacket as though reaching for my wallet but, instead, feeling for my Walther in its shoulder holster and releasing the safety catch. As he menaced me again I whipped the gun out and pointed it straight at his forehead.

'Drop the knife and back off otherwise I'll blow your fucking head off,' I shouted in German.

'*Nein, bitte, entschuldige'n bitte,*' he said in a pleading whine, all aggression gone at sight of the gun. '*Itch habe ein frau und kinde.*'

'Against the wall,' I shouted. 'Hands on your head.'

The knife clattered to the pavement. With my free hand, I frisked him for any other weapons, but he had none. I looked both ways up the street, but there was no sign of a Military Police patrol. Now that my adrenalin level dropped, it wasn't anger I felt, just a sense of resignation.

'*Absteigen,*' I said.

He turned around, unable to believe his luck.

'*Absteigen,*' I repeated, '*Raus! Schnell!*' Then I reverted to shouting in English: 'Go, you stupid fucker, before I change my mind!'

'*Danke, danke,*' he said. As he moved off his legs buckled and he stumbled, nearly falling before breaking into a run. I watched until he disappeared from sight before putting my gun away.

That night I had a confused dream in which a naked Lisa was cavorting with Chivers, while I stood apart, a passive spectator. The images were still with me when I shaved the next morning and I twice nicked myself. As soon as I could I rang the theatre desperate to hear Lisa's voice again, but although I got through she was not available to take the call. It was then that a telex came in from Nuremberg stating that Grundwall's trial had been set to begin in three weeks time and that I was subpoenaed to attend as a prosecution witness.

'Bloody inconvenient,' Graham said. 'Who is this character?'

'Ex-SS. I spotted him in a set of photographs the Yanks sent us. Turned out he was part of Mengele's team at Auschwitz.'

'How long will they keep you?'

'No idea. Never been to a trial before. As long as it takes, I imagine.'

'Bloody inconvenient,' he repeated.

Three weeks later I caught a courier flight to Nuremberg. It was dark when I touched down. A member of the British legal team met me and took me to the Grand Hotel, where most of the lawyers were housed. After I had checked in he gave me a thorough briefing on the procedures I had to follow, together with a file outlining the prosecution's case. I was also given photocopies of some of the experiments carried out by Mengele and his associates. After a quick supper I retired early and studied everything I had been given. Alone in yet another anonymous hotel room the realisation gradually sank in that I was on trial as much as Grundwall.

NINETEEN

Ironically, the nineteenth-century prison at Nuremberg, attached to the Palace of Justice, had been heavily damaged by our air attacks but was left still standing and it had needed extensive structural repairs before the trials commenced. All the accused were housed on two floors of one wing, and kept under twenty-four-hour suicide watch.

I was not allowed any contact with Grundwall, but I was granted permission to visit the cellblock and observe him through the small observation slit in the door. His cell was illuminated by a bare bulb hanging out of reach high up on the ceiling and kept burning night and day. It was sparsely furnished with an iron bedstead, a straw mattress, washbasin, slop pail, small table and wooden chair. Peering through the slit I saw somebody who bore scant resemblance to the man I had first encountered in that Hamburg bookshop. Grundwall lay on the bed in the foetal position, legs drawn up to his chest and seemed diminished in size.

'Does he give you any trouble?' I asked the burly young GI.

'No. Never talks. Just takes his chow without a word. Spends most of his time writing. The sooner they've tried the last one and I'm outta here the happier I'll be. Can't wait to get State side again.'

'Where's your home?'

'Austin, Texas. Know it?'

'No, I don't. I've never been to America.'

'Great country. Sure beats this shit hole.'

Grundwall's trial had been scheduled to begin the following day, but the young guard told me that, during the previous night, despite tight surveillance, a convicted prisoner given the death penalty had managed to commit suicide by hanging himself with a rope made from strips torn from his blanket. As a result all trials were temporarily suspended while an enquiry was held and the security measures tightened further.

'Pity they don't all top themselves,' he said. 'Save us a hell of a lot of trouble. Goodbye and good riddance.'

Left to my own devices, I was glad to accept an invitation to have a meal with one of the British team, a Major Jones. He voiced the same opinion as the young guard. 'Pity he cheated the hangman. Still, one less out of the way.'

With his sunken eyes and thinning hair, Jones had the haunted look of somebody who had been forced to witness too much horror, a surmise that proved true when he confessed he sometimes had to anaesthetise himself with a bottle of whisky at night – 'Just to blot out what I've been forced to listen to. D'you ever have nightmares?'

'Yes.'

'I have a recurring nightmare in which we lost the war, England is occupied by the Nazis and I'm the commandant of an extermination camp on Salisbury Plain, charged with gassing Jews from Golders Green.'

'Golders Green? Where's that?'

'A predominantly Jewish enclave in North London. That isn't the point. The point is that when I wake up I'm left with the question, "What if?" If we'd been defeated and occupied like France, would they have found some of us willing to embrace the same sort of horrors we're judging here? Think about it. After all, the Vichy French handed over many of their Jews.'

'What a bloody depressing thought,' I said.

'When this is over I never want to see the inside of a court room again. I shall emigrate.'

'Where to?'

'New Zealand, take up sheep farming, any bloody thing rather than be reminded of this.'

He pushed his half-eaten pork chop to one side. 'Whose trial are you here for?'

'A man called Grundwall.'

'Ah, yes, the good professor, otherwise known as SS Ober-gruppenfuehrer Grundwall.'

'Are you leading for the prosecution?'

'No. Westbury's down for that. Good man. Very thorough. What's your involvement?'

'I was the one who first identified him. I met him by chance, in a bookshop of all places. Seemed harmless enough. He was on the faculty at the university in Hamburg. Totally different from the SS types I'd been dealing with before.'

'Most of them look harmless enough out of their death's head uniform.'

'How many of them admit their guilt?'

'In all the time I've been here, 'Jones said, 'only one bastard admitted to the charges laid against him. Just one. Now, nobody has ever been put on trial without damning evidence – photo-graphs, eye witnesses, documentary evidence – and yet the majority still deny everything, the favourite defence being to plead they were carrying out orders from their superiors. That doesn't wash with me. Some of the ghastly *Einsatgruppen* squads, possibly, maybe, because they were recruited from infantry units, given plenty of booze and extra rations in order to stomach the killings until finally sickened by it. When that happened those who chickened out were sent back into the front line or else shot like their victims.'

I could not stop myself asking: 'Will Grundwall get the death sentence if convicted?'

'Depends. The majority of death sentences have been com-muted of late. That's another reason why I want out. Revenge eats into you. Instant revenge I can understand – camp survivors lynching their guards, yes – but once you institutionalise revenge it becomes as one with the crimes that prompted it. Every time I look in the shaving mirror I see a face I don't recognise, that's why it's time to get out. '

He downed his drink and contemplated the empty glass. 'That's enough philosophising for one night. This is on me.' He took out a wad of dollar notes secured with a rubber band. Seeing my look as he peeled off a few, he said: 'Nobody wants our official currency, but they love these. Don't we all? The Yanks are the new masters, so welcome to the next world order.'

TWENTY

It did not escape my notice that, with a certain irony, the Ten Commandments were engraved over the door of the courthouse and what struck me when I entered the actual courtroom was how cold it was, as though over long months the litany of horrors released had chilled the very panelling on the walls. I was directed to a seat in the witness section. There were a number of stenographers and translators but only a sprinkling of Press: the trials no longer commanded worldwide media attention: I had been told that after all the major players had been executed, the remaining trials held little interest save in Israel where they were still closely followed.

The first day, proceedings were delayed while the President and the four alternate judges heard submissions from the defence lawyer on a series of legal technicalities that were beyond my comprehension. When these were completed, the court was declared in session and Grundwall was brought in manacled to a guard, the manacles removed once he was in the dock, but two American Military Policemen remained on either side of him. I studied his demeanour but avoided direct eye contact as he looked around, taking stock of his surroundings. If he noticed my presence he gave no sign. I thought: it was his sperm that made Lisa, this man on trial for his life.

Grundwall took the oath in a low voice. Then Westbury rose and addressed him. 'Please state your name.'

'Karl Gustave Grundwall.'

'Speak louder, please.'

'Karl Gustave Grundwall.'

'How do you wish to conduct yourself, in German or English?'

'I am willing to answer in English if that is the wish of the court,' Grundwall replied.

'The choice is yours. You can use the facilities of the simultaneous translation. You will find headphones by your side.

'I will answer in English to the best of my ability,' Grundwall said. 'If I do not understand any question put to me I will ask for it to be repeated in German.' He spoke in an assured voice.

The President then asked Westbury whether Grundwall had been judged fit to plead.

'Yes, your Honour.'

'Karl Gustave Grundwall,' the President said, 'how do you plead to the charges brought against you?'

Grundwall began, 'Before I reply, I wish to state . . . ' but got no further. 'Defendants are not entitled to make statements at this stage,' the President interrupted. 'At this time there will be no arguments, speeches or discussion of any kind. You will simply plead either Guilty or Not guilty to the offences with which you are charged by the indictment.'

Grundwall lent forward, clutching the edge of the dock. 'I enter a plea of innocence. I stand here the victim of a mistake.'

'You must answer Guilty or Not guilty,' the President repeated. 'No other plea is acceptable by this court.'

Grundwall stared around as if seeking help from anybody present, before finally uttering 'Not guilty', first in English, then in German.

The President then addressed him. I had no means of telling whether it was a stock speech which he delivered to all those who came before him, but he delivered it as though for the first time and there was no mistaking the controlled vehemence in his voice.

'Karl Gustave Grundwall, you have been brought to this court to be tried under the jurisdiction and authority of the International Military Tribunal, charged with crimes against humanity in that you did unlawfully, wilfully, and knowingly commit war crimes as defined by Article II of Control Council Law No. 10. The totality of these crimes, which, over many months this court has been forced to hear and will no doubt continue to hear, is without precedence in history. You and others before you belonging to the infamous SS have stood in that dock to answer for atrocities arising from a sustained campaign of brutality such as the world has not witnessed since the pre-Christian era. Indeed some of these acts reached such proportions of bestiality that they aroused the sleeping strength of imperilled civilisation and acquired a worldwide familiarity. By virtue of the indictment under which you are charged this Tribunal will confront you with incontrovertible evidence of the foul and shameful treatment of concentration camp victims over a prolonged period. The prosecution will produce evidence, photographic and personal testimony to illustrate the methods employed to maim, starve, mutilate and kill. Such methods included male victims being immersed in freezing baths until their body temperature was reduced to minus 28 degrees centigrade, after which, close to death, they were "rewarmed" by hot baths and forced to have sexual intercourse with female inmates. Here Nazi degeneracy might be thought to have reached its nadir, but this was not the limit of degeneracy. It will be shown that you and your medical colleagues went further, progressing to experiments on living children as young as two years of age, subjecting them to such unimaginable horrors as to completely refute the universal Hippocratic oath the medical profession is sworn to uphold. In order that you be left in no doubt as to the substance and truth of such crimes as I have described, your trial will commence with the screening of filmed material, the authenticity of which has been proved beyond doubt. Please turn and face the screen.'

Grundwall now shuffled around to face the portable screen. The overhead light were extinguished and a court official started the 16mm projector. The film began with a train arriving at the Auschwitz railway siding, then shots of a new intake being disembarked, the packed bodies of men, women and children tumbling out of the cattle trucks and herded into lines by SS dog handlers. They were subsequently divided by sex and age into separate groups, the older women being the first group to be marched away. They filed past musicians in prison garb playing an accompaniment to their last journey. The grainy images had a sickening familiarity for me, for like most members of the British Army of Occupation I had seen many such compilations. The next sequence featured younger women, now naked, filing past an SS officer who made instant selections, some waved to the right, some to the left, infant children being forcibly removed from their mothers, any resistance savagely dealt with. The footage was without sound, giving it an added dimension of horror. Then it was replaced with a sequence in a hospital ward where half a dozen small naked children lay in metal beds without benefit of any covering. Three men in white coats partially unbuttoned so that their SS uniforms were clearly visible paused by the bed of an infant girl. Her head had been shaved. While examining her they appeared to be sharing a joke. The film changed to an autopsy room dominated by a stainless steel table and bearing a close similarity to the photograph that had first alerted me to Grundwall's involvement. Another small, naked girl was lying on the table and a man, possibly Mengele himself, administered an injection into her swollen abdomen. The child immediately went into convulsions, her abused body half rising from the table in a violent reaction. Finally, Allied footage, filmed post liberation, showing stacks of emaciated dead, pyramids of skeletal bodies layered in grotesque angles to each other, the skulls of some pushed into the sunken genitalia of others. Survivors, watched by shocked Allied soldiers, searched the swill bins for food. The film ended with image of a dead naked girl hanging on the barbed perimeter wire.

When the court lights were switched on again, the President called Westbury to commence the case for the prosecution. Like Jones, Westbury, by his general demeanour and the tone in which he put his questions, struck me as somebody who would never again believe in goodness. Months later I obtained a verbatim transcript of the trial, and it is from that record that I have been able to relive what took place.

Westbury began with: 'May this court take it you are familiar with the scenes in the film we have just witnessed?'

Grundwall gave a mumbled reply.

'Can you please repeat that?'

'No, I am not.'

'I put it to you again that the images in that film cannot be foreign to you.'

'I am not familiar with the exact images you have just shown me.'

'At the end of hostilities the British authorities forced civilians to attend screenings of such material. Did you attend any such screenings?'

'Yes.'

'With your wife?'

'Yes.'

'What was the general reaction to such screenings?'

'It varied.'

'In what way?'

'Many were shocked.'

'Were you and your wife shocked?'

'My wife did, I remember, express some doubts as to the authenticity of what we were being forced to witness.'

'Really? And you? What was your reaction?'

'I knew that all armies committed atrocities in the heat of battle. It is well known that the the Soviet armies behaved with particular brutality.'

'The events depicted in the film were hardly taken in the heat of battle,' Westbury said drily. 'They were far from any battlefield and showed examples of the day-to-day life in concentration camps.'

'I grant that certain elements may have reacted unlawfully when provoked.'

'And the film you have just been shown is an example of that reaction, is it? They were being provoked by defenceless civilians?'

Westbury waited, but Grundwall made no reply to this. 'Tell the court this, then,' Westbury continued, 'did you doubt the authenticity of the films?'

'I think the images were carefully chosen to give the maximum propaganda impact.'

'And yet they could not have come as a surprise to you, could they?' Westbury asked, opening another file. 'Because from September 1943 until February 1945 we can establish you were a member of the SS staff at the Auschwitz-Berkenau extermination camp.' He stopped and shuffled his papers, taking a long pause before speaking again. 'That being so, I wonder how you reconcile this fact with the statements you gave to two de-Nazification tribunals at which you stated you spent the entire war as a translator for the Ministry of Communications?'

'That was true at the outset. I was subsequently transferred.'

'Into the SS?' Westbury jumped in.

'Yes,' Grundwall murmured, then realised he had been trapped into the admission.

'You did not think it necessary to tell the de-Nazification Court of this transfer?'

'I took it that your records would be aware of my war service.'

'In the immediate post-war chaos details often could not be definitively checked.' He paused for effect. 'So you got away with it, did you not?'

'I don't understand what the expression "got away with it" means.'

'Our authorities were left believing that you spent the entire war with the Ministry of Communications. When they allowed you to return to your pre-war academic career they were unaware of your transfer into the SS and your posting to Auschwitz-Birkenau. That is what you got away with.'

Grundwall was silent.

'Since you were there, it therefore follows, does it not, that you must have witnessed at first hand incidents identical to those depicted on film we have all just seen?'

'No. That is not true.'

'What is not true?'

'I did not personally witness such incidents.'

142

'Are you saying you were unaware that there were six gas chambers operating round the clock at Auschwitz, and that in twenty-four-hour periods up to 20,000 human beings who arrived there could be gassed and cremated and you never looked upwards?'

'I don't understand the question.'

'On no occasion did you look up and see smoke rising from the fifty-foot chimneys?'

'I might have done.'

'But you did not make the connection?'

'I took it the chimneys were part of the heating plant.'

'Ah, yes, of course,' Westbury said with a curl of his lip, 'supplying heat for the benefit of the inmates of the huts. I believe one of the jokes prevalent amongst the camp staff was to say, 'The only exit is by way of the chimneys.' He picked up a new file. 'You have lived all your life in Hamburg, correct?'

'Yes. I was born there.'

I could tell from Grundwall's wary expression that he was unprepared for this sudden switch in the questioning.

'Were you aware that in order to exterminate two million Jews in 1942 and 1943, Reserve Police Battalion 101 was formed from middle-aged, middle-class Hamburg citizens such as yourself and was one of the battalions who carried out many thousands of these mass murders?'

'No, I was not. I have never heard of this Battalion 101.'

The President interrupted: 'What is this line of questioning intended to reveal, Counsel?'

'I wish to establish that many ordinary Germans, not necessarily fanatical members of the Nazi Party, were prepared to take part in the extermination of Jews and others deemed undesirables and that the accused was one such ordinary German who willingly joined the SS.'

After conferring with his fellow judges, the President replied: 'Very well, proceed.'

'Am I right in contending that the members of Battalion 101

and others such as yourself, allowed the genocide to proceed without complaint to anybody because one of the most frightening features of the Nazi regime was peer pressure and a culture of blind obedience?'

'I have already told you that I had no knowledge of Battalion 101's existence.'

'That was not what I asked you. I asked if you will concede that ordinary citizens such as yourself were prepared to turn a blind eye to the liquidation of the Jews.'

'I would not describe myself as typically ordinary. I am a scholar and an academic.'

'And an ex-member of the SS,' Westbury answered, 'so let me ask you this: did you recognise any of your fellow SS officers shown in the film?'

'No, I did not.'

'None of them?'

'No.'

'Perhaps these enlarged frames taken from the film will enable you to reconsider. I must remind you that you are on oath. It might also refresh your memory if I gave you their names.' He consulted another paper. 'SS Doctors Mengele, Cleber and Kremer.'

The enlargements were handed to Grundwall. He put on his spectacles, I remember, and peered at them for a long time before answering: 'I recognise Doctor Mengele, but I am not certain about the others. The camp administrative staff changed frequently.'

'It is known that the said Dr Mengele arrived at Auschwltz in May 1942 and remained there during the entire period you were also a member of the staff. In that same year, 1942, Dr Mengele commenced medical experiments on living Jews and others he deemed suitable. He used the pretext of medical science to carry out various shameful, potentially lethal experiments, in the main on children, particularly on twins. Were you aware that he was carrying out such experiments?'

'No, I was not.'

'Even though technically Dr Mengele was your superior and therefore you were answerable to him on a daily basis, you knew nothing of the work he was carrying out?'

'I knew that a separate medical facility existed, but I had no knowledge of the activities carried out there. My day-to-day responsibilities were confined to the health and welfare of the administrative staff and their families, the majority of whom lived outside the camp.'

'So are you saying that you did not know that some of these children who had outlived their usefulness to Mengele as a result of his experiments were dispatched with injections of phenol directly into their hearts and then thrown into the crematoriums?'

Grundwall swayed in the dock and one of the Military Policemen put out a hand to steady him. He answered in a whisper, 'I repeat, I had no knowledge of the procedures carried out in the special facility.'

'And are you also asking the court to believe that you never had regular social contact with Mengele?'

'That is correct.'

'I find that hard to believe. However, let us move on. Are you contending on oath that you were not aware of the true purpose of the facility headed by Mengele?'

'That is correct.'

'Again, it seems inconceivable there was no exchange of information between yourself and Mengele or that you did not discuss things with fellow members of the staff. I am seeking to establish how the administration of the camp functioned.' Westbury kept his voice even. 'Since you were part of that administration, it is not unreasonable to assume that, in order for the daily workings of the camp to function efficiently, there would have been regular exchanges between the various personnel involved. Yes?'

'If you say so,' Grundwall replied.

'It is not for me to say so, since I was not present. Let me ask you again: did members of the staff meet regularly in order to facilitate the smooth running of the camp?'

'Possibly.'

'That is not an answer,' the President interjected. 'The question warrants a Yes or a No. Did the staff regularly meet?'

Grundwall continued to stonewall. 'I did not attend every meeting.'

'Did you attend *any* is what the counsel is attempting to establish.'

'I may have done. I can't remember.'

'Carry on,' the President said to Westbury. 'The court will note that the prisoner avoided answering the question directly.'

'Let me ask you this then,' said Westbury, taking over again. 'What did you believe was the actual purpose of the camp?'

'That it was a correction facility for criminals.'

'I will give you time to reconsider your answer since it is patently false and you must know it is false.'

'That was the official designation.'

'I see. A "correction facility". And you had no problem in accepting that?'

'No.'

'I put it to you that Auschwitz-Berkenau and other camps of a like nature existed, not as "correction facilities" but as extermination facilities for the mass murder of Jews, gypsies, homosexuals and others considered a threat to the Reich.'

'I had nothing to do with that.'

'That is not what I asked you.'

Grundwall faltered. 'Will you repeat the question, please?'

'It was an extermination camp, was it not? One of many facilities built for the express purpose of the *Endlosung*, the "Final Solution".'

'The term "*Endlosung*" is not one I am familiar with.'

'You surprise me. Let me elucidate. In January 1942, during what subsequently became known as the Wannsee Conference, Reinhardt Heydrich was appointed as Plenipotentiary for the preparation of the Final Solution of the European Jewish question. At that conference the means of disposing of eleven million more Jews was agreed, and decisions taken to put in place the apparatus needed. Death camps were to be built in remote areas to carry out Hitler's stated aim for the complete annihilation of the Jewish population. Although remote, each site was to be serviced by a railway line. Camps were located at Cilmno, Belzec, Treblinka, Sobibor in the first instance and later the existing facility at Auschwitz was enlarged, an extension being built in the birch wood known as Berkenau. Hence all was in place for the implementation of the *Endlosung*. Is that now clear? It was sometimes referred to as *Judenfrei*. I am sure that term is familiar to you?'

Grundwall gave a mumbled 'Yes.'

'Then let me repeat my original question. Will you now agree that the term "correction facility" is a false description, and that your answer was a deliberate evasion?'

'It was not intended as an evasion. I believed what I was told.'

'You believed what you were told,' Westbury mimicked him slowly. 'How many times has this court has heard that defence? In other words you preferred to believe what you had been told rather than accept the evidence of your own eyes?' He paused for dramatic effect, letting Grundwall wriggle on the hook before searching for another file and extracting a photograph from it. He handed this to Grundwall. 'Will you confirm that is a photograph of the railway line and siding at Auschwitz?'

Grundwall examined the photograph, but took his time before agreeing.

'It was here that the line terminated, was it not? It was at this siding that trains regularly arrived crammed with a new quota for the gas chambers. As we witnessed on the film, the *selection* process was carried out immediately after they arrived. A number of the healthier young males would be saved for slave labour, but the majority would be gassed within a few hours, cynically led to believe they being taken to a delousing shower whereas, in reality, they were herded into death chambers and sprayed with the lethal prussic-acid asphyxiant known commercially as Zyklon B. So,' he continued relentlessly, 'do you still contend that these processes were unknown to you?'

I leant forward, concentrating on Grundwall's expression during this. I tried to imagine what was going on inside his head; how could he refute Westbury's systematic, clinical, stripping away of his supposed ignorance?'

'I had no personal knowledge of those procedures.'

'No knowledge?'

'I was never present when such alleged procedures were carried out.'

'They are not "alleged" to have been carried out. They were carried out on a regular basis, so whether you were physically present or not is immaterial. Let us take it step by step. You knew that trains arrived on a more or less daily basis, did you not?'

'Yes.'

'And that they brought new victims – or as you prefer to describe them, "criminal elements" – to the camp, even though a proportion were infant children and could not be so described.'

'I did not believe they were victims.'

'Really? What did you believe them to be?'

'It was my understanding that they were taking part in a relocation programme for undesirables.'

'That is an original way of describing it. They were "relocated" a matter of a few hundred yards before being murdered,' Westbury said dryly. 'Were you also unaware that these unfortunates underwent a selection process to determine whether they had an instant or slow death?'

'I have already stated I was never involved in the day-to-day running of the camp.'

'That does not answer me. Were you aware?'

'No.'

'Not even as a passive observer?'

'No.'

'I find that difficult to believe.'

'It is the truth.'

'I intend to prove it is less than the truth, since it defies logic. I shall produce witnesses who will testify that your superior, Dr Mengele, conducted his own selections, compelling victims to parade naked for him in order for him to determine who could further his experiments and that you witnessed this on more than one occasion. Do you wish to reconsider your previous answers?'

'I have already stated the extent of my involvement.'

'So, when infant children were selected and taken to Mengele's special medical facility, you had no idea why they had been selected?'

'I assumed they were sick children who needed medical attention.'

'You assumed.' Westbury drank from a glass of water. 'I put it to you that you are lying. Is it not a fact that your superior, Doctor Josef Mengele, who headed the *Shutzstaffeln* branch of the SS, determined what duties his staff performed, and that you were present when his experiments were performed?'

'All senior staff at the facility were compelled to be members of the SS.'

'That is not what I asked you. Were you or were you not present?'

'I was aware that he conducted clinical investigations in an effort to stamp out epidemics of typhus and spotted fever in the camp. Young children were always amongst the first to contract these diseases.'

'We are back to defining the degree of awareness. How aware were you?'

'Typhus was a major cause of death in the camp.'

'So was death by Zyklon B,' Westbury said with deadly understatement. 'I ask you again, were you a witness to the exact procedures used by Mengele?'

'Only as an occasional observer.'

'Ah!' Westbury exclaimed. 'At last we are moving closer to the truth. Let us try and define "occasional".'

I sat in admiration of Westbury's adversarial skills, the way in which he had slowly extracted admissions from Grundwall while at the same time I remained impressed by Grundwall's ability to stonewall until he was trapped.

Resuming, Westbury asked: 'Were you then only an "occasional observer" when Mengele, caused phenol, petrol, chloroform and air to be injected into children he deemed degenerate, causing death? That it was not unusual for him to dispose of a dozen sets of twins in this fashion, twins being his speciality, and that subsequently he ordered that the cadavers be boiled so that the flesh could be stripped from their bones and the skeletons sent to the Anthropological Museum in Berlin?'

Grundwall again swayed in the dock.

'I am waiting,' Westbury said.

Grundwall's response was inaudible.

'Say again, please.'

'I did not observe such procedures.'

'By choice?'

'Yes.'

'But I was under the impression, correct me if I am wrong, that you could not go against orders. It therefore follows that if Mengele ordered you to attend such experiments, you would have no choice but to obey. Yes?'

'I was often carrying out duties in another section of the camp and therefore unable to attend.'

'Let me put it another way. Whether you were able to attend or not, as a doctor, would you agree that such methods are not traditionally associated with the treatment of typhus or spotted fever?'

'I had limited experience as a general practitioner and therefore never gained any exposure to the standard treatment of typhus.'

'But during your limited time as a general practitioner you were surely not denied access to medical textbooks? True or false?'

'Yes.'

'Yes, true?'

'Yes.'

'So, tell me, did any textbook you consulted during your studies recommend an injection of petrol as a standard treatment for anything?' The chilling sarcasm in Westbury's voice allowed of no answer.

'I am waiting.'

Grundwall finally said: 'Will you repeat the question?'

'Willingly. I asked if anywhere in your studies you came across textual evidence of injections of petrol being used to cure any infectious disease?'

'No, I did not.'

'Therefore were you not appalled to witness, even as a casual observer, Dr Mengele treat typhus by such a method?'

'I had no influence over the way in which he decided on treatments.'

Westbury was not going to let it go. 'I ask again, were you not horrified?'

'I thought some of his methods were unorthodox.'

'So unorthodox, in fact, they killed rather than cured. How is it then you did not protest about his methods?'

'It was not possible for me to question his actions.'

'Not possible? Why?'

'All SS officers were required to swear an oath of obedience. You did not question the actions of your superiors.'

'But, as a man of medicine were you not bound by something stronger, namely the Hippocratic oath, even when you became aware of Mengele's special interest in twins and that he frequently injected a toxic agent into their eyes in a perverted quest to determine genetic differences?'

I could see Grundwall searching for some answer to this, finally coming up with: 'I acted as I was compelled to do under military law, which in a time of war took precedence.'

'Would you agree, then, that your passive acceptance of such practices meant that you condoned such acts?'

Grundwall did not respond and again the President intervened. 'The prisoner will answer the question.'

'I submit, it wasn't possible for me to interfere,' Grundwall said.

'By that, are you saying you were aware of what was taking place but were powerless or unwilling to condemn such matters?'

'Powerless.'

'It is a slender distinction,' Westbury said scathingly. 'Thus, *ipso facto* you became an accessory to the crimes committed.' He then switched his attack. 'Can we go back to your war service and establish how you came to be switched from being a translator attached to the Ministry of Communications to a commission in the SS. Is it possible you volunteered?'

'No. I was given no choice.'

'Do you accept that the SS was a body feared not only by enemies of the State but also the ordinary general public? That it was brought into existence for one purpose and one purpose only, namely to become an instrument of coercion and terror?'

'It was necessary to keep order in a time of total war.'

'But it was in existence before the war, was it not? And you must have known that, from the moment you wore the death's head insignia, it set you apart from your fellow citizens. Were you proud to wear SS uniform?'

'Proud?'

'Yes. Did it give you a feeling of superiority?

'I did not think of it in those terms. In any case I had no say in the matter.'

'No, that's right, you have said you did whatever you were told. And if you were required to observe the methods used by Dr Mengele to eliminate typhus, you again did as you were told.'

The Defence Counsel rose and objected. 'Counsel is leading.'

'I will rephrase that,' Westbury said. He took another drink of water. 'I put it to you that throughout you have sought to depict your own role as a passive observer, somehow unaware of the real purpose of the camp, somehow unaware that the SS was a component of the Nazi regime expressly dedicated to terror. Are you still of the opinion that Auschwitz was a correction facility for criminals?'

Grundwall answered slowly. He was now being ultra careful in his answers. 'You have demonstrated that it had a wider purpose about which I was not wholly aware.'

'A "wider purpose", that is an original way of putting it. Let me ask you this: can the court take it that in addition to the crematorium in the main body of the camp, you do not dispute the fact that the woods at Berkenau housed multiple crematoria?'

'I accept that.'

'Good. We are making progress. What do you think was the wider purpose of such installations?'

'I knew from my medical background that the most effective way of ensuring that a lethal epidemic is contained from spreading is by cremating infected corpses.'

I had to admire the way in which time and time again he wriggled off the hook Westbury dangled in front of him.

Westbury continued relentlessly: 'So are you are saying that the sole purpose of the crematoria was the containment of disease?'

'That was my understanding, although I was aware that not all deaths were the result of disease.'

'What were they the result of?'

'In the closing stages of the war the Central Government was forced to drastically reduce the food ration for the civilian population as well as those confined in the camp, thus the number of deaths was accelerated by malnutrition.'

'Is that another way of saying that the inmates were deliberately starved to death?'

'No, you are twisting my words.'

'I apologise. I am seeking to establish and for you to admit, what is borne out by the camp records, namely that taking out the numbers that could reasonably be attributed to disease and malnutrition, we are still left with thousands whose deaths cannot be so accounted for. How do you explain that?' Westbury waited. 'I repeat, as a medical man, how do you explain that?'

When Grundwall finally answered, his voice had flattened. 'I am of the belief that the Allied authorities deliberately exaggerated the numbers of dead as a propaganda exercise.'

As I watched and listened I tried to analyse my feelings towards him. Did I feel pity, revulsion, or anger that he had duped me? Was the spectacle of a man on trial for life something I could divorce from the love I felt for his daughter? Wars are made between governments, but fought by individuals between individuals. The fighting may have stopped but we were still locked in conflict, victor against vanquished. Westbury continued to whittle away for the rest of that day's session and although Grundwall had to give ground on several occasions, he fought every inch.

TWENTY-ONE

I found it difficult to sleep that night, my mind going over Grundwall's evidence time and time again. I had to ask myself whether he was a man lying to save his neck when faced with a capital charge, or was he, the father of the girl I loved, somebody trapped, forced, as he contended, to serve in the SS and posted against his will to an extermination camp? Could anybody of his culture and intelligence be in such a place and remain ignorant of its true purpose for more than twenty-four hours? Then, waking again in the small hours of the endless night, I began to closely examine my own motives. Because of Lisa part of me wanted him to be pronounced innocent, allowing me to return to her and for everything between us to be as before. From the moment the photograph had been placed before me I had known the dangers of exposing her father, that it would inevitably put the love Lisa and I had found for each other at risk of destruction, but I suppose I had clung to the slender hope that my identification of him would somehow prove a mistake. Yet even that pathetic excuse was a half-lie. I knew in my heart that I was not mistaken, that he had been in the SS, that he had been at Auschwitz and that a man of his intelligence could not have been deluded as to the real purpose of the camp.

I awoke exhausted, and found that when I shaved myself my hands were not steady and I nicked myself in two places. I returned to the court room with small pieces of toilet paper over the cuts and my thoughts were so jumbled because of fatigue that my memory sped back to the day when Charlie Boag had gone to his adulterous marriage to that sad girl in the same bloodied state.

Doubtless convinced he had acquitted himself well the first day, Grundwall looked more relaxed when ushered into the dock the following morning. This time the proceedings were opened by his Defence Counsel, a wiry little man named Fraser who spoke with a pronounced Scottish accent.

'Professor Grundwall, I understand you took a medical degree.'

'That is correct.'

'Where did you practise?'

'In Manheim, but only for a period of ten months as a locum.'

'What does the term "locum" signify?'

'A doctor who stands in on a temporary basis when the regular practitioner is absent.'

'And you only did this for a short period?'

'Yes. I could not obtain a permanent post and found casual work did not provide enough to support my family. By then my wife was pregnant with our daughter and I was forced to abandon a spasmodic medical career and obtained a teaching post which carried a regular salary.'

'I believe that at the same time you also attempted to pursue a parallel literary career?'

'I would not call it a career. I was fortunate enough to have a single collection of my poetry published. Although it was well received, it did not make my fortune.'

'But am I right in saying that your academic career prospered?'

'Yes, after a period at a school in Manheim, I applied for a post on the faculty at the Hamburg University and was accepted.'

'A post you occupied until the outbreak of the war in 1939?'

'Yes.'

'Which post you were allowed to resume at the end of hostilities?'

'Yes.'

'Let me turn to your war service. The prosecution has made great play with the fact that you did not stay in the Wehrmacht working for the Communications Ministry, but instead joined the SS.'

'I have already said in evidence that I did not join the SS voluntarily, but was directed into it.'

'Would you have preferred to have joined a fighting unit?'

'Had I been given the chance, yes, like my father in the previous war. But of course I had to go where I was told.'

'And you were eventually directed to serve in the camp known as Auschwitz-Berkenau?'

'Yes.'

'Prior to your arrival were you aware that such a camp existed?'

'No, I was not.'

'How was it described to you?'

'As a labour camp for criminals, and that because of my previous medical qualifications I would be responsible for the welfare of the camp staff.'

'And those, in fact, were your duties during your entire stay there?'

'Yes,' Grundwall answered confidently, obviously content with the line Fraser was taking with him.

'Therefore it came as a surprise to you to find large numbers of women and children being brought to the camp.'

Westbury was immediately on his feet. 'Objection. Counsel is leading.'

'Sustained.'

Fraser corrected himself: 'What was your reaction when you discovered that, in addition to the criminal element, women and children were also inmates?'

'It troubled me.'

The President looked up, frowning, from writing his notes. Quickly aware his response had been inadequate, Grundwall added: 'I thought it quite wrong.'

'Did you make your feelings known to Commandant Hoess?'

'Yes, I expressed my concern at the general unsanitary conditions.'

'And?'

Grundwall looked momentarily perplexed and Fraser asked: 'Did Hoess implement any material changes as a result of your concerns?'

'Yes, certain changes were made.'

Westbury again got to his feet. 'May it please the court? I find the accused's answers to this line of questioning deliberately evasive. It has already been clearly established that Auschwitz was an extermination camp. It is inconceivable that the accused could believe that women and children were criminal elements.'

'Yes, Counsel,' the President responded. 'I do not think the approach you are taking aids the accused's case.'

Fraser looked temporarily thrown and consulted his papers before continuing. 'How long was it after your arrival that you realised the true purpose of the camp?'

Grundwall had been answering quickly and confidently until this point, but now hesitated.

'Weeks, months?' Fraser prompted.

'Months,' Grundwall answered after a pause.

Westbury was again on his feet. 'Objection. I submit that the accused's answer is again in complete disregard of the facts. The vast amount of photographic evidence that exists clearly shows that anybody of average intelligence could not have been deceived as to the true purpose of the camp within days, if not hours, of arrival. The answers the accused has given insult this court. We are being asked to believe the unbelievable.'

The President nodded his agreement and said: 'I suggest, Mr Fraser, that you put the question again, in another form.'

Although obviously disconcerted by the interruptions, Fraser complied, asking: 'When you discovered the true function of the facility, what was your reaction?'

'Disgust and shock.'

'Did you share these feelings with your fellow officers?'

'No.'

'Why was that?'

Again, a hesitation. 'Unlike me, they were all committed SS and I did not share their ethos.'

'So did you keep your shock and disgust to yourself?'

'Yes. It was too dangerous to express opinions that conflicted with official policy, so I did not socialise with my fellow officers more than was necessary. The staff did not live on the camp but were quartered outside the fenced camp perimeter. Some, including Hoess, lived with their wives and families.'

'Your own wife and child, did they live with you?'

'My wife, yes, but only for a period. Not our teenage daughter. We had sent her to a relative in the countryside to escape the bombing.'

'How long did your wife stay in the camp.'

'Three months, perhaps. Perhaps a little longer.'

'And then what?'

'I persuaded her to leave and likewise stay with relatives. I sought to protect her.'

'What did you seek to protect her from?'

'I thought the atmosphere at the camp was proving injurious to her health.'

'Are you saying that your wife was equally shocked and disgusted by conditions in the camp?'

'No, she was never cognisant of conditions inside the camp because she had no first hand knowledge and never ventured beyond the married quarters.'

'Did you confide your own misgivings to her?'

'I decided it was not safe for her to be made party to my world. The fact that she was the wife of an SS officer did not automatically bestow immunity. Everybody was trapped in a vice of fear from informers. Even letters to loved ones were best "coded" for safety. Distrust reached paranoid levels. While I was there Hoess, the Commandant, had a senior member of his staff shot for expressing the view that the war could never be won.'

'Was your wife aware of the crematoriums?'

'She could not miss they existed. The chimneys could be seen from our married quarters.'

'How did you explain them to her?'

'That they were used to stem the spread of diseases like cholera.'

'Did you never reveal their real purpose?'

'No, I did not wish to frighten her.'

Fraser now asked: 'Did your wife ever meet Dr Mengele?'

'I think only on one occasion, when she arrived and we attended a welcoming party.'

'Was she ever made aware of Mengele's activities by you or others?'

Grundwall's reply was guarded. 'If I discussed his role with her it would have been to explain that he and his team were there to ascertain the causes and then contain the spread of various diseases.'

'Did the wives gossip amongst themselves?'

Grundwall looked puzzled. 'Gossip?'

'Did the wives socialise together?'

'Yes, some of them did.'

The President interrupted. 'Where is this taking us?'

'I am attempting to ascertain whether the accused's wife could have learned the true nature of Mengele's role from others,' Fraser said.

'Very well. I will allow it. Continue.'

'Could your wife have learned about the experiments being carried out from sources other than yourself?'

Grundwall said, 'Had she learned such things she would have discussed them with me. She did not.'

'By the end of hostilities the existence and purpose of Auschitz and the other camps had become common knowledge. At which point did you feel able to discuss them with Frau Grundwall?'

'I have already admitted that like the majority of the population in the occupied territories we were both compelled to attend news-reel screenings, and afterwards she questioned me. I remember she asked, "Is that why you sent me away?"'

'How did you answer her?'

'I said, "Yes, it was to protect you."'

'At that point did she question you in greater detail about your own role at the camp, since by then she must have been aware of the part played by the SS?'

'She accepted my word that I was innocent of any wrongdoing.'

'And your daughter? How was she affected?'

I leaned forward to concentrate on Grundwall's reply. 'My daughter knew nothing of my time at Auschwitz. This was something my wife and I agreed upon. As far as Lisa was concerned I had spent the entire war as a translator for the Ministry. She was totally unaware that I had any other job.'

Fraser consulted his junior in a whispered exchange before continuing. 'Let us now turn to Exhibit 764B, the photograph, showing you with Mengele and one other doctor. The prosecution maintain that it establishes you were present when he carried out experiments on children.'

Grundwall became animated, thumping the edge of the dock. 'That is untrue. I deny it categorically. I only ever entered Mengele's special block on Hoess's orders, and I never took part in any of his experiments.'

'You realise you are testifying on oath.'

'I do.'

'Then let me ask you again. Was there any occasion when, under orders or not, you personally and actively took part in the inhumane experiments instigated by and performed by Dr Mengele?'

'No, I did not.'

I thought, am I listening to the lies of a man fighting for his life, or should I believe him? If I had to sit in final judgement, which way would I vote?

'Thank you. No further questions for the moment,' Fraser said and sat down.

The President said: 'Are you ready to call your first witness, Counsel?'

'Yes,' Westbury said. 'I call Captain Seaton.'

I walked to the witness stand and took the oath. Grundwall's eyes never left me.

'Please give you name and rank.'

'Alex Charles Seaton, Captain, Intelligence Corps.'

'Captain Seaton, in April of this year were you serving as a member of a Field Security unit based in Hamburg?'

'Yes, I was.'

'What were your duties?'

'My main duties consisted of seeking out and interrogating ex-members of the SS, Gestapo and other proscribed organisations who were still at large.'

'And what was the object of such interrogations?'

'To identify the perpetrators of war crimes.' Then I added: 'It was often a question of sorting the wheat from the chaff.'

'How would you define "the chaff"?'

'Those who had so far escaped detection by assuming bogus identities.'

'And the "wheat"?'

'Those who, after interrogation, were given a clean bill of health and allowed to resume their civilian occupations.'

'In which category did you put the accused?'

'Neither, since he was never brought before me for interrogation. From his file I understand that he was twice questioned by others, and given clearance, but I had no knowledge of his history.'

Westbury handed the vital photograph to me. 'Have you seen this photograph before?'

'Yes.'

'Please tell the court the circumstances whereby it was first brought to you attention.'

'It formed part of a batch of material passed to us from the War Crimes department of the United States Army for cross-reference.'

'Did you examine it personally?'

'Yes.'

'And what was the result of that examination?'

'After studying it was my belief that one of the men shown was the accused.'

'Karl Grundwall?'

'That is correct.'

'On what did you base your identification?'

'Visual recognition. I had met the accused on several occasions.'

'Under that name?'

'Yes. But as Professor Grundwall.'

'How did that come about?'

'I had made his acquaintance by chance some months earlier in a second-hand bookshop where we discovered a mutual love of literature. Later he invited me back to his home.'

'Why did you accept such an invitation? That was surely unwise, if not in absolute contradiction of your duties as an Intelligence Officer in the Occupying Forces, wasn't it?'

'The rules regarding fraternisation had been relaxed by then. I thought he was an intelligent, cultured man and until our chance meeting I had had not had an opportunity to socialise with ordinary Germans. I welcomed the chance to discover how they had lived under the Nazi yoke.'

'That is what you believed him to be, an ordinary civilian?'

'Yes.'

'During these meetings did you have any reason to suspect that he was in fact an ex-SS officer who had chosen to conceal the role he played in the war?'

'None whatsoever. He had introduced himself as being a professor of philosophy on the faculty of the local university. Mindful of my responsibilities, I checked this before meeting him again and found he was indeed a member of the faculty.'

'Prior to that photograph being brought to your attention did the accused, by any casual remark or action cause you to change your first impression of him?'

'No. My role as an Intelligence officer demanded that I remained suspicious of anybody I came in contact with until satisfied of their innocence. I met with the accused on several occasions, but he never gave me any reason to doubt his sincerity. During talks we had he convinced me he was genuinely horrified by the revelations of the Final Solution.'

'He talked about the Final Solution with you, did he?'

'No. It would be untrue to say that he employed the term "Final Solution" to me. I think I was the one who first used it in conversation. In fact I remember him saying he was not familiar with the term. But he did question me closely about the concentration camps, in particular Bergen-Belsen since my unit had taken part in the liberation of that camp.'

'Did that seem odd to you?'

'No. It was my belief at the time that he wanted to probe my first-hand knowledge that the camps had existed and were not propaganda inventions. There was a body of sceptical German opinion that held to the belief that our photographs of the concentration camp dead were in fact photos of dead German civilians killed in Allied bombing raids, such as Dresden. Where Grundwall was concerned I felt his interest was motivated by a genuine collective shame and guilt he felt as a German.'

'Now, with hindsight, do you still feel his shame and guilt to be genuine?'

'I can't make any definitive judgement on that, but must leave it to this court to pronounce,' I said.

'Let us return to the photograph. Following your examination of it, what action did you take?'

'When, finally convinced of its authenticity and that my identification of the accused was positive, I made my opinion known to my commanding officer, Lt Colonel Machell. He in turn returned the photograph to the American authorities and asked them to carry out further verification checks. Subsequently he was informed my initial identification had been substantiated by the Jewish War Crimes Bureau who had also obtained positive identification from several Auschwitz survivors.'

'Armed with this confirmation, did you confront the accused?'

'No, I did not.'

'Why was that?'

'By then the matter had been taken out of my hands and in any case I was on leave in England while these enquiries were being carried out. By the time I arrived back in Germany I discovered Professor Grundwall had been arrested and was awaiting trial.'

'Thank you.'

Fraser rose to cross-examine. He began immediately with the line Machell had said the defence would use.

'Captain Seaton, what is your relationship with Lisa Grundwall, the daughter of the accused?'

'That of a close friend.'

'A close friend,' he repeated with emphasis. 'Would it be more accurate to describe it as a relationship of an intimate, sexual nature?'

Westbury was quickly on his feet. 'Objection. Irrelevance.'

'Sustained.' The President addressed Fraser: 'Counsel, I will allow a certain latitude if you pursue this line of questioning, but I must warn you I will rule out conjecture.'

'Thank you, my Lord.' Fraser turned to me again. 'Captain, you have admitted that you accepted the accuser's hospitality and visited his home.'

'Yes.'

'On how many occasions?'

'Two to the best of my recollection.'

'And on each of two occasions did you take him and his family gifts?'

'Yes.'

'What kind of gifts?'

'I gave him a paperback book the first time.'

'Nothing else?'

'Yes, I took them some coffee, cigarettes, soap and chocolate for them all to share.'

'Black market produce in other words?'

'No. I did not ask money for them, they were just modest gifts, part of my own legitimate entitlement but superfluous to my own needs.'

'Did you use such gifts to progress your relationship with the daughter, Lisa Grundwall?'

'No.'

'You did not think of them as bribes which would advance your cause?'

'No. I did not. In fact when first I visited the accused's home I had no idea he had a daughter.'

'Even so, would I be correct in saying that Fraulein Grundwall was grateful for the gifts you brought her?'

'Of course. She had been deprived of chocolate for a long time.'

'Can we turn to a further leave period which you spent at the *Gasthof Koch* in Krumpendorf, Austria. Were you alone on that occasion?'

'No. Fraulein Grundwall was with me.'

'Did you both occupy the same bedroom on that occasion?'

'Yes.'

'Did intimacy take place in that room?'

'We were in love.'

'I must ask you to answer the question.'

'I prefer to say we made love.'

The President chimed in at that moment. 'Counsel, I fail to see where these questions are leading us. We are not here to consider the morals of the witness, nor his relationship with the daughter of the accused. This is not a divorce court. Please confine your examination to matter pertinent to the indictments.'

Flustered, Fraser leafed through his papers and began again. 'Captain Seaton, you have stated that the accused expressed a sense of shame at the Nazi treatment of the Jewish population.'

'Yes. He spoke of collective guilt, which I took to mean that the entire German nation shared that guilt. He was of the opinion it would take a hundred years for the German nation to atone and that, even then, the crimes should never be forgiven.'

'Were you convinced of his sincerity?'

'At the time, yes.'

'Having heard his testimony in this court, do you continue to believe in that sincerity?'

I turned to the bench for guidance. 'The witness is not required to answer,' the President pronounced.

'Let me rephrase that,' Fraser said. 'You have heard the accused say on oath that he played no part in the crimes he is standing trial for. Did his answers convince you?'

'They are consistent with his general defence.'

'You believed him then?'

'I do not think it is up to me to believe or disbelieve. That is the function of those sitting in judgement.'

'But you must have formed an opinion.'

I looked to the bench, but the President was writing and allowed Fraser to continue: 'May I remind you, Captain Seaton, that the accused is accused of crimes which, if he is convicted, carry the maximum penalty of death by hanging. I would also remind you that you have stated that, prior to his arrest you did not consider him capable of such crimes. That is true, is it not?'

'I think you are over-stating what I have previously said. I could not consider him capable of committing crimes against humanity since, when my relationship with him began, I had no prior knowledge of his war service. To me he was what he said he was, namely a professor at the university who had served as a translator during the course of the war. At that time I was unaware that he had been an officer in the SS or that he had served in Auschwitz.'

'Has your opinion altered after listening to the accused's testimony.'

'My opinion is immaterial.'

'On the contrary, Captain Seaton. Please answer my question.'

'I am only here to give evidence, not to pronounce judgement.'

Fraser did not give up but continued to pursue this course, asking a number of questions in the same vein, but I still stone-walled and was finally allowed to stand down. The court was adjourned for lunch. As Grundwall was taken down to the cells he gave me one last, hard look.

TWENTY-TWO

When the court reassembled for the afternoon session Westbury called the first of his other witnesses, a small white-haired man of indeterminate age who walked slowly and obviously painfully with the aid of two sticks. I found his appearance profoundly moving for he brought back the moment when we first entered the horror of Belsen. He was sworn in with the assistance of an interpreter. Everybody in the courtroom donned headphones since he gave his evidence in his native language.

'Please give your name.'

'Josef Rajzman.'

'What is your nationality?

'Polish.'

'Are you Jewish?'

'Yes.'

'You have a number tattooed on your wrist, do you not?'

'Yes.'

'What does that tattoo signify?'

'That I was number 7568 in Treblinka.'

'Was that a concentration camp?'

'Yes.'

'And after Treblinka, what happened to you?'

'Because of the Russian advance we were force marched to Auschwitz.'

'When was that?'

'December 1944.'

'And how long were you in Auschwitz?'

'Four months, until we were liberated.'

'Have you any explanation why you survived while so many others perished?'

'God saved me.'

'What was your function in the camp?'

The word "function" confused Raizman, and Westbury changed it to: 'What were your duties in the camp?'

'I was a *Kapo*. I buried the dead.'

'And how did the dead you buried die? Did they die from natural causes?'

Rajzman listened to the translation, and then became agitated. 'No, no, no! They were murdered.'

'How were they murdered?'

'Gassed. Sometimes shot.'

'Including children?'

'Many children.'

'And women?'

'Yes, women. Many. Everybody was murdered.'

'Where did you collect the bodies from?'

'The gas chambers.'

'How about the medical block? Did you have to collect bodies from the medical block?'

'No, not allowed. *Verboten!*' Rajzman suddenly shouted, using a single word in German.

'When you are ready, please face the dock and tell the court whether you recognise the prisoner. Take your time.'

Rajzman peered hard at Grundwall.

'Take your time,' Westbury repeated.

'Yes, that is him.'

'Can you be more explicit, please?' Again Rajzman was confused by use of the word "explicit" and Westbury put the question another way: 'Can you name the prisoner?'

'Grundwall.'

'Was he a member of the staff?'

'Yes. SS Officer.'

'You are quite certain?'

'I never forget. Not their faces. Not anything. Never.'

'And you confirm that during the time you were held in Auschwitz he was still a member of the SS staff?'

'Until the last month. Not after. The SS left. Only the ordinary guards stayed.'

'Why do you think they disappeared before the camp was liberated?'

'Why?' Rajzman repeated loudly, swinging around to glare at Grundwall. 'Why do you think? They wanted to save their skins.'

'Did the accused leave the camp with the others?'

'Yes, all of them went. I don't see him again until now.'

'Thank you.'

Fraser cross-examined briefly. 'You have stated you were never allowed to enter the medical block.'

'I have said that, yes.'

'So therefore you cannot know whether the prisoner ever worked in the medical block or not, can you?'

The question had to be put to Rajzman three times before he fully understood. His voice rose again. '*Verboten*. I have said it was *verboten*. I am never inside that place.'

'Thank you. I will take that as No.'

Westbury's second witness was another Jew named Zeitlen, who came into the court wearing his prayer shawl. Painfully thin, more a walking skeleton, his physical frailty was not evident in the dignified manner in which he gave his testimony. He also admitted to having been a *Kapo* and that he had witnessed SS guards snatching infant children from their mothers as soon as they got off the trains.

'The babies were taken by the legs and smashed against a wall until only a bloody mess remained or else thrown into buckets of water and left to drown. The women were stripped naked and strung up, if they resisted, left to hang until they died and dogs set upon them, tearing them to pieces.'

'And you witnessed such events?'

'Yes. Every time a train brought new people there were such scenes.'

'What were your main duties?'

'We were there to reassure the new arrivals. Pretending.'

'In what way pretending?'

'That they were being taken to the wash rooms to be showered and de-loused instead of being gassed.'

'And they believed you?'

'Yes, we had to be good at our job or else we suffered the same fate.'

'Was that the normal procedure – the trains arrived, and you and your fellow *Kapos* accompanied them to the gas chambers?'

'At first they used trucks.'

'Why was that

'They had not built the big gas chambers so they backed up the trucks to an opening in the wall of a block close to the Commandant's office and pumped in fumes. In order that he could not hear the screams they revved up two motor cycles at the same time.'

'How long did it take them to die by this method?'

'Twenty minutes. Sometimes longer, it was not very efficient. That is why they started to make use of the Little Red House.'

'What do you mean by that? Tell the court.'

'It was a house in the fields at Birkenau. Just a house, which they sealed and made into a gas chamber. Later, when the numbers were too many they needed more room, so they did the same to the Little White House.'

'Are those the names the SS called them?'

'Yes. We were told to say, don't worry you are going to the Little Red House.'

'And afterwards, when they were dead, what happened to them?

'We dragged them to big ditches. To Lazaretto.'

'Lazaretto? What does that mean?'

'It was the nickname they gave it. Meaning, the "Infirmary".'

'I understand that those like yourself who carried out the task of disposing of the bodies wore armbands. Is that true?'

'Yes.'

'What sort of armbands?'

'They had the Red Cross sign on them.'

'The Red Cross?'

'Yes. It was a Nazi joke.'

'A joke?'

'Yes.'

'Are you saying that they made jokes about these things?'

'Yes.'

The President asked Westbury: 'Counsel, where is this line of questioning taking us?'

'May it please the court, I am seeking to establish that given that the accused was present in the camp when these hideous atrocities were happening on a daily basis, it stretches incredulity to believe he was unaware of them. I also wish to demonstrate that SS personnel viewed these events with indifference, as matters of no consequence, a necessary task to bring about victory in the war. They took the view they were not dealing with human beings, but creatures of a subspecies.'

The President conferred with his fellow judges before saying, 'Very well, we will allow your argument.'

Westbury asked Zeitlen if he recognised Grundwall. Unlike Rajzman, he did not hesitate and gave an immediate identification.

'Let me ask you this. In the course of your duties as a *Kapo* were you ever compelled to take live infant children to Dr Mengele's medical block?'

'Yes.'

Westbury said: 'Let me be absolutely sure on that point and ask you that again. You took live infant children.'

'Yes.'

'What age were these children?'

'Some two years old, maybe, others older, maybe four or five, I can't be certain. They did not look like children. They looked like old people.'

'Do you know why you took them to the medical block?'

'No, I never saw them again.'

'The accused has told the court that the reason these children were selected was to find a cure for the typhus epidemic raging throughout the camp. Do you agree?'

'Typhus was always present.'

'That is not what I asked you. I will put it another way. When you delivered children to Dr Mengele's, did you believe they would receive normal medical attention?'

'I don't know. You didn't ask questions if you wanted to stay alive.'

'And that is why you became a *Kapo*, to stay alive?'

Zeitlen lowered his head and said a Hebrew prayer before answering. 'Yes.'

'Were you given a choice?'

'Yes. A choice between life and death.'

'Did the other inmates hate you?'

'They didn't stay alive long enough to hate us,' Zeitlen said with chilling honesty.

Three further witnesses were called, all anxious to have their moment of retribution. One by one they identified Grundwall and there was little Fraser could do to dent their evidence. One of the three, a woman named Salomea Kaplan, who spoke good English, gave a detailed description of the selection process carried out by Mengele.

'He was always there early to meet the death transports, as if he could not wait to find new victims. Beautifully dressed, polished boots, gloves, like a film star. And he made the same speech to those herded in front of him. Always the same. "*Ihr geht's jetzt baden, nacher werder ihr zur arbeit geschickt.*" Every time the same, that is why it is fixed in my memory.'

'Translate for the court, please.'

She repeated the words once more in German then gave the English. "Now you are going to the bath house and afterwards you will be put to work." He pretended to give them hope. Afterwards he would begin to choose. The old, meaning everybody over forty and the young, meaning those under fifteen, were

173

sent to the left. I was healthy then, so I was sent to the right. Special children were kept back.'

'What do you mean by "special" children?'

'Any twins.'

'I see. Please continue.'

'While this was happening, while we were standing there in lines, ash was falling from the chimneys. Of course nobody knew it was human ash. And all the time the camp orchestra played. Then the *Kapos* marched those condemned to a building with a sign over the entrance in large letters: "*Bade und Inhalations raume.*" People believed what it said. Two hours later they were dead.'

'How was it you escaped?'

'Because I was young and able, I was put to work digging graves.'

'Was the accused ever present when the selection took place?'

She turned and regarded Grundwall. 'I think so, but they looked different in their uniforms, fatter, well fed.' She continued to study him. 'Yes, he was the one with glasses, like now. Sometimes he was there.'

'Thank you. Your witness,' Westbury said to Fraser, but Fraser declined to question her. Leaving the witness box she rounded on Grundwall, spat at him and cursed him in her native tongue.

At that point the President announced he would hear closing statements at ten the next morning and adjourned the proceedings.

TWENTY-THREE

I took my seat for the final session uncertain as to the eventual outcome. Studying Grundwall as he was brought into court, he again did not give the appearance of a man expecting the worst. On the contrary, he seemed composed.

Westbury rose to deliver a surprisingly short closing statement.

'The prosecution contends that the charges levelled against Karl Gustave Grundwall have been proven beyond reasonable doubt, and we therefore do not intend to burden the court with a recapitulation of the entire evidence. The accused is a scholar, a university professor of philosophy, and a poet . . . hardly a role model for a typical SS officer, yet it has been clearly established that for three years and one month he was an officer in that proscribed criminal organisation, as determined under Control Council Law No. 10. Although he has repeatedly contended that he did not join the SS voluntarily, but was conscripted and had no choice in the matter, it is the prosecution's view that this is open to doubt. What is not open to doubt, however, is that he served as an SS officer on the medical staff at Auschwitz-Birkenau extermination camp; that, further, he could not have been unaware of the true purpose of that camp, and that his evidence that he believed it to be solely a correction facility for the criminal element must be treated with the contempt it deserves. Central to his defence is that he had no personal involvement in the monstrous crimes committed in Auschwitz as part of the Final Solution and that he had no option but to be a reluctant, passive observer. Throughout he has maintained that he was ignorant of the perverted practices carried out by his superior, the infamous Dr Mengele, but again this strains credulity. It beggars belief that a man of Grundwall's undoubted intelligence, someone with academic and medical knowledge, would accept that Dr Mengele sought cures for typhus by injecting sufferers with petrol. His testimony on this point must therefore be treated as a deliberate lie. The question that must be asked is why then, just before the end of hostilities, did he deliberately falsify his records, fabricating a history of having spent the war elsewhere? These were not the actions of an innocent man, but rather the actions of a man with much to conceal. Had it not been for the vigilance of the joint Anglo-American Intelligence services, and in particular the initial identification by Captain Seaton, he would have continued to escape detection. He has never at any time shown the slightest remorse, but instead offered the plea that he was compelled to be a passive witness. Passive acceptance of crimes against humanity has already been ruled as no defence. We therefore ask for the maximum sentence this Tribunal is empowered to hand down.'

I made eye contact with Grundwall as Westbury concluded. He held my look for a few seconds before lowering his head. Fraser then commenced the closing statement for the defence.

'I submit,' he began, 'that the prosecution's case is not proven. No conclusive evidence has been produced to establish beyond reasonable doubt that Karl Grundwall was ever actively involved in the collective crimes for which he stands accused. He has admitted being one of the medical staff at Auschwitz-Berkenau and that his service there as an officer in the SS was mandatory, in the same way that a it would be mandatory for a British doctor serving with the Army Medical Corps to be commissioned and compelled to serve where directed.'

The President was quick to interrupt. 'Counsel, I cannot allow you to draw such a parallel. The Army Medical Corps is the humanitarian section of our armed forces and cannot be compared with the SS which was primarily a quasi-police force within a police state, given extraordinary and virtually unlimited powers which it exercised without regard to the laws of a civilised society.'

'What I seek to establish, my Lord, is the dilemma of an educated man compelled to accept a commission in a proscribed organisation and drafted to serve in Auschwitz. He had no choice since the concept of conscientious objection was not allowed in Nazi Germany.'

'Even so, your reference to a parallel situation between the SS and the British Medical Corps will be struck from the record. Proceed.'

'Thank you. On the first count in the indictment I submit that it has not been conclusively proved that the accused played any direct or active role in the experiments carried out by Dr Mengele. I further submit that the photograph which first prompted his arrest shows him as an observer only and that none of the witnesses could state positively that he was anything other than an observer. The prosecution failed to produce either still images or filmed footage showing the accused taking an active role in such experiments.'

Fraser painted a picture of Grundwall as a man who had been forced to remain silent in order to protect himself and his family. It was hardly an original or inspired defence, but given the weight of evidence against Grundwall, possibly the only course he could take.

'It is common knowledge,' he continued, 'that, during the Nazi regime, those who criticised the policies of the State or questioned the actions of their superiors were liable to the severest penalties, including death. Should the court so require, I will produce evidence that many members of the SS were imprisoned and executed for refusing to carry out orders. The credo of blind obedience was drilled into them from the moment they took the oath of allegiance. The accused's failure to protest at the actions of others may be taken as an act of cowardice to be treated with contempt, but it does not of itself imply or prove guilt. The prosecution alleged that the accused has shown no remorse, but I would draw the court's attention to the evidence given by Captain Seaton, who stated that the accused did express shame and a sense of collective guilt for the crimes committed by the Third Reich. I therefore respectfully submit that, on the main counts of the indictment, the case against Karl Grundwall has not been proven beyond reasonable doubt and that, justice demands a verdict of Not guilty.'

He sat down. I had watched Grundwall intently during this, but he had betrayed no emotion one way or the other. The President now addressed him. 'Before this court retires to consider its verdict, I must draw your attention to Article 24, under which a defendant can make a final, unsworn statement. Do you wish to exercise your right to make such a statement?'

'Yes, I do,' Grundwall said.

'Please proceed.'

He stared in my direction before speaking. 'I would like to emphasise once more that I am innocent of taking any active role in the execution of what has been termed the Final Solution. Until its meaning was explained to me, I did not know that such a plan existed, any more than I knew the uses made of the Little Red and White Houses at Birkenhau. I feel myself free of the guilt of ever having committed or furthered crimes against humanity. I am not a brave man and I knew that the fate of my wife and daughter always hung upon my actions, that any disobedience in obeying orders on my part would mean they would suffer grievously. Such dangers to them did not end when the war ended, for there were many elements, both foreign and domestic, intent on taking revenge. That is the sole reason I took steps to conceal my past when I resumed my academic career. My behaviour has been described as cowardice. I admit to this and I will carry the burden of that cowardice to my grave. For the rest of my life I must accept my share of the collective guilt, but from my clear recognition of the causes, the terrible methods and consequences of the war, I pray there will arise a new future for the German people which will one day obliterate this stain. I therefore throw myself on the mercy of this Court.'

The President merely nodded in acknowledgement, thanked the prosecution and defence for their conduct of the trial and ordered Grundwall to be taken down to the cells.

TWENTY-FOUR

At the end of the proceedings I went in search of Major Jones, eventually finding him in the large communal office where half a dozen stenographers were busy typing up the evidence.

'Can I ask you a favour?' I said. 'Am I permitted to see Grundwall now?'

'What would you want to see him for?'

'It's a personal reason.'

'I'd need more than that to be of assistance.'

'In the course of giving evidence I admitted that I have been having a sexual relationship with his daughter.'

Jones frowned. 'I see. Yes, well you can't get more personal than that, I suppose. However, it's not up to me. The Provost Marshal will have to rule. Normally it's not allowed, but now the trial's over, he might stretch a point in your case. I should warn you, he may not after the recent suicide.'

While I waited I tried to decide what I was going to say to Grundwall if I got the OK. Jones came back into the office and gave the thumbs up. 'He said, yes, except he'll deny it if anybody ever asks, so keep it short.'

'Understood. Thank you.'

A Military Police sergeant conducted me to the holding cells below the court. 'Rap on the door when you're through,' he said as he unlocked the cell. 'I'll be out here the whole time.'

Grundwall was sitting on the edge of his bed. He had the look of an exhausted man washed up on a beach. When I entered he searched for his spectacles and put them on. 'I expected you might appear,' he said. 'Do you have a cigarette?'

I proffered a packet. 'Of course. Here. Keep them.'

'You were always generous to me and my family.' There was no mistaking the sarcasm in his voice. I lit the cigarette for him.

179

'Have you come to commiserate or gloat?'

'Neither,' I said.

'Pity me, then?'

'I'd be less than human if I didn't.'

'I thought that was what has just been proved? That I'm less than human.'

'Look, this is a difficult meeting for both of us,' I said. 'Shall we try and not make it more so?'

'Perhaps more difficult for me than you.'

'I haven't come to discuss the trial. It's Lisa I want to talk about.'

'Ah, Lisa, yes. How is my Lisa?'

'I'm taking care of her.'

'Are you? Should I be glad about that? And my wife? How is she? I haven't been allowed to communicate with either of them.'

'As far as I know your wife is well. I sent her some money via Lisa, and I intend to go on taking care of both of them.'

'Your consideration knows no limits,' Grundwall said.

'I know you must hate me.'

'Is that surprising?'

'I've just listened to you justifying your actions, saying you had no choice. I had no choice either, in what I did.'

'Then that's the only thing left we have in common.'

'I came here in the belief that the one thing we still have in common is love for Lisa. So I ask a favour for her sake. I know you love her and she loves you. I also love her and I believe she returns that love. I want to marry her, but our marriage, if it goes ahead as I hope it will, would have no chance if she ever learned of the part I played in your present situation.'

'I imagine not,' he said. 'So what is the favour?

'That when next you see her or are allowed to communicate with her, you find it possible, for the sake of any happiness we might have together, not to reveal my involvement.'

Grundwall took a long draw on his cigarette, and then ground it under his heel when only half smoked, as though to show me he regretted accepting it from me. 'It's perhaps a mistake to mix happiness and love. They don't always go together.'

'Is that something you teach in your philosophy classes?'

Grundwall ignored this. 'And if I don't grant your request?'

'Then I imagine there's no future for me and Lisa.'

'It's not something I can promise,' Grundwall said finally. 'I must think about it. When am I likely to be granted contact with my wife and daughter?'

'I've no idea, but now the trial's over I imagine conditions will be relaxed.'

'And having sat through the trial, how d'you think they will deal with me?'

'I'm not a judge.'

'The prosecutor asked for the maximum penalty.'

'I thought your defence counsel put forward a forceful plea in mitigation.'

'He did his best, such as it was. But you heard the evidence. Do you believe me to be guilty?

'I think you are guilty of deception.'

'Ah, deception. That's the game we're both in, aren't we? After all, you deceived me with your friendship.'

'No, I took you for what you said you were until you proved me wrong.'

'And now, you want me to lie for you?'

'If you choose to call it a lie. But if you care anything for Lisa's future happiness I am asking you not to reveal the one thing that would destroy it.'

'Perhaps I would prefer her not to marry somebody like you,' Grundwall said slowly. 'Did that not occur to you? That might be the kindest thing I could do for her. And even if I were generous enough to lie for you, how can you be sure that at sometime, somewhere, somebody won't whisper the truth in her ear? Can you live with that time bomb, as I have lived with it, always wondering when the blow would fall?' He arranged his features into something approaching a smile. 'And when that happens, as happen it will, what price happiness then?'

'I love her,' I said, 'and that's the risk I must take. The choice is yours, I can only beg.'

'I may not have a choice. If the court is not inclined to mercy, then what you are asking becomes academic. Dead men are not in a position to grant favours, are they? So we must both wait and see. Philosophy has taught me able to face those events which are forced upon us, but not to foresee the outcome of those events.'

He lay back on the bed and closed his eyes, signalling that our discussion was at an end.

I stared down at him. 'You asked if I pitied you,' I said. 'I pity both of us.'

He did not reply and I went to the cell door and rapped on it. The sergeant let me out.

TWENTY-FIVE

I boarded a train to Hamburg, carrying sadness with me like unwanted luggage, thinking what a fool I'd been, what a fool to think Grundwall would do me any favours.

Opposite me in the carriage was a middle-aged Army chaplain with the beginning of a paunch and a smooth complexion that looked as though it had never been near a razor. I've always been uneasy in the company of gentlemen of the cloth and I'm not sure why. It may have something to do with my atheism or because I just cannot comprehend how anybody could spend their lives justifying what to me is a gigantic con. That and the fact that they push it to the rest of us as though they alone have the answer to the meaning of life.

As we settled into our seats he remarked on my Intelligence Corps shoulder flashes, and then asked in a soft West Country accent whether I was permanently stationed in Nuremberg.

'No, Father. I was just here to give evidence in a trial.'

'I'm not a Father in any sense of the word. Just a Church of England vicar. I'm Daniel, Daniel Saunders.' He undid his jacket, produced a silver hip flask and unscrewed the small drinking cup that capped it. 'Would you care for a taste? Single malt. My sister included it in her last parcel.'

'Alex Seaton,' I responded, accepting the offer of a drink. The neat malt burned the back of my throat when I swallowed.

He took a measure for himself and replaced the cap, then seamlessly resumed: 'When I think about these trials I remember something Talleyrand said. He held that war is not a condition between one man and another, but between state and state, in which individuals are only accidental enemies and therefore cannot be held responsible for the crimes they commit. You've been giving evidence, you say?'

'Yes.'

'Not an enjoyable experience, I'm sure.'

'No.' I suddenly felt the need to confide in a stranger. 'Certainly not in this case because I was responsible for this particular man's arrest. He was somebody I had previously trusted. An accidental enemy, I suppose you might say.'

'German?'

'Yes.'

'You say you trusted him at first?'

'Yes,' I said. 'I'd met him and his wife socially, and he deceived me into believing he was untainted by the Nazi years, a cultivated academic, one of the silent minority who had opposed Hitler. How wrong I was.'

'What made you change your mind?'

'A photograph. A photograph taken at Auschwitz, showing he had served there as an SS officer.' I broke off. 'Look, forgive me, I can't think this is of any interest to you and perhaps I shouldn't be burdening you with it.'

'It obviously weighs heavily on your mind.' He proffered the hip flask again. I shook my head.

'Well, because it isn't cut and dried. I have to confess something else, something of great moment. The fact is that when I got to know him and his family, I met and fell in love with his only daughter.'

'Did she know of her father's past?'

'No. I'm sure she didn't.'

'And does she now?'

'Only partially. But she does not believe he is guilty of any crimes.'

'What is he accused of?'

'Being part of the infamous Dr Mengel's unit at Auschwitz. Mengele was the monster who carried out experiments on children.'

'Did the trial reach a verdict?'

'Not yet, but from the evidence I heard I think his guilt will be said to be proven. There is always the possibility it will carry the death penalty.'

'Dear God, dear God,' he murmured and stared out at the desolate landscape we were passing through. 'Does she know that you were the one who exposed him?'

'No, not yet,' I said. 'But it can't be concealed forever. And then, will she ever forgive me?'

'Worse things have been forgiven,' Daniel said. He was silent for a while. 'I suppose for a long time now the love of God has been sufficient for my needs, so I'm hardly the best person to offer advice. Love, such as you have confessed to, is an unknown country to me. Not that I ever took the vows of celibacy . . . there was a moment when my life might have taken a different path, but it passed. It passed,' he repeated. 'Do you have faith? Faith in God, I mean?

'No, I'm sorry to say I don't.'

'Well, even without faith, God sometimes provides the answer. He doesn't withhold his love from anybody.'

'It must be comforting,' I said, 'to have such certainty.'

He shook his head. 'If I had certainty, I wouldn't question why God divides his mercy, why He lets a single child die of starvation in a world of plenty, why He allowed such places like Auschwitz to exist, why creatures such as Mengele aren't struck down like Lot's wife.' He fingered his dog collar. 'Wearing this doesn't bestow any special wisdom. If it did I might be able to offer you a solution.'

For the remainder of the journey we talked about less sombre topics. I only half-listened, turning over in my mind the best course of action and by the time we parted, I had steeled myself to what I had to do. Instead of changing platforms and boarding the connection to Berlin, I went to the Military Police post.

'Sergeant,' I said, producing my identity card, 'I need to get somewhere urgently, but I don't have transport. Can you help?'

He fixed me up with a spare Jeep and a driver who knew his way around and I directed him to Lisa's address. When we arrived outside the apartment block, the driver said: 'This area can be a bit dodgy, sir. Sergeant gave the OK for me to wait and bring you back.'

'Thank him, but I'll be fine. I can look after myself and I'm not sure how long I'll be.'

I followed an alley round to the entrance and mounted the dirty concrete stairs to the second floor. There was a smell of cabbages that took me back to the first time I had visited the Grundwall's flat.

Greta, not Lisa, opened the door to me.

'Ah, Greta,' I said. 'It is Greta, isn't it?'

'Yes.'

'Is Lisa in?'

'No, she is still rehearsing.'

'Can I wait for her?'

'Bitte, as you wish,' she answered without enthusiasm. As she stepped back into the light I studied her face. It wasn't a beautiful face, too hard for that, good bone structure, but a mouth not made for charm and the small, dark eyes suspicious.

'You like coffee?' Greta asked.

'Yes, if you can spare it.'

'Your money bought it.' There was a hint of resentment in her answer; a hint, too, of insolence. 'Only black, we have no milk or sugar.'

'Black's fine and I don't take sugar.'

I watched while she boiled water in a saucepan on a small gas ring.

'It's cold in here,' I said.

'Yes. Always. There is no heating in this block. We put on an electric fire at night, but it uses too much money.'

Now she took down a decorated tin and an earthenware jug from a shelf over the sink and carefully measured one tablespoon of coffee grounds into the jug.

'Are you going to join me?'

'No, we save ours for breakfast.'

'How is Lisa?'

'Can't you guess? She manages.' She poured the boiling water onto the coffee.

'Did she get my letters?'

'I think so, yes.'

'And you, do you have any work?'

'I am lucky. I work some days. Translating for the Commission.'

I held out my packet of cigarettes. She took one and I lighted it for her.

'Have things improved?'

'A little.'

'D'you have family?'

'My home was in Flensburg, but my father and brother are *tod*.'

'What about your mother?'

'She was killed in an air raid.'

'I'm sorry.'

The conversation petered out, until she asked: 'What d'you think will happen?'

'To Lisa's father? I don't know what the verdict will be.'

'Will your people execute him?'

'I desperately hope not for Lisa's sake, but of course he is charged with very serious offences. If he's found guilty, at the very least he'll certainly face a long prison sentence. But rest assured he was given a fair trial.' I immediately realised my slip in using the past tense.

'You mean it's over?'

'I believe so,' I lied.

Greta smoked half of her cigarette, and then carefully put it out and to one side. 'I hate what the war did.'

'Yes. It was bad for everybody.'

'Not so bad for you. We are left with nothing.'

'Well, it wasn't one sided,' I said evenly, 'and we are trying to put Germany back on its feet.'

'Half of Germany,' she replied.

'Because you invaded Russia and now it's pay-back time.' I

sensed that she would never be completely won over whatever I said. We sat in silence as the light outside the single window faded and it was another fifteen minutes before Lisa appeared. She stood in the doorway, amazed at finding me there, then rushed forward and flung herself in my arms.

'Why didn't you tell me you were coming? I've missed you so much. Do you have news about father?'

'He told me the trial's over,' Greta interjected before I could answer, confirming she had picked up on my chance remark.

Lisa stepped back. 'Over? It's over? Have they let him go free? Tell me they've let him go.'

'Darling, they haven't announced the verdict yet.'

'I know they'll find him not guilty. A woman in the cast reads cards. Today she did mine and said good news is on the way.'

'I'm sure the cards were right,' I said. 'I thought perhaps, if it's all right with Greta, I could take you out for a meal before I have to leave again.'

'Oh, yes, please,' Lisa said, then caught herself and turned to Greta. 'Do you mind?'

Greta shrugged. 'Do what you want, it's all the same to me.'

I felt I had to make some gesture towards her and took four cigarettes from my packet and lay them on the table. 'To make amends for us leaving you.'

'*Danke*.'

On the way down the cold stairway we encountered a young man on crutches. He had one leg missing and was wearing a battered Wehrmacht cap. I stood to one side to allow him to pass, but I heard him hawk and spit as we left the building. We walked through the ruined streets, Lisa holding onto my arm tightly, her head resting on my shoulder until I spotted a commissionaire in shabby regalia standing outside the entrance to a restaurant in the basement of one of the few intact buildings. He saluted me with an exaggerated flourish as we entered into a vaulted room decorated with pastoral murals. An obsequious Maître d' immediately took over and conducted us to a table.

'Would the Herr Captain and his lady guest like a cocktail?'

'We'll have some wine,' I said.

'Wine, of course, Herr Captain.' He produced a wine list.

'What d'you prefer?' I asked Lisa. 'Red or white?'

'You choose,' Lisa said. 'I don't know anything about wine.'

I studied the modest list. 'A bottle of number seven.'

'An excellent choice, Herr Captain.' His oily manner grated on me. He smirked at Lisa when spreading the napkin on her lap.

'I'm so happy,' Lisa said, reaching for my hand across the table. Her own hand was cold. 'I know they won't do anything to father because he's done nothing wrong. My mother would have known, wouldn't she? And if she'd known, she wouldn't have kept it secret from me. We've never had secrets between us. So I'm still sure that, like the cards said, it's going to be good news in the end. She's very good, this woman. Things she's told other people have come true.'

'Well, that's a good omen,' I said, trying to conceal the note of doubt in my voice.

'When I woke up today everything was so black and hopeless. And now it's all changed and I'm here with you.'

'I want you to be happy.' I reached in a pocket for my cigarettes. 'I noted Greta smokes,' I said, 'have you succumbed?'

'No. I'm tempted, but I can't afford the black market prices.'

'Are you getting enough to eat, did I leave you enough money?'

'Yes, more than enough. You're so good to me.'

'Greta was telling me she works as a translator. Does she have a boyfriend?' I was conscious I was making small talk, keeping away from the danger area.

'Somebody in Control Commission dated her once, but she doesn't believe in fraternisation. She was married to a bomber pilot who was killed.'

A waiter arrived with the wine, which he poured with a great flourish as though it was Premier Cru. I raised my glass. 'To us,' I said.

We studied the menu. 'Is that going to be enough for you?' I asked when she had made a modest choice.

'Yes. I don't eat much these days.'

'You should.'

'I tried to get permission to see father but it was refused,' she said, immediately reverting to the subject uppermost in her mind.

'I'm sure you'll be able to see him soon.'

'D'you believe in what the cards tell you?'

'I've never had mine read.'

'I believe in them. When my friend laid them out she said there wasn't a single bad one.' The look of trust in her face destroyed me. I thought, how to begin what I have to do? I started to say, 'Darling, whatever happens . . . ' but at that moment the food arrived. I took a few mouthfuls, then put down my knife and fork and began again, knowing that it could not be put off forever. 'You know I love you, don't you?'

Lisa looked up from enjoyment of her food, puzzled but smiling. 'Of course I do.'

'And that whatever happens I shall always love you.'

Her smile died. 'What could happen? When father's released everything will be right again.'

'What,' I said slowly, 'if he's not released?'

Now she stopped eating. 'Don't say "what if", don't say that.'

'Sweetheart, I broke my journey instead of going straight back to Berlin, so you'd hear certain things from me rather than anybody else.'

'What sort of things?' Her voice, her whole being, had changed.

'You once told me that during the war your father worked as a translator. That wasn't true. He was an officer in the SS.'

All the colour drained from her face. 'That's not possible.'

'I wouldn't lie to you. The reason he was arrested and put on trial is that he was part of the administration in the Auschwitz concentration camp.'

'No,' she said. 'No, they made that up.'

I shook my head. 'Darling, I was at the trial. Survivors from the camp identified him.'

Her face seemed to dissolve in front of me. She suddenly stood up, clutched at the tablecloth and sent her food and wine glass clattering to the floor. Unbalanced, she stumbled backwards, knocking her chair over. I was just quick enough to catch her as she fainted. The Maître d' hurried to the scene.

'Something wrong, Herr Captain?'

'Yes, my friend suddenly felt faint. Bring a glass of water.'

'Of course, at once.' He clicked his fingers at one of the waiters. '*Wasser schnell!* I hope it was not to do with the food.'

'No, the food was fine.' I took the glass of water and held it to Lisa's mouth. 'Sip this, darling.' When she had taken some I dipped a napkin in the glass, and patted her forehead with it.

One waiter righted her chair while another started to clear the broken crockery.

'Get me the check,' I said to the Maître d'. 'And I need to use your telephone.' I helped Lisa back onto a chair. 'Sit there until you feel better, darling.'

'*Bitte*, Captain.' He led me to a small office close to the kitchen. 'We have a good record for the food we serve.'

'Don't worry, I've said it was nothing to do with the food.' I dialled Machell's number, hoping I would find him in.

'To what do I owe this honour?' Machell asked. 'Where the hell are you ringing from? Berlin?'

'No, I'm in town, sir, and in trouble. I need a pad for the night. Is there any chance I could use yours?'

'What sort of trouble?'

'Personal.'

'Girl friend personal?'

'Yes.'

'Same girl friend you told me about?'

'Yes, only now it's desperate. I've just come back from Nuremberg and her father's trial.'

'I see. Right. Yes, OK. Borrow my place.'

'You're a real friend, sir. Are you sure?'

'Well, strange as it may appear to you, I still manage to sow the occasional oat. I shall try and rest my head on a friendly female for the night.'

'There is one other thing. I don't have any transport.'

'Now you're pressing your luck. Where are you?'

I gave him the name and address of the restaurant.

'Stay put. I'll come and fetch you.'

'How can I thank you, sir?'

'You can't,' Machell said. 'I'm too good to be true.'

TWENTY-SIX

Machell's set of rooms on the second floor of a rare, unscathed building was surprisingly opulent for somebody who went to some pains to shun any public ostentation. He showed me where to find everything before he left. Naturally he had provided himself with a well-stocked bar, and in addition the kitchen had an American fridge which actually worked and held most of the basics. The main room had some good pieces of antique furniture plus a pair of comfortable armchairs. As for the bathroom, that was marble and piping hot water came out of the taps, while his bedroom was the lair of a sybarite – an inviting, French-style double bed covered with a fur rug. I felt some guilt about turning him out.

'Help yourself to anything you want,' he said, 'especially the bar. I've always found drink to be the great panacea.' He had been discreetness itself on the journey, making no comment about Lisa's obvious distress. 'Good night, young lady, enjoy the creature comforts.'

Once we were alone, I led her into the bedroom, made her lie on top of the bed and covered her with the rug. 'I'll make you some tea with plenty of sugar,' I said. No longer crying, she stared at me as though a stranger. Returning with the sweet tea, I helped her to a sitting position, then propped pillows behind her before steadying the cup in her hands. She took a few sips, then gave me the cup and sank back.

I could not read her. There was nothing in her expression, not despair, just blankness. Feeling for her hand I found it was still cold. I went to the small kitchen and poured the rest of the tea away. There was a tin of Huntley and Palmers biscuits on the shelf over the sink and I stared at the familiar wording, thinking what a long way from home I had come to give unhappiness to somebody else. Then I helped myself to a Scotch from the bar. I had eaten little since leaving Nuremberg, but the neat shot had no effect. I could think of nothing but Lisa's pain. There was a photograph of a younger Machell in a silver frame on a side table, showing him in tropical gear with his arm around a dusky Indian girl. The print had a crease dissecting it suggesting it had once been folded and kept in his wallet. I stared at it, wondering if she was the mother of the love child he had once confessed to. Returning to the bedroom, I found Lisa had undressed and got under the covers. I shed my own clothes, climbed in beside her and cradled her as one cradles someone injured.

After a long time, she said, 'I wish I could die.'

'Don't say things like that, darling. There's always hope.'

'You don't believe that,' she said. 'I can tell by your voice. If they put him in prison, I shall die.'

'I won't let you die. I love you and I'm going to marry you.'

'Why would you marry me now?'

'Because nothing's changed between us. Nothing. We still love each other.'

'And that makes it all right, does it?'

I bent over her and put my lips on hers, but she did not open them to me. Then she started to cry again. 'Why?' she said between sobs. 'Why did it happen?'

'The war,' I said. 'The war did things to people. Everybody changed. I changed; it did things to me too. Nobody escaped, only those who died.'

'You said . . . they brought evidence against him. What evidence? I want to know.'

Still holding her close, I searched for the words that would not wound her further. 'Your father explained he was given no choice. Because he had trained as a doctor he was posted to Auschwitz and given the responsibility for the health of the staff and their dependents. Your mother joined him there for a time. Did she ever tell you that?'

'No.'

'Or talk about the camps?'

'Yes, but only when we were shown the newsreels.'

'So you know why they were brought into existence. They had one sole purpose. Hitler had decreed that the entire Jewish race was to be exterminated, together with gypsies, the mentally ill, anybody who threatened the purity of the race. All those who worked in such places, especially the SS, are held responsible.'

'I know father didn't commit any crimes, he couldn't.'

'But he was there, darling, while others did. He was there in the wrong place at the wrong time. There is a difference between armies killing each other on the battlefield and people being killed in cold blood simply because they are Jewish.'

As I stared into her innocent face I knew that if ever she was to understand the horror and misery of events beyond her comprehension I had to tell her something I had long buried, something I had never before revealed to anybody. It was my last throw of the emotional dice.

'I killed once,' I said and held her closer. 'Not on the battlefield, I wasn't in a fighting unit. But in another camp, the one we liberated at Belsen. I killed a Jewish woman, who might have been no older than you, except that you could only guess at anybody's real age.'

'Why would you kill somebody like that?'

'Because,' I started, and then realised that there was no "because": it was impossible to recreate the emotions of that time or adequately describe the horrors – only those who had experienced them and lived to tell the tale could give an approximation. Much of what we uncovered, such as instances of cannibalism, had gone unreported.

I began again. 'When we first entered the camp the stench was overpowering and we were physically sick. There were corpses everywhere, some with deep cuts in the small of their backs where attempts had been made to extract livers and kidneys by the starving to assuage their hunger. Others were piled high outside the huts, or else in little groups lying where they had collapsed and died. Five hundred a day still died after we got there and nothing we could do had the slightest effect because they were too far gone with disease and hunger. I saw children choke to death from diphtheria, women drowning in their own vomit, some of those who could still walk washing in water from a tank in which a dead child floated. Then this naked woman grabbed at me, jabbering in a language I didn't understand. Another inmate, a man, told me in German she was a Slav and that the week before the liberation the guards killed her baby as a last act before they disappeared. "What is she saying?" I asked him. "She wants you to kill her," he said as though it was a matter-of-fact, everyday request. "She is saying please shoot her. She has gone quite mad." '

Lisa started to cry and I felt her tears on my face as I clutched her to me. 'And did you?' she said.

'No, of course not. There was no way I could do that, but her poor demented face haunted me, and later that same day when I was on my own, I searched for her, finally coming across her kneeling in the filth beside a heap of unburied dead behind the crematoriums. I saw her pick up a dead infant and put it to her flaccid breast, as though she could suckle it. It was the saddest thing I had ever seen, sadder than the death of a friend who died beside me in the fighting around Caen. We all carried morphine in our battle dress . . . I squatted beside her, took the dead infant from her and injected a dose into her arm. She made no sound, just stared at me. I guess she was so weak that the injection proved lethal. I waited beside her until she died. Nobody saw me, or if they did, nobody cared, one more death amongst so many meant nothing . . . For a time I also went mad. I think we all did, because we had all been shown a vision of hell.'

Lisa's had begun to tremble long before I finished and now she shook as though in a seizure. I held her nude body close to mine until her spasms subsided. What happened next now seems hideously crude, the typical act of a male and maybe it was, but at that moment I think all I wanted was to calm her, or maybe it was that I believed that our days of loving were finished, so in

Machell's borrowed bed, I tried to stifle her tears by making love to her in an attempt to blot out both the past and present. As I entered her I realised, all too late, that I was not wearing a condom, but by then I could not have stopped. When the moment came it was so intense, bordering on pain, that it obliterated all else. I lay with my head nestled into her damp neck, spent with passion. Our bodies slowly relinquished each other, our heartbeats slowed to normal, and we drifted into merciful sleep.

We said little the next morning. I made breakfast for us and then walked with her to the stage door. When we kissed and parted, she said: 'I only feel alive when I'm with you. Make it all come right.'

'I'll try my best. What I'm going to do,' I said, 'as soon as I get back to Berlin, is rent an apartment for us. Then I can take good care of you all the time.' I foraged in my jacket for some money. 'Meantime I want you to have this.'

'I can't keep taking your money.'

'Yes, you can. Don't German husbands keep their wives?'

'I'm not your wife.'

'But you will be.' I pressed the notes into her hand. 'No good-byes,' I said. 'We don't say goodbye, you and me.'

I walked away from her quickly. I didn't look back, but I knew she would still be standing there, believing in me.

TWENTY-SEVEN

At breakfast, Rawnsley looked up from reading his week-old copy of *The Times* and said, 'Was Nuremberg fun?'

'Fun? No, I wouldn't say that.'

'How did your war criminal do?'

'He's not "my" war criminal.'

'Sorry, excuse me. I thought you had a proprietary interest. Your girl friend's father then. Did they decide to hang him?'

I wondered how much Graham had told him of my situation. 'No,' I said. 'I left before the verdict.'

Graham joined us at that moment and mercifully changed the subject. 'Ah, you're back, Alex. Does the name Chivers ring a bell with you?'

'Yes.'

'A major in the Control Commission?'

'Yes. Why?'

'While you were away the Military Police pulled him in during a brothel raid. He was in civvies, and turned very truculent, said he was there carrying out an official survey on morals. Absolute bollocks, of course, and they passed him to us to check him out. He gave your name as a close friend, said you'd vouch for him.'

'He's certainly not a close friend,' I said emphatically. 'I first clapped eyes on him in Hamburg, thought he was a pompous little prick, very full of himself. Told me he'd spent the war in some, hush hush place . . . Bletchley I think he called it. Meant nothing to me.'

'Have you seen him since?'

'Yes, but not intentionally. Once at the docks when I was going home on leave. Then here, in a nightclub, just before I went to Nuremberg. Always seems to be chasing some dodgy business deal. The last time it was a scam involving Leica cameras.'

Rawnsley came out from behind his newspaper. 'Doesn't take long for the spivs to start crawling out of the woodwork.'

'How did you deal with him?' I asked.

'He went back to Hamburg with a flea in his ear,' Graham said. 'Swore he'd put in a complaint at the way he had been treated. But I'm interested that he claimed to have been at Bletchley. I shall follow that up.'

'Was Bletchley something special?'

'Yes. Very special and still on the secret list. Blabbing about it is definitely not encouraged.'

At that moment an orderly joined us and handed me a Telex. 'It's from one of the prosecuting team I got to know,' I said, 'telling me that Grundwall didn't get the death penalty, but was convicted on the secondary indictment and given thirty years.'

'The right verdict in your view?'

'I don't know,' I said. 'Maybe thirty years is a death penalty to somebody like him.'

'So where does that leave you with your girl friend?' Rawnsley asked, making it obvious that my situation was common knowledge.

'I don't know. The defence made much of my relationship with her, and established I was the first to identify her father.'

'So he now knows it was you who sprang the trap.'

'Yes.'

'And we must assume that his daughter is bound to find out sooner or later?'

'Yes.'

'How will she react to that?' Graham asked.

'I don't want to speculate,' I answered. 'Or even think about it.'

'I think you should write and finish the relationship,' Rawnsley chipped in. 'Much the best, given the circumstances.'

'Yes,' Graham agreed. 'Pity they didn't give him the drop. One can forget the dead in time, but never the living. "*He who forms a tie is lost, the germ of corruption has entered his soul*" – Conrad.' Having delivered himself of this homily Graham became businesslike again as though quoting Conrad had embarrassed him. He handed me a thick folder. 'Decode this lot as soon as you can, please, and let me know what requires immediate action. And if you're at a loose end, let's have dinner tonight.'

I spent the rest of the day logging the contents of the folder. It was for our eyes only and dealt with Project Backfire, set up to locate and send back to England any German scientists who had worked in the Nazi nuclear field. The Yanks were likewise shipping home anybody with the same credentials they found in their sector. We were to disregard any questionable Nazi histories; all that mattered was their potential worth to us. The race was on to discover how advanced the German nuclear programme had been and to commandeer any knowledge.

Graham treated me to a meal at the Officers Club, where his conversation, far from discussing my ongoing situation with Lisa, was immediately dominated by his own demons.

'Never thought it would revert to the law of the jungle so quickly, Alex,' he said as soon as his choice of Burgundy had been swirled, tasted and accepted. 'We're on the back foot again, the ball's no longer in our court,' he continued, always prone to mix his metaphors. 'Naturally Whitehall is urging restraint, blocking any attempt for us to move up into another gear and get real. The word is, don't make waves, wait and see which way Moscow jumps. In other words do nothing until it's too late. Our pursuits have always been regarded with distaste by the FO. We're meant to stay off their sacred patch. I've invested my entire life in this game, Alex, and you know what I've ended up as? – A pen pusher, a bloody pen pusher.'

I thought: what the hell have I got myself into? As with Miller, the old guard seemed to singing the same dirge in the same key. They were all disillusioned, unhappy with their lot and the task they were faced with. For my part I found it difficult to take the spying game seriously. Real enemies used conventional weapons, mowed you down with machine-guns, and blew you skywards with booby traps. Dead-letter drops, clandestine meetings, talk of the "Firm", "Control" and "moles" remained the stuff of the nursery – as though those who practised the dark arts were still trapped in a *Winnie the Pooh* world inhabited by middle-aged Christopher Robins. I broached the subject cautiously because one never knew how Graham would react. 'Do you ever question the use of the whole business of espionage and counter-espionage?'

'In what way?'

'Did it ever occur to you that it has a touch of futility about it?'

'Futility?' Graham was immediately on the defensive.

'Well, put it this way, what in the last analysis has it ever achieved? It hasn't ever stopped any wars. In many ways guess-work intelligence has often been the justification for conflicts. Because everybody had a knee-jerk reaction to the same faulty script in 1914, it started the wholesale worldwide carnage. This time around we were badly adrift at Arnhem.'

'You're confusing intelligence with espionage,' Graham answered tetchily. 'Not the same thing at all. There'll always be failures; we don't practise an exact science, but that doesn't negate the need for us to exist. We were put on this earth to thwart those who pose a threat to our values and our way of life.' He was silent for nearly a minute, eating nothing but fiddling with his steak knife, then looked up and smiled. 'Don't mind me. I have to defend my reason to exist. Of course I question the whole mad business, never more so than today. While you were in Nuremberg learning the fate of your once prospective father-in-law, the cull that began with the murder of my girl, accelerated. We've started to haemorrhage agents, Alex. Firstly in Belgrade, somebody I turned, a blue chip investment with access to top-level Soviet thinking. Gone. Then a second in Warsaw, part of the same network. Somebody in the know is cleaning our stables. But where, that's the question?'

'Miller is convinced it has to be London.'

'Perhaps he's right. He may be a piss artist, but he's a canny old bastard. Perhaps we do have to start thinking the unthinkable.' He cut the fat from his steak and pushed it to one side. 'Maybe it's not so unthinkable at that. You don't appreciate how some of us came to be in this game, Alex. Nobody asked me what I wanted to do; it was taken for granted that I would go into the diplomatic, like my father and his father before him. I was slipped into the family business like drawing on an old glove. Nobody vetted me properly. Why would they? I looked right, had been to the right school, had the right accent. Somebody who knew Daddy took me out to dinner at Rules, made small talk about Len Hutton and the best way to tie a fly, anything but the actual reason for the meal. Well, I tell a lie. There was a moment when he casually enquired whether I had shed my Communist tendencies. Since I had no idea what was behind the question, I said I was working on it. I suppose he thought I was being flippant and dropped the subject.'

'Were you ever a Communist?'

'Never a card carrier but, yes, I flirted with the idea like most of my year, went to a few meetings with speakers like D. N. Pritt and Maurice Dobbs, both confirmed Marxists pushing the Popular Front. It was fashionable to be radical in Cambridge during the Thirties. We bought the idea of revolution, it felt dangerous and daring, like having your first French letter hidden in your wallet. Most of us despised Baldwin and Chamberlain. Those on the Left were the only ones actively fighting Fascism in the International Brigade. Despite that affinity, I wasn't a convert for long. I found something so infinitely dreary about the comrades parroting the official line. Anybody with a modicum of intelligence had to reject the crap they spouted. So in my case it was just a phase and I drifted away. But some didn't, they even managed to rationalise the Nazi-Soviet Pact. I mean, that was the ultimate test, wasn't it? If you could swallow that without vomiting, you could swallow anything – the show trials, the deliberate starvation of the Russian peasants, the purges, murders, the Gulags. Some did, God help us.' Graham lit a cigarette but immediately thought better of it and laid it on the edge of an ashtray. 'When the war came we were all scattered into various branches of the Services, but who knows where some of the committed ended up? Some, like me, must have been absorbed into the SIS. Who bothered to find out where our true loyalties lay? Are some still in place, lying low? After all, what body could be more perfectly designed to harbour traitors, given that the prime object of a secret service is to remain secret?' Graham allowed himself the faintest smile. 'You know, of course that, officially, we don't exist, have never existed since the day old Kell was given the job of inventing us. No statements are ever made to Parliament, our budgets never debated.' He retrieved the cigarette, holding it between his thumb and first fingers like an actress unfamiliar with a prop. 'God, I'd like to get legless tonight.'

'Why don't you? I'll see you safely back to the billet.'

'Because I can't, Alex. No matter how hard I try, drink only dulls me, never obliterates. Maybe one day they'll pack me off home in disgrace, a security risk.'

I liked Graham, he was the professional and my boss, but I couldn't read him with any accuracy. Just when I thought I was tuned in to his wavelength, the signal became corrupted. I suppose the truth was he was a victim of love, like me. In addition we were both trying to make sense of a peace that was still a war. I sat opposite him, listening with half an ear to his wandering dialogue while all the time my thoughts switched to Grundwall, wondering what his next move would be as he began thirty years incarceration. He had nothing to lose by revealing my part in his downfall to Lisa. It was the only revenge left to him.

I saw Graham safely home to his billet that night and when we parted he apologised for being such a morbid companion. 'Pity you didn't meet me in my best years, Alex,' he said gravely. He wasn't drunk or maudlin, just icy cold.

First thing the following day I rang Major Jones asking him to let me know in which prison Grundwall would be serving his sentence, so that I could pass the information on to Lisa. Then I went in search of Staff Sergeant Webb who ran our Transport pool and was generally regarded as the fount of all knowledge and was noted for slagging off the system that held us captive. He was in his usual form that morning, greeting me with, 'Sir, what Whitehall tosser decided we should now drive around in these?' He pointed to two gleaming new Humber Snipe saloons he had been servicing. 'That's a really brilliant stroke, ain't it, given they're the only ones in Germany. Why didn't they go the whole hog and paint "Secret Service" on the door panels?'

'You're right, but I dare say they're more comfortable than the crap they replaced,' I said. I was anxious to get on with my plan and send Lisa some good news. 'Tell me, Harry, where could I start looking for accommodation?'

'You want to move out of your billet, sir?'

'No. I want somewhere safe for my girlfriend.'

He winked. 'Great minds think alike, sir. I've just done the same for my own little fraulein. The place I found might also suit you. Owned by an elderly geezer who lives in the basement and lets out the rest of his house. I happen to know he's got one flat not spoken for. I pay him in stuff, like a bottle of schnapps or some baccy every week. Suits him, suits me.'

'Can you take me there, show me?'

'Sure, sir. But let's not use a Humber, they haven't been road tested yet, so if you don't mind, we'll take the Bedford.'

En route, he said, 'Excuse the liberty, sir, but are you married?'

'No, I'm not.'

'I was. My divorce papers came through finally. A Dear John letter caught up with me the night before we crossed the Rhine. Tried to get myself killed that night, but my number wasn't on a bullet. And here I am, ready to dive in again head first.'

He pulled up in front of a detached house in *Ploener Strasse*, a house partially hidden from the road by a screen of damaged trees with a faded grandeur about it.

'Who else lives here?' I asked.

'Apart from my girl? There's an old bird on the top floor, who keeps herself to herself and a bloke who teaches piano. I think the landlord is some sort of aristocrat because he's got a "Von" to his name. That's like the House of Lords over here, isn't it?'

He led me down a flight of stone steps to the basement doorway and rang the bell. There was a wait and then a stooped old man wearing several cardigans and a scarf wrapped around his throat opened the door. His face, under thin, yellowed strands of hair brushed sideways across his skull, had the quality of parchment.

'*Guten tag*, Herr Von Krenkler,' Webb said.

'*Guten tag*.' Krenkler stared past Webb to me.

Webb addressed him in German that left much to be desired, but Krenkler got the gist. 'This is one of my officers, Captain Seaton. He's interested in taking one of your flats, if one's still available.'

'*Bitte*,' Krenkler said. '*Bitte*,' and shuffled to one side allowing us to enter. He led the way through his quarters to the hallway. As we climbed to the first floor I heard the strains of Beethoven's Moonlight Sonata being picked out on a piano. The wooden stair treads were worn, the patterned wallpaper faded and peeling, yet redolent of an opulent past. Kenkler stopped outside a door on the second landing and produced a bunch of keys, studying them carefully before selecting the right one and unlocking the door. The room I entered was panelled, alternate panels decorated with bunches of flowers on a faded blue background. There was a marble fireplace flanked on both sides by empty bookshelves. The furniture was sparse, formal: a sofa and two matching armchairs covered in floral silk that had seen better days. A chandelier with some of its glass drops missing hung from the centre of the ceiling and the plaster cornice had gaps in several paces. I went through into the kitchen, a much smaller room, which in turn led into a bathroom. The bedroom was larger with a double bed in the French style like Machell's, together with an ornate wardrobe and side table.

'Yes, fine,' I said in German, without hesitation. 'I'll take it. What rent are you asking?'

'I am open to negotiation,' Krenkler replied. 'Will you be paying in cash or in other ways?'

'Cash.'

'Dollars?'

'No. British Army currency.'

He shrugged, obviously disappointed. Nobody wanted the Monopoly money we had put into circulation to try and dampen the black market. I named a figure which he agreed after short hesitation – although Baafs were not as welcome as US dollars, they were still money. I gave him a month's rent in advance. 'I won't be living here myself, I'm taking it for a lady friend, Fraulein Grundwall, but I will be responsible for all the rent and all outgoings.'

'It's no concern of mine,' Krenkler said, 'as long as you don't turn my house into a brothel.' As he pocketed the cash he gave me a sly smile. 'Do you ever have any spare coffee?'

'Possibly.'

'I can always give it a home,' he said, freeing two keys from his bunch. 'One for the main door and one for this apartment.' I didn't resent his transparent avarice, I was used to it, everybody in post-war Germany was on the make.

'Cunning old sod, slipping in that bit about spare coffee,' Harry said when we were outside.

'Can't blame him, I suppose. He must have seen better days.'

On the return journey I asked, 'Are you going to marry your fraulein?'

'Yeah, I expect so. Just worried if she'll fit in back home. Mind you, I found Blighty totally foreign the last time I went back on furlough. Not that I had much to go back to with the wife getting shagged by the local Air Raid Warden. I came across him in a pub while I was there. A right ponce. I thought about decking him, and then decided he was welcome to her. One thing's for sure, whatever happens I won't be going parking my heavy pack in Huddersfield when I get out of here. Might even pitch my tent in Berlin, learn the lingo properly, and find a decent job, because bet your life we'll put fucking Germany on its feet before we sort out our own fucking problems. What d'you intend when you get out, sir?'

'Tell you the truth, I don't know.'

Listening to him considering his future, it was brought home to me that mine would be decided by Grundwall. I wondered whether during his university lectures he had ever quoted Gauguin's *"Life being what it is, one dreams of revenge."* As he faced three decades behind bars, what else was left for him but revenge?

The next few weeks passed slowly. I wrote to Lisa every other day, reiterating that I wanted to marry her. A further Telex from Major Jones informed me that Grundwall's defence had lodged an appeal with the Allied Control Council. That body interpreted its duty as limited to considerations of mercy linked to a possible reduction of sentence, its members being judged not competent, in legal terms, to override the Tribunal's verdicts. In due course word came back that the appeal had failed and that Grundwall was being transferred to a prison outside Hamelin and would be allowed one visit a month. I saw that my only course was to confess my involvement to Lisa before her father got in first.

I began a new letter and after four drafts, I finally settled on this: *'My Dearest Lisa, I have just been informed that your father will shortly be moved from Nuremberg to a prison in the Hamelin area and will now be permitted visitors once a month. I know that you want to see him as soon as possible, even though it is a long journey from Hamburg. I will find out what documents and permissions you and your mother need and help with the fares.*

'Sweetheart, I realise that many of the things that happened during the war are incomprehensible to those who did not take part. The role your father played can only be understood if one accepts that the world is not black and white. Sadly, none of us can live life backwards and what happened, happened. Perhaps there is a God who will forgive all our actions. I wouldn't know, because I stopped believing in Him when one of my friends was blown to pieces in front of my eyes.

'I told you the story of the young Jewish mother I helped die so that you might understand that we all had to make terrible choices and that

the one I had to make at Belsen will always haunt me, just as what I have to now tell you may well end any love you have for me. I must take that risk because if we are ever to have a life together you must learn the truth from me and nobody else.

'Because of the job I had to do during and after the war, it was my fate to be the one who first uncovered evidence of your father's hidden past. In the course of my duties, I was shown a photograph taken at Auschwitz and to my horror recognised your father amongst the faces in a group of SS officers. At first I put my love for you before my duty and told nobody that I had identified him, but then I realised that if I said and did nothing it would be a betrayal of that poor Jewish girl and the many thousands like her. I also realised that by exposing your father, your love for me might not survive. You now know the choice I made and I can only ask you to try and understand that I owed a debt to the dead. Now you will make your own choice and I will have to live by your decision. I love you very much, and always will, but perhaps that will not prove enough. I pray it will, for if I were to lose you the rest of my life will be unthinkable.'

When I read it the following morning I saw all its inadequacies, but I knew I had to post it and risk everything. I sealed the envelope and handed it to the clerk in the Post Room on the way to the office I shared with Rawnsley. He was already at his desk and waved a languid hand in my direction as I entered. 'That character was never there,' he said.

'What character was never where?'

'That Control Commission bod, Chivers. A complete bloody phoney, never set foot in Bletchley. It really chokes me. We win the war against all odds and then entrust the peace to ghastly little shits like him.' He took up his pipe, pointed it like a pistol and mouthed a silent "Bang!" 'Put the buggers against a wall and shoot them, that's what I'd like to do.'

'I wouldn't stop you. What's the perfume you're wearing?'

Rawnsley, immediately aggrieved, said, 'It's not perfume, it's an aftershave I bought in the Yank PX. Very musky I thought. Don't you like it?'

'Not over much.'

Hurt, he began to fill the pipe from a leather pouch. 'Our leader wants to see you. Been in twice looking for you so don't keep him waiting any longer. He's become increasingly irritable, I find. Probably male menopause.'

'We could be about to fish in muddy waters,' Graham began as soon as I entered his den. 'Word is that somebody wants to come across.'

'Who?'

'We're giving him the code name Vanya. Maybe he'll prove to be a useful uncle, maybe not. Ever seen a production of it?'

'I'm sorry?' I said, all at sea. I could never get used to the way in which he jumped from one topic to another without drawing breath.

'The play, *Uncle Vanya*? You've seen it, surely?'

'No, I haven't.'

'Then you've missed the best Chekhov by far,' Graham pronounced, parading his knowledge. 'It gives a unique insight into human frailty.'

'You're saying this "Vanya" is a possible defector?'

'Yes. Possible. One of our scalp-hunters in Berne made the contact and he sounds hopeful. He met Vanya at a Soviet Trade Mission and during a heavy drinking session put out a feeler. Got a good initial feeling and subsequently engineered a one-on-one meeting in a safer location.'

'Who is this Vanya?'

'Colonel in the KGB, heavy hitter apparently, learned his trade in the Cheka. During the war ran a network of partisans behind German lines. His only son was a tank commander who was shot during one of the purges. Vanya was lucky to escape the same fate. That sort of sob story can be suspect, but our man believes his disillusionment to be genuine. With his tongue loosened, he boasted he had plenty to sell and after our man had helped him demolish a second bottle of Stolly, named his price, always a good sign if they're serious. Our man played it deliberately vague, said he didn't have the authority to take it further without getting back to London, but said we would be in touch if we got the OK. So, who knows? Could be a plant. On the other hand, could be a boost to our fortunes. We need a success after the recent failures. I thought you might like to cut your teeth on him, handle the next stage.'

'What's that?'

'Vanya's coming to East Berlin in three weeks for a trade fair. Always good pickings to be had at such events – new Western contacts, opportunities for blackmail.'

'Blackmail?'

'Yes. God, you're naïve. Classic KGB technique. Hone in on a likely target, get him legless, put him in a hotel room with a tart or rent boy, take a few incriminating snapshots on him on the job and apply the screws. I want you to go to the fair, meet him and form a judgement. Is he the genuine article or a dummy? We'll thoroughly brief you and provide you with a new identity. My first idea is to make you a salesman for British motorbikes. Know anything about them?'

'Nothing. Never ridden one.'

'Ah, well, I'll think again.'

'How will I recognise him?'

'We have photographs.'

Digesting this new development, I went back to my office and found some mail on my desk, two letters, one from home, and the other with a German postmark. I tore this one open. It was short, written on the back of a theatre call sheet, the handwriting uneven.

'*Mein Leibe Alex, please don't be angry, but I think I'm pregnant and I'm so scared what you will say. Tell me what I should do. I will wait at the stage door every day at one o'clock for you to ring me. Please ring as soon as you get this. I love you. Lisa.*' The last sentence was heavily underlined.

'You look as though you've seen a ghost,' Rawnsley said. 'Bad news from home?'

'No.' I walked to the window and read her note again.

'By the way, did you see the Labour government intend to cut our budget?'

'I haven't read the papers for a couple of days.'

'It's vital to keep up with the real world.'

I thought: the real world isn't in *The Times*, it's here in this note. I rushed back to the Post Room.

'That letter I handed in a little while ago,' I said to the post clerk. 'Can you give it back, I need to add something.'

'Sorry, sir, already collected.'

'How long ago?'

'At least half an hour, sir.'

'Where does the mail go from here?'

'Couldn't say for certain, sir.'

'Well, who would know? They must go somewhere, man. Find out.'

He disappeared for a while, but returned to say: 'No joy, sir. Nobody seems to know exactly.'

I agonised until it was lunch time, then rang the theatre stage door at exactly one o'clock only to hear the engaged tone. I re-dialled every two minutes but it was permanently busy. I had the number checked, all to no avail. Later the same day, around the time when Lisa usually finished rehearsals, I tried again. This time the surly stage-door keeper agreed to fetch Lisa and I finally heard her voice. 'Darling,' I said, 'I tried to phone at lunch time as you asked, but the line was always busy.'

'Everybody uses it.' She sounded flat. 'Are you angry with me?'

'Why would I be angry? Of course I'm not. I'll be thrilled if it's true.'

'It is true,' she answered. 'I saw a doctor yesterday. I'm so frightened, I wish you could come back.'

'I will as soon as I can, darling, but it isn't that easy . . . ' The connection suddenly went dead and although I re-dialled immediately, now the line was busy. After several more attempts,

I gave up. It was as if my future had been put into a code that I could not decipher. I rushed to buttonhole Graham just as he was leaving the building.

'How long before Vanya comes to East Berlin?'

'Eighteen days, why?'

'I know I shouldn't ask this, but can I have your permission to go to Hamburg for a quick visit, forty-eight hours at the most?'

'Why?'

'My girlfriend's just told me she's pregnant.'

'Don't go. Send her the money for an abortion,' Graham said coldly.

'I can't do that, she means too much to me.'

'Don't tell me you really want a child by her, given the family history? Children last a long time, Alex.'

'She still doesn't know the part I played in her father's arrest. A letter's in the post in which I confessed everything, and I need to get to her before it arrives if I'm to save our relationship.'

'Don't save it, save yourself from future grief,' Graham said.

'I have to try.'

He studied me for a few moments. 'Well, if you're so determined to ruin your life, obviously nothing I say will have any effect, so you'd better go. But, be back in forty-eight hours. Any longer and you're in trouble.'

'I really appreciate it, Graham.'

'You must have realised by now that my steely exterior hides a sentimental fool underneath. So, fuck off before I change my mind.'

I used a friendly WAAF in Air Control to get me a bucket seat on one of the daily Dakota courier flights. It was dark when we landed in Hamburg and once again I pulled rank and requested a car from Military Police to take me to Lisa's address. This time it was she, not Greta, who opened the door to me. She was in a dressing gown, bare footed, and her face blotched from crying. 'When you hung up on me, I thought it was all over between us, that I'd never see you again.'

'I didn't hang up, the bloody connection went dead and then the line was always busy.' I kissed her wet face. She was naked under her thin gown.

'And you're not angry?'

'Would I be here if I was angry? I'm going to marry you.'

'Why are you so nice to me?'

'I don't know. It must be that I love you.'

While we hugged each other, over her shoulder I scanned the room but, to my relief, I couldn't see my letter anywhere. I produced the bottle of wine I had brought with me. 'Come on, let's celebrate.' I uncorked the wine and poured two glasses. 'Sit on my lap. You remember I said I wanted you to leave here and be with me in Berlin? Well, I've already done something about it and rented an apartment for you.'

'You have? Really?'

'Really. Once you're there I'll be able to take proper care of you.' I put my hand on her stomach. 'Both of you. When you saw the doctor, did he say everything was OK?'

'Yes.'

'So that's good news.'

'Promise me you're happy about it.'

'I've already told you.'

Then, as though mention of good news had immediately triggered thoughts of her father, she said: 'Have they given a verdict yet?'

'Didn't you get a letter from me telling you all?'

'No, not yet.'

'Well, everything's in the letter, as you'll see when it arrives.'

'That they're going to set him free?'

As gently as I could, I said: 'No, sweetheart, they're not.'

Her face crumpled. 'Not?'

'They found him guilty.'

She wriggled off my lap and stood facing me. 'He's not guilty of anything, it's all lies.'

I held out my arms to her, but she did not respond. 'The

213

evidence against him was damning, sweetheart. He was convicted and given a long sentence.'

'How long?'

I hesitated before telling her, 'Thirty years.'

She swayed, uttering a cry like an animal and rushed to the sink where she bent over and retched. I went to her and supported her head until the spasms subsided, then helped into the only armchair. Her dressing gown gaped open, exposing her nakedness, but she made no attempt to cover herself, but rocked backwards and forwards. She was shivering and I fetched my army greatcoat and draped it around her shoulders. Reaching for her clenched fist I gently loosened the fingers one by one and held her hand in mine. Speaking slowly as to a child, I said, 'I've told you everything in my letter. When you get it you'll understand more.'

'I want to understand now.'

'All right. I'll tell you now.' I began to relate the contents of my letter, putting it in a way I desperately hoped would soften the final blow. She was silent until I had struggled through to the end, but her nails gradually dug into my palm. 'That's the whole story,' I finished. 'I promise I've kept back nothing.'

She pulled her hand away. 'And the part you played, does Vater know that?'

'Yes.'

'And you believe he's guilty?'

'The court found him guilty.'

'But what do you believe?'

'Is that important any more?'

'To me it is.'

'I believe he had a past he wanted to conceal but finally had to answer for.'

'You betrayed him,' she said. 'Why?'

'I've just explained why.'

'Because of that one Jewish woman?'

'Not just her.'

'Would you have done the same if it had been your own father?'

'Darling, that's not a fair question.'

'It is to me. Whatever he did or did not do, he'll always be my father. I shall never abandon him.'

'I'd never want you to.' I tried to reach for her hand again, but she would have none of it. 'We have a life, too, don't we?' She did not answer. 'Don't we?' I repeated. 'Doesn't the fact that you're carrying my child count?'

'I don't know,' she said. She was calm now, calm and cold. 'I don't know anything any more. When I see Vater, he'll decide for me.'

'Well, I'm certain he hates me, so I can guess what his answer will be. The only thing that matters to me is what you decide.'

'He will decide,' she said again.

'You say I betrayed him, but he was guilty with or without me, and he betrayed you by what he kept hidden. Of course you mustn't abandon him, I wouldn't want you to, but does that mean you're going to throw away what we have?' I waited. 'Does it? I have to know.' I searched her face for any sign that would give me hope. 'I haven't changed because of what has happened.'

'Perhaps I have,' she said flatly. 'How could it ever be the same again? It would always be between us.'

I became desperate in my efforts to win her round. 'Do you think I came here today thinking we could just turn back the clock and wipe out the past? I came because I love you and I want to keep you. Darling, we all have to live with whatever's handed to us. Life isn't a dance floor we can walk off if we don't like the tune being played. I came dreading what I had to tell you, but I thought that the love we have for each other could overcome everything. This pain will pass, I promise.'

'Don't make me any more promises. I'm tired of promises. You gave me something and then you took it away,' she said in the same dead voice.

'You mustn't believe that,' I said, but I might as well have been talking to a stranger.

'I shall do whatever Vater decides,' she said again. It had become a mantra.

'Am I no longer in the reckoning? Look at me. Look at me. I thought you loved me.'

'I do love you,' she said, 'but it's not enough any more.' She took my greatcoat from her shoulders and handed it to me like a hotel cloakroom attendant. It was a dismissal.

'I'd rather you hated me, than this,' I said. 'One can live with hate.' I put on the greatcoat and picked up my hat from the table. I waited, but she gave me no last-minute reprieve. 'I'll see that you and your mother get the necessary permissions to visit. Have you enough money for the fares?'

'We'll find the money somewhere.'

'Tell me if you can't,' I leant forward and kissed her cheek. It was like kissing a statue. 'Just take care of yourself.'

The same disabled war veteran we had encountered before was coming up the stairway and I stood to one side to let him pass. I felt as crippled as him, the sense of loss hollowing me like somebody who has been told he has a terminal illness.

TWENTY-EIGHT

Graham never asked me about the outcome of my visit, nor did I volunteer anything. Preparations for my coming trip to the Eastern sector occupied me during the following weeks, but I found time to track down and obtain the various permissions Lisa and her mother needed to visit Grundwall. I sent these to her, together with the location of the prison in Hamelin. Every day I searched the mail for an envelope with her handwriting on it, praying she had had a change of heart, but nothing ever came.

Having decided what my new identity should be, Graham provided me with a passport in the name of Alex Wilmot, a salesman for farm equipment, born in Boston, Lincolnshire. 'Better not to change your Christian name, avoids making any inadvertent slip. Likewise I settled on farming as an occupation so that you're on familiar territory. I take it you still remember your bucolic childhood?'

'Yes.'

'We'll be supplying you with a bunch of current trade brochures for tractors, combine-harvesters and other agricultural equipment, together with price lists and delivery schedules.'

'What happens if I actually take orders?'

'You accept them. The Firm has a covert department that will deal with them, but don't expect any commission,' he said with the faintest of smiles. 'Practise your new signature until you have it off pat; you're bound to have to sign in at the fair, and on any order forms. Remember, Vanya will be looking for any chink in your armour, just as you must be ultra aware of any in his.'

'Is Alex Wilmot married?'

'I thought not. Means another layer to remember.'

'But presumably he fought in the war?'

'Yes, we gave that a lot of thought. He served in a home ack ack battery and never went overseas.'

'What rank?'

'Sergeant, Royal Artillery. It'll all be in your file.'

He and Rawnsley put me through several mock sessions rehearsing me in the dialogue I could expect from Vanya, whose real name was Sergheyevich Vassiltchikov.

'The priorities you must quickly determine are (a) is he a plant? (b) has he got anything of value to sell? and (c) should we buy? Remember, if he tumbles you, Alex Wilmot is dead in the water, a non-person, nothing to do with us. As far as we're concerned you never existed.'

'Tell me the bad news,' I said as cheerfully as I could.

'Make doubly sure you carry nothing on you that connects you to your real self. When you smoke, smoke the British commercial brands, not any Army issue. Above all, don't sound keen, let him make the running. Happy so far?'

'No, but go on.'

'OK, let's walk it through step by step. Let's assume you've just met him. First you make certain it is Vanya.'

'How do I do that?'

'Our man in Berne gave him the passwords. At some point Vanya will ask whether you ever have snow in England. You'll reply, "Sometimes, but nothing like you get in Russia." '

'God, real schoolboy stuff.'

'Yes, well, schoolboy stuff, as you put it, is important,' Graham, said with a hint of annoyance. 'Don't mock it. Get it wrong and it's curtains. Right. Assuming you've got over that hurdle and had an initial discussion about the products you're promoting, then you suggest you go somewhere more congenial for a drink, and hopefully he'll take you to a bar or restaurant, preferably some-where noisy where you can talk. Even so, there could still be bugs. Has he got a flower in his buttonhole? Good place for a mike. A vase of flowers on the table or bar top, or fixed to the underside of the table.'

'Understood. Can I go back a bit? You said we'd have an initial conversation about farm machinery. Will he be knowledgeable about that?'

'He'll probably pretend interest for appearances' sake. He's playing the same game as you, don't forget. His cover is he's attending the fair as an official of their Trade Ministry. The fair's genuine enough, they're anxious to get their hands on Western technology and machinery.'

'Does he speak English?'

'Yes. And German.'

'Since he's a hardened pro,' I said, 'surely he'll know we wouldn't send a tractor salesman to recruit him.'

'Of course. What's your problem? He'll know you're not the genuine article. He's not interested in that, all he'll be looking for is proof that we've taken him seriously and taken it a step further. His main concern will be to be satisfied we can protect him once we've got him out. That and the financial consideration, of course. Money speaks louder than loyalty. If you're satisfied with his answers, you are authorised to assure him on both points. We will protect him once he's with us, give him a new identity and a payment of fifty thousand sterling in Swiss francs.'

'Christ!,' I exclaimed. 'I wouldn't mind a deal like that.'

'The fair lasts three weeks,' Graham said, ignoring this. 'If you come back with a positive reaction, we'll bring him across on the last day.'

'I don't care for you saying "if".'

'OK, "when" you come back.'

'How will you bring him across?'

'Once again it's all detailed in your file. You will instruct him to be in the loading bay area at noon on the final day. We're anticipating there'll be maximum activity on that day with everybody packing up. A white truck marked Mayflower Refrigeration AG driven by our Sergeant Webb will arrive with a consignment of American refrigerators, invoiced for the personal attention of Vanya. He will inspect them and pass all but one. The ones he accepts are then off-loaded, and the faulty one he has deemed unacceptable returned to the West. During his inspection he will have found a British passport complete with photograph naming him as Albert Chamberlain, electrician. This will be inside the ice compartment of the faulty fridge, sealed in the packet containing the guarantee together with five thousand dollars on account to give him confidence that we're on the level. Then he gets into the cabin beside Webb and they drive out.'

'Will that work?'

'There's bound to be chaos on the last day and if all goes to plan, Webb will reach the checkpoint just after the guards change over. All the paperwork will be in order and the new guards won't know that there was only one man in the truck when it came in. Once we've debriefed him and extracted our pound of flesh, we'll ship him out on a cargo flight, to live happily ever after. Or not, as the case may be. Who cares?'

He and Rawnsley took me through the plan several more times before they were confident I had mastered everything, paying particular attention to Vanya's photographs. My travel kit consisted of a second-hand English suit, shirt, tie and shoes, a well-scuffed wallet containing items such as a railway ticket stub, a Farmers Union membership card and a picture of Vera Lynn cut from a magazine. I still had a feeling of taking part in a fantasy with sinister undertones; Graham several times emphasised that if the operation went belly up, I was a non-person, abandoned to my fate. "Abandoned" was a word that inevitably led me back to the last time I had seen Lisa. 'I shall never abandon him' had been her mantra. I tried to picture what had taken place when she and her father had finally been reunited. What had his decision been? Had he insisted that she terminate the pregnancy? Abortion was a criminal offence in Germany; at his bidding would she resort to some dangerous backstreet job? Every scenario I conjured up led to a depressing conclusion.

The morning I was due to go in I carefully checked the interior of the car allocated to me. 'It's clean,' Harry Webb said. 'Been over it twice, sir. False number plates, full tank and the brakes are shit hot. But don't take my word for it, check it out and test it yourself.'

There was a scuffed fibre suitcase on the back seat packed with some toiletries (a bar of Yardley soap, spare Gillette razor blade, toothbrush and a tube of Maclean's toothpaste), a change of shirt and socks with British laundry marks and a quantity of trade brochures in a leather folder. The suitcase had a label attached to the handle giving my name and an address in Boston, Lincolnshire. I had also been issued with currency in used notes – the equivalent of a hundred pounds in Occupation currency and three hundred US dollars.

'Watch your back, at all times, sir,' Harry said, 'and don't forget Stalin is holier than JC.'

Feeling naked without my uniform and gun, I tested the brakes before moving off. Webb had done a great job and the engine was tuned to perfection. I followed the line of the canal then turned north onto Friedrichstrasse, heading for the American checkpoint. The GIs' on duty enquired the reason for my visit and examined my passport before waving me through. Leaving them I preceded across the uneven surface of Zimmerstrasse to the GDR barriers. The frontier police ordered me out of the car and took my passport into the control hut. Another demanded to know how much money I was carrying. I produced the notes, which were spread out on a table and counted twice. Before handing them back the policeman pocketed some of the dollars. It was quite blatant, no attempt to conceal the theft.

'We like dollars,' he said.

'Don't we all?' I wasn't going to argue.

'Do you have camera?'

'No.'

'Radio?'

'No.'

'The purpose of your visit?'

I indicated the brochures. 'I'm a salesman going to your great trade fair.'

He searched the car's interior and boot, opening my suitcase and rifling through the contents, then made me release the hood catch and examined the engine. Finally he trundled a mirror under the chassis; only then was my passport returned by his companion. I noted the passport had been marked on one page with a coloured pencil.

When I was allowed to proceed I drove around the concrete blocks until stopped by a *Vopo*. He too demanded to examine my passport before waving me through. An armed soldier raised the barrier and I entered East Germany for the first time. The trade fair was being held in a giant warehouse half a mile from the *Friedrichstrasse* railway station and had been given a make-over for the occasion. A large banner proclaiming the event stretched across the façade. I was directed to a parking space by an official and after retrieving my folder of brochures from the back seat, I purchased a ticket at the entrance booth, paying for it in dollars. Inside I was greeted by two uniformed, hatchet-faced women manning a stall extolling the virtues of life in the GDR and accepted the leaflets they thrust at me. I toured the fifty or more exhibits and although some displayed Western exports, most held products from the Communist bloc with a distinctly antique appearance, reminding me of items in rural museums devoted to the dawn of the industrial revolution. I thought it politic to do the rounds while keeping a weather eye open for Vanya. Martial music blared from loudspeakers, punctuated every now and again with official announcements, as watchful *Volkspolizie* circulated in pairs. Playing my bogus role, I distributed some of my brochures to the officials on the agricultural stall and was gratified to find that I could do a passable job of salesmanship. There was a refreshment area offering free food and drink and while introducing myself to my first dollop of caviar, I was suddenly tapped on the shoulder, turned and was aghast to find Chivers alongside.

'How about this, sport?' he boomed. 'Haven't seen Beluga for years.' He spooned a generous mouthful, a few eggs dropping onto the lapel of his shiny suit. 'Must tell you, just pulled off a humdinger of a deal. Fifty Praktikas at a price you wouldn't believe.'

'Do me a favour and fuck off,' I hissed.

Chivers jaw dropped, traces of caviar on his lower lip. 'I beg your pardon, who d'you think you're talking to?'

'I said, fuck off. You don't know me and I don't know you. Understood?'

'No, I don't.'

'Use your loaf for fuck's sake. I'm here undercover.'

I quickly walked away. Unnerved by the encounter, but thankful it had happened before I made contact with Vanya, I went back to the agricultural stall and found the same man I had approached earlier.

'Any interest?' I asked.

'It's possible we might be interested in tractors at the right price.'

'What d'you consider the right price?'

'Less than you quote here.'

'Well, I'm sure we could better it, depending on how many you order.' Beyond him I suddenly spotted Vanya making his way towards us. 'Give me some idea how many you're thinking of.'

'That will be decided by the Ministry. I merely pass on the information.'

The moment Vanya joined us the man became deferential. Vanya was wearing a superior blue serge suit with the ribbon of the Order of the Red Star in his buttonhole.

'We are discussing tractors, Comrade Commissar,' the man said. He handed my brochure to Vanya as I introduced myself.

'Vassiltchikov,' he responded and shook my hand firmly. Examining the brochure, he said: 'No Fordson's? I'm told the Fordson is a good machine.'

'We are the main agents for Massey Ferguson's, equally good, but I'm sure we could locate and supply Fordsons if they're your preference.'

'Who's to say what preference I have until I know the price?'

'Exactly, Comrade Commissar,' the other man said. 'I made the same point. The price is all important.'

Vanya said: 'We know you Western capitalists like to make a big profit, whatever the price. Are the ones you sell reliable?'

'Very reliable.'

'In all conditions? We have very bad weather in Russia. Have you any idea how cold it gets? Minus thirty degrees some years. You're from England, yes?'

'Yes.'

'Do you get snow in England?'

'Sometimes,' I answered slowly, 'but nothing like you get in Russia.' I saw Vanya's eyes give a slight flicker.

'Nothing is like Russia,' he said. 'Everything in Russia is bigger than anywhere else. Perhaps you and I can do business, perhaps not. No guarantees, but let's have a drink and find out.' To the salesman he said: 'Leave this to me, comrade. I know how to bargain with capitalists. Come, Mr Wilmot, let us find the vodka.'

As we walked towards the hospitality area we passed Chivers gesticulating to three dour-looking types. He broke off and glared at me.

'Who is that man?' Vanya asked, catching the look.

'Which man?'

'The one I saw you talking to a few minutes ago.'

'No idea. He came up and tried to sell me some cameras.'

'Is he one of yours?' he asked.

For a second he caught me off guard. 'If you mean, is he British, yes I think so, but I've never seen before today.'

'One should always be careful not to talk to strangers, don't you agree?'

'Absolutely.' At the refreshment table he did not wait to be served but grabbed an open bottle of vodka by the neck and poured two generous shots. 'To the German Democratic Republic,' he said.

'The German Democratic Republic.'

'And tractors,' Vanya said. 'May they soon be ploughing our fields.'

'Is the fair going well?'

'We have a lot of ground to make up. Our war brought terrible hardships.'

'Let's hope we can be of some help.' Mindful of Graham's advice, I started carefully, determined to sound and act the professional. 'Tell me, what is the average acreage of Russian farms? Are they in hundreds or thousands? I ask because I need to point you towards the right size of machine.'

'Tens of thousands.'

'I see. That's big by our standards.'

'As I have said, in the USSR everything is on the heroic scale.'

'Like your war effort.'

'What did you do in the war, Mr Wilmot?'

'I was in the British Army, the Artillery.'

'Where?'

'I served in a coastal ack ack battery in England for the duration. And you?'

'Infantry,' Vanya said. He took out a leather cigar case containing three dark cigars and offered one to me.

'I'll stick to cigarettes if you don't mind.' I produced a packet of Passing Clouds. 'Would you care to try one of these?'

'They're not strong enough for me.'

He lit a cigar then held out the still burning match for my cigarette. 'So, let's get down to business. How soon can you supply us?'

'Well, like you, many of our factories were badly bomb damaged, but we're gradually getting back to normal. We would of course give any order from you top priority. Delivery times would depend on the size of your order.'

'No, it would depend on the price. Quote me for two hundred.'

'Two hundred! Goodness, that would make my company very happy. If you're thinking in those numbers I'm sure my bosses will come back with a very attractive quote.'

'How are your bosses? Do they grind the workers into the ground?'

'No, those days have gone. Look, since I'm sure we are going to strike a deal, can I take you for a meal? It would give me great pleasure, but you choose where. I don't know East Berlin at all.'

'Sure, I know places. You want company?'

'Company?'

'Female company.'

'Oh, I see. I thought we would be talking business.'

'That is business,' Vanya said and roared with laughter, his face partially obscured as he exhaled a cloud of acrid smoke from his cigar. 'But I insist you will be my guest. I will show you real Russian hospitality. The Germans only know how to cook one thing – their goose.' He again laughed at his own joke.

'That's very good,' I said. 'I must remember that one.'

Vanya led the way out of the warehouse, waving aside the officials at the door when they asked for me to show my ticket. A uniformed driver was waiting beside a black limousine and Vanya gave him instructions in Russian. We sped through empty streets at high speed, with Vanya giving me a running commentary. 'Already we are rebuilding all this in our image and then we will repopulate it. Before long it will become Russian. Germany will never rise again, we will see to that. Our beloved Stalin made sure we got here first.'

'It must have been bloody at the end,' I said.

'They destroyed Stalingrad, we erased Berlin. How does the expression go? Tit for tat, yes?'

We drew up outside what appeared to be a large private house and the driver hurried to open Vanya's passenger door. A Russian soldier snapped to attention and saluted as we entered. I had a sense of foreboding. Inside, the circular marble hallway, dominated by a portrait of Stalin, opened into a small anteroom. This led into a much larger room which was the restaurant. We were conducted to a side table in one of the alcoves. Remembering Graham's warning, as I sat down I dropped my sheaf of brochures. Bending to retrieve them I checked the underside of the table for a bug, but could see nothing untoward. 'This is very impressive,' I remarked as a waiter immediately brought a carafe of vodka. There were no flowers on the table.

'What shall we drink to?' Vanya asked when he had poured two glasses of vodka.

'How about "to happy conclusions"?' My hand was clammy and the glass almost slipped out of my grasp.

'Or "Journey's End"?' Vanya responded with a straight face.

Now the cat and mouse proceedings begin, I thought. Both of us watching for chinks in the armour, as Graham had put it. Vanya was sure to be an old hand at mind games. I knew I was about to spar with somebody who had survived by keeping one step ahead of others.

'You say things are bad in England. How bad?'

'We're virtually bankrupt, having pawned the family silver to pay for the war.'

'What the Yanks called "Lend Lease", yes? What d'you think of the Yanks?' Before I could frame an answer, he gave his own opinion. 'They take everything, but that will end. Soon we will be spoken of as God's own country instead of them. Soon we will overtake everybody, our beloved Stalin will see to that.' He switched abruptly to another subject. 'What are conditions like for workers in England?'

'The new Labour government is bringing in measures to improve their lot.'

'Your Labour party is imitation communism, not even a half-way house.'

'You think so?'

'Don't you?'

'It's all new to us because many were shocked when Churchill's party was voted out. Everything is in short supply. We still have food rationing.'

'In Leningrad our people ate rats and dogs during the siege,' Vanya answered. 'That's what we call short supplies.' A waiter hovered by the table. 'Let me order for you. Dog is not on the menu today.' I was getting used to the fact that his sense of humour was very basic. He ordered rapidly in Russian, but I had no idea what he had chosen for me.

'So, shall we talk tractors?' I asked after he had poured more vodka.

'All in good time. One should never be in a hurry to take important decisions. Agreed?'

'Except I have to make a living. My employers want results.' My response seemed so weak. I thought: are we both going to talk in riddles? 'Just a suggestion, but perhaps, it would be a good idea for you to visit England and inspect the product before placing an order? As our guest, of course, all expenses paid.' When he did not react, I asked, 'Is it easy for you to travel abroad?'

'It can be arranged. Everything is possible if the will is there. Would I be paid for this visit?'

'Paid?'

'A commission?'

'I'm sure that wouldn't present any problem,' I answered, trying to keep my responses casual. 'Is the idea of such a visit attractive to you?'

'It could be if it holds benefits.'

We were served hot Borsch with coarse black bread and we both ate in silence for a while.

'This is excellent,' I said. 'I've never had it before.'

'Did I not tell you? Russian food is good for the soul.'

After I took the last mouthful I asked: 'Exactly what sort of benefits would you be looking for?'

'Certain assurances.'

'As well as a commission?'

'Of course.'

I found myself floundering, knowing that now I had to move the dialogue onto a different level. This, together with the knowledge that I was on enemy territory – the restaurant was so obviously the preserve of top Party officials – there was always the possibility that I had been led like a lamb into a trap. Even if the table wasn't bugged, hidden cameras could be filming everything. Toying with my spoon, and pushing calm at him, I said: 'We're just fencing with each other, aren't we?'

'Are we?'

'Oh, I think so. But I'm used to that,' I continued, attempting to give the impression we were equally matched. 'If we meet your demands, my company usually looks for a long-term business relationship benefiting both parties. That inspires confidence. If I go back and ask them to grant you favourable terms, it would be reasonable, would it not, for them to expect a return gesture?'

I waited as the soup plates were removed and we were served with generous helpings of meat and cabbage. 'It comes down to mutual trust,' I resumed.

'So, how do we go about achieving that trust?'

'It begins here at this table,' I replied, becoming more confident. 'So you lead. Tell me what you would want.'

'No, you tell me what they would give,' he fenced.

'Luxuries.'

'Such as?'

'Enough to enable you to enjoy a much different life style.'

'And where would I enjoy that?'

'Your choice. But the first question they'll ask, of course, is whether your credit is good.'

He stopped eating and took out his cigar case, selected one and bit off the end. 'One accumulates a lot of credit in twenty years. It would a relief to cash it in and buy some security for one's old age.'

'Can you show them an indication of what you've accumulated? Something I could take back with me?'

His cigar case lay between us on the table. 'I thought you might ask that,' Vanya said. 'Help yourself to my last cigar, but don't smoke it until you get home. It will remind you of our pleasant meeting.'

I extracted the last cigar, held it to my nose as I had seen others do, and rolled it between my fingers before carefully tucking it into a breast pocket.

'Let's talk about specifics,' Vanya said. 'Assuming I have provided your people with enough to convince them of my credit rating, what is the next step?'

'Well, we deal in a variety of other goods. One of our subsidiary companies exports American refrigerators. It so happens a consignment of these is due to arrive here at noon on the final day of the fair in a truck with the name "Mayflower" on it. In your capacity as a Ministry official you could make it your business to inspect them.'

'Why would I do that?'

'To make certain they're all in good condition. You could reject a damaged one.'

'You think one might be damaged?'

'I'm sure of it. Delicate things refrigerators when they're transported over rough roads. The ice compartments always need careful scrutiny.'

'The ice compartment?'

'Yes. Where they put the guarantees and instruction booklets.'

I felt reasonably pleased at the way in which I had explained the plan.

'Guarantees are important,' Vanya said. 'Is there a time limit on them?'

'No. They're good for life. I think you'll find ours very generous.'

Vanya flicked his drooping cigar ash onto his plate. 'And what happens to the faulty refrigerator?'

Now I took the biggest risk. If he was playing with me then I was dead in the water, as Graham had put it. If, on the other hand, he genuinely intended to defect, then the final step of the plan had to be put to him. 'Eventually,' I began slowly, 'it will be returned to the factory in the United States. The delivery truck will be driven in by one man, but he could have a companion as he drives out.' I paused to let this sink in. 'The new guards will not think anything odd about this.'

'So who is the second man?'

'I leave that up to you.'

'Noon on the last day of the fair, you say?'

'Yes.'

Vanya signalled a waiter for the bill.

'Whatever you decide I enjoyed meeting you,' I said. 'Thank you for your hospitality.'

'Oh, this is your hospitality,' he said, pushing the bill across the table. 'We need all the hard currency we can get.'

'Of course.' I settled in dollars. It was a small price to pay to bring the ordeal to an end.

Vanya's car drove me back to my vehicle in the parking lot at the fair.

'Do you think you will place an order?' I asked him as we parted.

'I will study the proposal and price,' he said and surprised me by kissing me on both cheeks, though whether this was an affirmation or because we were being observed I had no means of telling.

TWENTY-NINE

'Lucky,' Graham said suddenly.

'Sorry?'

'I've just remembered the name of the cat.'

'What cat?' I said, baffled. It was entirely typical of Graham to break off in mid sentence and introduce a completely new topic . . .

'The one we had when we were first married. A tabby. Did you ever have a cat?'

'We had dogs. There was a cat, yes, a Tom, but you don't keep cats as pets on a farm. He was a good ratter, went feral in the end. What made you suddenly think of that?'

'Association. You playing cat and mouse with Vanya.'

'The only time I felt he was serious was when he said it would be a relief to cash in twenty years' credit. For "credit" read information.'

Graham said, 'Old pros like him are figure skaters who judge the thickness of the ice under their blades before striking out. The microfilm in the cigar he gave you was middle-grade stuff, nothing special. Still, I wouldn't expect him to pass over the crown jewels at this stage in the relationship. We must wait and see if he shows on the day. You did well from all accounts. Bringing some-body in from the cold is never easy.'

'There is one other thing. Guess who turned up at the fair? That arsehole Chivers who tried to fool us that he worked at Bletchley. Isn't that a coincidence? I told him to piss off before he blew my cover.'

'I always hate coincidences,' Graham said. 'They're seldom what they seem.

'Did anything else emerge about him?'

'Well, he was called up in 1942, only did his six weeks initial infantry training with the Essex Regiment, and was then discharged on medical grounds. Shaved his armpits, maybe, who knows? No record of him ever applying to be a fighter pilot. That was another piece of bullshit he gave you. The trail goes dead after that until he surfaces over here in the Control Commission and turns up too often for comfort where you're concerned. I've sent word to Machell at your old unit, to pull him in and have a chat. Could be that he turns out to be just a serial liar, but you never know.'

Waiting for the last day of the fair, I remained consumed by my anxiety over Lisa, unable to mentally wipe clean my final image of her. Over and over again I relived our last meeting, examining everything she had said like a forensic scientist searching a cadaver for clues to a death. I weakened and phoned the stage door number, and although I got through once, I was told she was not available. The shell of my life had been removed. I read once that true lovers never accept finality, or "closure" as the buzz word now has it. Such a stupid expression, I've always thought, since love, if genuine, is never subject to closure. We may move on but we never completely forget.

On an impulse I went to find Harry Webb. He and his team were readying the truck he was to drive to the East sector. A stencil of the "Mayflower" logo had been applied to both sides of the vehicle and half a dozen refrigerators were waiting to be loaded.

'Got a spare vehicle I can borrow?'

'Of course, sir. Take one of the Humbers,' Webb said, 'they've been checked out.'

I drove myself to the apartment I had rented for Lisa. As I pulled up in front of the house I saw a small boy sitting on the porch steps attempting to mend a crude wooden replica of a bomber plane. He scrambled to his feet as I approached, hiding the plane behind his back.

'Let me see,' I said in German.

He handed it to me. One wing hung loose from the fuselage.

'You need glue,' I asked. 'Do have any glue?' He shook his head. 'Here.' I held out some money. 'Buy yourself some.' Fear was replaced by surprise on his face as his hand closed over the notes. Without a word, he ran off.

Letting myself in, I heard the same Beethoven sonata being practised. I mounted to the second landing and entered the empty apartment. Looking around I thought, this could have been our bedroom, here she could have cooked us a meal, the other, smaller room could have been the nursery. I slumped down in a corner of the main room, my back pressed against the flaking plaster and stayed there for over an hour, chain-smoking, wondering what her days were like, whether by now she had visited her father and what had passed between them. Was she still carrying my child or had Grundwall ensured that he had the last word and persuaded her to find a way to abort? Above me, as though by thought transference, the unknown pianist began playing the song from *The White Horse Inn*. I felt cut off from everything and everybody – the recent encounter with Vanya seemed to belong to a doppelganger masquerading as me. Stubbing out my final cigarette, I exited the apartment and walked down to the basement. When Krenkler shuffled to the door at my summons, I handed him both keys.

'I'm returning these,' I said. 'My friend will not be coming after all.'

Krenkler said, 'I cannot give you back your money.'

'That's OK, spend it on vodka.'

Krenkler expression changed; he had obviously been expecting me to insist on partial repayment, but I just wanted out.

Returning the car to the garage I found that Webb was still working.

'Care to join me for a night on the town, Harry?' I said.

'Never say no, sir. I'm your man, soon as I've cleaned up and made myself respectable.'

We ate in a restaurant Webb had sampled before where the food was indifferent but the beer good. He drained his second stein and asked, 'This trip I'm going to make, sir. Fancy he'll show?'

'We're hoping he will.'

'Can't imagine what it must be like to take a step like that. Here I am wondering whether to put down roots here and he's about to turn his back on his homeland.'

'Are you worried about bringing him out'

'Yes and no. Makes a change from routine, something to talk about in years to come. Can't be as dangerous as Caen.' He veered off the subject and said, 'Forgive me asking, sir, but has your girlfriend moved in yet?'

'No. She's not coming after all. I returned the keys today. It didn't work out,' I said, cutting off further discussion. 'Let's go on somewhere. Got any suggestions?'

'Depends what you're looking for.'

'Oblivion.'

'Sorry, sir?'

'Don't keep calling me sir. We're off duty. My name's Alex. What am I looking for? Somewhere a bloody sight livelier than the Salvation Army canteen.'

'Right, Alex.' He used my Christian name awkwardly. When I had settled the bill for our meal, he drove me to nightclub in a side road off the *Kurfurstendamn*. Here the décor looked as though the designer had given up halfway through the make-over, the walls painted in lurid colours and decorated with Klimt prints. The tables had miniature flags of the three Allies on them and were grouped around a small dance floor where a few couples were gyrating slowly to recorded music. The waitresses were dressed in scanty outfits with pink bows in their hair. The manager advanced on us.

'*Guten abend, mein Herrs.*' He escorted us to a table one the edge of the dance floor. 'You wish champagne?'

'No. Bring a bottle of Scotch,' I said.

'Of course, *mein Herr.*'

When my eyes became accustomed to the dim lighting, I could

make out half a dozen women of indeterminate ages at the bar, all dressed to impress the punters. A couple of them glanced in our direction.

'This OK?' Webb asked.

'Sure.'

The Scotch, when it came, had a label I did not recognise. I poured two measures that old Machell would have approved of.

'To your safe return, Harry.' It burnt my throat as it went down. Two women joined us. The brunette asked: 'You wish company, gentlemen?' Her companion was a mousy blond.

'Why not?'

The brunette sat down next to me. 'I'm Inga,' she said, 'and my friend is Marlene.' Her friend, a fairly obvious dyed blond made sure that Webb didn't miss her eye-watering cleavage as she sat down.

'Well, Inga, would you like a Scotch?'

'D'you have champagne?

'Is that the house rule?'

She glanced to where the manager was hovering. 'Champagne is very nice.'

'Well, we mustn't deny you.' I signalled to the manager who was already half way to us. 'Champagne, *mein Herrs*?'

'How did you guess?' I said.

'You are British, *ja*?' Marlene said. She had a lisp.

'British to the core,' Webb answered.

'British are always so polite. We like British very much.'

'Marlene, eh?' Webb said. 'They wrote a song about you. Do you know Lily Marlene?'

'Oh, *ja*.'

'Big favourite of ours too.' Webb launched into a few bars, and the girls clapped their hands in exaggerated delight. Then Inga followed him in German.

'Sounds better in German,' I said, when she had finished.

'*Bitte*?'

'Much sadder,'

'Ah, yes, very sad,' she agreed.

'Shall I give them "We'll Hang Out the Washing on the Siegfried Line"?' Webb said.

'Maybe not.' The champagne arrived and was opened with a flourish despite the cork coming out with a plop rather than a bang. 'Bottled yesterday, was it?' I said. He took this with a smile.

The girls raised their glasses. 'Down the hatch,' Inga said.

'Ah, you've said that before, haven't you?'

'*Bitte?*'

'Never mind. *Skol.*'

Neither of them were great lookers, but they were pleasant enough. I listened as Webb chatted them up in his fractured German, which produced giggles. He was entirely at home, the typical British squaddie who knew his way around. I envied him.

'You are very quiet, you do not like me?' Inga said.

'Yes, I like you.'

'You wish to dance? Is good music, I think.'

'Very.'

I took her onto the cramped dance floor. She immediately pressed herself against me and I felt the warmth of her body and caught a whiff of the cheap cologne was wearing. Whether it was just the whisky or holding a woman in my arms for the first time in weeks, I found I was aroused. When the number came to an end we remained on the floor waiting for the next record.

'Are you lonely?' she asked.

'I've been lonelier.'

'I like you very much. Do you like me?'

'Yes, you're a very nice girl. Where are you from?'

'Before I am living in Leipzig. You know Leipzig?'

'No.'

'Is a beautiful city, but no work there.'

The next number was a slow waltz and again she danced with the lower part of her body pressed into me. When the music ended and we returned to our table I said to Webb, 'Shall we divide and conquer?'

'Sounds good.'

'The evening's on me, Harry.' I put some notes down on the table. 'Here, this should handle it. Have a good time. Let's go someplace else,' I said to Inga.

She took me to a house half a mile from the club where she lived in the basement. The living area had a divan bed in one corner covered with a fur throw, and in one corner there was a curtained-off kitchen area. The moment we were inside she killed the overhead light and switched on a small bedside lamp, filling the room with an orange glow, which she doubtless believed clients thought erotic.

'Do we settle the money first?' I asked.

'As you wish. I trust you. The British are always generous. *Bitte*, make yourself comfortable.' She disappeared into the bathroom.

I sat on the bed and noted a packet of condoms and a German Bible on the small table beside it. I removed my clothes, folding them neatly and placing them over the back of a chair. Naked, I got under the fur and waited for Inga's reappearance. When she reappeared from the bathroom she was wearing a pink robe which recalled the candlewick bedspreads my mother's generation thought the height of fashion. She let the robe drop to the floor, revealing a figure that owed more to the art of corsetry than to Nature. The contrast between her body and Lisa's immediately weakened my ardour. Inga joined me under the fur and reached down to fondle my flaccid penis before sliding down to fellate me. I willed my body to respond and her practised ministrations eventually produced the desired result. As soon as I was hard, she reached for a condom and expertly rolled it down my penis, then sat astride me and guided me inside her. For a few moments it seemed that I could perform, but then my erection collapsed.

'I'm sorry,' I said.

'You don't find me attractive?'

'On the contrary, and it's nothing to do with you. I've had too much to drink,' I said, wishing that was the real reason. The truth was the moment she had begun to writhe above me in simulated passion, disgust had replaced desire.

'You rest, then we try again. Yes, next time I make sure it is good.'

I lay back on the thin pillow, but when she again tried to rouse me I gently lifted her head from my groin. 'Don't,' I said. 'It's not your fault. I'll still pay you, don't worry.'

I swung myself off the bed, desperate to escape. I removed the limp condom and put on my clothes. Inga watched me impassively. I handed a generous amount of money to her.

'*Danke,*' she said twice.

Once outside I relished gulping in fresh air, happy that I had not fully betrayed Lisa, even though she would never be aware that I had strayed close to the brink.

THIRTY

'What time is it now?' Graham asked, wiping the eyepieces of his field glasses with a handkerchief.

'Just gone twenty past one.'

On the day when the East German Trade Fair was due to close we were in one of the Humbers, carefully parked so that we had an uninterrupted view of the East German Control point. There was a fair amount of traffic coming and going but, as the minutes ticked by, no sign of our white van.

'How far is the drive from the fair warehouse to here?'

'It took me roughly half an hour,' I said.

'Then they should have appeared by now if everything went to plan.' Graham refocused the glasses and swept the checkpoint again. 'More than the usual number of their bloody police around. Not a good sign.' From long habit he spoke softly, as if there was a danger of being overheard, then handed the glasses to me. 'Take a look.'

I adjusted the range to my own eyesight and zeroed in on the border guards marching stiffly along the line of the sandbag emplacement, carbines slung. A battered Opel had been stopped at the first control hut. The driver had been ordered out and prodded at rifle point into the hut by one of the *Vopos* while his companions searched the car. He eventually reappeared, allowed to get behind the wheel, then was ordered out again and given a body search before finally being allowed through.

'They're being extra thorough and jumpy today,' I said. 'Why, I wonder? Do you think they've got wind of our man?'

'Who knows? When you live by a siege mentality, everything and everybody is suspect.'

We sat in silence for another fifteen minutes staring straight ahead. There was a lull in the traffic; a few cyclists came through, but no vehicles.

'Difficult race to understand, the Germans,' Graham said suddenly. 'They're such a mixture. A poisonous mixture – all Brahms "Cradle Song" one moment, soothing and treacly, and then they switch to Wagner's booming sturms. And think how quickly that mob over there switched from Adolf to Uncle Joe. Change of uniform, change of philosophy, no problem. A few years ago those goons would have been wearing SS gear and herding Jews and Communists into the gas chambers . . . You can't believe how a whole nation could be taken in by that obscure charlatan with a Charlie Chaplin moustache. Of course it was all wonderfully stage managed – the Nuremberg rallies, the torch-light parades, the carefully designed uniforms . . . ' He was about to launch into one of his long philosophic monologues when I interrupted him.

'Our van's just appeared.' I handed him the field glasses and he fiddled with the focus, exclaiming, 'Jesus! Can't see a bloody thing. Your eyesight must be lousy.' He adjusted the glasses to his own vision and studied the scene. 'You're right. I can read our phoney Mayflower logo. It's just been halted at the first barrier.'

'Can you make out Vanya?'

'Well, there are two bodies in the cabin. Yes. They've both got out, Webb and another and they're both being directed into the hut. All very casual. Guards relaxed. One has gone to the rear of the van and is looking inside. Wait, wait!'

'What is it?'

'Another car has just pulled in front of our van. Black saloon, standard KGB issue. Came from behind the hut, obviously kept in readiness there. Three characters getting out of it. Doesn't look good.'

I took the glasses from him and quickly refocused. The three men Graham had mentioned were grouped to one side of their vehicle. Webb came out of the hut first, followed by Vanya. 'Both Webb and Vanya have reappeared,' I reported, 'and are walking towards our van.' As they got closer the three men made their move, closing in on either side of Vanya and bundling him into the saloon. I saw Webb react and run to the van. He managed to jump in behind the wheel and gunned the engine, accelerating towards the barriers. The guards started shooting out his tyres. After a couple of hits the van immediately veered crazily, but Webb managed to keep going and crashed through the first barrier. The sound of a siren carried to us and a further burst of gunfire came from the observation tower. I saw the windscreen on the van suddenly become opaque. Two more guards ran out and dropped to a kneeling position, pumping sustained automatic fire into the van which finally spun out of control and crashed onto its side by a bank of sandbags. The *Vopos* rushed to it and pulled out Webb's body.

'They've got Harry,' I shouted. 'The bastards have got Harry.'

Webb's body was quickly dragged out of sight and the black KGB saloon backed out and drove away. It was all over as quickly as it had begun.

'Oh, Jesus!' I said. I felt as though I had been watching a cinema trailer which didn't reveal the plot but showed the action highlights.

'That was all staged for our benefit. They knew we'd be watching,' Graham said. 'Let's go.'

'Go?'

'Yes, it's over and they know we're here somewhere, observing it.'

Reluctantly, I turned the ignition key and swung the Humber's wheel, reversing out of our space.

'What happens now?' I asked.

'They'll lodge a complaint about a violation of their border controls. We'll deny any knowledge or involvement. End of story.'

'That's it?'

'That's it.'

'Are you saying we're powerless to do anything?'

'Webb knew the risks. He knew nobody plays by the Queensbury rules. The body might be returned to us in due course. Maybe not.'

'Don't you care?'

'Of course I bloody care. I sent him in.'

I drove in silence for a while, reliving Webb's last moments, thinking to the night we had spent on the town with a couple of whores. Thinking, too, of a second flat in Krenkler's building that would now be vacant.

'Who d'you think blew the whistle?' I said finally.

'Could have been Vanya himself. Maybe he never intended to go through with it, just baited a trap which we fell into. Wouldn't be the first time. Then again he might have been serious, but got careless. We shall never know. Or, the worst scenario, somebody on our side gave them the tip-off. However you look at it, we fucked up.'

'Who knew except us?'

'London had to know and give approval.'

'So it could be that there is a mole?'

'Alex,' Graham said tersely, 'don't ask me questions I can't bloody answer. I'm as sick as you are. Webb was one of the best. But he took the job knowing he wouldn't get any help if it went wrong. And it went wrong.'

'How can you live with that?'

'I live with it because the game we're in requires me to. I do what I'm told to the best of my ability until they put me out to pasture. Then I'll have the rest of my life to mull over the insanity of it all. What you witnessed this afternoon is the dirty end of a dirty business, and if that doesn't sit with your conscience, get out while you can.'

'I might just do that,' I said slowly.

THIRTY-ONE

As predicted, the Soviets lodged a strongly worded condemnation about the incident and, in turn, our authorities blandly denied any knowledge or responsibility.

'How will we ever know whether Harry's dead or alive?' I asked.

'We won't unless they deign to tell us,' Graham replied. 'And we can't enquire about a man whose existence we've already denied.'

'Oh, bollocks, he was a serving British soldier.'

'No. The day they shot him he was a civilian working for a bogus refrigeration company.'

'We're talking about a man's life, for God's sake. What d'you tell his next of kin?'

'That he was killed in a car crash. His life will go into the Marie Celeste file, end of story. MI6 doesn't award posthumous gongs.'

'It's all madness. Madness.'

'Alex, I agree, but the object of the madness is to keep secrets. Take that away and the whole edifice collapses and we're out of a job.'

'God,' I said, 'you're such cynic.'

'Am I? I prefer to call myself a realist.'

That night I made an effort to get seriously drunk, seeking to obliterate some of my demons, but the alcohol barely dulled me. The recurring image of Webb's dead body being dragged out of the van made me realise that I was a fool to believe I could ever share Graham's values. Harry hadn't given his life for a cause, he had been a pawn sacrificed in some perverted game of chess. Graham might be able to accept the outcome without questioning the morality, but I couldn't.

The following morning he said, 'I've been thinking about your own situation in view of what happened. It's a dead cert they got you on film either at the trade fair or the restaurant Vanya took you to, which renders you a liability here. If I were you I'd put in for a posting elsewhere, some cushy desk job in a warmer climate.'

'What if I want out altogether? Didn't you say "if your conscience troubles you, get out?" '

'And does your conscience trouble you, Alex?'

'Yes. Yours doesn't, I take it?'

'I cannot afford a conscience, Alex.' He smiled as he said it.

That last remark decided me. Without telling anybody of my intentions, I packed an overnight bag and had one of our drivers take me to Templehof. I hung around at the airport until I managed to secure a seat on the last flight out to Hamburg. It was dark when the DC7 touched down and this time, since I was technically AWOL, instead of bumming a lift from the Military Police, I managed to find a rare taxi to take me to Lisa's flat and instructed him to wait.

Greta opened the door to me.

'If you were expecting to see Lisa,' she said, 'she isn't here.'

'Is she at the theatre?'

'No. She no longer lives here, thanks to you.'

I ignored the antagonism. 'So where does she live now?'

'With her mother.'

'Where? In Hamburg?'

'No.'

'Where then?'

'I cannot tell you.'

'Cannot or won't?'

'She told me not to give it to you.' There was a note of satisfaction in her reply.

I said, 'It's vital I see her.'

'Maybe not to her.'

'Just tell me where she is. Please.'

'I can't help you.' She went to close the door.

'Well, tell me one thing: was she well when last you saw her?'

'As well as could be expected. You should know about that.'

Now a young man appeared behind her. 'Anything wrong?' he asked in German.

'No,' Greta answered. Then to me: 'Don't waste your time looking for her, Englishman. She's finished with you.' The door was slammed shut.

For minutes afterwards I remained on the stairway, my back pressed against the peeling wall, trying to decipher what Greta had meant when she said "as well as could be expected". Did she mean Lisa was still carrying the baby or that she had aborted it?

I had the taxi driver take me to the theatre where I questioned one of the production staff.

'*Ja*, Lisa, she left,' the man told me.

'Any idea where she went?'

'No. We don't see her any more.'

I bribed the stage-door keeper in the hope that she might have left a forwarding address with him, but again drew a blank. I had a sudden longing for the familiar and told the taxi driver to take me to the *Haupbahnhof Platz*. The *Hotel Kronprinzen* had been patched up and the adjacent bombsites cleared since I was last there, but there were no rooms available and I tried the Atlantic Officers' club. There I struck lucky. When I had stowed my gear and had a wash I went down to the bar. There was a noisy party in progress in the adjoining dining room and the raucous behaviour of others enjoying themselves grated, punching home the bleakness of my own situation. I sat at the bar nursing a drink; memories of Lisa swirled around in my mind, my body remembering too much.

I looked up to find the ubiquitous Chivers standing beside me and anger resurfaced as I remembered our last encounter at the trade fair.

'Well, fancy,' he said, 'look who's here. I was hoping our paths would cross again.'

'Why was that? Thinking of flogging me a dodgy Leica?'

'You know why. I didn't care for your attitude the last time we met.'

'You didn't?

246

'No, it was totally out of line. You were bloody offensive and I want an apology.'

'Oh, piss off, you boring little man, or I'll tell you what I really think of you.'

'Let me remind you, I hold a superior rank.'

'Really? You mean the one you bought off the shelf?'

'I'm warning you, Captain.'

'OK, you've warned me, now go away and let me enjoy my drink before I get really offensive.'

'I'm not leaving until you apologise, otherwise I shall take the matter further. I don't intend to let it rest until I have satisfaction.'

'Is that supposed to frighten me?'

'If you know what's good for you, you'll apologise.'

I said, 'Don't threaten me. You forget it's my job to suss out dubious pricks like you, and I sussed you the first time you came into my orbit. You were never at Bletchley, that claim is as bogus as your put-on posh accent.' From Chivers's changed expression I saw that this had struck home. 'And for your information, I wasn't in East Berlin for my health and you probably blew an undercover operation. As a result one of my best men bought it.'

'How was I to know that?' Chivers blustered, no longer so sure of his ground.

'No, you were too busy with another of your scams. What's it going to be next? Flogging diluted penicillin? I hear there's a killing to be made there.'

'I don't have to listen to this and, by God, I'll have you for slander.'

Faces were turned in our direction as he raised his voice.

'Oh, get knotted you pathetic cunt,' I said as I stood up and pushed past him, spilling the remains of my whisky on his immaculate uniform jacket.

'You did that deliberately!'

'If only,' I replied as I left.

'I have witnesses,' Chivers shouted after me.

There was a knock on my bedroom door an hour or so later

and I answered it to be confronted by two Military Policemen. The sergeant saluted.

'Captain Seaton?'

'Yes.'

'Sir, we have to ask you to accompany us to the Provost Marshal's office.'

'What for?

'A charge of assault has been laid against you, sir.'

'Assault?'

'Yes, sir. By a Major Chivers, sir.'

'He's not a real bloody major. He's in the Control Commission.' The sergeant fidgeted, uncertain as to how to proceed.

'Right, you have your orders, so we'd better go.' I picked up my beret and they stood to one side to let me to exit first.

The Provost Marshal was a huge Scot called Reid who spoke in a gravelly Glaswegian accent that was difficult to penetrate. 'I gather you ran into a bit of trouble with one of our Control Commission johnnies. Bloody bane of my life. He's charged you with making slanderous remarks to a superior officer in front of witnesses and deliberately throwing a glass of whisky over him.'

'I wish it had been deliberate, but I wouldn't waste good Scotch on somebody like him. As to the slander, this is a character we're in the process of investigating. He alleges he spent the war in some hush hush outfit, but we've established that's a lie. I last saw him in the Russian sector of East Berlin while I was engaged in an undercover operation which went wrong. It's possible his presence there at the same time was the reason it went belly up and one of my team died as a result.'

'His statement says you abused him with foul language.'

'I called him a cunt and a prick, if that's what he's referring to. Nothing foul about that, just describing him accurately in two ways.' I surprised myself at how relaxed I felt about the whole thing.

'Had you been drinking, Captain?'

'Yes.'

'Heavily?'

'Not more than usual. I walked out of the bar without falling over and went to my room, where your men found me. They didn't have to carry me here.'

'Look, Seaton, between you and me, having met the man I wouldn't disagree with your description of him, but he's pressed charges and I haven't got any option. Are you stationed here in Hamburg?'

'I was. Now I'm in Berlin.'

'Field Security?'

'Not any longer. I'm MI6 now.'

'Ah!' Reid made a grimace. 'Well, you'd better return to Berlin, report the incident and await developments. I'll pass the papers to your superior and let him deal with it. Give me his name.'

'My head of station is somebody called Green.'

'What rank does his hold?'

'He doesn't have one. He's Foreign Office.' I gave Reid the details of our headquarters.

'Fine. Officially, I've advised you of the charge and possible consequences. Do you want to give me a statement of your version?'

'Maybe not. Never say anything that can be used against us, isn't that right?'

'Fair enough, I agree, laddie. I can't wait to show a clean pair of heels to this country and get home to the Isle of Bute. Ever been there?'

'No, sadly I haven't.'

'You should. Wonderful place. Well, good luck, laddie.'

'Thank you, sir.'

'Not at all. You're one of us and we look after our own.'

I saluted and left.

Later, when the charge papers eventually arrived on his desk. Graham asked, 'Couldn't you have steered clear of him? What on earth possessed you to get involved in a fracas with that character?'

'He started it. Demanded an apology for the way I treated him at the trade fair. That got me on the raw, and I more or less accused him of being the cause of Harry Webb's death. Which may not be too far from the truth, because Vanya spotted him and asked questions.'

Graham studied the papers. 'The charges are (a) conduct unbecoming of an officer in that you used obscene language and (b) you threw a glass of whisky in his face.'

'I accept the former, but as to throwing whisky in his face, that's bollocks. I accidentally spilled some on his jacket. Actually, I should have decked him. I was itching to.'

'He claims to have witnesses. Obviously I'll have to pass these papers to London.'

'Will I be taken out at dawn?'

'You'll certainly get your wrists slapped and it'll count against your advancement. However, my accompanying report will give our assessment of Chivers's dubious cv.'

'You assume I want advancement. I don't. Harry Webb's death has concentrated my mind. He was sacrificed for what? So that we could bring some bloody defector over to our side, pick his brains and keep the spy industry going? Well, fuck that. I can't take Harry's death in my stride like you. I'm not a natural for this game. It's all so bloody pointless and cynical; we win one war then start organising for the next.'

Graham said: 'Are you sure the real reason you're disillusioned isn't because of Grundwall and his daughter? Isn't that it? In your heart, you're regretting having turned him in?'

'No, that isn't the reason.'

'I think it has a lot to do with it, whether you admit it or not.'

'I didn't have a choice,' I said. 'The choice was made for me way back, in another place. That American war correspondence made it crystal clear to me.'

'Which American war correspondence?'

'The woman you asked me to take sightseeing. She said, "God left early in Buchenwald, if He was ever there." That summed it up for me.'

'Show me a time in this war when He didn't leave early,' Graham said.

THIRTY-TWO

All my anxieties were still concentrated on Lisa. In the eight months since the photograph of Grundwall overturned my life she had occupied my every waking thought and life without her was not tolerable. Again and again I relived our last sad meeting. Unable to accept the finality of our parting, I still clung to the misguided belief that true love always had a romantic ending. I dreamt of the idyllic time we had spent together in Krumpendorf, the delight I had experienced in seeing her perform on stage, the cry she gave when shaken by orgasm. Everything about her haunted me.

Taking a weekend pass I scrounged a spare Jeep from the transport pool and drove myself to Hamelin determined to test whether Grundwall might, despite everything, agree to see me and reveal Lisa's condition and whereabouts. I had a gut feeling that if we could only be reunited my love would be potent enough to surmount the past. I kept harking back to a remark Machell had once made about leaving a love child behind in the Punjab. Did my own love child still pulse in Lisa's womb or was I destined to bore strangers in my old age with stories of what might have been?

Hamelin was a city whose name I had been familiar with as a child after discovering the fairy-tale legend of the Pied Piper. It had been left relatively unscathed during the war. On arrival I went to the Military Police requesting directions to the prison where war criminals were housed on the pretext that I had to conduct a further interrogation of one of the inmates.

On arrival at the jail I requested a meeting with the prisoner governor who turned out to be a burly Texan Colonel named Altman who, far from being put out by my unannounced visit, greeted me warmly and immediately poured me a lethal shot of his private stock of bourbon. I think he was bored with his post-war job and couldn't wait to get back to the homeland.

'Who have you come to interview?'

'A man you're holding named Grundwall,' I said. 'We've got an ongoing situation, still searching for other SS personnel who served with him at Auschwitz. Never know, I might be able to prise some information out of him.'

Altman's expression changed. 'Grundwall? Didn't anybody brief you beforehand?'

'Brief me about what?'

'You've had a wasted journey, Captain. He's no longer here.'

'You mean he's been moved elsewhere?'

'Yeah, you could say that. Moved permanently elsewhere. He hanged himself.'

I drank some of the bourbon before I was able to respond, my thoughts winging back to another time and another death: Brigadier Hirst had snuffed out his own life because of an arcane code of honour – had Grundwall killed himself because he had finally acknowledged his guilt? 'When, how long ago?' I asked.

'Have to get my people to look it up if you want an exact date, but my recollection is it was about three weeks to a month back. We put some of the newer arrivals on suicide watch but, after evaluation, he wasn't considered a major risk. We were wrong, but on the other hand he's saved taxpayers a lot of money. Still, your people should have been informed, but that's typical. Every-thing takes an age to filter down.'

'What happens in circumstances like that? Are the families allowed to take the body away, or are they buried here?'

'Depends whether we can trace any relatives and whether they can afford the expense of shipping it out; otherwise we bury them in an unmarked grave.'

'And in his case?'

'Let me check. As you can imagine I don't actually give a fuck once they're crossed off my list.'

While he left his office to consult a member of his staff I figured

Grundwall must have hanged himself around the time I was in East Berlin meeting Vanya. Not that it made any difference when he did it, he was gone, out of it and now my major obsession was how I could trace Lisa's present whereabouts.

Returning with a log book, Altman said: 'His wife was informed of the facts of his death as required. But we don't send flowers,' he added with a grin. 'Subsequently the daughter and a man stated to be a relative, came here to make arrangements for Grundwall's coffin to be shipped to his birthplace, a small town near Brunswick. More than that I can't tell you. Any use?'

'Do you have a current address for his wife?'

He consulted the log book again. 'All his record shows is the Hamburg address where he was first arrested. Nothing else. Is it important for you to trace her, now that he's dead?'

'Probably not,' I lied. 'Well, thanks. Sorry for taking up your time.'

'Give your lot hell for not checking before they sent you down here.'

'Don't worry, I will,' I said, playing along with the myth that I had come on an official mission.

'Well, at least let me treat you to some decent chow before you go back. I had some prime steaks flown in from my home state yesterday. Cut like butter.'

Although I enjoyed his generous hospitality, half-listening to him discoursing on the various blessings of life in Texas, my own thoughts constantly returned to what I could or should do next. Lisa had made it clear she never wanted to see me again for exposing her father and whatever slender hope I still harboured at being able to change her mind, his suicide seemed destined to put the final nail in my coffin. The realisation that she was now lost to me forever induced in me a fear greater than any I had experienced during the fighting outside Caen. Many times since I have thought of my unrequited love for Lisa as being like the unending absence caused by death. Throughout that friendly, well meant, meal I felt more and more disengaged from the life I had been leading; what consumed me as Altman described the American dream he would be returning to, was the realisation that Grundwall's suicide had brought everything full circle, and circles have no ending. From that chance, innocent, meeting in a bookstore I had been sucked into the nightmare of his past and now, sitting at a stranger's table within the prison walls where he had ended it all, I saw with hideous clarity that, in bringing him to justice, I had fashioned my own tragedy. The choice I had made to expose him may have revealed his crimes but it had also resulted in the destruction of my own happiness.

Any journey that ultimately proves fruitless always seems to double the distance travelled and my return trip to Berlin was no exception. I had gone to Hamelin if not with high hopes at least with some expectations. Although I felt no residual guilt about Grundwall's demise, the absence of any clues to Lisa's present whereabouts or the fate of my child left me horribly deflated.

Once back in Berlin I found I had been docked a month's pay as a result of the charges Chivers had levelled against me, the incident duly marked on my record sheet. I was also required to have an interview with the General commanding Group, a character in his late forties who wore a black eye patch, treated me as a wayward son who had strayed, but could be saved.

'Apart from this recent and isolated incident, Captain Seaton, I see your conduct has been exemplary throughout your service. You're exactly the sort of officer we want in a peacetime Army. Your records state you were first promoted in the field, which is highly significant. Your present rank is not substantive, but I could help there. In the normal course of events you could expect to make major within five years but who knows how far somebody with your qualities could go? You have the profile we badly need if we are to consolidate the peace. The Army is always here to help. If you have a personal problem, let's discuss it confidentially. It won't go further than this room. Do stand at ease. Are you married?'

'No, sir.'

'Family?'

'My mother and father, sir.'

'And they're still alive, are they?'

'Yes, sir.'

'Money problems?'

'No, sir. Except like everybody else I wish I had more.'

He smiled and fingered his eye patch. 'Until now your life has been cocooned by the Army, has it not? It's natural, inevitable, that after coming through a long war, you should feel uncertain as to the future. We all do. The way ahead is certainly going to be a challenge, but that is why people such as you are needed for the task. That's not flattery, just a statement of fact. A career in the Regular Army should not be dismissed lightly. It offers security, a superior life style that separates you from the humdrum. I would be failing in my duty if I did not make every effort to persuade you to sign on for a long-term commission.'

The rosy prospect he dangled in front of me had the reverse effect from what he intended. The more the he rattled on, the more I wanted to test the waters of the unknown sea of civilian life. I needed to put distance between me and the country of Lisa's birth. I listened politely to his arguments, for they were well meant, but they did not change my mind. I stuck to my guns and set in motion my determination desire to leave the Army for good.

My discharge papers came through ten weeks later, weeks I used to try and discover any clues to Lisa's whereabouts, but drew nothing but blanks. She seemed to have disappeared, swallowed up by the shifting tides of the homeless and stateless in a divided Germany, leaving no trace. I finally had to admit defeat.

With my gratuity and some back pay I was entitled to, I departed the Army with £345, more money than I had ever possessed. I delayed telling my parents what I had done; I lied, writing to them that I was taking up a new position which would mean I would be out of contact for a few weeks. I wanted some breathing space in which to take stock of my life.

On the eve of my departure I had a farewell dinner with

Graham in the same restaurant in the French sector where our relationship had begun.

'So, the deed is done,' Graham said. 'You've chosen this moment to leave what will probably become the only growth profession in the West. So what next?'

'I've no idea.'

'Haven't you made any plans?'

'No.'

'None at all? Doesn't that scare you?'

'Not yet, but I'm sure it will. Like you, I made plans once but they didn't work out.'

'Well, let's keep in touch. You've taught me a lot, Alex.'

'Me? What could I have possibly taught you?'

'That principles count. The required Establishment teaching is that principles are for those without ambition. If you want to prosper in the corridors of power, never give a straight answer when an obscure one will suffice. Dissemble until such time as questioner has forgotten what he originally asked.'

'But you've often spoken out,' I said.

'No, and on the one occasion I did it worked against me. So let that be my last piece of advice to you. By the way, I've never asked you this, did you vote Labour?'

'Yes. Yes, I did. Although I thought it a pity they couldn't continue with a National government that had held up well during the war, I decided that a change might be a good thing.'

'Do you still feel that?'

'Not sure.'

'Wait until you get home and sample it. Both major parties are only interested in absolute power in order to be corrupted absolutely.'

'I shall miss your cynicism, Graham. It's been a breath of fresh air.'

'Or flatulence maybe? I've gone beyond mere cynicism, I'm now totally disillusioned with everything and everybody,' he said with one of his enigmatic smiles.

And on that note we parted for good, because we never did keep in touch although by chance I came across his name in a copy of *The Times* when he was awarded a knighthood. My last act before leaving Germany was to post a letter to Lisa care of the Hamburg theatre asking for it to be forwarded. Whether it was, or whether, on receipt, she chose to ignore it, I was never to know.

When I arrived in Harwich I was quickly made aware that my life had irrevocably changed. Dragging my heavy duffle bag, I made my way to the Custom sheds. Overhead the gulls swooped low in the grey sky as they too searched for booty. A middle-aged Preventive Officer with an apology for a moustache singled me out. 'Anything to declare, Captain?'

'I don't think so.'

'You don't think so? No cigarettes or booze?'

'No booze, just a few cigarettes.'

'What d'you call a few?'

'Fifty.'

'How about cameras?'

'No,' I said.

Beyond the shed a departing ferry sounded its mournful Klaxon, like a funeral bell.

'Open your duffle bag, please, Captain.'

I obliged. He rifled through the contents and took out a package wrapped in brown paper. 'What is inside this, Captain?'

'An inkwell.'

'Inkwell? Show me, please.'

I opened the package and explained: 'A souvenir. I took it from Josef Kramer's room at Belsen.'

He gave me a quizzical look and turned it over in his hands. 'Why would you want this as a souvenir?'

'I guess to remind me of the horrors I left behind.'

'Are you on home leave?'

'No. Happily I'm being demobbed at last.'

'And you have nothing else? No jewellery for a girl friend?'

'No jewellery, no girl friend.'

Still not inclined to believe me, he thrust his arm down to the bottom of my duffle bag and rifled around but this time produced no further treasures to interest him. 'Right,' he said curtly, obviously disappointed. 'You can go, Captain.'

'Thanks for the welcome home,' I said, but the sarcasm was lost on him.

I made my way to the platform where the London train was waiting. A cold wind blew in from the sea, swaying the chains hanging from the giant cranes. I bought a copy of that day's *Express* at the newsstand and was surprised how thin it was. I decided I would treat myself to a last bit of privilege and went in search of a First Class carriage. Stowing my gear, I was joined by a 2nd Lieutenant my own age wearing the wings and red beret of the Parachute Regiment. He immediately put his feet up on the opposite seat, loosened his battledress jacket and offered me a cigarette. 'On your way for demob?'

'Yes,' I said. 'You too?'

He nodded. 'Thought it would never come. Are you looking forward to it?'

'Yes, I suppose so, though I guess it'll feel odd not to be wearing a uniform after all this time. A leap into the unknown, like your first jump I imagine.'

'Nothing's like your first jump,' he said. 'You've trained for it, looked forward to it, and then when you actually have to do it, you wonder if you're insane. Mind you, the second is the worst because by then you know what to expect. Can I take a look at your paper?'

'Sure, go ahead.'

He glanced at the front page headlines. 'Oh, great! Old Bevin promises we'll all get a job. Give me a break. Is there one waiting for you?'

'Not really.'

'Me neither. I'm going to blow my gratuity taking my girl to the seaside for a dirty week. Don't intend to get out of bed for forty-eight hours.'

A few minutes later our train pulled out of the station, gradually picking up speed as it passed rows of identical houses such as a child might draw, just basic boxes. Their small back gardens all had sandbag-topped Anderson shelters sunk into the patch of lawn, the flower beds now given over to vegetables. There was little evidence of bomb damage in that part of Essex and it wasn't until we reached the outskirts of Colchester that I saw fields scarred with bomb craters, here and there a ruined building, a church with its steeple chopped in half, a burnt-out warehouse. The roads seemed like narrow twisted ribbons compared to the autobahns I had left behind. As the train sped through country halts, in the patchwork of fields small children paused in play on tops of concrete blockhouses and waved. The passing scene, so unlike the country of the damned I had left behind, mesmerised me. My head lolled against the grimed carriage window and I lapsed into an uneasy cat nap, only waking when we were entering the grey outer rim of the metropolis. Here everything was uniformly drab, the pedestrians in the streets like Lowry stick figures. I felt I was coming home to a foreign city that had been left unfinished, that those who first designed it had lost heart halfway and settled for a formless chaos. I opened the carriage window and gulped in sooted air.

'Where's your home?' the Lieutenant asked as we both began to gather up our belongings.

'Lincolnshire.'

'Coventry, me. Ever been there?'

'No. Coventry took a pasting, didn't it?'

'And how. My mother and little sister were both killed when the house bought it. So I'm going to my girlfriend's place in Oxford. Handy if I ever get to university.'

'Well, I wish you luck.'

'Likewise. Good to meet you. Least we made it, didn't we?'

The train pulled in beneath the shattered glass dome of Liverpool Street station, our carriage stopping in front of an old, defaced poster warning that Careless Talk Costs Lives. I walked with the throng to the barrier, past a Nestle chocolate machine empty now of the penny bars I had bought as a child. A crowd of relatives and girlfriends was waiting to greet the passengers and I felt a tinge of envy as a pretty blonde rushed forward to embrace my travelling companion.

I had a railway warrant entitling me to travel to the Aldershot depot and there complete the demobilisation procedure, so I took the Tube to Paddington and caught another train. Once in the depot, my measurements were taken and I drew a suit, a pair of shoes, a shirt, pairs of socks, a tie, a Trilby hat, a food ration book and another of clothing stamps.

Outside the depot touts were offering to purchase the entire collection for a few pounds. I gave one of them the Trilby hat for free, having decided that it made me look ridiculous, then it was another train back to London at the end of a long day. I checked into the YMCA at Tottenham Court Road, which even in those far-off days was known to be a favourite haunt of sexual predators, but by then I was too tired to care. The following morning, I went for a walk and eventually found a small cinema showing a French film, *Mayerling*, starring an actress I had never heard of named Danielle Darrieux. It was the first French film I had ever seen.

That night I dreamed I was lying in bed beside Lisa, both of us dressed like the doomed lovers of Mayerling and I had my service revolver pressed against her temple. I awoke before I pulled the trigger, sweating and disorientated, unable to get my bearings for several minutes. As I gradually became aware of where I was I thought back to Germany, to the rooms I had occupied there, first in the *Hotel zum Kronprinzen*, then the brothel-like accommodation in Berlin and, most of all, the room where Lisa and I had often made love in the afternoons.

THIRTY-THREE

The following morning I sent a telegram to my parents telling them that I was back in circulation and returning home, preparing to tell them a fiction about having been on one last secret mission to account for my long silence. When I eventually told this fiction, I made light of the fact that I had resigned my commission.

'I'm sure they were sorry to lose you,' was all my mother said. She was just so happy to have me home for good. Both my mother and my father had further aged since my last visit, my father in particular was more hunched, his face drawn and lined, his hair above the plimsoll line of sunburn, thinner.

'You did more than your bit, if you ask me,' he said. 'And you didn't come home with a German bride like some, though I expect you left a few broken hearts behind from what you told me last time.'

'Not really,' I said.

'Our prisoners of war finally went back.' He lit one of his cheroots and I noticed how twisted his fingers were as he cupped his hand around the match. 'So, until you decide what you want to do, I'd appreciate a bit of help around the place. I'm not trying to make up your mind for you, don't think that, it's just that I don't get around to things as fast as I used to, do I, mother?'

'You do as well as anybody else,' she replied, ever loyal.

'Of course,' I said. 'I need some exercise.'

I couldn't sleep that first night I was home and in the small hours I crept down to the kitchen and made myself a cup of tea, using the iron kettle that stood on the blackened stove that was never allowed to go out. By the light of the paraffin lamp, I studied the room – the pine dresser stacked with odd pieces of crockery, the worn wooden chairs, the large zinc sink fed by a single cold

261

water tap – and I wondered how my mother had managed all the years, seldom taking a holiday, she and my father always at the mercy of the elements, always tied, like jailers, to the needs of the animals. I tried to imagine them being in love when starting out in marriage. Thinking of them as they now were, settled into a placid companionship (when had I last seen them kiss?) I tried to trace the map of their love, but they had left me few signposts. Where, in which room, at what time, had they joined together to make me? Had my father come in sweating from the fields, suddenly gripped with the urge to procreate, or had it been just an act of familiarity between two people who shared the same bed?

Awaking early and disorientated in my old bedroom the following morning, it was several minutes before I realised where I was. The room was bright; sunlight hit the wall opposite my bed, the shadows of leaves forming shifting patterns. There was a familiar smell of lavender polish and the bedclothes had a downy softness that came from being washed in rainwater. I lay listening for the familiar hum of traffic that had characterised my stay in London, but the only thing to break the silence was the insistent cry of a wood pigeon. Rising, I went to the open window. Beneath me half a dozen Rhode Island Reds were fluttering to escape as the rooster made repeated attempts to mount them; beyond, the flat landscape stretched to the horizon and the regular beat of a pumping station engine in a distant fen reached me in the still morning air. I felt rested and at peace.

After the ample fried breakfast my mother cooked for me, I parcelled up my demob suit and drove into Woodhall Spa. I parked in front of my old school where in the playground the children were at morning break, one group of small boys flicking cigarette cards against the wall, another group playing "fives". I was surprised how small the school building was, indeed how small all the neighbouring Victorian houses appeared. I watched the scene for a few minutes then walked to the general store. Pausing just inside the doorway I drank in familiar scents before going to the middle-aged woman behind the counter.

'Mrs Hundleberry?'

'Yes.'

'Alex Seaton.'

She clapped a hand to her mouth. 'Good gracious. I'd never have recognised you. My, how you've grown. Are you home on leave?'

'No, I'm out for good at last.' I put my parcel on the counter. 'If you won't be offended I thought perhaps this suit might fit your Charlie. I seem to remember he was about my size.'

'Bless you, my duck, but my Charlie's dead,' she said. 'He died in a Japanese prisoner of war camp.'

'I didn't know. I'm so sorry, forgive me.'

'Nothing to forgive, it was a kind thought and he'd have appreciated it. You were always good friends, you two. Up to all the mischief.'

'Well, perhaps you can find a home for it elsewhere. Give it to anybody you like. How is Mr Hundleberry?'

'He's gone too, my dear. Two years ago come March. Now there's only me keeping this going. Still, I manage.'

'My parents didn't tell me. They're not good letter writers,' I said lamely.

'No, well, folks don't want to write bad news, do they? Enough of that around. We had the lovely Air Force boys stationed in the big house. I used to lie in bed at night counting the planes taking off, then counting them home again. Course some didn't come back, more's the pity.'

I felt compelled to buy something. 'Do you still have any of those . . . what d'you call them? Pinafores? I thought I'd take one for my mother.'

'I've got a few somewhere.'

She disappeared into the dark recesses of the cluttered shop and came back with a selection of three flowered-patterned aprons. I chose the brightest. 'What do I owe you? And how many coupons d'you want?'

'None from you, my duck. I don't bother with them stupid things.'

'Well, don't get into trouble.'

I gave her seven and six for the pinafore, and bought a bottle of whisky for my father.

Next I drove to the Kinema in the Woods, remembering as a child the excitement of the once weekly visit and where, if you paid the top price, you sat in deck chairs. The posters outside were advertising *The Seventh Veil*, starring James Mason and Ann Todd. I mooched around the village for a while longer, reminding myself of old haunts, and then drove home. In between aiding my father, this was the pattern I followed for the first six months, sometimes venturing further afield, reminding myself of places and scenery that had once been the extent of my world. Many of the adjacent farms had the same air of neglect as ours: rusting equipment half buried in nettles, here and there a hay wagon with a wheel missing, everywhere evidence that the war had denuded the countryside of old skills. On the first Sunday after my return, I accompanied my parents to the evening service in the simple Wesleyan chapel that stood isolated on the road to Walcott Dales. A sudden cloudburst bounced noisily off the corrugated iron roof, drowning out the hymn singing while it lasted. I had no surge of religious belief but carried off a pretence for my mother's sake, kneeling in prayer, but not praying for a renewal of faith, just for some answer that would make sense of the rest of my life.

As the months went by the tempo of my day-to-day existence gradually changed. Working alone mending the gaps in the wire fences enclosing our land, or else mucking out the stables and fetching fresh hay for the two Shires, the unaccustomed physical exertion calmed my previous restlessness, and my bare arms acquired a tan, the muscles tautened and I enjoyed a new feeling of well-being. I slept well and let my beard grow, my skin softened from washing in rainwater taken from the butts. There was the long-forgotten pleasure of seeking out hidden nests in the hedgerows and bringing back a bowl of fat, brown eggs, but I found I still could not bring myself to wring a chicken's neck. I went into Spalding one market day and came home with a black Labrador I named Harry.

'Funny name for a dog,' my father said.

'I suppose so,' I said, but volunteered no explanation.

Some nights we took shotguns and a torch and killed rats in the shed where giant Bramley apples were stored in a sea of chaff. I fell into the unhurried rhythm of the countryside where events were dictated by the weather as though I had never left it. With every passing week geographical memories of Germany receded, though a day never went by when I did not think of Lisa and feel the pain of loss. Alone in the fields I sometimes stood still, seeing again the room she shared with Greta, seeing her face taut with rejection as I left for the last time.

When my father and I were working together it was always my job to fetch our lunches and a flask of tea. When I returned from the house on this particular day he was not where I had left him. I shouted for him but got no answer. I first looked in the stables then went to the Dutch barn, but there was no sign of him there. It was the dog who led me to him, zig-zagging ahead of me to the lean-to where the tractor was kept. As I turned the corner I saw my father lying with part of his body under the connected harrow. I went through the motions of feeling for a pulse on the side of the neck, and then opened his faded shirt and placed my hand over his heart, but I could not discern any sign of life. Although blood from a gash above one eyebrow had riveted down one cheek, I doubted if this had been the cause of death, it seemed more likely that he had suffered a massive coronary. Clenched between the first two fingers of the right hand, his last cigarette had burnt itself out, searing the calloused skin. I prised the butt free and then eased the body clear of the harrow before closing his eyes. Drained by the suddenness of it all, I sank down, resting my head against the tractor's wheel arch, while I thought how I should break the news to my mother. I stayed there for quite a while and a rooster strutted into view and stood crowing as though incensed by finding another present. Harry stretched out on his belly at a distance and whined, sensing the presence of death. When, finally, I got up and walked to the house I found my mother in the diary, churning butter. I went to her and took her hands from the handle. 'Come inside, Mum,' I said, 'I have to tell you something.'

'I can't leave this now.'

'Yes, leave it.'

'What, what's happened?'

'Dad's had an accident. Come inside and sit down.'

Her voice and expression changed. 'No, tell me here. What sort of accident?'

'A bad one,' I said.

She made a cry like a wounded animal. 'How bad? Tell me. Show me where he is.' Before I could stop her she ran out. I chased after and it took all my strength to hold her. 'There's nothing we can do,' I said. 'He's gone.'

She struggled free and started to run across the yard, scattering the chickens. Seeing it was useless to try and stop her, I followed. When I caught up with her she was cradling his body and wiping the blood from his face with the edge of her apron. 'He wouldn't have known anything,' I said. 'It must have happened instantly because he was fine when I left him, right as rain, talking about us all going to Skegness next week.'

She rocked to and fro. 'He always worked too hard,' she said. 'I told him time and time again, but he'd never listen.'

'That was Dad,' I said. 'Always his own man.'

'We can't leave him here.'

'I'll call and get help.'

'You make the calls, I'll stay with him.'

'No, come back inside, please, Mum.' I helped her to her feet and led her back to the house and seated her in a chair.

'The butter won't have churned,' she said.

'Doesn't matter. You sit here.' I made her a cup of tea with plenty of sugar then made the calls that had to be made. Two neighbours came and we brought my father's body into the house and laid him out on the bed. Later our GP arrived, made his examination and signed the death certificate and afterwards took me outside.

'Will there have to be a post mortem?' I asked. 'I hope not, for my mother's sake.'

'I don't think so. See, there was a history, Alex. He had a chronic murmur. A couple of times in the past year I told him to ease off. I said to him, give up the fags and the whisky too, but I don't think he took any notice.'

'Did my mother know?'

'Only if he told her. I certainly didn't give out any hints.'

I made arrangements for the funeral. My mother did not want the body to be removed to a chapel of rest and refused to go to bed but sat beside his body all through that last night. Her main concern was that he should be dressed in his best suit before being put into the coffin.

As the news travelled a succession of neighbours came to give their condolences.

'Flowers,' his mother said. 'What sort of wreath would be right?'

'Did he have a favourite flower?'

'He used to buy me roses on our anniversaries.'

'Well, roses would be perfect.'

She never cried in front of me, but the shock and grief had visibly changed her, she seemed suddenly smaller. In the days before the funeral the house acquired an extra layer of silence such as descends on the land after a heavy snowfall. The funeral was well attended, the small chapel packed with friends, many of whom were strangers to me. I gave a short Address, frequently stumbling over the words as the finality of the occasion struck home. Afterwards we held a small wake in the house, and then I and my mother were alone again.

'What will happen?' she said, fingering the cards she had removed from the wreaths. 'What will happen to the farm?'

'Nothing. Nothing will happen. I shall stay and look after it.'

'You couldn't manage it on your own.'

'Then I'll hire some help. Don't worry about that now.'

'You're sure? You told him you wanted to do something different before.'

'Well, that was before. I'd changed my mind.'

'Were you able to tell him before he died?' she said.

'Yes,' I lied.

THIRTY-FOUR

For the next two weeks after the funeral I concentrated on sorting out my father's affairs and preparing the information for probate. Save for a small legacy to the RAF Benevolent Fund, the simple will gave everything to my mother. He had kept a crude ledger in a school exercise book, everything meticulously noted in his sloping handwriting and the final balances married with the bank statements. A separate exercise book locked in a box listed the cash sales of surplus eggs, butter and bacon sold in the village on the black market. When all outstanding debts had been paid, the bank account was in credit for just over a thousand pounds. The mortgage on the house had been paid off, although there was an annual rent on the extra land he had leased at a later date. After doing the sums I calculated there was no immediate need to worry but obviously I had to ensure that the farm stayed solvent. I knew that I could not maintain it single-handed and would need help so my first priority was to find and hire a live-in waggoner.

Mrs Hundleberry's shop had always been the village pump where word of mouth quickly circulated, so I made my needs known to her. She came up with a name a week later, a widower named Jack Warrender whom I vaguely remembered. Warrender had been made redundant from his previous job and, as a result, had lost the tied cottage that went with it. In return for board and lodgings and a salary just over the going rate, the deal was struck. Warrender was able to turn his hand to most tasks, was good with animals, and had the experience that I lacked.

I knuckled down to the harsh regime that we shared between us, rising while it was still dark, lighting the boiler fire to warm the mash for the horses, feeding household swill to the pigs and attending to other necessary chores before going in for breakfast. That first season we were fortunate, the beet harvest commanded a good price, the sow gave birth to a healthy brood and the potato yield was up on the previous year. I traded up the old tractor for a later model, and when funds allowed, converted one of the upstairs rooms into a bathroom with an inside toilet, something my mother had wanted for years.

Warrender had a taciturn nature, for he was that rare soul, a man content with his lot. He ate his meals with my mother and me, but for the most part kept to himself. On Sundays when he finished his chores he set his fishing lines along the river bank while he went to morning service and invariably returned to find a catch of bream. It was a simple life we all shared, light years away from my previous existence in occupied Germany and when I was working alone in the fields under the wide, sheltering sky, a sudden longing for Lisa would stab me like a knife. Where was she now? Had she given birth to my child? In desperation I wrote to my old boss, Graham, and asked him to feed Lisa's name into the system and tell me if anything showed up, but he drew a blank. It was still so easy for both the innocent and guilty to disappear in that shattered country, the vaunted Nazi bureaucratic efficiency no longer operating and the process of putting the structure of society together again proceeding slowly. The only reminder of my past came in a letter from Machell saying that he had finally been pensioned off and had moved to a seaside cottage in Dorset where I would always be welcome. 'Let me have news of you if you feel like it,' he wrote. 'Don't end up like me, bored out of your skull.'

Although the life I was leading took me further and further away from the world of occupied Germany, I couldn't help thinking what a long journey it had been from the Normandy beaches to this – a journey from innocence to disillusion, marking me as indelibly as the tattooed number on a Holocaust victim's wrist. Sometimes I was convinced I could smell the stench of Belsen as I relived the moment when I injected the lethal dose of morphine into the wasted arm of that grief-demented *Unter-menschen*. In all probability she had been the same age as Lisa, when I ended her misery. Ah, Lisa, it always came back to Lisa. Sleepless in the still small hours of the night when rats scurried in the eaves, images of her came crowding back. Sometimes in my dreams I walked myself through the empty rooms of that unused Berlin flat I had rented in joyous expectation of furthering our love. At other times I turned in my bed expecting to see her lying beside me. Visiting the chaff house, the scent of rotting apples would immediately transport me back to the cider press in hills behind the *Gasthof* at Krumpendorf where I had first discovered the meaning of happiness.

Mostly my day-by-day life had a monotony, dulling my senses, but I was jolted back into reality by the changes in my mother; she started to neglect herself and her memory came and went like a lighthouse beacon, now illuminating what she trying to recall, now swinging away into darkness. The deterioration was most marked as she went about her normal household chores: the most mundane tasks confused her, she would make the tea with a kettle that had not boiled, lay the table with four places instead of three, addressing Warrender by my father's Christian name. Once, coming in after a day in the fields I found her making a bonfire of furniture in the yard. These eccentricities caused me growing concern and a few weeks later she slipped in the new bathroom, cracking her head against the toilet. Concussed and bleeding profusely she was taken to hospital and there she went downhill very rapidly. I visited her daily but the accident seemed to have accelerated her mental deterioration and now she was like a trapped, birdlike creature lying motionless in the white nest of the hospital bed. At times she treated me as a stranger; if I held her hand she pulled it away as though I was personally responsible for her condition. There were moments when I saw nothing in her face but anger. The pattern was the same whenever I saw her: no glimmer of recognition and the only time she spoke she called me by my father's name. It was hard to reconcile the silent, immobilised, resentful creature with the person who had loved and nurtured me since birth. She lingered for three months before finally being released from her nightmare of non-existence.

This time I had no wake after her funeral, but returned to the silent house and sat in the unused best room which still retained its musty smell. There, alone, I demolished half a bottle of whisky and thought about the whole business of living. Ever since coming home I had been consciously acting out a lie, pretending an affinity with the land so as not to offend my parents, but now both had gone I no longer had any need for such deception. I could not see myself taking the same, long route to the grave as my father. The war years and the time spent in the occupation had released me from the bondage of familiarity and for an all too brief period I had glimpsed a future to be shared with the daughter of an enemy before the chance revelation of her father's past changed all my tomorrows. The loss of Lisa still filled my being and as I sat there in the family "best" room that had seldom been used, I saw my life as a book borrowed from a library I had been forced to return before finishing it. I knew I had to escape from the suffocating sameness of life on the farm though I had no idea of where I would escape to. Any decision being preferable to a slow drift towards apathy, the next morning I determined to put the house, land, livestock and chattels on the market. I know one is supposed to feel a lasting affinity with the place of one's birth, and maybe some people do, but I harboured no such sentimentality.

It was over two months before a suitable buyer appeared, a man not unlike my father in appearance, or at least how I remembered my father when younger: the prospective purchaser had the same weather-beaten features, revealing calloused hands when he rolled his hand-made cigarettes. He paid the asking price with only the minimum of argument and afterwards I suspected I had pitched my price too low. From the proceeds I gave Warrender £1000 which he told me would enable him to buy himself a place to live if the new owner did not want to employ him. I walked away without looking back and took a room in a small B & B hotel in Coningsby while I thought out my next move. The sale of the house had provided me with a measure of financial security for the first time in my life, but the sea change in my fortunes proved difficult to come to terms with. Service in the war had matured me in some ways but left me inadequate in most others; the Army cocoons you from the realities of life; without that shield, I lacked any positive qualities as a civilian, the skills of an interrogator of ex-SS members being of little commercial value in the England of 1948. The problem was that my age group had been socially immature when called up; before any of us had a chance to decide what we should do with our lives, the conflict decided for us. Many of those who had came through unscathed, now found themselves rootless, alienated from the post-war world of those who had not had front-line experience of the fighting. We had witnessed violent death, delivered death in return and would never again take our own mortality for granted. Often when jerked awake in the middle of the night from a particularly disturbing dream, I would again relive the moment when I helped that victim of Belsen to die.

The instant, self-congratulatory mood in the country produced by the victory had gradually evaporated as we were forced to accept that the war had bankrupted us, the most obvious manifestation being that rationing was kept in force; class wars, the most damaging of peacetime conflicts, still flourished because it was impossible for the new government to deliver its promise of equality for all. Free dentures maybe, but while the rich might be less rich, the poor remained poor. There was a sense that the majority were morally tired, that the long war, culminating in the use of the atomic bomb, had changed all the rules governing human behaviour. I was no exception.

On an impulse I wrote to old Machell and asked if he had a spare room for me to come and stay for a few days. His reply saying I would be very welcome came by return of post. 'I'll have a couple of fierce mahoganies waiting for your arrival,' he wrote. 'The solitary life has little to commend it.'

He had ended up in a bungalow in the small Dorset village

of Mothercombe, just outside Plymouth. Before setting out I searched for a bottle of whisky to take him. It was rare enough in those days but I finally struck lucky in a Woodhall pub where, at a price, the landlord parted with a rare bottle of Johnny Walker blue-label: the war-time black market mentality still coloured the lives of many. Having disposed of my father's ancient Wolseley when I sold the house, I took a train to London and then caught a connection to Plymouth. The trains were still crowded and I stood in the corridor for both journeys. Once at my final destination I was fortunate to get the last taxi outside the station and, after quoting over the odds, the driver agreed to take me to Mothercombe – I was discovering that the previous "we're all in it together" camaraderie had reverted to the old status quo.

The exterior appearance of Machell's bungalow was unprepossessing, lacking the traditional thatched roof of picture postcards, or roses arching the doorway, but welcoming smoke went straight upwards from chimney, indicating a warm interior and he greeted me on the threshold with a crystal tumbler of whisky in each hand.

'Good to see you, sir,' I said.

'Oh, God, let's dispense with rank, we're both in mufti at long last. Call me Roy. Down the hatch and to hell with the pall-bearers.' We drank a toast to each other before I had set foot inside, which seemed a good start.

He had done his bachelor best to furnish the cottage with a collection of comfortable, if eclectic, furniture and the spare bedroom he showed me to was warm and welcoming, if sparse, with a collection of sea shells arranged on the window sill.

We sat in two odd armchairs on either side of the log fire. In the beginning I felt oddly ill at ease; we had hardly been intimates before, our different ranks determining that I had always treated him with deference; that and the age difference between us now proved an initial restraint. After a lifetime of uniforms, he seemed to have shrunk, the civilian clothes – a weathered Harris tweed jacket with leather patches on the elbows, Jaeger check shirt and baggy trousers – gave him a strangely diminished look. No longer the officer we had all looked up to, now he was just another civilian.

The good plain fare he provided that first night had been cooked and brought in by a neighbour he referred to with a wink as "my merry widow". 'I think she may have designs on my body, such as it is – a case of the naïve pursuing the uneatable, or words to that effect, paraphrasing Oscar Wilde.' A decent bottle of claret further loosened our tongues over dinner, and it became more and more obvious that he welcomed having somebody with shared experiences to talk to at long last. For my part I felt a sudden rush of affection for him; he was, after all, the man who had brought me through the war intact, and it was a relief to be with someone with whom I could have an intelligent conversation about shared interests. Warrender had had many qualities but intellectual stimulation was not one of them.

'Have you kept up with any of the others, "Betty" Grable, for instance?'

'Ah! the estimable Betty!' he exclaimed, his face lighting up as though I had just named his best friend and I began to appreciate the extent of his isolation. Roy's "Battersea Dog's Home" unit had been his family and now we were all scattered to the four winds. 'I did hear he had gone into the Foreign Service, very suited to his personality. Most diplomats I have come across were pedants. Still, he had his qualities, you all did. I was very fortunate to see out the war in such diverse company. Sadly you're the only one who has stayed in contact, although I did write to everybody in the unit, telling them of my present whereabouts. I guess everybody wants to forget.'

'Not everybody,' I said. 'and not everything. You can't forget everything. Do you, like me, look back and think how strange it was after the war ended, when we lived in that charred city? I shall never forget the cold that winter. The cold and the deaths in the streets every night.'

'Yes. If defeat is an orphan, victory also has its limitations.' He looked at me over his wine glass with a quizzical expression. 'And some compensations, of course. Can I be rude and ask how your own life is, dear boy? I seem to recall you got your knickers in a twist about a little German girl. I met her once, remember, when you needed to borrow my Hamburg apartment? Did that relationship have legs?'

'No,' I said.

'Ah, sorry to hear it. I remember you were very keen on her at the time.'

Although it was strange to have Roy describe my feelings towards Lisa as just 'keen', I was grateful to him for bringing her into the conversation, since any mention by others brought her back into sharp focus.

'Her father was ex-SS, wasn't he? I was impressed that you were smart enough to pick him out from a photograph.'

'Was it that all that smart? I wonder. Maybe I should have kept quiet. He could have lived the rest of his life as a university professor, the man I met by chance in a bookshop who happened to have a daughter called Lisa that I fell for.' Speaking her name aloud for the first time in ages rekindled a life I thought I had left behind forever. 'When my identification exposed him and he was subsequently arrested and tried, she never wanted to see me again.' The floodgates of memory having been opened, I had an overwhelming desire to unburden myself further. 'I constantly ask myself, did I do the right thing? I knew real happiness before that photograph turned up on your desk, but it changed everything forever.'

'You couldn't avoid doing your duty,' Roy said evenly.

'Was it duty or was it misguided?' I said. 'I agonised for hours. I was just about to go home on leave, remember? So I dumped the decision onto you. That wasn't duty, it was cowardice. The whole process was set into motion while I was away, which I misguidedly thought let me off the hook. But I was wrong. Nothing went away, and on my return everything became more complicated because he had already been arrested and charged. I hoped my part in it had been hidden, that I had escaped any personal involvement, but then I was ordered to give evidence at the trial.'

'Nobody could escape,' Roy said. 'We were all involved.' He got up and put more logs on the fire. 'You've never talked to me much about the trial. Were you convinced of his guilt?'

'He was definitely on the staff at Auschwitz but denied any involvement with Mengele's experiments. Perhaps that was true, perhaps it wasn't, who knows? But, yes, I thought his guilt by association was proven.'

'Did his daughter know you had been at the trial?'

'Not at first, but I had to tell her in the end and that I believed in his guilt.'

'But she didn't?'

'No, there was no way she could accept that the father she loved was part of the Auschwitz horror.'

We were both silent for while, staring into the spitting fire before Roy asked, 'Don't tell me if you don't want to, but you once intimated a child was on the way.'

'Yes.'

'And?'

'I don't know. I wish to God I did. I've no idea whether she had it or not. Her father could have persuaded her to abort, probably did. He hated me at the end. Why wouldn't he?'

By now I was sufficiently pissed to ask: 'Once when you were in your cups, Roy, you confided you sired a love child during your early days in India. Do you ever think about that time?'

'Oh, yes, in the still hours of the night.' He waved a hand towards a framed sepia photograph of a young Indian girl on the mantelpiece that I had first seen in his Hamburg apartment. 'As you can see I still have a keepsake after forty years.'

'Your daughter?'

'No, that's the mother, the reason for turning me into a child molester. They were all so colourful, so bloody desirable, those young Indian girls, unlike the expat European wives, and I was lonely.'

'How old were you at the time?'

'Twenty-eight.'

'And the girl?'

'Difficult to say. Sixteen, maybe. They mature earlier in India.'

'It must have been romantic.'

'Lust isn't always romantic,' he said with a conspiratorial smile, 'but, yes, at the time there was an element of romance.'

'Did you ever see your child?'

'No. I was given a Blighty posting before the baby was born. I got word back from a mate that it was a girl and for a couple of years I sent money to provide for them both. No idea whether they ever received it.' He took the photograph from the mantelpiece and studied it as though for the first time. 'So long ago, another world, which of course it was before Partition. All gone now. Funny thing lust, love, whatever you want to call it. Lands you in no end of trouble, as you well know. I did think of going back and trying to locate them, but decided that wouldn't be a good idea. For a start I'm not cut out to be a father and, assuming I found them, they wouldn't know to deal with a strange old fart like me. The India of today isn't the India I knew.'

I've found that most people, once they have a sympathetic audience, can't resist bring airing a few family skeletons. There is pride in historical misdemeanours. 'At least you have a photograph to remind you,' I said. 'I don't have any of Lisa.'

'Maybe just as well. I don't know that there's a great deal of comfort in photographs.'

'And after her? Did you never find anybody else?' It crossed my mind that perhaps this was a question too far, but he didn't take offence.

'Well, I bedded a few over the years, but none of them led to a lasting relationship. I guess I was too selfish, too set in my ways, hence my present status. However, don't let's travel any further down my memory lane. Changing the subject, you say you've sold the farm, turned your back on all that, so what's next for you?'

'I was hoping you might have some ideas or advice.'

'The only advice I can give you is try not to end up like me, having nothing to look back on except plenty of incident, but no substance.'

I protested: 'How can you say that? You had a distinguished career.'

'Did I? I wonder. You're looking at somebody who surrendered his entire life to the Army. And in return for what? A pension of sorts, just enough to enable me to rent this place and keep myself fortified with plonk. But a quote "grateful" unquote country doesn't really value characters like me. If anything we're an embarrassment, especially to our current Labour masters who've never had any love for the armed services. We're the uniformed face of the Establishment. I got the CBE as a farewell gong but it doesn't absolve me from paying income tax on my pension. Now, listen, enough of me, surely a bright young chap like you can turn his hand to anything?'

'If only I knew what. I didn't have time to figure out a career before being called up.'

'OK, but *before* you were called up, didn't you have some particular ambition?'

'Not really. It was always taken as written that I would spend the rest of my life on the farm. My father had promised to hand everything over to me. Then I went abroad for the first time, saw how others lived, and it changed me. Wasn't it the same for you at my age?'

He shook his head and, as he filled our glasses yet again, the firelight showed up the spider's web of broken veins on the back of his hand. This, more than anything else, made him old in my eyes. 'I escaped my origins for different reasons. As soon as I was the permissible age, I joined up as a bandsman. You see, unlike you, I didn't have a settled home life. Not to put too fine a point on it, my mother was a whore. Ghastly thing to say, but true. When I came home from school there was always a new "uncle" in the house.'

'What about your father?'

'Oh, he'd already fled the coop by the time I was seven. Never saw him again. The peacetime Army was my salvation. I served in Africa first, the King's First African Rifles, then was posted to India where I discovered I was a natural at languages and gradually worked my way up the promotional ladder, finally managing to get transferred into the Intelligence Corps. That proved my salvation because it threw me amongst characters who had some direction in their lives and it rubbed off on me.'

We talked a long time that first night and he seemed anxious to reveal further insights into his inherent loneliness. As with Hugh Dempster-Miller and Graham Green, Roy gave off an aura of somebody unfulfilled; all three belonged to a breed that, I suspected, would eventually die out. People like me belonged to the war generation, compelled to do our bit by the conscription laws, but Roy and the other two had gone voluntarily into the service of the nation, devoting their lives to a concept that was now thought of in certain quarters as reactionary, a throwback to the days of the Empire. Listening to him describe his past, I doubted whether all those years ago, when he had given his heart to a nubile Indian girl, he had ever thought he would end his days alone in a rented bungalow, regarded as a dinosaur by the new liberal elite, his only comfort an occasional visit from somebody like me. It was there, sitting beside the dying embers of his log fire and making a dead soldier of the whisky I had brought, I knew I had made the right decision for my own life. Despite still not having a clear idea of the direction I would take, I knew the fault lines to avoid.

I stayed with him for another two days and although he tried to persuade me to prolong my visit, I was anxious to get away: there was element about his nostalgia for the past that had become burdensome. I wanted to escape memories of the war. Reminders were too painful and all routes led back to Belsen, Grundwall and, of course, Lisa. I felt sorry for Roy having to eke out the remainder of his days in a coastal backwater; unlike me, the Army had been his entire life and I understood why he still needed to retain even tentative links with the past, but it was a past I wished to shed.

Before leaving I accompanied him for a last stroll along the nearby deserted beach. I noticed he didn't find it easy to walk on the wet sand and kept having to pause and catch his breath. He suddenly spotted an addition to the shell collection in my bedroom. 'A few exotic specimens are washed up on this coast, carried from God knows where by the tides, since they're not indigenous to these shores.' He held it out for me to admire. 'Funny to think that a creature once lived inside that. Then one day it poked its head out and was consumed by a predator. I often feel that my life has been like that, encased and protected for most of the time then, when I ventured beyond the conventional, I was consumed by regrets.' It was his idea of a joke, and although I shared his laughter, I recognised the sad truth behind his words.

As he prattled on about the times he had left behind I began to form an idea of what I could do with my life. It was as if my subconscious had brought me full circle from that chance meeting with Grundwall in that Hamburg bookshop. Lying awake in Roy's sparse guest bedroom the thought of working amongst books appealed. It was certainly preferable to other options. With my modest amount of capital I was now in a position to invest in a bookshop of my own. En route back to Coningsby I bought a copy of the the *Bookseller* from a station bookstall and that night I carefully studied the small ads giving details of bookshops for sale, discarding any that indicated they wanted a partner because I was determined to chance my luck and strike out on my own, come what may.

It took two subsequent issues of the magazine before I spotted an advertisement that struck the right note: '*Going Concern. Well established business in Surrey village. Forced to sell because of bereavement. Good general stock and faithful clientele. Premises would allow for enlargement. Two-bedroomed, self-contained flat above the shop and Lease with 20 years to run. Fully audited accounts available for bona fide purchaser. Please contact owner Box 76.*'

I wrote requesting more details and stating that I was in a position to take an immediate decision and pay cash if satisfied. The existing owner replied within a week and enclosed the previous year's accounts, showing that, after deduction of rent, staff costs and utilities the turnover had produced a net profit of some £1500. The written-down stock was shown as £4000 and he was asking £7000 to surrender the lease and the contents. I answered saying that, subject to viewing the premises and the stock, I would be prepared to make a firm cash offer of £6750.

THIRTY-FIVE

The shop proved to be in the hamlet of Englefield Green, a village bordering the fringe of Windsor Great Park and the more affluent areas of Virginia Water and Sunningdale. It nestled in the middle of a row of the usual eclectic collection that once characterised British villages before the supermarkets put many of them out of business: a butcher, fishmonger, grocery, iron-monger, small café, patisserie, off licence and a chemist. The bookshop's double-fronted façade badly needed a coat of paint, but the interior was clean and well arranged, the stock neatly divided into categories with a special area catering for children. A small garden in the rear led to a lock-up garage and store room.

Mr Rufus Godwin, the owner, was in his late fifties and had an eccentric appearance – bearded with long pepper-and-salt coloured hair gathered at the back of his head in a ponytail secured with an elastic band, sandals, thick woollen shirt, mittens and corduroy trousers – the whole reminded me of photographs I had seen of Lytton Strachey. Opening with, 'Ever owned a bookshop before?' he did not wait for my answer but continued, 'Can I give you a cup of my speciality coffee? Java beans that I grind.'

'Yes, thank you. And to answer your other question, no, this is my first venture into bookselling, but it's something that always appealed.'

'Well, let me straight away level with you and point out the pitfalls,' he said while he busied himself preparing his brew. 'Running a bookshop is a labour of love and certainly not a way to get rich quick. All booksellers, me included, are mad masochists who put the love of books before everything else. For most of the year you'll just tread water. The only time you'll make a profit are the three months leading up to Christmas when the great British public suddenly decides that books solve the gift problem even if the majority of them don't read themselves. Still, look at it this way, selling books is better than being in a bloody nine 'til five office job or working down a coal mine. Mind you, you'll be lucky if you only work nine `til five but at least you don't have to answer to anybody else.'

'How d'you decide what stock to keep?'

'Trial and error. Once you've found out what your regular clientele are likely to go for, you add to the basics. Most of the major publishers send their reps to visit once a month, and one of the big wholesalers comes round in a van every week enabling you to keep stocked with what's selling. But never be without the basics – dictionaries, Beatrix Potter, Agatha Christie, local Ordnance Survey maps, Bibles and prayer books for when kids take their first Communion. Oh, and Enid Blyton, don't run out of her. Despite what the literary snobs say, she's always a seller. The rest is up to you. Put your own stamp and taste on the stock you decide to carry because the majority of customers won't have a clue what to buy and want you to guide them. But be circumspect, know your customers. For instance, the vicar's wife won't thank you if you recommend *The Well of Loneliness*.'

'Not a book I know.'

'You haven't missed anything. It was a *cause célèbre* when it first appeared.'

'Why?'

'A hymn to Sappho. Dull as ditchwater, unreadable in my opinion. So be on your guard, people around here can be a bit straight-laced when it comes to reading about sex.' He grinned at me over his coffee cup. 'Not that you'd think so, judging from the local divorce rate. Hope that doesn't put you off. When I first opened up, oh, fifteen years ago, I was less cynical about the shopping habits of the great British public. I've come to the conclusion that now most of them don't buy books for pleasure, but from duty. It's the age of the unread coffee table book and having the latest best seller blatantly on view they think bestows a certain social *cachet*, even if they never open the bloody things. It was different during the war; then people were desperate for the printed word even though most of it was published on toilet paper and wouldn't last.'

'What happens to the ones you can't sell?'

'If you're lucky and on good terms with the rep, he'll take the duds back. Give you another tip. A lot of the big bookshops treat the reps like dirt. Me, I've always made a point of making them feel welcome, always offering a cup of Java. Pays off. Mind you, there'll be times when you're stuck with a title that nobody wants. In that case, admit defeat, cut your losses, put it in the post-Christmas sale at a knockdown price.'

He handed me my coffee and watched as I took the first sip.

'Is that the best cup of coffee you ever tasted?'

'Lovely,' I said, although it didn't taste any different from what I usually drank.

'Talking of Christmas,' he continued. 'Christmas is tricky. You have to order children's annuals early in the New Year and it's difficult to predict which ones they'll buy by the time December comes round again. Very often it's decided by what's been on telly during the year.' By now he was in full flight. 'Owning a shop means that you provide a village pump where customers come to gossip rather than make a purchase. Never expect everybody who comes through the doors to buy, bookshops aren't like that. Don't do the hard sell, you'll frighten them. Guide them if they ask but otherwise leave them alone. And get used to the fact that some days you won't see a soul. Nobody will come through the door except the postman with a sheaf of bills. You'll get the usual quota of eccentrics, the odd book thief and certainly a few garrulous bores. I call one of my walking wounded from the local sanatorium "Lady Macbeth". Never buys anything but looks in the doorway and shouts "Is it safe?" When we tell him it is he walks through the shop and washes his hands in our cloakroom. I indulge another one who steals an Enid Blyton paperback every time he manages to give the slip to his minder. Quite harmless, poor soul. There's another, a peer, who comes in and give me stock market tips. "I've just told my broker to buy ten thousand Rio Tinto, you should do the same." The poor sod hasn't got a pot to piss in, just living in the past. They're all harmless, but they can be exhausting some days.'

He took me out to lunch that first meeting and continued to give me sound advice on how to survive. Far from putting me off, by now my appetite was whetted and I couldn't wait to shake hands on the deal. Before leaving he gave me a crash course in how to contact all the suppliers and showed me the flat over the shop which was certainly sufficient for my needs and I agreed to pay him extra for the furniture and chattels.

'Will you miss all this?' I said.

'Yes, I'll miss certain things, but after my wife died the fun went out of it. We were two of a kind, my wife and I. She loved books as much as me. I shall use the money from the sale to emigrate, go to our daughter's in New Zealand.'

Godwin promised he would urge his solicitors to push for early completion on the sale for he was obviously anxious to be shut of his previous life. I spent my last half an hour with him inspecting the stock I would inherit. 'I'm impressed,' I said, picking out a volume. 'Not many shops would still carry Aldington's *Death of a Hero*. It's an omen because I took a copy of this to war with me.'

'Yes, wonderful book but sadly he's out of fashion now. People didn't like his attack on that phoney, Lawrence of Arabia. I always tried to have an element of the unexpected. Sometimes, like that one, they stick on the shelves for years, but then you get a sense of triumph when somebody comes in and asks for a book they didn't expect to find. That always made my day.' He thrust the Aldington at me. 'Have it. After all it's yours now, or soon will be.'

I departed full of excitement, feeling I had made the right decision, yet for some reason on the return journey the memory of Charlie Boag swam into my mind and I thought about the way things had worked out for both of us. I remembered his dream of owning a restaurant and the day he'd bigamously married his stateless girlfriend. I had my bookshop but whether he ever achieved his restaurant was doubtful. How far away it all seemed. Memories of Charlie inevitably meant that all paths led back to Lisa, for both unfinished stories were linked to the *Gasthof* by the lake at Krumpendorf.

Having resolved to give the shop a new name, I came up with *Book Soup* which I felt had real originality and character. A local sign writer incorporated this into a design on wood which I had fixed over the entrance door when I finally received the lease that made me the proud, if nervous, owner. The first thing I did was to give the façade a coat of paint and examine the stock I had inherited book by book, weeding out any that betrayed the fact they had been on the shelves too long. These I put into an "Opening Sale" marked down to a maximum of £5, which I hoped would attract fresh customers. On opening day I served wine bought from the off licence next door. Disappointingly, there was no mad rush through the doors and those that did come to look me over, sorted through my bargain remainders as though they were pieces of rancid meat and most of the bargains remained unsold. It was in many ways a baptism of fire, and although I retained my initial sense of excitement at being my own master, I remembered Godwin's warning that his clientele had conventional tastes. Given the location this wasn't surprising; the surrounding area was, after all, an affluent Conservative enclave, a haven for golfers and bored wives who were strangers to their own kitchens. As I was to learn over the next few years this didn't translate into tribes of avid book lovers storming my doors. Godwin had warned me that some of the locals treated the shop as a village pump, a few of them using the shop as a bank to cash modest cheques. I had an early visit from 'Lady Macbeth' who stared at my strange face from the entrance and shouted rather alarmingly, 'Why don't you walk like a lady?' There was no answer to this. He then ignored me and proceeded into the toilet area to cleanse his hands. I didn't mind his visits if there was nobody else in the shop because it usually broke up an arid morning. I followed Godwin's advice and went out of my way to be nice to the succession of publishers' reps who came touting for business at regular intervals. Like most commercial travellers they had an unenviable job, but in the early days I allowed myself to order far too many titles, seduced by their well-honed sales talk. I settled into the routine of my new life and, although, because of my inexperience, I found it demanding since, every day, there were fresh problems to solve, I felt I had made the right decision. Unlike the farm there were no animals to feed in freezing temperatures at dawn, no crops ruined by inclement weather, no crushing loneliness of working in the fields without companionship, though I had to admit that there were moments when the small talk of customers parched the soul. But, having burnt my boats, the possibility of failure had to be pushed to the back of my mind. Most evenings I either cooked a desultory and uninspired dinner for myself or else ate out in one of the local restaurants. I tried hard to become part of the local wallpaper and be accepted, but it was often a monastic existence. I so wanted to make my shop a treasure house that people would visit from afar once the word got around; a shop full of the unexpected, not just the usual best sellers; a shop where customers stayed longer than they had planned and never left empty-handed. That was the ambition, but it was a long time before it became reality.

I spent hours studying publishers' catalogues, deciding which of the forthcoming titles I would take a punt on, and subscribed to the *Sunday Times* and the *Observer* to keep up with the most influential reviews and ensure that I did not miss out with the new generation of writers. This was still the time when good literature counted for something. Fine novels with searing honesty about the war were starting to appear quicker than they had after the 1914–18 conflict. In films, a disrespectful, kitchen-sink school of *cinema vérité* was challenging the old order, born of a growing sense of impatience that the promised changes had not come fast enough for, despite the welcome that had greeted the new Labour government, the years of austerity remained with us.

As Godwin had predicted I did not get rich quick, but the life suited and fulfilled me. Maybe long hours working alone in the Lincolnshire Fens had helped condition me to accept the lack of companionship and have a fatalistic attitude to life. Once my parents had died I no longer had to pretend a belief in religion. What I had witnessed during the war and the occupation had made me reject the conception of a merciful God. A God who allowed the horrors of Auschwitz, Belsen and Dachau, echoed what Beth Eriksson had once said to me: 'He left early.' I never wished to deride the comfort others obtained from their religion, but Christianity's image of a crucified man bleeding to death on the cross, seemed to me to do nothing other than epitomise the cruelty inherent in the human race from all time.

Even though I never entered into another intense relationship, as time went on I enlarged my circle of friendships and there was no lack of opportunities. I had two or three short-lived flings which went nowhere. On one occasion I took a girl for a dirty weekend at a hotel in the New Forest, but it rained on my parade for the entire two days and the girl went to bed in a diaphanous purple nightdress which totally extinguished any passion I harboured. Nowadays it would be fashionable to say that my bout of impotence stemmed from the emotional scars from my affair with Lisa, just as many paedophiles justify their actions by pleading they too were abused as children, but the truth is I never met anybody who attracted me sufficiently. I did not live the life of a eunuch, I was not unhappy, I had sex, but it amounted to little. Everybody today seeks to find reasons for the foibles of human sexual behaviour, but often the truth is that for some people relationships are just too complicated, they can't be bothered to take that first step. True love had been wiped from my life, I had been delivered from its illusion.

One Saturday morning, when I had been running the shop for two years or more, a Sunbean Talbot convertible drew up outside and a smartly dressed, attractive woman got out and came into the shop. After looking around she asked me to recommend some new novels. I gave her my views on several and she purchased four without much ado, paying by credit card, in those days still quite a rare event. I asked her if any of her purchases were presents and if so could I gift wrap them? 'No, they're all for me,' she said, flashing a diamond-encrusted wrist watch as she wrote her signature on the credit card slip. 'All I seem to do these days is read novels. Too much time on my hands. You might say I'm bored,' she said, looking me straight in the eye. I checked the signature on the credit card and saw it had been issued to an Annabel Chivers.

'I knew somebody with your surname years ago,' I said as I handed it back to her. 'When I was in Germany, in the Army of Occupation.'

'Could be that you came across my dear husband then. He was in something called the Control Commission, I think.'

'Possibly,' I said. The way in which she subtly emphasised the word "dear" was a further clue that this was a lady looking for extracurricular amusements.

'But there wasn't enough money in it for my Kenneth. Came home and made a pile in property.' Again she gave me the impression that although she enjoyed the spoils, she was not totally enamoured of the provider. I racked my brains to try and recall whether my Chivers's first name had been Kenneth.

She came back regularly and always bought several new books, never looking at the price, the sort of customer that gladdens a bookseller's heart. 'I can't tell you what a difference finding your shop has made,' she told me. 'It's an oasis in an otherwise local desert. Before, I used to have to schlep all the way to Harrods.'

'Where do you live?'

'Amongst the ghastly racing set, most of whom were bottled in the Dark Ages. Royal Ascot.'

'You don't like horse racing?'

'You have to be joking. All those Hoorays. Kenneth revels in it of course, says he makes most of his business deals there.'

'He's in property, you say?'

'Yes, parking lots, rows of derelict houses, stuff like that if you can think of anything more boring. Nothing interesting like running a bookshop.'

Every time she pushed out signals that she was available. Although desperate to find out more, I was careful not to probe her too much about her husband. Then again on a Saturday morning, a white Mulliner two-door Bentley Continental drew up in front of the shop and I saw that there was a man behind the wheel. When Mrs Chivers came in to choose her weekend reading, I made an excuse to go outside and search for a book in the window display and took a good look at the driver's reflection in the glass. Although he had put on weight since the time in Germany, the man in the Bentley was unmistakably the Chivers I once knew. He stayed where he was, smoking a large Havana, while his wife made her purchases.

'Anything here that might interest your husband?' I asked her.

'You have to be joking. The only things he reads are balance sheets.' She glanced outside then casually asked, 'Do you ever take a day off?' Again I detected a hidden agenda behind her question.

'Not really. Well, Sundays of course and I'm thinking of staying shut Mondays, give myself a long weekend break.'

'Doesn't your wife help in the shop?'

'There isn't a wife. I'm not married.'

'How come, an attractive man like you?'

'I think it's known as lack of opportunity,' I said.

It was a month before her next visit. She waltzed into the shop looking fit and sun-tanned and exuding the scent of some expensive perfume.

'You've obviously been somewhere hot and exotic,' I said.

'Barbados. Lovely beaches, but otherwise boring. I was starved for something to read there since the only reading matter on offer in the hotels are moth-eaten Agatha Christie paperbacks, not my cup of tea. What have I missed?'

I showed her the novels that had come in after her last visit and, as usual, she bought three or four without glancing at the prices. It was then that she surprised me a second time by suddenly saying, 'I asked Kenneth whether your name rang a bell and could he have come across you while you were both in Germany.'

'And did he say he had?'

'He thought your name was vaguely familiar. Could you two have met?'

'Always possible,' I said glibly. 'It was a fairly tight community. Ask him if he remembers a production of *Charley's Aunt* in Hamburg not long after the war finished because I distinctly recall bumping a Major Chivers in the Control Commission on that occasion. Then I came across the same man a couple more times. Curiously, he was keen on property deals even then. Tried to get me involved at one time, but I didn't fancy it. I felt it sailed too close to the wind.'

'That sounds like Kenneth,' she said. 'But, as long as he pays the bills I don't enquire too closely as to what he's up to. We keep separate lives.'

Even though I found her attractive and sensed she was waiting for me to make a move, I hesitated to take it further despite the thought that it would have been poetic justice for me to have had an affair with Chivers's wife. I just didn't have the stomach for it. Revenge, I think, is only justified when taken at white heat; I still believed Chivers had contributed to the betrayal and death of poor Sergeant Webb, but I had no proof, I just remembered him as a thoroughly unpleasant character. Now that I was content to be part of a small, tight community, where gossip of any relationship quickly made the rounds, it seemed stupid to put all that at risk for a quick and probably dangerous shag that in the end couldn't go anywhere but down. Chivers, I was sure, had the fiscal clout to make life extremely difficult for me, so I continued to stonewall his wife's charms even at the risk of losing her valuable custom. And that, sadly, was what happened. I think a tepid and unreturned flirtation with the village bookseller eventually lost all attraction for her and she took her credit card elsewhere. For a time I occasionally glimpsed Chivers's Bentley with its customised KC 1 numberplate winging its way around the area and years later I was not unhappy to read he had been tried and sent down for being a major player in a Ponzi-type pyramid scheme that involved selling parcels of non-existent land in the Cayman Islands to the gullible. I imagine his wife's extravagant life style was severely curtailed. What goes around, comes around.

THIRTY-SIX

Love, it is said, lives on in the ruins of time, and it's a mistake ever to believe that the past will remain forever silent.

My more or less celibate life in Englefield Green was placid and uncomplicated. For the most part I think I was happy, though happiness is always subjective. I was content in being my own master. Though bookselling was not the most lucrative or glamorous of occupations, it suited me and had many compensations, not the least of which was the fact that every day brought parcels of new titles. As a book lover I never lost the excitement of unpacking them and wondering whether my instincts would prove right: would this novel rush out of the shop and prove to be a hit? I often made the wrong choices since taste in literature, as in all things, is fickle.

So it was that one day, the shop empty of customers, I brewed myself some coffee and began unpacking the latest batch of arrivals. I always tried to give a share of my orders to the smaller publishers, those who offered a platform to authors neglected by the mainstream houses. I particularly remember an enterprising firm called Calder and Boyar's whose list mostly contained lesser-known European writers. This particular day, I unwrapped a copy of a memoir translated from the German. The title page carried the name of a female author, Elizabeth Danziger, which meant nothing to me, but the dust-jacket blurb stated that the author had spent her formative years during the war as an evacuee from the Allied bombing, becoming an actress during the post-war occupation. It stated that her life had been devastated when she learned that her father, far from being an ordinary Wehrmacht soldier as she previously believed, had been an SS officer attached to the infamous Doctor Mengele's staff at Auschwitz concentration camp. The blurb went on to describe she '*struggled to come to terms with the revelation that a loved parent was accused, tried and convicted of taking part in the Holocaust.'*

Some dread premonition made me turn to the Index and found there was a whole section devoted to Grundwall, Karl, Frau Grundwall and Grundwall, Lisa (née Danziger). I let the book fall from my hands and sat there, stunned. Never in a thousand years could I have imagined that the past would catch up with me in this fashion. When I had recovered from the initial shock, I put the 'Closed' sign on the door and sat down to read the rest of the book. I had no idea whether the English translation was faithful to the original, but the narrative had a stilted feel to it, cold, as though it had been written by somebody hollowed out. The story told how, following her father's suicide in jail, the author had suffered a mental breakdown and spent a period in an institution where she met, fell in love with and subsequently married the doctor who nursed her back to health. Resuming her acting career, she had achieved a measure of success in the emerging German film industry. There was no mention of her ever having a child and only one oblique reference to me: I was not named, nor was there any hint that we had had an affair, just a bald paragraph describing how, during the post-war occupation she had formed a friendship with a British soldier in order to survive and that it was this same soldier who was ultimately responsible for bringing her father to trial as a war criminal. *'Nobody,'* she wrote, *'can have any idea of the devastation this event wreaked on our lives, especially since, as a family, we had all trusted this soldier and yet he was the one who betrayed us. When my father was arrested my life came to a full stop. There was no way I believed he could have been guilty of the charges laid against him for he was too good a man, and the sentence he was given of thirty years was harsh and inhumane. The final horror, which hastened my mother's last illness, was when despairing of his lot, he took his own life.'*

I don't know how long I sat there in the fading March light, borne back into the past like Gatsby, ignoring the occasional customer who rapped on the door, thinking of that moment when

I made the choice between love and conscience. Only time lost held any reality for me as I remembered that room in the *Gasthof* at Krumpendorf where once brightness fell from the air and I believed happiness could last forever. I wondered if that belief ever repeated itself or had I spent whatever luck we are given on this earth? It had been such a long journey, leaving me to wonder where did they all go, those dreams of permanence? But as I swam from the shores of yesterday, there was nobody to tell me.